Speed Demons MC

Book Five

Jules Ford

ISBN: 9798872255710

Copyright 2023 by Jules Ford

All rights reserved.

Cover Design by JoeLee Creative
Cover Model: Robbin
Photographer: Wander Aguiar
Formatting by MD Foysal Ahmed
Proofreading by Nicola Thorpe
Editor: Nicola Thorpe
With thanks

Dedication

For my sweet baby angel, Annabelle, who helps me
with the Googly thing.

Love you lots like jelly tots.

XOX

Other Books by Jules

Speed Demons MC

Bowie

Cash

Atlas

Snow

Breaker

Colt

Stone ~ Coming Soon

Soulless Assassins MC

Tyrant's Redemption (Co-author Raven Dark)

Note to Readers

This one took a while.

Sowweee.

This book contains a dirty mouthed biker who likes a bit of control.

If this is offensive to you, please back away.

If this isn't offensive to you, grab a wine and prepare to read this book one handed.

wink face emoji

Oh, and this book also contains a bit of violence, but they are bikers...

You can find Colt's play list here –

https://open.spotify.com/playlist/58Go17XFK49gHif T71cFu3

Character List

SPEED DEMONS MC

OFFICERS

President, John 'Dagger' Stone

Vice President, Xander 'Cash' Stone

Sergent At Arms, Danny 'Atlas' Woods

Road Captain, Kit 'Breaker' Stone

Treasurer, Xander 'Cash' Stone (acting)

Secretary, Abraham 'Abe' Decker (original member)

Enforcer, Gage 'Bowie' Stone

Tech, Colter 'Colt' Van der Cleeve

MEMBERS

Kit 'Snow / Breaker' Stone

'Shotgun'

'Chaps'

'Reno'

'Fender'

'Brew'

'Arrow' (was 'Boner')

PROSPECTS

'Sparky' (deceased)

Noah 'Billy the Kid' Hart

ORIGINAL MEMBERS

Don 'Bandit' Stone (deceased)

OLD LADIES

Adele Stone, ex-wife of John 'Dagger' Stone

Sophie 'Stitch' Green, partner to Danny 'Atlas' Woods

Cara 'Wildcat' Landry, partner to Xander 'Cash' Stone

Layla Jane 'Doe' Hardin, partner to Gage 'Bowie' Stone

Kennedy 'Kitten' Carmichael, partner to Kit 'Snow / Breaker' Stone

Iris Decker, wife of Abraham 'Abe' Decker

Freya Stone, daughter of John Stone, sister to Xander, Gage and Kit

Abigail, best friend to Freya

Rosie Woods, sister to Danny 'Atlas' Woods

CHILDREN

Sunshine Hope Stone, daughter of Layla Hardin and Gage Stone

Willow Stone, daughter of Layla Hardin and Gage Stone

Kai Carmichael, son of Kennedy Carmichael and Kit Stone

Kadence Carmichael, daughter of Kennedy Carmichael and Kit Stone

Gabby Thomas, daughter of Rosie Woods and John Thomas

DJ Thomas, son of Rosie Woods and John Thomas

Seraphia Reid, adopted daughter of Iris and Abraham Decker

Mason Gray, adopted son of Iris and Abraham Decker

OTHER CHARACTERS

Mayor Robert Henderson, mayor of Hambleton

Elise Henderson (nee Bell), wife of Mayor Henderson

Robert Henderson Jr (deceased), son of Elise and Robert Henderson

Anna Bouchard, salon owner

Tristan Forbes, salon employee

Callam O'Shea, owner of O'Shea's Bar

Donovan O'Shea, brother to Callum and Tadhg

Tadhg O' Shea, brother to Callum and Donovan

VIRGINIA CHAPTER

Jameson 'Hendrix' Quinn, President

Nate 'Blade' Hollister, Vice President

Jacob 'Iceman' Irons, Enforcer

Adam 'Pyro' Reyes, Enforcer

Damian 'Diablo' West, Sergeant at Arms

Patrick 'Trick' O'Brien, Road Captain

Luca 'Gambit' Ortiz, Treasurer

Joey 'Scout' Rivers, Secretary/ Tech

Grayson 'Bones' Locke, Doctor/ Medic

William 'Will' Quinn, Wise Man/ Chaplain (Hendrix's father)

MEMERS

'Picasso' (Cass)

'Rockabye'

'Mac'

'Hammer'

'Ghost'

'Fletch'.

PROSPECT

Gopher

Table of Contents

Prologue

Dagger ~ Twelve Years Before

The roar of tailpipes echoed through the dive bar, drowning out the chorus of female voices emanating from the jukebox, ye-hawing about how they were gonna put their man back in the goddamned fucking saddle.

My back stiffened slightly as catcalls and hollers permeated the air, thickened by the stench of cigarettes and stale beer. Slowly, I slid my hand inside my leather jacket.

Glock. Check. Knife. Check.

I ducked my head, pulling the baseball cap lower to cover my eyes.

The only way the Burning Sinners would expect me to be sitting in a bar on their turf, having a beer like it was the most normal thing in the world, was if some fucker had rumbled me. By the sound of Thrash's shouts getting closer, I knew someone had been getting chatty.

I often came here to recon, always wearing a cap, staying quiet and in the shadows. Too much alcohol led to loose lips, and loose lips sunk ships, at least when it came to the Sinners.

My MC, the Speed Demons, were well-trained. Every brother knew to never talk about club business outside Church. The Burning Sinners didn't have that discipline, and thanks to their lack of training and too much beer, I knew exactly which bastard to look for, except he wasn't there.

Seemed his daddy was about to enter the fray, though.

I swallowed bile down as the double doors flew open so forcefully they slammed against the walls. My stare rested on Thrash—the Sinners' Prez—who sauntered into the bar, followed by Dog, his VP, and Ratchet, one of his enforcers, who was tweaking like he needed a fix and fast.

Thrash scanned the room, eyes eventually reaching me and doing a double take. He held up his hand, a silent order to lower the music. The second it quietened, he called over, "You take a wrong turn, asshole?"

Snickers rose through the room, every eye turning with interest toward the stand-off.

I knew I was in a trouble. Every other time I came here, I'd flown under the radar. Maybe I'd gotten complacent. Too late now, though. The only thing I could do was act like I planned the entire fucking thing.

Making a show of lounging nonchalantly back in my chair, my stare flicked over Thrash and the minions by his side. "When we handed operations over to you, it was on the premise you kept your bullshit away from my town. Am I right, or do you need to phone a fuckin' friend?"

Thrash's eyes narrowed. "You've gotta lotta mouth for someone who's outnumbered and outgunned. Spit it out, Dagger. What ya bleatin' about now?"

I sat forward, elbows to knees, hands dangling down, never taking my stare away from Thrash. "Some

2

kids were partyin' in the woods just West of Hambleton when one of the girls went missin'. Some big fucker jumped her when she went to pee, then he assaulted her just yards away from her friends. Threatened to kill her if she called for help."

A hush fell over the room.

"I feel bad for the poor bitch," Thrash sneered. "But it's nothin' to do with me or mine."

"Ain't it?" I curled my fingers around the neck of the beer bottle, a ready-made weapon if I needed it. "'Cause word on the street is that your boy was the one who did it. The girl described him to a tee, even down to the scar on his chin." I sat straight again, glancing around the bar. "Been overhearin' some shit since I've been here too, Thrash. Seems Bear's got some explainin' to do."

Thrash's lip curled. "Bullshit."

"Nah," I retorted. "All true. Your boy's a fuckin' pervert."

The other man's face reddened as murmurs and whispers rose up. "You gotta fuckin' nerve comin' into my bar and accusin' my boy of that shit," he roared.

I cocked an eyebrow like the brazen motherfucker I was. "Save the bluster. All you need to do is hand Bear over, and we'll be good."

Thrash looked around at the bar full of people, whispering between themselves at my accusations. It didn't look good on him, Bear, or his club. The Burning Sinners were no choirboys. In fact, they were the source of every goddamned drug flowing through the county. Still, Thrash couldn't afford to be publicly associated with a rapist, especially when it involved his boy.

"Everybody out!" Dog hollered.

Of course, Thrash would make everybody leave. He wouldn't want the entire bar to overhear the shit I had to say. The only problem was, I was a sitting duck.

Beer bottle still in hand, I got to my feet, watching as the patrons began downing their drinks. My stare fell on a figure hunched over the bar, beer in hand, scrolling on his cell phone. Our eyes caught for a split second before his blue-eyed stare lowered.

A jolt of recognition went through me. It felt like I knew the kid. But his dark blond hair and good looks didn't put me in mind of anyone in particular.

My gaze flitted to the woman who'd been cleaning glasses behind the bar. She threw her cloth on the counter and reached down for her purse, before turning and disappearing through a back door.

Boots shuffled across the beer-swilled floor. Hushed conversation faded to silence as the main doors opened, and the patrons spilled out into the warm night air.

I took in the scary-looking fuckers before me.

All three were tall, though only Dog was built in a way that concerned me. Undoubtedly, they could all look after themselves, but when it came to brute strength and fighting talent, they had nothing on me. Though admittedly, three against one were shitty odds.

Thrash shot his brothers a furtive look before his eyes rested on me again. "I dunno whether you're brave or just plain fuckin' stupid, comin' into my turf and talkin' smack about my boy."

"You know what he is, Thrash," I bandied back. "He's gotta screw loose. Bear walks around believin' he's untouchable. You need to get him in hand before he goes too far."

Thrash's face twisted into a snarl. "Are you fuckin' crazy? The Sinners rule the southern counties. Your goddamned club gave up your diamond, we didn't. We're fuckin' outlaws. What do you expect?"

"Your son's a fucking pedophile!" I bellowed. "He came into my town, breaking our deal, and touched an

4

underage girl against her fuckin' will. That shit don't stand."

"What the fuck you gonna do about it?" Thrash taunted, holding an arm out each side. "Seems to me you came to a gunfight packin' a knife. Three of us, one of you. I reckon we could shut that lyin' mouth of yours up permanently."

"Ain't lyin'," I challenged. "You know what Bear is; if you don't stop him, he'll only get worse."

Thrash took a step closer. "He's my son. And I ain't lettin' the likes of you run around bad-mouthing him. You're sore because we've taken all the Demons' business over. What's up, Dagger, missin' the life? Tryin' to get your deals back? Is this your way of makin' it so organizations won't deal with us?"

"We passed the illegal shit over to you on the condition you kept it away from Hambleton," I reiterated. "Seems you're the one breaking our deal by lettin' your pervert son's ass into our territory."

"Fuck you," he spat. "You've gone too far this time. Can't believe you came solo. If you think I'm letting you walk out of here, you're fuckin' crazy."

Pulling my shoulders back, I clenched and unclenched my fists. "Keep your fuckin' boy away from that girl, or I'll put a bullet between his eyes. The Speed Demons don't like dirty perverts in our town."

Dog grabbed a beer bottle from the table next to him and smashed it against the wood, leaving the end a broken, jagged edge. Eyes narrowed he pointed it toward me. "I'm gonna rip you a new asshole."

"Bring it on, motherfucker," I spat.

"You gonna take us on solo?" Dog casts a glance around the room. "One against three? Seems like a doozy to me."

I felt a smirk take over my expression. "If three of you knew a lick of what you were doin', I'd worry. Instead, I find all my fucks flyin' away."

5

The scrape of a chair sounded from the direction of the bar.

All eyes slashed toward the scruffy length of wood to see the guy I noticed earlier rounding it. "I've been listening to your convo, and I find myself not taking too kindly to grown men hurting little girls." His gaze swung to mine. "Got your back, friend."

I jerked a nod of gratitude. As he strode toward me, I caught a glint of metal at his throat as the light bounced off his dog tags. Immediately, I felt a sense of kinship toward him. Myself, hell, most of my club were ex-military. He was one of mine. "You can walk away. Nobody would think less of you. I appreciate ya, but it's not your fight."

He drew up next to me, eying the three Sinners sizing him up. "Ain't leaving."

It took everything in me to keep the smile off my face. I moved closer to the kid's side. A whir came from the jukebox as a record fell. The needle bounced onto it with a thump before the bars of 'Rock the Casbah' thudded through the speakers.

I grinned, wriggling my fingers in a beckoning motion. "Come to fuckin' Daddy."

The Sinners moved surprisingly fast. Thrash circled around me, blocking my six and picking up a stool. With a roar, he swung it at me.

Ducking, I managed to narrowly avoid having my head taken off, before turning, yanking it from his hands, and swinging it back at his head. With a resonating thud, it glanced off the side of his face. Thrash let out a yowl as the metal leg sliced a wide gash across his cheek, sending him careening into the bar.

"You're done," I growled, raising the stool again to crack the back of his skull.

"Watch your back," the kid yelled.

A sharp pain slashed across my shoulder. I dropped the stool and brought a hand to the sleeve of my tee to find blood trickling down my arm.

"Fuck," I snapped, rounding on Dog, who was still holding the broken bottle. I focused my mind on blocking out the dull ache radiating from my shoulder.

A split second was all it took to be caught off guard again as Dog grabbed for me. I went to jerk my head back to catch his face, but I hit air. I turned to see my new friend almost throwing him across the room.

"You're a dead man," Dog snarled, finding his balance.

"Bring it," the dude retorted in a low, toneless voice.

I caught a flash of black creeping up on him from behind. Before I could warn the stranger, Ratchet grabbed my bud around his throat.

Thrash slowly got to his feet and rounded on me. A smirk covered Dog's face as he threw a sucker punch, making me drop to my knees with a groan.

Thrash tugged my hair and yanked my head back. "Say adios, motherfucker."

My eyes fell on the stranger, standing taller than the Sinner who had hold of him. With a roar, he broke Ratchet's hold, twisted around, gripped each side of the enforcer's head, and headbutted him hard.

"Watch your back, kid," I shouted, but it was too late. Dog punched the stranger in the kidney before grabbing him and slamming him chest first into the bar.

The stranger gave a pained grunt, then smashed his head back into Dog's face, making him fly backward. My new bud whirled around and followed with a punch to the jaw, then another, until Dog yelled in pain and crumpled to the floor.

Jesus Christ. This kid was the shit.

Thrash's arm tightened around my throat while Ratchet rushed the stranger. The kid spun around, leaped into the air, and caught the enforcer across the face with a roundhouse kick.

"You're dead, you fuck," Thrash roared.

Taking advantage of the distraction, I reached into my pocket, pulled out my gun, stood to my full height, and butted it against Thrash's temple, releasing the safety with a *click*. "Really? 'Cause it seems like you're the one swimming in a big pool of shit right now, Thrashy boy."

He froze, his arm falling from around my neck.

The stranger reached into his pocket and pulled out a Glock as Dog moaned from the floor. My new bud pulled his boot back and kicked him hard in the head.

I watched in morbid fascination as an angry graze bloomed across the Sinner's skin before he passed out.

Catching the kid's eye, I moved to his side, my stare gliding toward Thrash, who stood rigid with fear. "This is the only warnin' you're gonna get. Keep your business, and your pervert son outta Hambleton, or next time it'll be more than two of us. Feel me?"

Thrash's eyes slid over his two brothers, still knocked out on the floor, and jerked a nod.

"Y'all take care now." I glanced at the kid and gestured toward the main doors of the bar in a silent command.

We approached the exit, leaving the other prez to bring his guys around.

My hand went to my shoulder, trying to see how nasty the wound was. Judging by how much blood covered my fingers when I pulled them away, it was cut pretty deep. It didn't bother me though, my ol' lady was good with a needle. I just had to get back to the compound without being shot at by a Sinner, 'cause I had no doubt Thrash was already rallying the troops.

The warm night air smelled fragrant, a relief after the stench of booze and sweat from back inside the bar. The place was situated just outside Mapletree in the middle of nowhere, so at least we didn't have anyone nosing into our business.

The stranger pulled some keys from his pocket, twirling them around his finger as he headed toward a beat-up old Harley Bad Boy.

"Hey," I called to his back. "Thanks for your help in there."

He stopped, turning to face me. "You gonna be okay? Your shoulder's bleeding like a motherfucker."

"It's just a scratch," I assured him. "Where did you learn to fight like that? Military?"

He nodded. "Yeah, and boarding school."

Laughter bubbled up. This guy was a trip. "Where are you headin'? It's probably safer for you to get outta Mapletree. After what just went down, the Sinners will be gunning for both our asses."

The kid ran a hand through his dark blond hair. "I'll find a motel and bunk down for the night."

Suddenly, the clouds parted, and a beam of moonlight shone down on the kid, lighting him up. He looked to be in his mid-twenties. Dark blond hair, blue eyes, tall, and built. He had swagger, no doubt some residue from his military training.

"Good luck, man," he said, jerking his chin before turning back toward his bike.

Something slid through my chest, a feeling.

This kid had guts, and it wasn't just about how he'd backed me up. It was more. Something about him reminded me of an old army bud who'd saved my life back in the day. A bud I owed everythin' to. It wasn't often you'd come across a man who'd fight on the side of good when the odds were stacked against him.

"What's your name?" I called over.

He threw his leg over the saddle of his bike before his stare rested back on me. "Colter."

"You AWOL?"

"Nah," he denied. "I left the right way."

9

"Why?" I enquired.

He shrugged nonchalantly. "They couldn't keep up with me."

The sound of tailpipes roared in the distance. "Follow me," I ordered. "I know the back roads. I'll take you to my MC compound. It's the least I can do after you just had my back. You'll be safe there."

His eyes narrowed. "You a biker too?"

I grinned. "Yeah. I'm President of the Speed Demons MC."

"Are you like them?" he asked, nodding toward the bar.

"Nope," I replied. "My club's decent. None of my men would touch a kid. If they did, they'd meet the Reaper."

His eyes narrowed while he assessed me. Finally, he said, "Let's go."

I swung my leg over my bike and started her up. "You heading somewhere? To see family? A girl?"

He pulled the strap to his helmet tight. "Got nobody to see."

"Okay, Son. I'll take you to meet my brothers. I've got boys around your age. You'll like my club. A lot of us are ex-military. We're on the right side of the law—mostly. We work hard and reap the rewards. You interested in stayin' a few days? Maybe see if you like us?"

He shrugged. "Guess that'll be okay. Ain't got nothin' else."

I started my engine and craned my neck to take in Colter. A warm feeling settled in my chest. "That's where you're wrong, Son." I grinned. "You got me now."

Chapter One

Colt

The buzz of my cell phone cut into my train of thought. It had been going crazy for the last few minutes. My gut leaped, nerves shooting through me as I stared at the small, square electronic device.

Everything inside me screamed to look, but I was determined to ignore it.

Usually, the brothers' antics didn't warrant my scrutiny, but the WhatsApp conversation wasn't a brother telling his ol' lady what time he'd be home.

It was *her*.

My mind began to wander, questions of who she was messaging popping through my brain as I simultaneously conjured up the image of long, dark, glossy hair, ripe for someone to ball into their fist, and warm, golden-brown eyes that managed to see inside my fucked-up soul. She was petite, ass like a peach, and had so much lip that sometimes she drove me to drink.

Freya Stone was gorgeous, mouthy, and a pain in my ass, though admittedly, I kinda liked it.

I jumped slightly as another buzz came from the cell. Curiosity and years of crippling OCD got the better of me. Letting out a soft curse, I grabbed it, clicked the side button, and stared at the screen.

Charlie: Are we still on for Below Zero 2nite?

Freya: Wish we could stay home *wink*

Charlie: I can't be held responsible 4 the dirty things I'd do 2 U

Freya: Wow!

Charlie: Can't w8 2 eat that sweet pussy

Freya: OMG Ure making me so hot

Charlie: I'll make ur pussy soaked b4 the nite is through

Charlie: I'll pick u up from the bar and we'll go back 2 ures

Freya: Gotta get back 2 work. TTYL

A fire razed through my chest. My lip curled, fingers tightening around the cell before I pulled my arm back and launched it against the wall, snarling as a loud splintering sound filled the air, and it shattered into tiny pieces.

My jaw clenched hard as granite.

What the fuck?

Staring sightlessly at the dent I'd just made in the wall, I rubbed at the ache in my chest.

Freya fucking Stone drove me crazy. When had she started getting random dick? And who the hell was Charlie? My hands clenched into fists as my brain conjured up the image of some pretty prep boy all over her.

I knew the type. I grew up with them. Hell, back in the day, I was one of them.

Freya Stone needed an intervention. She was too pretty, too lippy, and too fucking wild. It looked cute on a teen, but she was in her twenties now; Jesus, she was training to be a goddamned doctor.

With a quiet growl, I reached into my desk drawer and grabbed a packet of antacids. Popping three out, I shoved them in my mouth and started chewing, my mind still tripping over what I'd just read.

It was times like these I wished I didn't have to monitor this shit.

Admittedly, I watched Freya's cell much more closely than the brothers', but I had to. She was so fucking beautiful and always seemed to attract trouble.

For years, I'd watched her date randoms and bruise hearts. Freya didn't set out to hurt people, but for whatever reason, her relationships got to a certain point, and she ended things.

And every time she did, I'd find myself breathing a sigh of relief.

I'd watched the club's princess morph from a pretty teenager into a beautiful woman.

There were rules stating she was off-limits, so I knew we could never be anything, but it didn't stop me from wanting to punch a wall every time I saw her on the arm of some fucknut who could never be worthy of a girl like her, like this fucking Charlie guy, for instance.

The burn in my gut crept into my chest, forcing me to pop another antacid and toss it into my mouth.

Motherfucker.

The echo of footsteps sounded from the hallway, and Breaker appeared in the doorway. He noticed the smashed pieces of cell phone scattered on the floor and barked a laugh. "What did that cell phone ever do to you?"

I scrubbed a hand down my face. "Your fuckin' sister will be the death of me."

"What's she done now?"

"Some asshole's sextin' her," I bit out. "And she's lapping it up."

Break brought a hand up to cover his grin. "How many cell phones have you destroyed this week?"

I got up to retrieve my SIM card from the broken remains of my cell. "Too fuckin' many. She's your sister. Can't you do somethin' about her?"

"Fuckin' chill." He laughed. "Why ya so pissed?"

"She'll put me in a mental asylum." I sat at my desk and ran a hand through my hair, before reaching into my drawer to grab one of the backup phones I kept in there. "How am I meant to keep her safe when she's fuckin' around with random assholes?"

Breaker blew a hard breath before perching his ass on the edge of my desk. "Look. Do I like the idea of my little sister fuckin'? No way. But what do you want me to do, Colt?"

"She's too damned young." I placed the SIM card in the new cell.

Breaker's head reared back. "She's twenty-fuckin'-four!"

"Who's twenty-fuckin'-four?" a voice asked from the door.

I turned to see Cash standing at the threshold, his arms crossed over his chest and his eyebrow cocked.

"Freya," Breaker's lips thinned. "Colt's tryin'a cockblock her again."

Cash held up a hand, face hardening. "Do *not* talk about my sister needin' to be cockblocked."

Breaker folded his arms across his chest. "Like I said to this prick. Freya's a fuckin' adult, and she's allowed to have a sex life, and at least while she's gettin' it in Colorado, she's not moping over Colt."

My eyebrows slashed together. "The fuck you say?"

"Oh, come on," Breaker rolled his eyes. "She's crushed on you for years. Don't tell me you haven't noticed. I mean, my head's been riddled with PTSD, and I still saw it."

Something shifted inside my chest.

"You better not say that in front of Dad." Cash winced. "He'll flip."

Break shrugged. "He'll get over it. Freya's been in love with Colt since she was a kid."

"Whoa!" I protested, holding up a hand defensively. "Let's calm the fuck down now. Freya's not in love with me. I'm too old for her," I sniffed, "anyway, she never said anythin'."

"For someone so smart, you're a goddamned idiot." Cash muttered, turning to Breaker. "Dunno why we're even wastin' time discussing it. He hasn't got the balls to claim her. Eventually, she'll marry some stuck-up asshole and not give him any more attention, then he'll see the light, but it'll be too late."

A prickle ran down my spine. "Your pop would beat me to fuck if I touched Freya."

He shrugged. "Wouldn't give a fuck if it was Cara. Nobody would keep me away from her."

"Same with Kitten," Break mused. "I'd pick her every time."

"For somebody so perceptive, you can't see the forest for the trees." Cash shook his head at me frustratedly. "Come on. We need to get our asses to Church."

I stood, slipping my backup phone into my pocket, and followed the boys out of my office.

Prez had warned me off Freya since the day I joined the club, and I respected him enough to listen. It sounded weird even to my own ears, but Freya was my best friend. I'd always loved her like a sister, but I had to admit that over the last few years, our relationship had changed.

"Here we go," Breaker muttered as we reached the door to Church. He held his thumb up to the electronic pad on the wall, waiting for the buzz of the locks disengaging before walking in.

Greetings went up as I followed the boys inside, and we all exchanged chin lifts.

"Where's Prez?" I asked.

Atlas shrugged. "Fuck knows. It's not like Dagger or Abe to be late."

Cash checked his watch. "They're not technically late. It's us who're early for a change."

I sat and pulled my cell phone out of my pocket to check my messages. My thumb hovered over Freya's name, wondering if Charlie fucknut had messaged more bullshit.

"Prez'll knock you out if he sees you on your cell," Atlas muttered.

"Workin'," I replied. "I'm your tech man. It's what I do."

The SAA cocked an eyebrow. "Bullshit. You're probably sextin' some bitch."

I laughed. "What the fuck do you know 'bout sextin'?"

Atlas puffed his chest out. "You think I don't send my Stitch some racy shit? I'm the fuckin' king of sextin'."

Breaker looked at him curiously. "Do you send her dick pics?"

"Couldn't fit it in the shot, brother," Atlas boasted as the door flew open and Prez walked in, followed by Abe.

"Couldn't fit what in the shot?" Prez asked as he sat in his chair.

"My dick," Atlas informed him.

John froze. "What ya takin' pictures of ya dick for?"

"To send to my Stitch," the SAA told him.

Prez's head reared back. "You dirty fucker." His nose scrunched up like Atlas was giving off a bad smell. "Gonna tell Soph to share the pics with me so I can pin that shit up all over the clubhouse. You're fuckin' shameful."

"That's what I was saying. My dick's too big to get in the shot," Atlas explained.

John turned to Abe, who'd sat looking at Atlas with interest. "Can you believe this fuckwit? Sayin' his dick's too big to get on camera."

Atlas shrugged. "Got nothin' to prove to you fuckers, but Sophie likened it to a Coke can."

"Huh?" Bowie said.

Cash sat up straight.

"Fuck me," I muttered.

"Coke can?" Breaker confirmed.

Atlas smirked. "Yip."

Prez rubbed his beard thoughtfully. "Show me."

Atlas's eyes rounded. "Fuck no. I'm not sittin' in Church and whipping my cock out."

"Well, you gotta show us now, boy," Abe insisted. "You can't say shit like that then leave us hangin'."

"Hanging like Atlas's dick, ya mean." Bowie snickered.

"Bet it's a choad," Cash mused. "It's probably thick as a motherfucker, but two inches long."

Atlas smirked. "Ain't got no choad, asshole. It gets to a twelve on a good day."

Abe barked a laugh.

"What do ya mean 'on a good day'?" Dagger demanded.

"It's a ten-point five bordering on eleven most days," Atlas explained. "But when my Stitch baby gets me really riled up, it gets to twelve."

Dagger's eyes narrowed on Atlas's crotch, and he gestured toward it, repeating his request. "Show me."

Atlas smirked. "Your family's obsessed with dicks."

Prez stood, palms to the table. "Bet it's all bullshit. Bet you're hung like a damned church mouse underneath all that swagger."

Atlas got to his feet, hands going to his buckle. "How about a little wager? Hundred bucks."

Prez glanced at Cash. "Go get the tape measure, Son."

The Veep's head reared back. "I'm not touchin' that thing. I'll get a fuckin' rash. Have you seen the chicks he used to run with?"

By then, Atlas's belt hung open. He went to his fly, popping the buttons open one by one. "I reckon I'll take my Stitch out for a nice dinner with my extra hundred." He dropped his jeans, a loud chink emitting from the belt as it hit the deck. With a flourish, Atlas then dropped his shorts and jammed his hands to his waist. "Take a peek, motherfuckers," he crowed.

I looked down and froze.

Yep. Atlas had an abnormally big dick.

It hung down his hairy-assed thighs, thick, pink, and veiny. I was surprised he was groomed; honestly, Atlas didn't seem the type to care. I had to admit Sophie was right when she likened it to a Coke can. He'd have made a fortune in porn.

"Fuck me," Bowie said, voice strangled as he leaned down to examine Atlas's crotch.

Abe started choking.

Cash's mouth dropped open, his eyes rounding.

"Bet that makes Sophie's eyes water," Bowie muttered, grimacing.

Abe barked another laugh.

I winced at the thought of Atlas's monster cock going near any of my orifices.

"I'm surprised poor Sophie doesn't walk with a limp," Abe added.

"Poor bitch," Cash breathed.

A thought came to me. "You know, statistics say that one man in a billion has a penis of ten inches or over. There's approximately three point nine seven billion men in the world, which means Atlas is one of four men in the entire world with a huge cock."

Chuckles filled the air.

I sat back in my chair. "Those statistics aren't totally accurate, though. Measuring every living man, especially those in Africa, South America, or Asia, is impossible. Indigenous people still live in small tribes without contact with the outside world. For example, the Sentinelese who live on the North Sentinel Island are the most secluded. Thousands live in the Brazilian rainforests and still have no contact with civilization. Some people live in Papua New Guinea with languages and customs the Western world has never encountered."

The room fell silent, every eye trained on me.

"How do you know all that shit?" Prez asked after a minute.

"By reading, watching quiz shows and documentaries. Though I learned that stuff in school." I informed him.

"Fuck me," Atlas muttered, pulling his jeans up. "All I learned at school was the best way to play hooky."

"That explains a lot." Prez laughed. "It's not like you could play many sports lugging that huge dick around."

Abe roared a laugh.

"Didn't need school," Atlas retorted, fastening his jeans. "May not know all that encyclopedia shit, but at least I've got street smarts."

"Yeah," Prez retorted. "And Colt's got everythin' smarts."

"Didn't you go to some stuck-up private school?" Bowie asked me.

I stared at him, weighing up how much I should say. This shit was always tricky to navigate. Prez knew I was from a wealthy family, but he didn't know to what extreme.

"Yeah, my family's got some bank," I told Bowie, who was looking at me expectantly. "But I hate all that bullshit."

"You're crazy," Cash said, shaking his head. "Why the fuck would you wanna be a biker when your folks are as rich as the Rockefellers?"

I rolled my lips inward to stop blurting out that the Van der Cleeves made the Rockefellers look like fuckin' paupers. I hated the thought of my brothers treating me differently, which was what every person I'd ever encountered did the instant they found out who I was.

Fuck that.

"That's not quite right," I replied, ignoring the underlying insinuation. "We're nowhere near the Rockefeller's league." I wasn't bullshitting. We had billions more than them. I had a trust fund alone worth millions. I gave most of the dividends to charities.

"Change of subject," I announced, turning to Breaker. "Ed's doin' well at Grand Junction. He sailed through his first week. Nina says he's not an addict, but they've gotta work hard to get him outta the mindset he's in."

"Thanks for checkin' on him, brother." Breaker gave me a hard clap on the back.

A slow smile spread across Prez's face. "Good fuckin' job, Colt. When Kit told us about Ed and all the shit he'd been through, I felt we needed to do more as a club. It's terrible how our military's treated when they pop smoke. My own fuckin' son went through hell because he fought for his country. I never got offered help when I returned from the Marines, and you all know how crazy my pop went after 'Nam."

Breaker leaned forward to address Prez. "Been thinkin' about that. I wanna talk to Nina about startin' a program for the men who're discharged from Grand Junction but haven't got anywhere to go. The construction company always needs labor, and the military's work ethic is as good as you'll find. A decent job would help 'em mentally and physically."

Prez stroked his beard thoughtfully. "It'll be a good way to expand the club, too." His eyes slid to Atlas. "What do you think, Supercock?"

Laughter rose through the air.

"I ain't gotta problem with it," the SAA replied, ignoring Prez's diss. "Ninety percent of the brothers are ex-military; it's why we organize so well. Remember that day the Sinners attacked? They didn't stand a chance 'cause of how we mobilized."

"It's a great idea," Abe added. "We can offer jobs, homes, even a family within the club if they need it. Don't hurt that we also get good men out of it."

"Cash? Bowie? What do you think?" Dagger asked.

Bowie nodded. "I'm good with it."

"It's a great idea in principle." Cash turned to Breaker. "You think you can swing it?"

"Yeah," he replied confidently. "Nina may wanna visit with a coordinator to check us out and see what we can offer. It won't suit everyone, but men like Ed, who've lost everything, would be grateful for a chance."

"Right then." Dagger rubbed his hands together gleefully. "So we start with Ed. You go down, see where he's at. The club will sponsor his treatment; we'll take it from there. While you're down there, you can check Freya's gettin' her packing organized."

"Gotta say," Abe interjected. "Glad our princess is comin' home. Been worried about her down there all alone with all the Sinner's shit goin' on. She all set to start her internship?"

Prez's mouth thinned. "Says she wants some time out. Reckons she'll apply for the intake startin' next summer. She's talking about movin' state again."

"Why?" I barked, my gut giving an odd, painful twist.

"'Cause assholes like you, Pop, and monster cock over there don't let her live her life." Breaker turned to address Prez. "Colt just smashed up another cell phone, gettin' all pissy at her."

Dagger's mouth twisted. "What did she do this time?"

"You don't wanna know," I muttered, lip curling.

"Did it involve a dude by any chance?" Atlas asked dryly.

My eyes slashed to the SAA.

He didn't miss a trick. Atlas may have looked like a fuckin' meathead, but he was sharp as a blade under all his muscle and bad attitude. I shifted in my seat, uncomfortable under the SAA's unwavering stare. I couldn't shake the feeling that he saw straight through the walls I'd carefully constructed over the years.

Breaker sighed audibly. "Timing couldn't be worse, what with the Sinners' bullshit. I feel like I should be here for Kennedy and the kids. Hate the thought of leaving them, especially after what happened with Kady."

I must've had a brain fart because my mouth suddenly engaged before my brain. "Why don't I go?"

Atlas's hard stare narrowed on me.

"You okay with that?" Prez asked.

"It's no problem," I assured him, even though my inner voice screamed at me to shut the fuck up. "I can see to Ed in the daytime, then hole up in a hotel room with my laptop at night. I can work just as easily from

Colorado. I'll get on with lookin' for that license plate in my downtime."

"Sounds like you've got it all figured out." Prez leaned forward, elbows to the table. "While you're there, do me a favor and make sure Freya's winding things down before she leaves. She hasn't called or visited since Kennedy jumped in front of that car. Make sure she's not gettin' caught up at med school, or with volunteering at the hospital."

I made a face.

"What's the fuckin' problem?" Prez demanded. "Thought you and Frey were buds. You're always goin' down to visit. Jesus, anyone would think I'd asked ya to jump off the side of the Grand fuckin' Canyon."

I sighed, knowing I had no choice. "Course I can look in on her. Just have to think about how to fit everythin' in, is all."

"If it's that much of a problem, leave the license plate bullshit until you get back," he ordered. "Family first, every time, Colt. You know that."

"I do, Prez," I agreed. "But I'm so close."

"It'll keep." His tone softened. "You need a break anyway. We've worked you to the bone since that night we followed Stafford. You're playin' the stock market, chasing down that goddamned SUV, and organizin' the buildin' schedule for the new homes."

"I can take over the buildin' schedule," Abe offered. "I should'a been doin' it in the first place."

"You dealt with recruitment, as well as buying, and organizing delivery slots for the materials," Breaker reminded him.

"Yeah. But I'm up-to-date now. I can take over the schedule." Abe turned to me. "Thanks for takin' that shit on. Have a fuckin' break. See to Ed, then take a week to see your folks or somethin'."

I almost shuddered at his words.

A week with my dad was seven days too long. He'd say I was wasting my life, and imply I was an embarrassment to my mother. He always told me that if I wanted to run for the Senate, I needed to get a real job or take a government position.

The thought of following in his footsteps left me cold.

I could've joined an agency. The CIA and FBI had been actively trying to recruit me since the day I'd left Army Intelligence. But I popped smoke for a reason. There were too many restrictions and too much red tape. Working for a government agency meant going back to square one. The FBI, especially, tortured the shit out of me to join their ranks, but I kept turning them down.

I was a lone wolf. I didn't play well with others.

"You still drivin' over to Laramie this weekend?" Abe asked Dagger.

Prez jerked a nod. "Yeah. The Cowboys are playin' the Longhorns. It'll be a good game. You should come, bring Iris. She loves her football."

"She won't cheer on your team." Abe laughed. "I know it's college football, but she's from Missouri. A Chiefs girl through and through."

"You planning any trips for her?" Atlas asked.

"Yeah," Abe replied. "They're playin' the Broncos at the end of October. Then we're doin' the December game when they play the Patriots. It's her Christmas gift."

"I reckon my Kady girl will turn into a Chiefs fan soon," Prez muttered. "There's me thinkin' I could get the kids into the Cowboys like their Grandpop."

Breaker's face scrunched up. "I imagine she'd be into the Raiders, seein' as she was born in Vegas."

Prez cocked an eyebrow. "Nah. Kady will be all over the Chiefs now. Did you see Taylor at the goddamned stadium cheerin' Travis on? Nearly fell off my chair."

"Who the fuck's Taylor?" Cash demanded. "Never heard you mention him before."

Prez rolled his eyes. "Are you fuckin' simple? Swift! Taylor Swift!"

Silence fell over the room.

"I'm shippin' those two," Prez continued, a faraway look falling over his face. "Imagine their beautiful, tall as fuck, singing, tight end babies."

"What the fuck are you goin' on about? And what's ships gotta do with it?" Bowie demanded, his tone confused.

Prez puffed his chest out. "Kelce went on his podcast, shot his shot with Taylor, and asked her to his game. She rocked up to Arrowhead on Sunday and went out with him after they beat the Bears. If they get together, little Kady will stan 'em. She loves Tay Tay, and I'm takin' more of an interest in what the kids are into. I got one of those alert things set up on my cell about her."

"Who the fuck's Stan?" Atlas said with a grunt. "You're talkin' like a teenage girl."

Abe chuckled.

Cash's lips twitched.

Bowie turned to me. "What are you doin' setting up alerts for him? He'll be runnin' around the clubhouse squealin' like a fuckin' NSync groupie."

"Showin' your age there, Bo." I laughed. "I never set up shit, and I sure as fuck didn't teach him how."

Prez's face tightened. "Kai helped me. We looked at the Googly thing. Step-by-step instructions right there."

I barked a laugh. "Ya mean Google?"

Prez waved a dismissive hand. "You know what I mean."

"Jesus," Atlas griped. "He can google his shit but can't pronounce it."

"You fuckers give me a headache," Prez rumbled. "All you talk about is dicks and reality shows. As soon as I get down with the kids, you yank my chain. It wasn't long ago you assholes were takin' Church time up talkin' about English bitches and fuckin' Zinfandel."

"Ya mean Scandoval," I interjected. "Zinfandel's a type of wine." This I knew 'cause I'd seen it served at many a stuck-up dinner party.

Prez waved a hand. "Ya know what I mean."

Abe's head fell back, and he shook his head at the ceiling. "Jesus Christ. You fuckers are makin' my brain bleed. Is there any other business, or can I get back to work?"

Dagger looked around the table expectantly. "Well?"

Silence.

"Church is closed." Prez smashed the gavel into the sound block. "Fuck off the lotta ya." His eyes came to me, and he gave me a chin lift. "You stay put. Wanna go over what I need from you in Colorado."

I checked my cell while chairs scraped, and the guys filed into the corridor. Without thinking, I clicked on Freya's name. I didn't notice the knot in my gut until I saw no more messages between her and fucknut Charlie, and it unraveled.

"Atlas," Prez called as the SAA approached the door.

Atlas turned back. "Yeah?"

"Mind you don't trip over your massive dick on the way out." He laughed.

Atlas's lips flattened as laughter came from the corridor. "Fuck off," he rasped, leaving the room, and slamming the door behind him.

Prez turned to me and chuckled. "Fucker's never gonna live it down."

I put my cell down, lifting my stare to Prez. "Everythin' okay?"

He sat back, rubbing his beard. "You still keeping tabs on Freya?"

I nodded.

"Any sign she's seein' anyone?" he asked.

My gut dropped.

"Some dude called Charlie's sniffin' around, but I can't tell how serious they are."

He nodded thoughtfully. "Check it out while you're down there. I know you're busy, so see to Ed, then see to Freya. Take time off the other stuff."

"We need to know who's behind the trafficking of those girls, boss," I insisted. "Are you sure you want me to take a back seat?"

He raised his eyes to the ceiling and sighed. "Just do what you can. I know we need to get to the bottom of what's passin' through town, but Freya's not herself. Ever since she broke up with Sully, she's been quiet. It's not like her, and I'm worried, especially with her bein' so far from home." He leaned forward, eyes boring into mine. "Need you to spend some time with her. Make sure she's okay. You may get more outta her than me or her brothers. Try and get her to open up and report back. Feel me?"

Fuck.

The last thing I needed was to play babysitter for Freya fucking Stone. For a start, she had too much lip for her own good. Her opinions were strong, and she didn't hesitate to make them known.

Our friendship had faltered since I'd been seeing Lucy. Freya stopped coming home. I suspected why, especially after what Cash and Breaker told me earlier. It hurt me that I hurt her, but there was no way around it.

Still, I couldn't tell Prez that.

Freya was the apple of his eye. He was determined she was gonna get hitched to some lawyer or doctor. He didn't want his little girl with a biker, and I saw his point when I thought about all the bullshit the ol' ladies and kids went through. Still, if anyone could keep Freya safe, it was a Speed Demon. I reckoned she could do a lot worse. We revered our ol' ladies.

But my loyalties lay with my Prez. I didn't want Freya to do something she'd regret. At least if I had an excuse to turn up, she wouldn't think I was cockblocking her which, frankly, I intended to.

Decision made; a weight suddenly lifted from my chest. "I'll have a little chat with her, bossman. See where she's at."

His expression softened. "Thanks, brother. I knew I could count on you. There aren't many men I'd trust around Freya, but you two are friends, and you seem to understand her. I can't tell you how happy I am to have someone I can rely on around my baby girl."

A lump formed in my throat.

John Stone gave me something nobody else ever had. His trust and loyalty. It wasn't about what I could do for him or how good I could make him look. It was about friendship and brotherhood.

I'd never known it before. I was born into a world of reputation and fake bullshit. What I had from John Stone was authentic and pure.

And I couldn't let him down unless I wanted to lose what the Speed Demons gave me.

Family.

Chapter Two

Freya

"You're a fucking baddie," my friend Abigail crowed as the Uber drove away. "Colt won't be able to resist you." She took her cell from her purse, aimed the camera at me, and clicked. "That'll do it," she muttered, her fingers flying over her phone.

"No more sexting, Abi. Colt will work it out if you overdo it." I reached out to take the cell from her. "He's smarter than the average biker."

She flipped her phone around to show me the screen. "Chill out. I took a Snap, that's all. It's on Instagram, Facebook, and TikTok. I tagged the bar, too, in case he wants to track you down." She grinned as her cell buzzed. "Notifications already coming in about the hot girl. Colt will see everything." Abigail grinned. "That outfit's fire, and your hair looks amazing in that slicked-up ponytail. You're totally giving off sexy, edgy vibes."

I looked down at my black body suit with side cutouts, camo utility pants gathered with elastic at my ankles, and black strappy sandals. "Is it too slutty?"

Abigail's stare flicked up and down me. "Yeah."

I smoothed my pants down. "Perfect. Just the look I was going for."

"You look sexy as fuck," Abi added. "If Colt doesn't show up to rescue you from yourself, at least you'll have all the guys in the bar to choose from. You know what they say: the best way to get over somebody is to get under somebody else."

"If reading that shit doesn't make Colt pay me a visit, I don't know what will," I muttered. "You couldn't have set up those sexy texts any better. He's been monitoring my cell since I was sixteen, so there's no doubt he's seen them."

Abi smiled. "He'll turn up for you. It wouldn't be the first time you've teased him, and he's arrived like a white knight to save your virtue."

I opened my mouth to reply when I was interrupted by a series of pings coming from my pocket. I fished out my cell to check the notifications and smiled when I saw the ol' ladies' WhatsApp group going crazy with messages.

Kennedy: Jesus, Frey. You'll give John a fkg conniption in that outfit.

Cara: Cash just saw it and nearly choked to death. :D Good job.

Layla: I think you look beautiful, honey. XOX

Kennedy: Someone's looking to get laid 2nite. LOL

My fingers flew over the keyboard. Smiling, I typed,

Freya: Thanks, girls. I'm going to a bar with my friends. You guys are good 4 my ego. I'll

message 2morrow. Love u.

Notifications pinged again with a flurry of messages from the girls who told me to have a good time. I cleared them and slipped my cell back into my pocket before turning to Abi. "The picture's getting around already."

"Good." She grinned, jerking her thumb across the street to where a thumping bassline echoed from the bar, along with chatter and laughter. "Can we go? I'm gonna die of thirst."

"Come on." I linked my arm with my friend's and picked our way across the street in sky-high heels.

Abi was Thelma to my Louise, Clyde to my Bonnie, a partner in crime in all ways. She made me laugh my ass off most days, which was no mean feat considering we were usually hangry and overtired. Our final year of med school was just as hellish as everybody said it would be.

"I love this place," Abi said excitedly as we approached the lit-up bar. "It's so fucking slick. Makes me feel like I'm going to a rockstar after party."

"Well, we *are* gonna be rockstar surgeons one day, so it's fitting." I laughed.

"And we're fucking hot," she added, grabbing the door and ushering me inside.

A wall of warmth hit me as soon as I stepped over the threshold.

Beautiful men mingled in groups at the bar while even more beautiful women packed the dance floor. Glasses clinked, and laughter filtered through the bassline of 'Desire' by Years and Years, a song I recognized from a Zac Efron movie I'd watched the year before.

Below Zero was an old, renovated manor house. The architect must've been a genius because, somehow, they'd managed to keep the original features but added glass and steel to bring it up to the twenty-first century.

A voice called my name as we approached the bar.

I turned to see our friends sitting on a massive couch against the back wall with small, round tables with stools on which our friends and colleagues sat.

Zuri stood up and waved us over. "Saved you two a seat."

I pointed to the bar. "We'll get a drink first. Do you guys want one?"

"Got you a beer, Princess," a deep voice murmured from my back. "You know the rules: stick to beer when you're out at bars."

Slowly, I turned and looked up into ocean-blue eyes. My hurt lurched the same way it did whenever he walked into the room.

The corners of his mouth curled into a subtle smile, as if he knew the effect he had on me. The warmth of his gaze felt like a caress against my skin.

It had been so long since I'd seen him because I'd stopped going home, and when I did, I avoided him like the plague. It hurt too much.

I fixed a look of surprise on my face. "Colt! What are you doing here?"

He cocked his head and shot me the lady-killer grin that made me weak at the knees. "Thought I'd check you were stayin' outta trouble. It's been a while, right?"

I studied his beautiful face, and my heart flipped inside my chest as memories of Colt assailed me.

I was a girl of twelve when Dad first brought Colter Van Der Cleeve to the Speed Demons compound. The instant I caught sight of his dark blond hair, boy-band good looks, and cocky smile, everything inside me thudded to life. Colt was different from the other Speed Demons. For a start, he turned out to be uber intelligent, which was my catnip, seeing as I'd grown up in an environment where men used their fists rather than their brains.

Even as a girl, I gravitated toward him, and over time, Colt became the person who helped me with homework because nobody else could keep up. We discussed everything from psychology to anthropology. We watched True Crime shows and debated the intricate facets of human behavior until our voices became hoarse.

Colt challenged me at every turn and made me think for myself.

Then, on my sixteenth birthday, I ran out of the clubhouse to see him casually sitting astride his bike, wearing Ray-Bans, and oozing more sex appeal from his pinky than Jax Teller did in his entirety. He told me to get on the back because he was taking me for cake.

That was the day I fell head over heels in love with him.

"I'm on a job for Prez," Colt said, pulling me away from my memories. "Ol' ladies mentioned you were comin' here tonight, so I thought I'd stop in and see ya."

"Oh. Well, that's nice. You haven't been to see me for months." I didn't mention the fact I'd never told the ol' ladies I was coming here. I *knew* he'd been watching my cell. I'd overheard him and Cash chatting about it when I was home last. It was just as well I had another phone I used for private messages I didn't want the club to see.

"Thanks for the beer." I smiled brightly. "But I'm gonna get a margarita."

"Nope," he said dismissively. "You know better."

"What are you, my daddy?" I teased.

"Babe," he rumbled. "You comin' to bars like this, lookin' the way you look, you gotta know these assholes will be like bees around honey. You gotta keep a clear head. A wasted girl is a vulnerable girl. Plus, it'll be harder for someone to fuck with a beer bottle than a glass."

My heart fluttered. "I'll be fine. I'm with my friends. They wouldn't let anything happen to me."

"Drink your beer, Princess," he ordered quietly.

I gazed up at him, wide-eyed and innocent. "Yes, Sir."

Fascinated, I watched as a red spot appeared on each of his cheeks. His eyes raked down my body as if he'd never seen me before. "You're trouble, Freya Stone."

My lips twitched. "Have you only just worked that one out? Thought you were smart."

"Not as smart as your fuckin' mouth, Princess," he rasped. "I may shock you one day and put it to better use."

"Promises, promises," I sassed. "It's good to see you, Colt. But don't think for a minute I'll let you cockblock me. I moved here to escape from my dad, brothers, and a hundred uncles staring down every boy I brought around."

"Well, that's fuckin' unlucky seein' as you're movin' back."

I smirked. "I've still got a week. A lot can happen in that time."

"Not if I can fuckin' help it," he muttered.

"What's that supposed to mean?" I asked casually, taking a sip of beer.

"You're goin' home, Princess, so there's no point you startin' anythin' with any of the fucknuts here. Plus, I've missed you. I'm over the moon you're comin' home at last."

My heart bloomed. "I've missed you too, Colt."

Our eyes locked. Goose bumps scattered down my arms, and a spark passed between us. My stomach pulled toward him, the same way it had since I was a teenage girl, dazzled by Colt's charm and intelligence.

I knew I played games with him; hell, he played games too. We pushed each other to test how far we could go before one pulled back—usually him, and every time it destroyed me because I loved him so hard but only got scraps back.

A flash of red appeared by my side as Abi sidled over, looking between me and Colt with a knowing smile. "Hey, you!" she exclaimed, rolling up on her toes to kiss Colt's cheek. "What brings you here? We were only saying today that we haven't seen you for a while."

"Hey, Abigail," he rumbled. "Came to keep you two outta trouble."

"Hope you brought bail money," she said dryly as the opening bars to 'Closer' began to pound through the bar, and she clapped her hands excitedly. "I love Ne-Yo!" Grabbing my hand, she pulled me toward the dance floor. "Come on, girl."

Within seconds, we hit a swell of bodies, joining in with the whoops and hollers as Ne-Yo's sweet tone filled the air, and we began to move in time to the bassline.

Heat warmed my back, and I knew he was watching. Colt's physical effect on me sometimes made my breath catch.

Abi pulled me to dance beside some dude who kept smiling at her. His friend noticed me and made a beeline, eyes glued to my hips as I moved them in time to the music.

I was startled as solid arms snaked around my waist from behind, and I heard a deep voice rasp, "Fuck off!"

The dude looked crestfallen but knew he was no match for Colt because he slinked away instead of trying his luck.

"Fuck, Princess. Can't take you anywhere." Colt's chest pressed flush against my back, sending a shiver down my spine.

I turned in his arms and slid my hands up his shoulders until my fingers locked around his nape. "I can handle myself. I grew up a long time ago."

His hands rested on my hips, and he matched my rhythm, pulling me closer to him. "I handle you better. I can't help wanting to protect you." His ocean-blues stared into my soul as he sang along to the words as we danced.

My heart bloomed inside my chest, and my skin felt heated and itchy. I squeezed my thighs together to alleviate the ache between them. My stomach tumbled as his fingers dug deeper to pull me closer like the song suggested.

His eyes held mine, a small smile tugging at his mouth. He drew me into his body, the lyrics on his lips as he whispered them against my ear.

As if in a trance, I leaned up and softly pecked his lips before pulling away and snuggling into his chest. Colt smelled expensive. I knew his cologne was over a thousand dollars per bottle, pricey even for my pocket. It was citrusy with a woody undertone. Beautiful, just like him.

I pressed my face into his throat and discretely breathed in his scent.

As if on cue, I felt his body stiffen.

I knew it wouldn't last. We'd been here so many times. We'd laugh, get close, have a beautiful moment, and then he'd retreat, physically and mentally. It was unsettling how easily he pulled me in, like the moon pulled the tides, but it was those crazy moments that kept me hoping.

Being close to him like this was equal parts pure bliss and pure torture.

Gently, he pushed my arms down, pulling back to study my face. "Gotta go, Princess. Got work to do. I'll take you home now."

I shot him an incredulous look. "I've been here thirty minutes. I've finished school, and I'm not volunteering at the hospital until Monday. There's no way I'm going home this early."

"It's a bit late for you to be out." He frowned. "And I don't like the fact you're drinkin'."

My eyes bugged out. "Say what now?"

He flattened his lips.

"Umm. You know I'm twenty-four, right, Colter? Well over the legal drinking age and honey, my dad stopped sending me to bed early when I hit thirteen."

"Come on," he cajoled. "Just think you could be outta those heels soon and all tucked up safely in bed."

I smirked. "Or I could dance with some hottie and ask him to tuck me up instead."

A low growl emanated from Colt's throat, and he grabbed my elbow. "Say your goodbyes, Freya."

"Hey!" Abi called out, stepping toward us. "You going already?"

"Yeah. Colt's making me go home." My lips curved seductively. "Isn't that right, Daddy?"

He visibly gulped.

"You can't go." Abi widened her eyes innocently. "Charlie will be here soon."

I bit back a laugh, almost choking as Colt's body stiffened.

"Freya!" He growled, cracking his neck from side to side. "Let's fuckin' go!" His fingers dug into my arm, and he tugged me toward the exit.

"Bye, babe," Abi called after us. "Don't do anything I wouldn't."

I craned my neck, laughing and stumbled in my heels. "Colt!" I snapped. "Slow down. My shoes are hurting me."

The next thing I knew, I was hauled into the air, and my ass hit a table.

Colt lowered to his knees and began to undo the straps of my high heels. "Dunno why you wear these things." He eased one shoe from my foot before going to the next. "You'll break your neck. I won't always be here to save you, Freya."

My heart swelled. "Yeah, you will. You'll always be my hero."

His eyes lifted and met mine. "You set me up, didn't ya?"

Leaning forward, I swept a lock of thick, dark blond hair out of his ocean eyes. "You deserved it. How would you like it if I invaded your privacy? I don't look at messages between you and your girlfriend."

Slowly, he stood to his full height—the straps of my shoes swinging from his fingers—and dragged me into his arms. "That's 'cause I don't gotta girlfriend."

I wrapped my legs around his waist, clinging to his neck as he walked us both out of the bar and into the cool fall night air. "What about Lucy Bloom?"

He didn't meet my eyes. "Not my girlfriend."

I rolled my eyes.

Last year, I thought something would finally happen between Colt and I until the day of Bowie and Layla's wedding when he got close to Lucy Bloom, the town's florist.

I got it. I was off-limits. Dating me would cause issues for Colt with the club. I loved him enough to want him to be happy, even if it wasn't with me, so I tried to move on by dating a doctor from Baines Memorial.

Sully was a great guy, but I knew he wasn't *my* guy, so I ended it. He wanted more than I was willing to give. Leading him on wasn't fair.

Watching Colt with Lucy affected me. I couldn't eat or sleep. My stomach ached, and it hurt to breathe. After a while, it seemed easier to avoid going home altogether. He still visited me occasionally, but never talked about her, despite the fact he'd been seeing her for months.

"It's just as well I had plans to come down anyway," he muttered, reaching into his pocket for his keys. He opened the passenger door and dumped me onto the seat. "If not, I would've tanned your ass for that shit. It's not funny."

Swinging the door closed, Colt jogged around the hood and hauled open the driver's door. "You know how busy I am," he rasped, sliding into the car. "The fuckin' Sinners are causing me headaches, but instead of concentrating on that, I'm runnin' around Denver pullin' you outta bars." He jerked his seat belt on, looking at me disappointedly.

I rolled my eyes, pulling my belt and clicking it into place. "I repeat. I'm an adult, almost a doctor. I never asked you to pull me out of the bar and I don't need a babysitter."

Colt started the engine and drove toward the main road, checking both ways before he joined the light flow of traffic heading downtown toward my apartment. "You need to grow up, Freya."

I flinched slightly at the sting in his words. "Do you know the average age of med school graduates?"

"Late twenties," he muttered. "Usually around twenty-eight."

Ugh. Of course he knew, clever bastard.

"Right," I agreed. "How old am I?"

He glanced right. Colt's eyes were half-mast. If I didn't know better, I'd have thought he was eye-fucking me.

"Twenty-four," he said sarcastically. "Your point?"

"My point, Colter, is that I'm the ever youngest graduate in the school, except for one guy a few years ago who also graduated at my age. People start med school at my age, but I'm graduating. Does that sound like somebody who needs to grow up? All I've done since my first day of junior high is work my derrière off. Do I go out? Yes. Do I go out excessively? No. If I did, there's no way I'd be in the position I'm in now."

"Is that why you're taking a year out?" he asked, tone biting.

I banged the back of my skull against the headrest. "Dad's been talking."

"Just as well, seeing as you didn't confide in me." He leaned forward, looking right to take the turn off. "Usually, you tell me everythin'."

"I haven't seen you," I said softly.

"So, pick up the damned phone, Freya. Or visit once in a while."

My throat thickened.

How could I tell him I couldn't go back home and watch him and Lucy together? How could I tell him it broke me inside every time he smiled at her like he should've been smiling at me?

"What else has he been saying?" I asked quietly.

"Nothin' much except you're looking at takin' an internship out of state," he murmured. "But what I can't seem to work out is, why?"

My eyes lowered to inspect my nails.

"Lots of reasons," I said evasively.

Because of you.

Because of her.

The words sat on the tip of my tongue, but instead, I told him the other reason. "I want to be a trauma surgeon. I don't want to train at a large hospital with fifty other interns all vying to assist with the same surgeries. I want a small teaching hospital or at least to work alongside a good surgeon who's willing to share their knowledge and expertise."

"Where ya lookin'?" he gritted out.

I sighed. "Oregon, Cali, Virginia, and Maine."

Colt's fingers gripped the steering wheel so tightly his knuckles turned white. "No."

"Not your choice," I said quietly. "My other option is to enlist."

He banged the steering wheel with his palm. "No!"

My jaw dropped, eyes widening with confusion at his outburst. "It's not your business!"

"You're not fuckin' enlisting, Freya," he snapped. "Get that idea outta your head. Your dad would flip, and so would your brothers. Jesus, look what it did to Kit."

"I wouldn't be taking lives," I retorted. "I'd be saving them. It's hardly the same. And anyway, enlisting would be a last resort. I'd only do it if I didn't get into a training program I wanted."

Colt glanced at me before indicating to turn into the parking lot of my apartment block. "Your dad won't have it. He'd cut you off."

I skewered him with a look. "Do you think Dad cutting me off scares me? I've still got my inheritance from Bandit. You're as bad as him trying to control everything I do. You've got a lot of opinions for someone who dropped me like a hot fucking potato as soon as his little girlfriend arrived on the scene."

"Already told ya, she's not my girlfriend," he bit out, pulling into a parking space. "And I'm aware you don't like her. You've made that obvious."

Colt was right. I didn't like Lucy; she had everything I wanted. But the reason for my dislike wasn't that. "She's a bitch, Colt. She's jealous of our friendship," I told him, unclipping my seat belt.

He barked a laugh. "Shouldn't be a problem seein' as she's got no say in who I'm friends with. Can't you come up with somethin' better? That's weak, even for you."

My throat heated.

"What do you mean, even for me?" I demanded. "You think I'm weak?"

"I didn't mean it like that—"

"Save it," I snapped. "Should've known you'd screw me over for easy pussy. Why change the habit of a lifetime?" I swung the door open and jumped out. "Fuck you, Colter." I slammed the door closed, lip curling as I stomped for the apartment entrance.

What an asshole.

His fucking girlfriend looked down her snooty nose at me at every opportunity she got. She was the most condescending bitch I'd ever met, apart from Sydney Barrington, which wasn't surprising, seeing as they were friends.

Jamming my key in the lock, I opened the door to my apartment block and stepped inside just as Colt started the engine. Then, I waited until he drove past me before raising my arm and giving him the finger.

Fucking asshole.

Chapter Three

Colt

I woke at five, unable to fall back to sleep. My mind was full of Freya Stone and not just our argument. The memory of the way she kissed me on the dance floor at Below Zero kept floating through my head, and every time, I had to will my half-chub to go down.

Eventually, I gave up. Staying busy was the key, so I cracked open the laptop and started digging. Anything to stop thinking about our dance and how her body fit mine so perfectly. The feel of her had become imprinted on my mind.

Eventually, I'd managed to push all thoughts of Freya to one side. By eight o'clock, I'd exhausted all the databases I could think of trying to find the car that chased Atlas, Bowie, and Breaker. The next step was tricky, so I waited until eight-thirty before I dialed Prez's number. With a grimace, I clicked my cell onto speaker mode and laid back on the hotel bed.

"Yo, Colt," he barked. "Got anythin' for me?"

"Sorry, Prez. The license plate doesn't exist according to all the legal sources. Usually, I wouldn't risk hacking into places we shouldn't, but even they didn't throw anything up this time."

"Were you careful?" Prez asked.

"As careful as I could be, but you know there's a chance they'll see my footprint."

There was always a risk involved with hacking into government agencies. They had people on the payroll who were almost as good as me. If I was caught, there'd be consequences, and they'd no doubt be dire.

"I fuckin' hate this." Dagger heaved a frustrated breath.

"I've done this shit before," I said reassuringly. "The Feds haven't caught onto me yet."

He let out a snort. "Colt, I trust you. Diggin' doesn't worry me. What's makin' my ass nip is the chance you might goddamned find somethin'."

I scraped a hand down my face. "I know. But at least we'll have a heads-up. The last thing we need is to be sittin' ducks."

"Yeah." He expelled another hard breath, pausing briefly before asking the question I'd been dreading. "Have you seen Freya yet?"

The image of her kissing me floated through my head again at the mere mention of her name. "Yeah," I muttered, gut nosediving. "Tracked her down to a bar and took her home. Didn't want her vulnerable when she'd been drinkin'."

Prez laughed. "She's lived away from home for years and always kept herself safe. Though, I gotta say, I like that you're protective. It's good she's got another big brother."

I tugged at my collar and reached into the nightstand to grab my antacids. "I've watched Frey grow up. I feel a certain kinship to her."

"When you goin' to visit Ed?" Prez asked.

I popped an antacid into my mouth, thanking the heavens Dagger had moved on to another subject. "Within the next few days."

"Where are ya?" Prez demanded.

My mouth twisted. "The Thompson in Denver."

"Why didn't you stay in Grand Junction? Surely, you're gonna see more of Ed than Freya. Logistically you've kinda screwed yourself. For a smart guy, you've gone and fucked-up there."

A weird feeling crept through my gut. Prez was right. Why did I hole up in Denver?

"Anyway," he went on. "It's probably good you're staying there. Want you to take Freya to visit Ed at some point."

I thrust an impatient hand through my hair. "Why?"

"Soph wants her to speak to Nina about a treatment plan. Kit had one when he came home, and she thinks it'll benefit Ed, especially as she reckons he'll have more problems settling. Poor guy's been homeless for so long, she thinks it'll be harder for him to integrate."

"I can get the info for Doc," I offered.

"Sophie reckons it'll be easier for Freya to relay the details. You probably won't recognize the medical terms. Freya's familiar with 'em 'from Kit's treatment plan. All the details have gotta be right."

"I'll call her now," I told Prez. "See when she's free."

"Good man," he said proudly. "Oh, and call Lucy too, will ya? She turned up here for you last night. Snooty bitch just walked into the bar like she owned the goddamned place. Atlas is pissed."

I scrubbed a hand over my face.

What the fuck was she playin' at? It wasn't the first time she'd shown up at the compound uninvited. Maybe I should've called to tell her I was here, but we didn't have that kind of relationship. In fact, I'd made it clear there *was* no relationship, we were casual at best, an on-tap fuck at worst, and honestly, her blow jobs weren't good enough to make me put up with the rest of her bullshit.

I was only with her for convenience, so appearing at the clubhouse with no invite was a massive no-no, especially after I'd told her never to do it again after the last time.

Maybe it was time to reassess my situation. Pussy was one thing, but when it was attached to a sneaky cunt, it lost all appeal.

"Leave it with me," I told Prez. "I'll make sure it doesn't happen again."

"Good man," he replied. "Gonna go get coffee. Keep me posted, yeah?"

"Later, boss," I said, ending the call.

This was all I needed. I had Freya threatening to enlist while Lucy acted like a stage one clinger. Jesus, why couldn't it be the other way around? At least Freya could hold an intelligent conversation. I fuckin' loved our late-night chats about Milton and Shakespeare. Lucy wouldn't know the difference between Macbeth and Henry V if she got smacked in the face by the books.

I'd call Lucy later. First on the day's agenda was to get Freya back onside. I didn't feel right when we argued.

The ringing of my cell pulled me from my thoughts.

I looked at the call display to see the caller ID had been withheld. My skin prickled with an ominous feeling. For a split second, I thought about declining the call, but I knew my OCD would kick in if I didn't know who it was.

I clicked the green icon and held the cell to my ear. "Who's this?"

"Colt," a deep voice greeted. "You don't text. You don't call."

A sharp ache stabbed through my temple. I needed this like I needed a limp dick. "What the fuck do you want, Shepherd?"

A low chuckle came through the line. "It's Agent Shepherd to you. We need to catch up, Colt. It's been a long time."

Tom Shepherd was an old military colleague of mine. We were in the same unit and worked together on missions. He was nearly as good as me with computers. I heard he popped smoke about a year after me and immediately got recruited into the FBI.

All the government agencies had been trying to acquire me since I left the army. I joined the Speed Demons and managed to disappear for a while. It was Shepherd who caught up with me eventually. He'd been a pain in my ass ever since.

"We are buds," I replied. "But you keep buggin' me to join your pig agency, and it bores me. You need to change the goddamned record."

"How about I promise to be good," he offered. "Meet with me. We've got serious shit to talk about. You're in Denver, right? Staying at the Thompson? We can meet up for a drink."

My gut tightened. "Not meetin' you for shit."

"Aww, don't be like that. Thought we were friends," Shepherd cajoled. "I've got something important to talk to you about."

"Fuck off, Shep. There's nothin' you've got to say that I'm interested in. I've told you, I'm not an agency kinda guy, never will be. I'm happy where I am, so tell your boss to fuck off." I disconnected the call and fell back on the bed with a curse.

What a shit show.

The damned Feds sniffing around was all I needed. Shep's tone made me feel uneasy. Something definitely felt off.

I rubbed at my temple, trying to ease the tension headache forming.

There was no point stressing about it. I had shit to do. Ed needed sorting. I had to call Lucy and tell her to back the fuck off. And I had amends to make with my princess. On top of all that, I had to find the illusive goddamned license plate.

Cell phone still in hand, I clicked on Freya's name, even though I knew the stubborn woman wouldn't pick up for me.

Her voicemail came on.

"Freya," I barked. "I'll be there in an hour. Got shit to discuss." I dropped my voice to a deeper tone. "If you're a good girl for Daddy, I'll bring coffee."

My heart lurched.

Fuck. Fuck. Fuck. Where did that come from?

Clearing my throat didn't stop my stammer. "Umm, right, well, I—I—Guess I'll umm see you soon?" The cell phone almost slipped from my hand as I tried disconnecting the call. I had to scramble to catch it.

What the fuck was going on with me today? Fucking Shep had unsettled me more than I realized.

Cursing out loud, I finally clicked the end call button, my insides cringing at the words I'd just uttered.

One thing was for sure. I needed some fucking sleep. That must've been it, overtiredness. Also, I had to end shit with Lucy. My heart wasn't in it, and it never would be. It started off okay, but over time, it turned into just sex and even that was mediocre. The stuff I liked in bed was reserved for women I cared about, not for randoms who wouldn't be around for long.

Also, there was the added complication of not being able to get Freya's kiss outta my head. Why couldn't I stop thinking about the feel of her lips on mine? Or the way she tasted?

Every time I tried to picture Lucy, an image of Freya popped into my head, and my heart would swell with emotion.

I was losing my goddamned mind.

Throwing my legs over the side of the bed, I took a steadying breath before standing to grab my wallet and keys.

It was time to get a fuckin' grip. I had coffee to fetch.

One hour later, I rocked up to Freya's apartment block, Starbucks coffee in hand.

Luckily, a woman appeared at the entrance trying to navigate a stroller, so I didn't have to go through the indignity of begging Freya to let me up through the speaker system on the wall.

I grabbed the door, holding it open for the woman with my best 'I'm trustworthy' smile. "Morning, Ma'am," I said brightly with a polite nod.

"Thanks." She looked up at me suspiciously. "Are you visiting?"

"Yes, Ma'am. I'm here at the invite of Freya on the first floor. I'm a friend of the family."

She looked relieved. "Oh, yeah. I know Freya. Tell her Rachel said hi."

I politely inclined my head and slipped inside. Then, after securing the door, I climbed the stairs to the first floor.

Freya and I hadn't left things on a good note, but I reckoned she'd be sweet if I gave her Starbucks. My princess loved her coffee.

I reached the top step, headed toward Freya's door, and pressed my finger to her buzzer. Ten seconds passed, and nothing. "Freya!" I called, pushing the buzzer again.

Two voices whisper-shouted from inside. I recognized Freya's voice, but the other one wasn't only unfamiliar, it was male.

My skin grew hot. I clenched my jaw so tight it ached. "Freya!" I bellowed. "You better get your ass out here before I kick the fuckin' door down."

"Go away, Colt," she called through the door. "I'm busy."

A bolt of fury flashed through my chest. I dumped the coffee holder on the floor, pulled a leg back, and kicked her door so hard it rattled on its hinges.

Freya shrieked.

I kicked the door again before whacking it with my palm. "Open the door. Now!"

"Fuck off!" she called out.

My nostrils flared, and I began to boot the door repeatedly until it flew open.

It was bad enough that Freya stood in the hallway wearing a short, pink, silky robe. But what really made me rage was the asshole Jersey Shore clone who stood behind her.

My stare skimmed down her body, hands clenching when I saw her hard little nipples poking through the thin material. Her shiny hair fell in disarray as if she'd just been thoroughly fucked.

With a snarl, I stormed inside, grabbed the asshole's collar, and pulled him out to the hallway. "What the fuck are you playing at?" I demanded, getting in his face.

The asshole squared up to me. "You're a fucking lunatic. Freya told you to leave, so *fuck off*!"

I grabbed him by the collar. "Did you touch her?"

His lip curled. "Are you for goddamned real? I'm her mechanic. I'm here for her car keys."

My head whipped toward Freya. "Are you sick?" I demanded, eyes dropping to her robe.

"No," she said, tone full of disdain. "I went down to start my car, but it was dead. I went under the hood to look for loose wires and got covered in grease. I called Christian to get a tow, and then hopped in the shower to clean up before he arrived."

"I was on my way back from a job," he muttered. "It only took me five minutes to get here."

Freya flashed him a small smile. "Thank you for coming out so early. I'm really sorry about this."

His mouth flattened. "It's okay. He's not the first jealous boyfriend I've come across. I'll call to let you know the problem, and we'll take it from there." He gave her a smile, turned on his heel, and jogged down the stairs, shooting me a glare as he went.

I smirked, giving him a cocky finger wave.

Fucking prick.

"Oh my God, you're such a child," Freya muttered as she walked back into her apartment. "You've just humiliated me, and I've probably lost a good mechanic too. Do you know how hard it is to find someone reliable who won't try and fuck me over because I'm a woman?"

I picked up the coffee and sauntered after her, nostrils still flaring. "Why didn't you call me about your car?" I followed her into the living room. "I could've looked at it."

Freya whirled around to face me, eyes flashing. "Don't you ever do that to me again?"

I dumped the coffee cups on the table. "Asshole shouldn't have been here." My eyes dragged down to her beaded nipples. "You're almost fuckin' naked."

"It's just tits, Colt." She pursed her lips.

"It's not just tits, Freya. It's your tits," I growled. "You need to cover 'em up and stop fuckin' parading around half-naked."

She rolled her eyes.

"And another thing. Next time your car fucks up, you call me! Even if I'm in Wyoming, I'll come down and sort it."

She looked to the heavens and blew out a huge sigh. "What about my door?"

I shrugged. "I'll get it fixed."

"But that means I can't go out all day."

I tilted her chin up with my finger and shot her my tried and tested sexy grin. "Tell ya what, Princess. We haven't had a couch day for ages. Why don't I order food in, and we'll watch movies for hours, just like old times?"

She hesitated.

"Come on, baby girl," I crooned. "I've missed spending time with you."

All tension visibly left her body, and she gave me a begrudging smile. "You're ridiculous."

My eyes darted between hers. They were mesmerizing, almost the same shade as the fine brandy my father used to serve to his cronies after a dinner party.

My mouth went dry as I noticed her long, thick eyelashes flutter. Lucy overdid hers with extensions, whereas Freya's were natural and pretty. My cock twitched when I caught the scent of deep amber with floral notes—Coco Chanel.

It was my favorite perfume. I'd bought Freya her first bottle when she was eighteen. Even so young, the expensive, elegant scent suited her perfectly. She wore it like she wore everything else, with class.

Our eyes locked. I felt the pull between us stronger than ever. It was a force I'd been ignoring since the day she turned twenty-one.

My fingers swept from Freya's shoulder to splay across the back of her neck. Her skin was soft and smooth, the tone unlike anything I'd seen, a light olive with a golden hue that made it gleam. My heart tugged, and I leaned forward to graze my nose across her throat.

"You smell amazing," I said huskily into her skin.

Freya froze.

I traced the tip of my nose across her jaw, inhaling again. I couldn't get enough. "Baby, you're so fuckin' se—"

Freya's ringtone pealed through the air.

"Jesus!" I jumped back as if I'd been burned. My jaw dropped, and my eyes shifted to Freya, who studied me, her beautiful eyes languid.

"Err—Umm." I almost swallowed my tongue.

My princess whipped around and grabbed her cell from the table, her fingers tremoring as she lifted it to her ear. "Hello?" She turned her back on me, speaking into the phone with a shake to her voice. "Oh, oh, hi, Christian. The alternator?" She paused then, "Yeah, that's fine..."

My hands balled into fists. I tried to regulate my breathing, though the galloping of my heart made it a challenge. My cock kicked in my jeans, and I realized I had a fuckin' half-chub.

Swiftly turning, I concentrated on anything other than Freya. I settled on the mental image of a school nurse who was the double of Miss Trunchbull, and thank God, it worked.

Half stunned, I switched on her TV and clicked through the menu to look for a movie, except I couldn't concentrate. All I could think of was the softness of her skin under my fingertips, how right it felt to touch her.

I almost groaned out loud.

Freya was my boss's daughter, my best friend's little sister. Going there wouldn't only be immoral but also suicidal if the club ever found out.

No fucking way.

A lone tear ran down Freya's cheek as the closing titles faded from the TV screen. "It's such an amazing movie." She sniffed. "Poor Big Mike."

At some point during the movie, we'd gravitated toward each other. We'd started out on opposite ends of the sofa but had somehow inched closer.

Freya sat with her back against my front, and my arm slung casually around her waist.

God only knew how it happened. We always watched movies cuddled together, so maybe it was just habit that drew me to her.

I gently threaded my fingers through her long, glossy hair. "Baby. It's okay. The rich white folk saved the disadvantaged black kid and made him a football star. All's well in the world."

She twisted around to look up at me. "Stop being such an asshole. Where would Big Mike be now if the Tuohys hadn't saved him from the laundromat and the pouring rain?"

I shrugged. "Probably would've ended up playin' for Alabama, who became seven-time national championship winners. Obviously, he went to Ole Miss 'cause of the Tuohys and Miss Sue. It's their fault he ended up being the twenty-third pick in the two thousand and nine drafts. If he'd have gone to Alabama, he'd have wound up a top ten pick in the draft, which would've got him a hell of a signin' bonus. Oher missed out on some good endorsements. He could've been an NFL great if he'd gotten into the right team."

"But the Tuohys gave him a family," she protested. "Nothing's more important than having people in your corner."

"Is that why he's suing them?"

"Huh?" Freya's mouth fell open.

"Yeah," I went on. "Oher reckons the Tuohys made him sign a conservatorship after he turned eighteen and took advantage of him. So, it begs the question, what if they took him in to prey on him and make money from his athletic abilities?"

"Oh my God," she whispered.

I nodded. "Michael Oher says the movie portrayed him as illiterate when, in reality, he graduated college with a criminal justice degree. He says the way he was portrayed was humiliating and they fucked him over."

Freya cocked her head, thinking hard. "But when they took him in, he didn't play football. They're the ones who got him on the team by appealing to his protective instincts."

I gazed down at her, almost in awe.

Anyone else would've agreed with me when I bamboozled them with facts, but not Freya. I loved the way she challenged me. Loved how she debated and put her point across. Her intelligence was the thing I loved most about her. She never bowed down to me, even though I was usually the smartest person in the room.

"Just remember it's fuckin' fictional," I muttered. "When ya gonna realize life ain't a rom-com? Shit happens, and most of it's not good, Princess."

She laughed. "You're so jaded. Sometimes nice things happen. It's all ying and yang. We get good, and we get bad. Life balances out in ways we can't control, Colt. Often, when everything seems lost, other things happen to help us find our way again."

Jesus, this girl.

Freya had always possessed a touch of spirituality, probably due to her mom who one minute was away with the fairies, and the next, could be holding a knife to your ballsack while cussing like a pirate.

Freya, on the one hand believed in medical science, which, by its own definition, was based on physics and biology. But she also believed in the human spirit, karma, and in people being reincarnated, each time to learn lessons and do better.

She was right in what she said—I was jaded—but there were reasons behind my attitude and beliefs, just like there were reasons behind hers.

"Think about it, Colt," she continued. "You told me you were lost after leaving the military, but soon after, you met my dad and found a home. See? Ying and yang."

My heart bounced in my chest.

Freya was an enigma. Maybe that was why she fascinated me so much. She was the town's it girl. Beautiful, confident, a social butterfly. I loved that side of her, but my favorite version was intelligent Freya, who watched movies with me wearing a robe and no makeup.

I reached out and tucked a stray lock of hair behind her ear. "You're beautiful, and I don't even mean on the outside, though that part of you is stunning. But the most gorgeous thing about you by far is your heart."

Her eyes softened and she beamed. "You're a charmer, Colt Van Der Cleeve."

My chest settled, and I noted how she glowed with vitality. Without a thought, I cupped her jaw and leaned forward until I felt her breathing gently. I wondered how she could get air into her lungs when she'd robbed me of all breath.

A low hum warmed my blood and I watched, mesmerized, as Freya's eyes dropped to my mouth. An urge hit me, and an invisible force pulled me closer until our faces were a hairsbreadth away.

I nuzzled her cheek, heart racing at the thought of kissing her pillowy lips, of touching her tight little virgin puss—

A loud buzz from the door cut through the room as her phone also pinged with a notification.

I sprang back like someone had thrown cold water over me.

"*Fuck*—umm—I—I'll get that," I stuttered, lifting Freya from under her arms and throwing her away from me.

She let out a shocked little squeak as she hit the back of the couch.

"It's probably the dude come to fix your door. Yeah—umm, that'll be it. The door." Jumping up from the couch. I glanced back and almost jizzed in my jeans when Freya stared at me with wide eyes and half a boob popping out from her skewed robe.

"Get fuckin' dressed!" I barked. Turning, I hurried down the hallway, rubbing the tight feeling in my chest where my heart galloped.

Fuck. Fuck. Fuck.

Approaching the front door, I pulled it open with so much force the already broken handle came off in my hand.

The guy standing there bent down to inspect the damage. "I'm here to repair this, though I think you'll need a new frame as well as a door."

"Fix it," I demanded. "I want the best, most secure one you've got in stock."

He stood to his full height, sucking a breath noisily through his teeth. "It's gonna cost ya."

I scrubbed a hand down my face, trying to get myself under control. The urge to turn back around and drag Freya into her bedroom was overwhelming.

"Don't care," I replied. "I'll go to your store now and pay. Get it done today, and I'll throw some extra in for your cooperation."

A slow grin spread across his face, and he gave me a thumbs-up. "You've got it, friend."

"Don't leave until it's done. Want that door as hard to break into as Fort—fuckin'—Knox," I ordered, returning to the living room.

I needed to get the hell out and try to get my head around what had nearly just happened between us, and more to the point, what the fuck it meant. Slipping my jacket on, I patted my pockets, checking I had my phone and keys before doing the best thing I could think of for us both.

I turned, and fucking ran.

Chapter Four

Freya

Grabbing my keys and phone, I walked through the hallway and slipped out my new front door.

I'd waited for Colt all day yesterday, but he hadn't returned, even though I sent him a voice note. It killed me to make the first move regardless of him being the one who ran scared.

The last thing I wanted to do was chase after him, especially after what had nearly happened—twice. I knew it had spooked him; I was spooked too.

Abigail lived one floor above me. We chose our apartments together to stay close. I liked having her nearby, especially in times like these. I'd messaged her last night and told her what had happened, and she was seething on my behalf.

Before I could knock, an arm flew out, grabbed mine, and pulled me inside. "I'm making margaritas. You can chop the limes."

I followed her into the kitchen. "It's ten A.M. A bit early, even for you."

"It's wine o'clock somewhere." She shrugged, pouring some tequila into her smoothie maker. "Anyway. We never get weekends to ourselves. I want to make the most of it."

She added lime juice and an extra glug of triple sec, switching on the machine. "How are you feeling?" she shouted over the loud whirring noise.

Moving to the counter, I grabbed a lime from the fruit bowl and began chopping it into segments. "I'm okay," I yelled. "Happy I've finally gotten somewhere. A bit confused, though."

She turned the machine off, removed the lid, and poured the mixture into a big jug. "Go out with somebody else," she suggested. "No point waiting for a guy who's treating you like an idiot. There's nothing like almost jumping your bones then bolting like Usain to make a girl feel like a douche." She pursed her lips. "Colter Van Der Skeeve is on my shit list."

I laughed, watching as she reloaded more tequila, triple sec, and lime juice into the smoothie maker. "You throwing a party?" I asked, lips twitching.

She waggled her eyebrows. "Let's see how drunk we can get before we pass out. We could always ask some hotties to come and party." She poured the fresh mixture into the jug. "Are those limes done?"

I held up the dish. "Yes, mi'lady."

She grinned and did a little ass wiggle. "Then it's margarita time."

We grabbed some glasses, put everything on a tray, and moved into the lounge.

Abi glanced at me and must've seen something in my face because she murmured, "He'll regret running, babe. Don't sweat it." I sat on one side of the couch, watching her place the tray on the coffee table and pour us both a drink. "Maybe, but what if being together was never in the cards for us? Pulling away now would save a lot of heartache and stop me getting over-invested."

Abigail handed me a glass, and we did a cheers. "You've been invested since you were a teenager, Freya Stone. You're not fooling me."

"It was going so well, Abi," I explained. "He was feeling it, I could tell. We were so close to our first kiss that I almost fucking squealed in delight. As soon as the door fitter arrived, the asshole couldn't get out fast enough. He didn't even say goodbye, and if I'm honest with myself, it makes me second-guess his intentions."

"What do you mean?" Abi asked.

"Colt hates authority. It was why he left the army. Being in an MC suits him because he can live free and still use his skills. Except even an MC has a hierarchy. Bikers live free and don't conform to society's rules, but there are still rules, for example, touching me."

"Interesting," Abi said thoughtfully, taking a sip of her margarita. "So maybe being with you is a way to act out and not conform."

"It could just be a thrill for him." I shrugged.

"That's all very well," Abigail murmured. "But it doesn't explain his jealousy over Christian being at your place. There has to be some feelings on his part, or else he wouldn't care."

I slumped back. "Yeah. I guess so. Colt's charming, and he looks like a dream, so it's easy for people to forget how dark his life can get. There's a side to him he doesn't let many see. He's always on the dark web, and we all know what nasty shit goes on there."

"Jesus," Abi breathed. "He must see stuff we can't even begin to imagine. How the hell did he get so deep into that shit? Didn't you tell me once he's from a society family?"

I nodded. "I don't know the details, except Colt's father fucked him over when he was young. He left and never returned. I think that's why he doesn't make easy friendships. He's an integral part of the club but shies away from getting close to anybody except my dad, brothers, and me. He's one of the boys, but there's a distance there too."

Abi grinned. "The lone wolf hacker. A man of mystery. It's no wonder you're so hung up on him." She took a sip of her margarita and grimaced. "I'm suddenly not feeling this. Wanna go out? I'll take you to the auto shop to check on your car, and then we can go out for lunch."

"It beats sitting in all day waiting for Colt to get his head out of his ass," I said thoughtfully.

"Go out with Christian," Abi suggested. "He keeps asking you, and it'll make Colt jealous."

I worried my lip nervously. "You didn't see the way Colt threw him out of my apartment. I thought he'd kill him."

Abi shook her head at me. "The signs are there, Freya. God knows what's in his head that keeps him away from you. I'm telling you; he's caught feelings. I could see it last night at *Below Zero*. He just hasn't woken up to it yet—"

She was interrupted by my ringtone.

I grabbed my cell from the table, eyes widening when I saw it was Colt. "It's him!" I shrieked, nearly dropping the damned thing. "Oh my God. What do I say?"

Abi grabbed my phone and jabbed a finger to it, cutting the call. "You do nothing."

"Jesus, Abi," I exclaimed. "Why did you do that?"

She cocked an eyebrow, an evil grin spreading over her face. "Because it's time to pull away. The blond god knows you're interested, and you've shown him you've got the goods. Now, we make him chase you. The first rule of psychology is, if you take something away from somebody, they'll want it even more."

My ringtone pealed again.

Abi glanced at the display before holding it out for me. "Big Daddy."

I winced. Not the person I wanted to chit-chat with. Still, I clicked the green icon and put the phone on speaker. "Hi, Pop. You okay?"

"Freya!" My dad barked. "I'm good. You seen Colt?"

An uneasy feeling pinged in my stomach. "I'm great, thanks, Dad. So good of you to ask."

Silence fell for a moment. "Sorry, sweetheart," Dad rumbled. "You doin' okay? How's your packing going?"

"Good," I replied carefully. "Why are you asking me about Colt?"

"He's not answerin' his phone," Dad muttered absentmindedly. "Gotta say, I don't like him not bein' around. I didn't realize how much I'd miss the asshole. Your brothers are doin' my nut in, and Atlas won't leave the doc alone now her pregnancy's showin'. Kennedy's got too much lip, and Kit won't put her in her place. He's so goddamned whipped. I need to talk to Colt. He's the only one I don't wanna punch except for Kai, Kady, and Sunshine."

I laughed softly. "Says something that you get on better with the kids than the brothers."

"Yeah, Frey. It says the brothers are goddamned fucknuts." He heaved out a frustrated breath. "Colt said yesterday he saw you. Did he mention what he was doing today?"

"No," I said, purposely keeping my voice breezy. "Colt doesn't discuss club business with me."

Dad paused again, asking, "Do you think he's gotta girl down there?"

My stomach dragged. "Why do you ask that?"

I dunno," Dad muttered. "It's not like him to leave me hanging. Maybe he's with a woman and doesn't wanna answer the phone."

Looking to the heavens for help, I blurted, "Isn't he seeing Lucy?"

"Yeah, but no," Pop muttered thoughtfully. "That's not goin' anywhere. It's been months, and it's still casual. She's doin' shit to piss him off now too, so I can't see it lasting much longer."

I tamped down my excitement and tried to stay cool. "I don't know, Dad. I'm not there enough to know what goes on."

"Yeah. I know." His tone lowered. "How's Denver? Have you met anyone yet?"

"I meet people all the time," I said softly. "But I haven't met anyone special." *Except for your computer whiz kid.*

"You're young and beautiful, Freya," he told me. "There must be doctors at your hospital. It's fuckin' crazy how nobody's locked you down. You should've stuck with Sully. He treated you well. I liked him, thought he'd make a good husband."

I made a gagging face. The last man I'd end up with was someone John Stone approved of. "I'm working long hours, Dad, and I'm hardly ever in Wyoming. It wasn't fair on Sully to carry things on. He's a nice guy and deserves a woman who's present."

"He's seein' a nurse now," Dad said, almost accusingly. "You missed your chance."

I rolled my eyes. "I'm happy for him. He deserves to meet a nice girl."

"Could've been you," Dad muttered.

"No, Dad," I said quietly. "It couldn't. When I meet the right person, I'll know. Until then, please stop trying to force men on me who you think I should go out with. How would you like it if I paraded women in front of you and expected you to date them?"

"I just want a better life for you, Freya," he said, his tone low. "Never want you to worry about bein' snatched or hurt. I want you away from all this bullshit."

"I get it, Dad, but I'm in the life already. If I get snatched, it's nobody's fault but the people who take me. You can't control everything; nobody can. What's so bad about falling for a biker anyway? You don't think any less of Cara or Sophie for being ol' ladies. The Speed Demons are good men who idolize their women. Why *wouldn't* you want that for me? I could marry a politician who'd cheat or abuse me. At least a brother would have respect."

"Over my dead fuckin' body," Dad ground out. "I've told ya. I want you outta the life. It's no place for a woman."

"But it's a place for Mom, Layla, Cara, Sophie, Ned, Iris, Ashley, and all the other ol' ladies," I challenged. "Maybe you just don't believe I'm strong enough."

"Freya..." Dad warned.

I rolled my eyes. There was no point arguing. We'd had the same discussion since I was fifteen. My mom, Iris, and even some of the officers thought Dad's views were strange, but he wouldn't back down.

"I'm gonna go," I said softly. "If I see or hear from Colt, I'll tell him to call."

"Freya," Dad murmured. "I just want you safe. If anythin' happened to you, I dunno how I'd cope."

Tears welled in my eyes. "I know, but there's nowhere safer for me than with you and the club. Why can't you see that?"

"I don't want a life for you where you're constantly lookin' over your shoulder."

I laughed. "I'm always gonna be the Prez's daughter, sister, or something. That won't change, whoever I end up with."

Dad gave a big sigh of frustration. "So, tell me, which brother you interested in?"

"Nobody," I said a little too quickly.

"So, it's a moot point then," he said sarcastically. "You're givin' me shit for no reason. Why can't you, for once, just gimme a break instead of givin' me high blood pressure?"

Dad always did this. I'd never known a person more adept at emotional blackmail. My dad was one of the best men I knew. He was also one of the most manipulative. I guessed it came with being the President of an MC.

"I have to go," I said. "We're going around in circles."

"Okay," he acquiesced. "I do love ya, Frey. Can't wait for you to come home. I miss my girl."

"I love you too, Dad," I replied softly, sighing as I ended the call.

If my dad had his way, I'd be married to a doctor or lawyer, churning out babies, and eventually turn into a Stepford wife. That life suited some women, but if that was what I had to settle for, the least I wanted was to do it with a man of my choice and not his.

He didn't choose for my brothers, so why did he think he could choose for me?

My gaze went to Abigail, who was studying me sympathetically. "Don't look at me like that," I protested. "You know what my dad's like."

She made an 'eek' face. "Daddy Stone loves you, but by God, he's hard work."

I laughed. "And I'm trying to get myself mixed up with another biker. What am I thinking?"

"We all know what you're thinking with Freya Stone," Abi said tightly, nodding at my crotch. "And I think it's fabulous. Now go and get ready. We've got car repairs to chase, lunches to eat, and a world to put to rights."

My phone pealed again.

I looked at the display and froze.

Colt.

Abi snatched the cell from me. "Go and get ready! I've told you the plan; now stick to it." She held up the phone. "You're putting Colt on ice for the foreseeable. You hear me?"

I bit my lip in thought.

Abi had never steered me wrong before. Maybe she was right, and I should make myself less available to Colt.

I smiled and nodded. "Yeah, babe," I murmured, suddenly grateful for my friend. "I hear you loud and clear."

Chapter Five

Colt

Switching off the engine of the SUV, I leaned back and scrubbed a hand over my face.

I'd fucked-up.

Was running from Freya the day before my finest moment? Hell no, but it was better than going back into that room, bending her over the couch, and fucking her brains out. But what really drove me crazy was, in the cold light of day, the whole fucking her over the couch thing didn't seem like such a bad idea.

What did I expect? To stay over? Have a morning cuddle before we made coffee and ate breakfast while reading the morning paper?

I'd holed up in my hotel room and worked all day and into the night. It wasn't until the next afternoon when I raised my head and decided I needed to get out for a while. I drove to the mall, then went to the nearest burger joint before picking up a few things and returning to my hotel.

And here I was.

My eyes slashed to all the fucking bags beside me on the passenger seat.

Even when I tried to escape Freya, she ensconced herself in my head. Every time I bought something, subconsciously, I had her in mind.

Finally, I'd given up the ghost and headed to Nordstrom. I wandered into the ladies' designer department and bought a pair of black, red-soled, high-heeled pumps, cock hardening knee-high boots, and a large calfskin tote, all Louboutin. Then I bought the biggest bottle of Coco Chanel I could find, along with matching body spray, soap, and shower gel.

Fuck my life.

Now, instead of running for the hills away from Freya, all my mind could conjure up was the sexy little princess wearing those boots for me with a see-through black bra and nothing else.

I gently banged the back of my skull against the headrest a few times.

Shit. Shit. Shit.

It went without saying I was confused as fuck. Freya had somehow gotten into my head, and the fucker of it was, I liked her being there. There was more to our friendship than just...well... friendship. What that was, remained to be seen.

Reaching to grab the bags, I threw my door open, exited the car, and slammed the door shut. As I beeped the locks, I heard footsteps crunching on gravel from behind.

Whirling around, I saw a tall, dark-haired, suited man approaching and let out a curse. A low growl escaped my chest, and I stopped dead. "What the fuck do you want now? Didn't I tell you to fuck off? Do I need to get an injunction?"

He raised both hands defensively, a cocky grin splitting his face. "Is that any way to greet an old Army buddy? Just came to say howdy, Colt. See how you're doin'."

I looked up at the heavens, asking God, *why the fuck me*? The last thing I needed was the goddamned fucking FBI sniffing around.

"Thought we could go for a drink," he suggested. "Catch up. See if you've been in contact with any of the boys from the unit."

My gut burned.

I reached into my inside pocket and pulled out my antacids. "Thought I made it clear I didn't wanna talk on the three thousand occasions your stalker ass called my cell. See what you fuckin' do to me, Shepherd?" I said, throwing a small tab into my mouth. "You give me goddamned heartburn."

"You must be allergic to somethin'," he said with a nonchalant wave. "You always were pretty sickly, even when we served together."

"Yeah, I'm allergic to fuckin' FBI who get all up in my grill. You're what makes me goddamned sick. Get it over with. What do you fuckin' want?"

"Just to go for a drink, Colt. Have a little chat. We need to discuss what we're gonna do about you digging into places you shouldn't be."

My gut dropped into my ass.

Fuck.

"You here to take me in?" I asked, tone low.

He shook his head. "No. If I was, you know it wouldn't go down like this. We'd lock up all your MC brothers, including the hot little president's daughter. Just little incentive for you to keep an open mind." His lips thinned. "Be warned, that could still be an option if you don't give me a meet."

My chest tightened.

"How about that drink?" He gestured across the street. "There's a bar there. What do you say? You with me?"

My shoulders slumped. "I guess I don't gotta fuckin' choice."

Shepherd laughed, nodding toward the bar across the street. "I remember when you first came to Intelligence. Talked all nice and proper. Now you sound like a thug. You've been with that biker gang too long."

"Ain't a gang," I retorted, starting for the bar. "We're just a group of men who like to ride. The Demons are businessmen, not outlaws. You don't got a clue about my club."

Shepherd checked the road for cars before we headed across the street. "I know your club's mainly on the right side of the law now, but it didn't used to be. Bandit Stone was a fucking lunatic. It's only been the last ten or so years that you've been legit. I wonder how legit, though, seeing as you're hacking every law enforcement agency you can crack. You've left yourself wide open this time."

My gut twisted.

Fuck. Fuck. Fuck.

I'd been looking for the vehicle involved in the chase for the last twenty-four hours by dipping a toe into a few databases and testing the waters. I was positive I hadn't left a trail. Maybe Shepherd was bluffing. Either way, I wasn't about to admit shit.

"Don't gotta clue what you're talkin' about. I'm in Colorado to help out a military veteran the club sponsors." I opened the door to the bar, gesturing for Shepherd to go first. "Gotta do better if you're tryin' to pin your bullshit on me." I nodded toward the counter. "Beers are on you."

"You're richer than the Queen of England," Shepherd bandied back.

"I'd say considerably. But you dragged me here, asshole. The FB—fuckin'—I can pick up the tab."

I made my way to a row of booths on the left wall, taking the seat farthest away from the bar. If this was gonna go the way I thought, I didn't want anyone overhearing shit.

Sweat clung to my back, and I pulled my tee away, telling myself to calm the fuck down. A SWAT team would be knocking on my door if the intent was to take me in. So I wondered what this little meet-up was all about.

I sucked in a breath, trying to steady my heart rate.

Adrenaline served a purpose. I used it to focus on keeping my mind clear. If talking was all Shep wanted to do, I'd need to have my wits about me. Suddenly, I wished I hadn't snuck out of Freya's place yesterday. I'd have done anything to be with her rather than sitting in a run-down bar, wondering if I was about to get busted.

The Feds had been actively trying to recruit me since the day I popped smoke. I'd been careful as all hell to cover my tracks; they'd already recruited a bud of mine against his will. They'd built an entire case against him and threatened the poor dude with life in prison unless he joined the ranks.

Needless to say, he chose the agency.

A bottle of Bud hit the table. "Assuming you still drink that," Shepherd muttered, sitting opposite. He took his cell phone from his inside pocket and placed it on the table.

"You waitin' for a call?" I enquired, taking a nonchalant swig of beer.

"Maybe." He put his own bottle to his mouth, his calculating eyes never leaving mine.

I held his stare. I'd learned a long time ago to never show fear, especially to men like Shep. We'd been good buds back in the day. I'd even go so far as to say I liked him, but I liked my MC brothers more. My loyalties lay with my club, not the pigs.

"Do you remember that time I deciphered code incorrectly and nearly got an entire marine unit blown up in Iraq?" he asked, tone low.

I nodded, taking another swig of my beer. "Thank God you had me to save the day."

"Yeah," he concurred. "I couldn't have lived with myself if those men had died. It wasn't about getting court-martialed or even demoted. Those men's deaths would've been on my hands."

"I think about that day a lot," I said quietly. "The Iraqi Government had terrorist links. That code was designed to fool us. You shouldn't take that shit on."

"Not gonna take it on because I don't need to." Shep sat back in his seat, eyeing me carefully. "You did me a good turn back then, so I'm gonna do one for you now. The agency wants you, Colt. They've wanted you in since the day you left Intelligence. They won't let it go, and because you're tapping into our database, you've put yourself on their radar and given them leverage."

Ice ran through my veins. I tightened my fingers around my beer to hide the telltale shake. "Go on."

Shep shot me a sympathetic look. "You must've known it wouldn't last forever, Colt. They've been waiting a long time to catch you out, looking for your weak spot. They've been digging and got info on your club. There was no way they'd let you go your entire life, wasting your talent in an MC. The second you joined the Speed Demons, your days were numbered. You're too big a threat."

My skin prickled. "What have they got on my club?"

"Robert Henderson the Fourth died of suicide just over a year ago. His father, the mayor, has friends in high places. He's like a dog with a bone and won't let his son's death go. The local law enforcement is under pressure to open the case back up. It can go one of two ways. The FBI can either bury it, or they can come down and arrest all your club officers under the RICO Act. Several members were there at the time. They all gave evidence."

"They won't find anythin'." I grinned. "That sick fuck put a gun to his head 'cause he knew he'd get locked up as a pedophile. He couldn't take it."

Shepherd's eyes met mine. "Colt. They want you, and they'll do anything to get you. Evidence can always be found, whether it's legitimate or not."

My gut sank.

When I walked away from the military twelve years before, I knew this could happen eventually, but I'd gotten complacent. Though, honestly, they would've caught up with me regardless. They'd even take down the club to get to me.

I was fucked.

"I helped you once," I croaked. "Now help me. Is there any way out?"

"I've tried," he assured me. "I held them off for as long as I could, but when you went on your little hacking spree, you signed your own warrant."

I scrubbed a hand over my face. "How long have I got?"

"I'd say three months."

A cold tremor ran through my body.

There was so much work to do, the club was at war, they needed me. "Can you get me six if I cooperate?"

"I'll try." He leaned forward, arms to the table. "It's not as bad as you think. You don't have to give up your club brothers, Colt, not entirely. What you do on your own time is up to you, as long as it's not illegal."

The thought of Atlas working alongside an FBI agent almost made me laugh out loud. Not long ago, some of the older members dealt in guns, women, and drugs for the club. There was no way I could stay in the fold.

I rubbed my forehead, trying to think. "Nah. It's an all-or-nothing deal. I can't be a Demon and a Fed. Even if Prez had a brain fart and allowed it, the members wouldn't work alongside me."

"What if having a foot in both worlds meant you could help them?" he asked.

I barked a laugh. "The club would take the help but still wouldn't accept me."

"Sorry, Colt." Shep grimaced. "If it's any consolation, I met a good woman when I joined. She was a witness I questioned for my first case. Ended up married with two kids. Joining the FBI doesn't mean life ends."

My mouth twisted. "Life as I know it will end. And you know me, I'm not the marrying type."

Shepherd shook his head, smiling. "You're crazy. I've seen that piece you've got in your bed. Freya, daughter of John Stone. Graduated with one of the top med school scores in the country. Has her pick of internships. Brains and beauty. You're a bit old for her, but still, you'd be crazy not to lock her down."

My pulse quickened. "What do you know about Freya?"

He smirked. "Been tailing you for a week. Saw you take her home from the bar the other night."

My hackles raised. "You keep her out of it, asshole."

"I guess that depends on you, Colt," Shep muttered. "The higher-ups would have no problem wrecking her career before it's even begun."

I tamped down the burn rising through my chest and studied Shep closely to determine how far I could push. "Tell me about the FBI. What would I even fuckin' do there?"

He let out a snort. "You'll get the pick of the jobs. The Assistant Director's been watching you for years. Maybe you should think about what you want and tell them. When they get you, they'll wanna keep you happy, Colt. Remember, you've also got some leverage. You need to tell them what you expect."

As much as the thought of leaving the club behind made me wanna curl up and weep, I couldn't ignore the spark of interest that ignited in my gut.

I'd have the authority to do things I'd only been able to dream of at the club. I loved my life, but I had to admit, being a Speed Demon didn't challenge me.

Being a biker wasn't in my blood. As much as I liked the guys, I wasn't a team player; I was a loner. I'd never played well with others; even now, I had my own office and holed up there unless I had Church or info to relay. I'd stayed at the club for John, and the love and respect I had for the patch and the brotherhood, but that didn't automatically make me a good brother or a decent biker.

"Why did you hack into our database, anyway?" Shep asked. "You must've known there was a chance of getting caught. Didn't you know they were onto you? What was important enough to risk your freedom for? You've avoided getting caught for years, and now you're blatantly sticking your nose into places that have gotten you in a world of shit."

I sat back in my chair, eyebrow cocked in challenge. "Why the fuck would I tell you that?"

Shep shrugged. "What if I could help?"

Or what if he ran back to the FBI and alerted the dirty ones we were onto them?

I had to give him something. If we were gonna be colleagues, I'd need to show some trust. "I was tryin' to look up a license plate. Couldn't find it on the regular databases, so the Feds were the next logical step. The way the license number's been set out reminds me of government plates."

"Give it to me," he ordered. "I'll help."

I studied Shep's face for any duplicity.

If the vehicle was FBI, it could point to dirty agents. Did I really want to let Shepherd in on it? What if he was involved, and this meeting was a ploy to dig up what the Demons knew?

Jesus. I hated all this espionage bullshit. It made me feel like I was out on a limb. Had enough of it in the Army. Hell, it was the main reason I left. Spying was a complete head-fuck.

My mistrust must've been written all over my face because Shep took one look at me and leaned forward. "You think we've got dirty agents," he bit out, more as a statement than a question.

"Maybe." I blew out a hard breath. "I'm not sure. Sometimes, nothing's as it seems. But what I know indicates we've gotta big trafficking ring affecting Southern Wyoming, and a vehicle I can't trace was involved."

Shep scraped a hand down his face. "If the ring's as big as you say, someone high up must be turning a blind eye, or we would've taken them down. Or maybe we're already working on it. Give me the plate details, let me run it, and I'll see what I can find."

I sat back, noting the glimmer in Shep's eyes. He seemed desperate for information. I knew him well enough to understand his curiosity. Smashing a ring like this would be a feather in his cap, and taking down dirty agents may even land him a big promotion.

It hit me that Shep was right when he said I had leverage. The FBI had marked me, and I knew I'd have to leave my home and MC family, but maybe I could do it on my terms.

"I'll give you the license number, but I need your word you'll keep me in the loop. I wanna protect the club; information equals power," I said thickly. The thought of leaving the only place I'd ever known loyalty made me wanna puke. But at least I could go out giving my boys what they needed.

"Done," he agreed.

"Second," I croaked, throat filling with emotion. "I want six months. Between you fuckers and a rival club, the Demons' backs are against the wall. They need me."

"I dunno, Colt," Shep protested nervously. "The higher-ups want you now. I had to fight to get you three months."

I leaned forward, almost baring my teeth. "Get it agreed, or I swear on everythin' holy, I'll walk out of here and disappear for good, and your fuckin' agency will never get me."

Shepherd held up his cell. "I'll try. I'll even let you listen, asshole, so when my superior tells me I'm canned, and he's sending a fuckin' SWAT team down to pull your ass in, you'll know exactly what I put on the goddamned line for you."

I sat back, folding my arms across my chest. "Make the fuckin' call."

He jerked a nod, unlocking the cell before he stabbed a few buttons and held it to his ear. After a minute, he barked, "Boss. It's Shepherd. I'm with Van Der Cleeve. He's agreed, but there are conditions."

Over the next few minutes, I listened as Shep bartered and pleaded with his boss—and I guessed my soon-to-be boss too.

A sick feeling slid through me when it hit me: I wasn't a Speed Demon anymore. The powerful rush of emotion almost made me keel over, and my chest felt as if it was on fire.

The last twelve years of my life were my happiest, but it would all end soon.

Freya's face flashed behind my eyes, and my heart clenched.

What the fuck was I meant to do without my princess? Who'd give me shit when I acted like a dick? Who'd demand I got some shut-eye when I'd stayed awake for three days chasing a lead. Who'd challenge me, if not her? Who'd care for me unconditionally?

If I refused the FBI, they'd do something to make me change my mind, like pinning Robbie's death on the club. It was a given that Prez would take the heat off Bowie. I couldn't watch my brothers slowly be picked off one by one, especially when I could stop it.

The FBI, CIA, and the Secret Service had objectives and did their best to attain them. I understood it. I'd lived it in the military and knew how it worked. In some ways, the club was the same. Sacrifice one to save the many.

Who knew one day I'd be the sacrificial lamb. But if I did leave the club, at least they'd survive.

My thoughts went to Freya again, and I immediately felt the gut punch. Then, the clouds inside my head parted, and a ray of light shone through.

I wouldn't be a Demon anymore.

Freya wouldn't be off-limits to me.

I wasn't stupid; I knew what we had was special. A new kind of awareness had been growing between us for a while. The thought of her with someone else made me ache, hence why I'd rushed down here to stop her sleeping with some random, and I had to ask myself why?

Clarity hit me like a sledgehammer, and a thread of excitement weaved through me as the doors in my mind that were previously locked down tight started to fly open.

My thoughts of Freya and what could be, drowned out the conversation happening before me. So when Shepherd finally ended the call, I had no clue what had been agreed.

My forehead creased questioningly. "Well?"

"You've got six months, Colt," he told me. "Not a day longer."

"Right." I exited the booth and got to my feet, a spring in my step and ready to jet.

"Where you going?" Shep asked. "Don't you want to know where to report to?"

I leaned forward and clapped him on the shoulder. "Gonna send you the license plate number. You dig and get back to me. As for the rest, it can wait." I turned toward the exit.

"What the fuck?" he called to my back as I walked away.

My feet halted, and I turned, scraping a trembling hand through my hair.

Everything was out of control. I needed to pull it back so I could think straight and plan my new future. I needed Freya; she was the only person who could get my head back in the game.

"I've got six months before I hand my life over to you fuckin' assholes," I declared. "I'll be in touch about the car. In the meantime, you can hang tight. I gotta girl to see."

Chapter Six

Freya

The day had been emotional since the second I'd opened my eyes, so I was exhausted by the time Abigail and I arrived home.

"You okay?" Undoing her seat belt. "You're quiet."

I relaxed back in the passenger seat. "I'm just thinking about Colt. I'm at a loss with the way he runs hot and cold. I thought we were friends, but he acts like I'm a pariah. I don't know what's going on."

"Give it time." She leaned across the middle partition and grabbed her purse from the back seat. "For years, he's seen you as a sister. The jump to something more must be jarring for him."

My heart sank. "Maybe I should give up the ghost. Colt's got a girl, anyway."

"She's not his girlfriend," Abi protested. "The way I see it, if he hasn't made it official after ten fucking months, he's not that into her."

"True." I sat straighter in my chair. "It's not like he's rushing her down the altar. She's so catty, Abs. She's sweet as pie when she's in the shop or if the men are around, but it doesn't take her long to change her tune when it's just me and her."

Abi shot me a curious glance. "You're no pushover. I dunno why you don't just cuss her out. It's not like you to be such a fucking doormat."

A smile curved my lips. Abigail didn't blow smoke up anyone's ass. She said what she meant and meant what she said. "Thanks."

"What's the matter with you?" She rolled her eyes. "Tell her to fuck off."

My lips tipped up. "You're right. I've let Lucy Bloom get away with her bullshit because it was easier to get along with her than not. Colt chose her, and I didn't want to be a bitch just because I'm jealous. It's not her fault. Maybe I overcompensated."

"Stop being so fucking noble. You can't let that shit slide, Frey. If she's an ass, be an ass back. People will treat you the way you let them. I'm shocked you let her get away with it. You're a biker princess, start fucking acting like it."

"Love your pep talks," I murmured. "Thanks, Abs."

She laughed. "Babe, you've helped me through many a romantic liaison. It's the least I can do after all the nights you've sat and drowned my sorrows with me. All you need to remember is this. You're Freya fucking Stone. Colt would be lucky to have you."

"Love you, Abs," I murmured.

She turned to face me, smiling. "Stop being all gooey. You know I hate that shit."

I laughed just as my ringtone filled the car. Leaning down, I grabbed my purse and fished my phone out. I knew it was him. I felt it. He'd been calling me all day, each voicemail message getting angrier.

I turned my cell so Abi could see the caller ID. "Answer or not?"

She checked her watch, smirking. "It's been more than twenty-four hours. I think you can answer now. Remember what I said. Colt's gonna be mad at you. Be sweet back, but don't apologize. Let him know you're Freya fucking Stone, and you've got a life."

I nodded, took a breath, and clicked to accept the call while putting it straight onto the speaker. "Hey!" I said breezily. "I've just seen all your missed calls. Everything okay?"

Abi's smirk widened.

"Where the fuck have you been?" Colt demanded.

"Went to check on my car, grabbed a bite with Abi, then we hit the gym." I kept my tone light. "Have you had a good day?"

"No." he snapped. "Been tryin'a get a hold of ya. Why didn't you answer your goddamned phone?"

"I had it on silent," I lied. "We've just got back. Jeez, Colt, chill out."

Abi's face turned bright red with her attempts not to laugh out loud.

"What ya doin' tonight?" he asked.

"Going to a bar with Abi," I lied again.

"Cancel," he demanded. "I'm taking you out."

My friend's eyes widened, and she punched the air.

"Hmmm. I don't really like canceling plans. Abi's relying on me. She wants me to be her wingwoman because you dragged me out of *Below Zero* on Friday night. Can we do it another time?"

Abi squeaked.

"Cancel," he repeated, louder this time. "I'll pick you up at eight."

"I dunno," I murmured undecidedly. "Maybe I'll just stay home. I'm tired."

"Eight. Be ready," Colt barked before disconnecting the call.

Abi burst out laughing. "Oh my God." She chuckled. "You played that one perfectly. I thought he was about to have a stroke."

I sat back in my seat. "I can lead a horse to water, but I can't make it drink. I've done what I can. Now, he has to take the initiative. If nothing happens tonight, I'm done. I can't be around him and act like we're only friends. We're more, and he knows it. He's known it for years. I'll lay it on the line tonight, and he'll either be in or out."

"I think he'll surprise you, babe. By the tone of his voice just then, he wasn't happy you weren't available for him. The plan's working." Abi counted off on her fingers. "One, you showed him you weren't a kid anymore and made him see you as a woman. Two, when he acted like an ass, you pulled away, effectively showing him you wouldn't take his crap. You know when we can't have something, we want it more, it's human nature. Three, you just showed him you wouldn't wait around, and that he's dispensable. Now, he sees you as a challenge he's got to overcome." Her lips curved evilly. "Now, the last part of the plan happens tonight."

I winced. "What are you gonna do?"

She cackled a laugh. "You're gonna make Colt pant after you. Tonight, Freya fucking Stone will turn some heads and show Colt there are plenty of men who'll snap you up if he doesn't." She waggled her eyebrows. "I think it's the perfect time to bring out the red dress."

A slow smile spread across my face. "Yes!"

Suddenly, my cell phone beeped with a message. I looked down at it and grinned. "He's bringing out the big guns, Abs." I turned my cell around for her to show her the message.

Colt: I've booked Rioja. Wear something nice.

"How the hell did he get into Rioja at short notice?" Abi asked.

I grinned. "Knowing Colt, he probably hacked their computer system."

"Jesus," she breathed, fanning her face. "He's hot as Hades. All that swagger, blond hair, and attitude, mixed up with all the subterfuge gives me cunt flutters."

I laughed. "Why do you think I'm in this god-forsaken position?"

Her eyes narrowed. "So, tonight's plan is a red dress, attitude, and big clit energy."

"Definitely," I agreed.

"Then why are we sitting in the car?" she demanded. "Let's get moving. We've got a man to snare."

I nodded my agreement. I'd teach Colt to walk out on me. By the time the night ended, I'd make sure Colter Van Der Cleeve had a fucking conniption.

Chapter Seven

Colt

At one minute to eight exactly, I rapped on Freya's new door.

I'd picked well. This one was much sturdier than the other. There were three locks instead of two, which were much better quality, so her landlord shouldn't go loco about the replacement. Nobody would be getting past this motherfucker unless she invited them.

Footsteps sounded from behind the door, and I caught myself holding my breath because when Freya dressed up, she always looked stunning. She didn't need to do much; all the basics were there, but she could transform into a siren with just a little makeup.

The door flew open, and my jaw dropped, all breath leaving my body, or maybe it all flowed to my cock alongside my blood because suddenly, it stood to attention like a new recruit on his first day of training.

Freya had styled her hair into a loose bun at the back, but she'd left a few strands falling sexily around her face and neck. Her eyes were framed with black liner, flicked out so sharply they could've fuckin' stabbed a man. Her cheeks were stained the same color as her glossy red lips. But the thing that made my cock weep was her dress.

It was fire-engine red, skin-tight, cut low across her firm little tits, held up with one strap diagonally across her chest. My gaze dropped, and I almost choked. The dress had been cut out, showing a generous amount of side boob.

I stood stock still with my mouth hanging open. The sound that left my throat sounded something like, "*Huhoiughhhh.*"

Freya's bright red lips curved into a sexy smile. "I just need to put my shoes on and grab my purse." She turned, and I froze at the sight of her ass swathed in skin-tight material, swaying seductively as she walked.

I almost fell to my goddamned knees.

Within seconds she sashayed back up her hallway wearing red sandals which crisscrossed up her goddamned leg so fucking sexily that my brain filled with images of me undoing those delicate little straps with my teeth.

"Ready?" she asked brightly.

Suddenly, my brain whooshed back into my head. "You need a coat," I rasped.

Freya shrugged a smooth, tanned, bare shoulder. "I'm hot-blooded. I'll be fine." Stepping out, she turned, locked the door, and walked ahead of me toward the stairs.

My cock jumped around like it had a life of its own. It hadn't been this out of control since I turned twelve and started jerking off to Kelly Le Brock from the movie 'Weird Science'.

I looked to the heavens, breathed hard, and cursed.

My princess and me had a lot to discuss tonight. My conversation with Shep and how she'd ghosted me all day made me realize a few things.

I'd taken my feelings toward Freya for granted, and tonight, it was gonna stop. Life was about to change for me. Whether I liked it or not, new opportunities had arisen, the main one being *her*.

She looked so fuckin' sexy I couldn't think straight. How had I resisted her all this time? How hadn't I said 'fuck the rules' and done what I wanted to do years ago?

How the fuck would I keep my hands off her?

Things didn't get any easier when we got to the restaurant.

As soon as we exited the car, two guys walked past us. Their necks craned as they walked past Freya. "Evening, gorgeous," one of them said.

The fire that sparked to life the instant I saw her burned hot. "Fuck off," I snarled.

Freya laughed. "They were only being friendly, Colt. Chill out. Sometimes, you act like an old man." Her glossy red lips twisted. "Thinking about it, you're probably there already. You're heading toward forty, right?"

I skewered her with a look. *Jesus.* "I'm thirty—fuckin'—six."

She shrugged. "Close enough." She threaded her arm through mine, and we headed up the street toward the restaurant. "I thought someone your age would have more patience."

I unthreaded our arms as we approached the restaurant, grabbing the door and opening it for her. Without a thought, my fingers went to the small of her back, a lover's touch, guiding her toward the maître d, who stood at a desk talking to a waiter.

A trail of goose bumps erupted down her back, and my cock kicked at how beautifully she responded to my touch. My imagination went crazy thinking about all the other places I could give her goose bumps, and my jaw clenched.

The maître d's eyes fell on Freya and widened briefly before he composed himself, giving us a friendly smile. "Good evening, Sir... Madam. What name, please?"

I shot him a cold stare. "Van Der Cleeve. Eight Thirty."

He nodded. "Very well, Sir. This way please." He took two menus from a pile and headed toward the restaurant area. We followed, all eyes turning to Freya. The men stared appreciatively, and the female ones filled with cold jealousy.

Without thinking, I caught her hand and brought it to my lips.

Fuckers needed to know that I couldn't stop them from looking at my Princess, but by God, they'd never get to touch her.

Freya's head whipped toward me, her eyebrows pulling together. She went to say something, but I shook my head at her. "Don't say a fuckin' word, Princess."

Her lips curled into a slight grin, but she didn't open her mouth, and thank God because my nerves were already on a knife-edge.

It had taken one damned day for me to do a one-eighty. Twenty-four hours for my mind to go from never wanting to stick my dick into Freya Stone, to never wanting anyone *but* me, to pop her sweet little cherry. Meeting with Shepherd had put things into perspective because I'd gone back to the hotel and thought long and hard about what, and who, I wanted.

When Freya opened the door, all the questions I'd pushed down for years bubbled to the surface. Was being with Freya really a betrayal? I'd proven myself ten-fold to my Prez over the years. If we got together, who would we really be hurting? Wouldn't it be better to make sure she was looked after?

She wasn't a kid anymore. She was old enough to make her own decisions. The only way I'd betray my club was if I mistreated her, and I'd never do that.

We approached a table toward the back wall. *Good, some privacy.*

"Here we are," the maître d said, gesturing toward it with a flourish. "One of the best tables we have." He glanced at me curiously. "Sir, do we have the pleasure of hosting one of the New York Van Der Cleeves?"

I held Freya's chair out for her, my fingertips lingering on her back as she took her seat. "Conrad is my father."

The maître d beamed. "Excellent, Sir. Welcome to Rioja. Your waiter will be with you shortly. Can I get you anything from the bar?"

The maître d gave me a nod at the choice of wine I ordered and then disappeared.

Glancing around the room, I noticed most eyes still on Freya, and my chest twisted.

"New York Van Der Cleeves?" she asked quietly, eyes sparkling. "That's hilarious."

My eyes fixated on her plump, red mouth, wondering if the color would look good smeared around my dick. I pulled at the collar of my button-up. "Is it hot in here?"

Freya's eyes softened. "I'm not overly hot."

"That's a matter of opinion," I retorted under my breath.

"Sorry?" she said, leaning forward slightly. "I didn't catch that."

My eyes dropped to the curve of her tits. "You'd need to wear clothes to feel the heat, Princess."

She glanced downward. "Don't you like my dress?"

My cock kicked like a motherfucker, my balls growing painfully heavy. "You know I like your dress, Princess. You enjoyin' your little game?"

She dipped her chin and looked up at me, her golden eyes full of innocence. "I don't know what you're talking about. This dress was the only thing that didn't need cleaning, and to be fair, you didn't give me much notice."

I lounged back in my chair, eyes burning into her. I decided to test the water. Freya had thrown me signals for years, but could she truly handle me? I knew she was a virgin—if I was honest with myself, it made the possessive part of me roar with satisfaction—but I needed her to understand what being with me entailed.

"You know exactly what you're doin', Princess," I said huskily. "You're playing with fire. If you're not careful, I'll spank your ass raw."

I almost groaned at how her eyes gleamed, and the way her little pink tongue darted out to lick her bottom lip.

"You don't scare me, Colter." Freya leaned forward until I could see the gentle swell of her breasts.

Saliva pooled in my mouth.

"Oh, Colt." She waved a nonchalant hand. "I was raised in a biker club. Do you think I haven't seen everything? Spank my ass all you want, I don't care. I know you'll take good care of me."

Sitting back, I studied her closely.

Freya was full of bravado. She'd never fucked nor played me. There was a ring of truth in her words though. She'd grown up witnessing things most girls would never have a clue about. The clubhouse was tame these days, but only since the kids had been around. Just two years ago, the Speed Demons' bar was a veritable den of iniquity. Growing up, the Demons' princess had probably learned more than most adults knew.

"Is that what you want, Princess?" I asked, chest rumbling with pleasure.

She opened her mouth to reply but was interrupted by the waiter approaching.

Picking up my menu, I scanned it, before ordering appetizers and mains for the both of us.

Freya smiled, watching him walk away. "You always know exactly what I'd order."

I nodded slowly. "Because it's always the same as I'd fuckin' order."

Her smile widened. "Remember when you used to take me to the mall. I'd always wanna go to a burger joint, but you'd insist on taking me to nice restaurants."

My chest tingled with warmth. "I knew you'd go places. I was certain one day you'd be better than the club. Didn't want you to be overwhelmed by rich people, so I showed you how it was done."

"You always looked out for me; you still do. Is it any wonder I have feelings for you?" Tears glimmered in her eyes, making my heart clench at the sadness I saw there.

A fire burning a hole in my gut.

She looked up at the waiter who approached us with our wine. I declined to taste it, telling him to pour. Freya's gaze transfixed on mine, and my heart thudded painfully at the thought of passing up on the promise of her.

I liked women. Over the years, I'd been with redheads, blondes, and brunettes. Tall, short, thin, plump, and everything in between. But I'd never been so fucking horny as I felt sitting in that restaurant looking at Freya Stone. God only knew how, but she'd made me want her above every other woman. Granted her red lips, red dress, and heaving tits did it for me, but there was more to her too. Freya's entire essence pulled me in, and fuck me, I didn't want to escape. I knew touching Freya was playing with fire, but being burned suddenly didn't seem too bad.

Picking up my glass, I swirled the wine around thoughtfully. "We'll see how it goes."

Freya's smile froze on her face. "What?"

"We'll do this on the proviso you adhere to my rules." I sipped my wine before placing the glass back on the table. "Want me to continue?"

Freya nodded, almost dumbstruck.

"One," I began. "I'm here for another week. It doesn't give us long to get to know each other. We'll decide after the week if we move things to Wyoming. If we do, it'll be difficult to keep our relationship under wraps, but that's the way it's gotta be, at least for a while. I don't want us to come out only to end things a month later. I don't wanna hurt ya, Freya, or anyone else. Do you get me?"

Hurt flashed behind her eyes.

"*Do you get me?*" I repeated with a harshness to my tone I didn't often use with her.

She tipped her chin up. "Yes."

"Good girl." I took another sip of wine, mentally noting how her cheeks bloomed pink at my words of praise.

Interesting.

"Two," I continued. "It'll be between me and you. No chatting with the ol' ladies. No secret late-night revelations to anyone. If it gets back to the club, they'll kill me, and it'll cause problems between you and your dad. He'll cut you off, Freya. You'd be fucked." I didn't add that she needn't worry because I'd look after her financially if it came to it. She needed to be aware of the pitfalls.

"I won't tell a soul," she breathed before cocking one eyebrow. "Anything else?"

I'd been dreading this part of the deal, but I knew if me and Freya did this, it'd be all or nothing. She needed to know long-term what I needed from her, even if it made her uncomfortable. She had to be okay with my next request and understand how seriously I meant it.

I leaned forward to look directly into her eyes. "Princess, I fuck a certain way. You have to be okay with it 'cause it's a dealbreaker for me."

Silence fell over the table for a full minute until she asked, "What do you mean?"

I paused briefly, eyes still staring intensely into hers. "I like control, Princess. You do what I tell you when I tell you. I may push you to places you feel uncomfortable. If that happens, you tell me, and I'll stop, but if I stop, I walk away 'cause there's no other option for me."

Another pause.

"Explain," she murmured, shifting in her seat. "I need to understand. Do you mean like BDSM?"

I shrugged. "Maybe we'll dip a toe into it. I may tie you up, but that's probably as far as it'd go, unless you asked for more, which we'd obviously discuss. My kink's more about control. I could use toys, I may tell you to dress for me, or I might edge you. At some point, I'll probably make you wish you'd never asked me to fuck you, Freya, but what I'll never do is physically hurt you."

I watched her think about my words, holding my breath.

"I know you'd never hurt me," she finally surmised. "There's nobody I trust more than you." She tilted her chin proudly. "Can I ask something?"

I jerked a nod.

"Do you do that with Lucy?"

My chest twisted at the slight catch in her voice.

I hadn't. Our relationship—if that's what you could even call it—was casual. I only showed my preferences to women I was close to, and there'd only been one serious relationship before Freya. I didn't wanna discuss Lucy; she wasn't important.

I replied with a slight shake of my head.

I dunno why I felt like such an asshole. I wouldn't have looked twice at Lucy if I even suspected something could happen with Frey. I'd gotten bored with the club girls before I even finished prospecting, so, over the years, I got together with a few of the girls from town because I didn't want the same snatch all my brothers had railed. And if other women were in the picture, I could convince myself—and everyone else—there was nothing between me and Freya.

Reaching out, I took her hand, splaying our fingers together. "I'll end it with her. Lucy's not important."

Freya rolled her eyes. "Of course she is. You pulled away from me for her."

I stroked her thumb. "Not for her, Princess. For *us*. Could feel you reeling me in, but I wasn't ready."

Freya lifted her gaze and bit her lip before whispering something that made my cock harden to iron. "What if you change your mind? We got closer before, and you fucked me over for her."

My heart almost leaped into my throat. "I won't change my mind."

She looked up at me, all big brown eyes, red, pouty lips, and glowing tanned skin. "Can I think about it?"

My gut tightened.

What if, after everything, she turned me down? What if I'd left it too late?

Her eyes fell over my shoulder. "Thank God. Our food's here."

I watched the waiter set everything down before I topped up our wine glasses and took a big swig. "Anything else you wanna ask, Princess?"

Freya picked up the small fork for her lobster and crab cakes, eyeing me curiously. "No. I think you made everything clear. I just need time to think." She delicately took a small mouthful of food, rolled her eyes back, and moaned.

I imagined her groaning the same sound as I slid inside her tight little virgin pussy. My cock wept, and I almost came in my shorts.

"What is it you need to think about?" I demanded gently.

"I don't want to lose what we have now," she replied softly. "Everything would change between us. You mean a lot to me; you always have, and I don't want to lose that."

My heart gave a kick. It was crazy how days ago, Freya had given me goo-goo eyes, and now I was the one almost begging. I could understand her reservations, but I was in it for the long haul.

"You've also gotta think about the fact that eventually, we'll also have to come clean to the club," I reminded her. "If we get caught, your dad will slit my throat. And the last thing I want is your relationship with your family and the club to get screwed up. I wanna take time for us to see how we work before we piss everybody off, but we have to be careful."

Freya picked up her wine glass and took a sip. "I understand, and I don't want your relationships fucked-up either, Colt. And I certainly don't want you to lose your place in the club."

I felt like an asshole for not being completely honest, but I still needed to wrap my head around what had happened with Shep. Everything had gone at light speed, and I still needed to catch up.

"We'll deal with it as it comes," I reiterated. "But me leaving the club is our only option."

She furrowed her brow. "I want to think about everything you've said."

I scraped a hand down my face, expelling a hard breath.

My Princess had a stubborn side; I'd experienced it countless times.

I wasn't proud of the push and pull I'd created, but I couldn't help the circumstances we found ourselves in.

Over the last few days, I'd allowed myself to finally look deeper. Freya wasn't a kid anymore. She was a beautiful, caring, intelligent woman. I wasn't the settling-down type, but if I had her, that would change.

"What made you ask me this tonight?" she asked curiously. "You've always shied away from me before. You've done a complete one-eighty."

I pushed my plate away, suddenly losing my appetite.

How could I tell her about the shit show I found myself in? At this stage, telling her about Shep was out of the question. I didn't know the details yet, and there was no point in worrying her.

"It's been challenging for me to leap from friends to something more," I admitted. "I've felt it for a while but didn't let myself go there." I rested my arms on the table, thinking how to word everything. "We both know there's a special bond between us. When you were growing up, it was a brotherly feelin' I had for you. It hasn't been easy to jump from that to something romantic. I'm not sayin' I didn't feel it; I just didn't recognize it had changed." I smirked. "Then you answered the door in that damned dress."

Freya laughed.

Shaking my head, I picked up my fork and stabbed my filet. "Eat your goddamned food."

She laughed again. "Yes, Sir."

My cock almost exploded.

Fuck my life.

Two hours later, we were getting ready to leave. I'd just paid the bill, smiling to myself at the other bottle of wine Freya had polished off. It didn't bother me. I wanted her to relax and not stress about what I'd offered earlier. And I liked tipsy Freya. She lost all her inhibitions.

As I stood to help her up, my cell phone rang.

Pulling it out of my pocket, I checked the screen and saw a private number calling.

My eyebrows slashed together. I hated these calls; the fuckers were virtually impossible to trace. Knowing it would bug the fuck out of my OCD if I didn't know who called, I motioned to Freya to sit back down. "I'll just take this," I told her, holding up my phone. "Won't be long."

She smiled and sank down into her chair.

I moved toward a small corridor leading to the ladies and men's rooms. It was quiet and in view of our table, so I could keep an eye on Freya.

Clicking the green icon, I held it to my ear. "Hello?" I heard silence, then a click as the call dropped in. "Colter Van Der Cleeve?" a familiar voice asked.

Raising a hand, I rubbed my temple. I needed this like I needed a limp dick. I cleared my throat before muttering, "What the fuck do you want now, Shepherd?"

A low chuckle came through the line. "Just wanted to let you know I've got news on the license plate. It's definitely Federal. I'm trying to track down which department it belongs to."

"Are they dirty or undercover?" I asked tightly.

"I don't know yet. If it's an undercover job, it's a good one. Not even I can find any intel. If the Feds are dirty, I'll need to escalate it. I suggest you try to keep your club away from it, at least until I have something more to tell you."

I glanced over at Freya and froze when I saw our waiter leaning on the table, chatting to her. My chest caught alight when she laughed at something he said. "This is all I need," I muttered, not just meaning our conversation.

"I'll get to the bottom of it," Shepherd promised. "You need to give me more time."

My eyes stayed on the waiter flirting up a storm with Freya. My jaw clenched tight as I watched him write something on a piece of paper and slide it across the table toward her.

My heart burned with an emotion I couldn't quite place and subconsciously didn't want to. The fucker had some balls giving Freya his number when she was out with me.

"Need to go," I replied, watching the waiter smile down at my princess before turning on his heel and returning to the kitchen. "Get diggin'. Need everything you've got asap." I ignored his protestations and ended the call while glaring toward the kitchen.

That asshole waiter had tried to get my girl while she was on a goddamned date with *me*. My nostrils flared as I breathed through my nose to calm my shit, but it didn't work.

I stalked through the restaurant, ignoring the looks the other diners shot me as I headed toward the kitchen. Fists balled up, jaw ticking. I probably looked like a crazy motherfucker.

Shoving the door to the kitchen open, I scanned the room. The chefs were cooking, calling out orders to each other as they put plates on the pass.

"Hey," I called out. "I'm lookin' for the waiter who serves table sixteen? Wanna give him a nice tip."

"He's out takin' a break," one of the workers shouted through the noise, nodding toward an open door at the back of the room.

"Obliged," I replied, going over and slipping through the door into the fresh fall air.

I turned and spied the fucker standing over to my left, leaning back against the wall, blowing smoke rings into the air, eyes on his cell.

Without a word of warning, I marched toward him.

He jumped, turning his head, eyes widening as he saw the anger pounding from me. "Err, Sir. I don't think you're supposed to be back here—"

Letting out a low growl, I threw my fist into his face, not as hard as I could, but hard enough to show him I wasn't a happy fuckin' diner.

His head snapped back, and he let out a low moan, clutching his nose. "Hey. What the fu—"

"That's for puttin' your moves on, my girl," I snarled. Grabbing my wallet, I pulled out some hundreds and threw them at him. "That'll cover your medical bill, but here's your tip. When a man's out with his woman, giving her your phone number is a sign of disrespect. Get me?"

He stared up at me, eyes round with fright, and nodded furiously.

"Have a nice fuckin' night." I turned and sauntered back through the kitchen to the restaurant, hands still clenched to fists by my sides.

I knew I'd overreacted. Jesus, he just put the moves on Freya, like all men did when it came to a beautiful girl.

But it wasn't just any beautiful girl; it was my girl, who I'd watched grow from a pretty teen to a unique, beautiful woman. It hit me that I didn't want any fuckers' hands on her but mine.

I just wanted to get her home and out of the sight of asshole men who thought it was okay to disrespect her and disrespect me.

Freya belonged to me now.

Chapter Eight

Freya

Two hours after *the* conversation, my stomach still fizzed and popped.

At last, Colt wanted me. Finally, we'd gotten somewhere, and I struggled to contain my excitement.

He'd gone to take a call, so, with shaky hands, I pulled my phone from my purse and messaged Abigail.

I knew I said I wouldn't tell anyone, but there was no way I'd leave Abi in the dark.

I'd just put my cell away when Colt appeared at the table and downed the dregs of his drink. "Get your shit, now. We're goin'"

The light feeling inside suddenly turned heavy. "What's happened? Are you okay?"

He pulled his jacket from the back of his chair, his movements jerky. "Move it, Freya."

I blinked up at him, eyebrows drawing together. "Who called you? Was it Dad?"

He looked at me pointedly, ignoring my question.

My blood cooled.

We'd had a great dinner and laughed, joked, and talked about old times. What the hell could've gotten Colt so worked up?

I stood with a slight wobble from the effect of the wine. Picking up my purse, I smoothed my dress and started slowly for the door.

"Wait." Colt slid an arm across my shoulders, guiding me toward the exit. "Don't want you tripping over."

My eyes raised to meet his. "I'm perfectly capable of walking out of the restaurant."

He let out a humorless snort. "What's the matter? Worried your boyfriend will see?"

My eyebrows drew together questioningly. Colt made no sense, and I didn't want to make things worse. I didn't understand what had made him so angry with me? What had I done?

I kept my mouth shut. I didn't want to make Colt even more pissed, but I also didn't like him speaking to me that way. He needed to tell me if I'd done something wrong, so I could make it right, instead of acting like a dickwad.

A small wave of hurt washed through me as we approached the exit and walked out into the cool night air toward the car. A group of young guys walked past but didn't say anything, probably because of the rigid set of Colt's jaw and the fury flashing through his eyes.

A cold shiver ran down my spine.

What the hell had happened when he stepped away from the table?

Colt clicked the key fob as we approached the car, and the lights flashed in the darkness as the locks disengaged.

"In," he ordered.

Jesus.

"What the hell's your problem?" I demanded, flinging the door open. My indignation flared at how he spoke to me. He was starting to push his luck. I prided myself on being understanding, especially regarding Colt, but I was no pushover.

He was heading into dangerous territory.

I slid into my seat, pulled my seat belt across, and clicked it into place before shooting Colt a quick glance as he started the car and sped out of our parking space.

The light caught his knuckles, and I did a double take. A couple of them were split and bloody. "What happened to your hand?" I asked, leaning forward to examine them more closely. "Did you get into a fight? Is that why you're in a bad mood?"

He kept his eyes on the road, his face like thunder.

My stomach churned.

I didn't like him driving so aggressively. I'd seen some awful sights in the ER because of dangerous driving. Colt was usually careful when he drove me anywhere. It was confusing, to say the least.

I kept my mouth shut, not wanting to make him madder. The evening had been so perfect. One minute, he put me on cloud nine, and the next, he brought me crashing back to Earth. How could everything have gone downhill so quickly?

I jutted my chin up. Screw him. I didn't need this treatment. I didn't need him.

It didn't take long for the car to speed into the parking lot of my apartment block. Colt had driven so fast that he'd knocked five minutes off the journey.

I leaned forward to open the door the second the tires squealed to a stop.

"What's the hurry," he snapped. "Can't you wait to get upstairs and call your asshat boyfr—?"

My head whipped around to face him, hand still on the door handle. "I don't know what your tantrum's all about, and quite frankly I don't care. You've disrespected me tonight, and it's made me wonder if I've been very wrong about you."

He let out an angry snort. "Likewise, bitch."

My breath caught, tears flooding my eyes.

I'd heard the word bitch for as long as I could remember. The brothers it used in many ways: jokingly, angrily, and lovingly. It was part of biker culture, and the Speed Demons used it as a term of endearment because they didn't usually speak to or about women in derogatory ways.

I never dreamed I'd hear Colt weaponize it against me.

The biker princess in me wanted to slap his face, tell him he was an asshole, and to leave me the fuck alone. But the girl who'd loved Colt for as long as she could remember just wanted to get out of there before he let me down even further.

"I think we can safely say that after tonight, our friendship's done." My voice sounded husky, probably due to the heated emotion hitting the back of my throat. I opened the door and went to get out.

Colt's hand came out and grabbed my arm, stopping me from moving. He turned to me, sneering, and clipped out, "I saw him give you his phone number." He leaned toward me and snatched my purse.

"Hey!" I shrieked. "Give that back."

Ignoring me, he snapped the clasp open and started rifling through it. "All night, you've had assholes falling over to talk to ya. They even detoured past our table to get a closer look. I don't fucking like it, Freya. Now, where's that phone number? I'm gonna burn the fucker."

My mouth fell open as suddenly, everything fell into place.

He was jealous.

I couldn't work out why though. I'd waited years for him; why would I jeopardize everything?

Colt brought out my insecure side and a lack of control. I'd never known him to get possessive over the women he dated before. Lucy had lasted the longest, but Colt didn't bat an eyelid even when she talked to the brothers. He usually seemed detached from her, almost irritated when she draped herself over him.

One time at the clubhouse, after he shook her off, she flirted with Shotgun, and Colt didn't even notice.

I hadn't welcomed any attention at all tonight. Hell, I didn't notice it half the time. Colt needed to grow up and stop being a dick to me over something I couldn't control.

"I can't stop men from looking at me," I stated coldly. "Maybe I shouldn't have worn something quite so revealing, but why should I wear a burlap sack because grown men don't possess the manners to control where their eyes wander? Is it really on me, or is it on them? The waiter gave me his number, but I didn't keep it." I snatched my purse back, got out of the car, slammed the door closed, and turned to my apartment.

Colt wound the window down and called, "Freya. Come back, we'll talk."

"Fuck you, Colt," I yelled, craning my neck to look at him. "Forget everything I said. I wouldn't touch your ridiculous ass if you paid me."

"Freya!" he shouted.

"Check your card receipt," I called over my shoulder. "Make sure the restaurant didn't overcharge you." With a toss of my hair, I let myself into the building, my heart aching as I heard the engine rev before the car sped away.

I walked up the stairs to my floor, trying to make sense of what just happened.

Guys gave me their numbers, now and again, mostly at work. I never kept them though. Sometimes, it was easier to placate somebody than make them feel inadequate by rejecting them outright. I knew I was pretty, but I didn't hold value in beauty because looks faded. I prided myself on working hard and being kind. I wasn't perfect, but I wasn't an asshole, either.

Colt obviously thought the worst of me. He froze me out and called me a bitch without even asking me what happened. Jealousy was a natural reaction, but he could still have behaved respectfully.

I wondered if he'd even bother looking at the receipt like I'd suggested. He'd see the number on the back of it in *his* pocket, not mine.

I let myself into my apartment, locking up behind me while cursing the entire male species. Maybe I was doomed to remain a virgin for eternity, though it didn't feel like a bad thing after Colt took his shitty mood out on me.

Turning off the lamp I'd left switched on in the living room, I went straight to my bedroom. I undressed by the bathroom light, grumbling about how Colt had been so quick to doubt me.

I grabbed my cell, clicked on a playlist, and smiled ruefully as the opening chords to Mark Ronson's 'Late Night Feelings' filled the bathroom.

Oh, the irony.

I jumped slightly as a loud bang came from the door.

My gut screamed it was Colt, but still, I wasn't sure if I should answer it. I didn't want to see him if he thought he could take his bad mood out on me.

I froze as the buzzer sounded.

Ugh. He'd wake all my neighbors if he carried on banging like a crazy person. A buzz filled the air again and again before the sound fractured through my apartment continuously.

Something fired in my belly. With a curse, I stomped to the hallway and checked the peephole.

"I know you're in there, Freya," he rasped. "Open the door, please."

My shoulders slumped in defeat. With a deep sigh, I unbolted the locks and pulled the door open. "What do you want, Colt?" I folded my arms across my chest, my eyebrow lifting in question.

His beautiful eyes locked with mine. "I was a dick."

I tapped my foot impatiently. "And?"

Colt scraped a hand over his face. "I'm sorry."

My eyes narrowed. "Thanks for the apology. I'll call you." Colt's face fell when he saw me step back and shoot him a snooty glare before slamming the door in his face.

He called my name, but I ignored it. I turned on my heel and stomped into my bedroom.

What an asshole. If Colt thought he could speak down to me and call me names, he had another thing coming. I'd been so excited over dinner when he finally made his move, but it went up in flames within hours. He frustrated me to the point where I wanted to scream.

I turned to walk into my bathroom when suddenly, out of the corner of my eye, I caught a figure looming in my bedroom doorway.

My heart plummeted, every muscle tensing as I opened my mouth and let out a piercing scream.

A strong hand clamped across my mouth, another cuffing the front of my neck and pulling me back into a hard body. "Ssshh, Freya. It's me," Colt rasped. "Not gonna hurt ya."

My entire body slumped until all that held me up was Colt's hands. "Jesus," I groaned through his fingers. "You scared the life out of me." I babbled. "What are you doing here? How did you get in? I don't fucking want you here."

His mouth rested on the shell of my ear. "I'm sorry, baby," he whispered, turning me to face him. "I got a key from the guy who fitted the new door."

My eyes met his ocean-blues and filled with tears.

"Freya," he murmured, looking horrified. "I'm sorry. I didn't mean to upset you. I dunno what came over me. I just got so fucking angry."

Maybe it was delayed shock, an adverse reaction to being so frightened. Or was it because Colt frustrated me so much I couldn't think straight.

Not a half hour ago, he treated me like an idiot, and now he stood with his arms around me in my bedroom like it was the most natural thing in the world.

His neck bent until his forehead rested on mine. "You drive me insane, Freya. God knows how, but you've broken down walls that took years to build. You make me feel raw and exposed. Half the time, I dunno if I should tan your ass or kiss you stupid. You've got me all tied up inside, and I don't know how to unravel."

My heart fluttered. "I feel the same. But you can't treat me the way you did tonight. I don't deserve that shit."

"I know," he replied, tipping my chin up to look deep in my eyes. "I'm a jealous prick when it comes to you, baby. You burn me up inside." His eyes flickered between mine, full of emotion I'd never seen from him before. After what seemed like an age, he lowered his head and softly took my mouth.

I melted, and my heart unfurled inside my chest like a flower on the first day of spring. Finally, he'd kissed me. I'd waited eight years for him, and it was everything I'd dreamed of. My mind went back to the years I'd tried to make him see me, and I burrowed deeper into him, never wanting to let go.

I whimpered softly and slid my hands around his neck.

His lips were soft but firm. He coaxed my mouth open with his and tangled his tongue with mine. His moan was full of need, making my knees turn to jelly as he strengthened the kiss, moving his lips like he was half starved.

I tangled my fingers into his hair and pulled him closer, sighing contentedly.

Colt's hand went to my hip and tugged me into him. I gasped as his thick, hard cock hit my stomach through his jeans.

With a groan, he broke our kiss, pulling away gently. "I know I'm askin' a lot, and I know you don't like my rules, but tell me you want this. I'll give you everything I can, but you gotta say yes first."

I felt a slight flutter deep in the pit of my stomach as a shiver of desire went through me.

I'd squirmed in my seat in the restaurant when he said he wanted to control every aspect of me. I couldn't believe he was proposing to give me what I'd asked for, but there was also the risk of my heart smashing into pieces if it got too heavy, and he walked away.

Colt was my dream man. He kept me on my toes and was so intelligent I sometimes struggled to keep up with him. No man had ever made me feel like I could take on the world except Colt. The thought of us being nothing made my throat burn and feel like half of me had been ripped away.

At least I'd get this part of him, even if we may have been on borrowed time.

I couldn't help admitting I was curious about the things he told me in the restaurant. If I was honest with myself, I liked the idea of Colt taking control of me. Plus, he'd given me the option to stop at any time.

That had to count for something, surely?

What if this could be the start of something special?

Colt pulled away slightly and nipped my bottom lip. "Is this what you want, Freya? You've gotta tell me."

Studying the face that had haunted my dreams since I was fifteen, I concentrated on the blood rushing through my veins and the buoyant feeling in my chest.

Colt made me feel things I'd never experienced before. He made me excited to be alive.

A smile curved my lips, probably the first genuine one I'd felt in years. "Yes."

His shoulders slumped with what appeared to be relief. "I'm sorry I got angry, baby. You drive me fuckin' crazy." His hand slid down to rub my pussy outside my clothes. "Has any man touched you here at all?"

Cheeks on fire, I shook my head, too ashamed to speak. The only person who'd ever touched me was me.

"Look at you," he said thickly. "The minute I touch this pussy, I'm breakin' all the rules. Do you like the thought of that, Princess? You wanna be bad with me?"

My pussy clenched at the mere thought of the forbidden shit I wanted us to do. Biting my lip, I nodded.

"I'll break every rule for you, Freya, every law in the land 'cause you saved all of it for me. I can't give you the same, baby, but I can promise from now on, everything I am belongs to you. Do you understand?"

My heart overflowed with emotion. "Yes."

"Good," he rumbled. "Now, be a good girl and get in the shower."

My heart jumped, and my eyes widened. "Are you staying tonight?"

A sexy grin spread over Colt's face. "Yeah." He slid the hidden zipper at the back of my dress down and pushed it off my body until I stood in just my red panties and shoes.

I shivered, self-consciously crossing my arms across my chest.

Slowly kneeling, he unfastened my heels, lifting my feet to remove them. "We're not goin' all the way tonight, baby," he said huskily, brushing against my body as he stood to his full height. "Tonight, I'm gonna feast on your beautiful body, and you're gonna blow me. You ever done that before?"

I shook my head nervously.

Colt's smile widened. "Gonna have the time of my damned life teachin' you how to give head." He nodded toward the shower. "Get in. I'll join you in a minute."

Almost dazed, I hurried into the bathroom, shimmied out of my panties, and turned the shower on, waiting for the water to heat. My mind raced with thoughts of Colt, wondering how it all went from zero to a hundred.

After ten years of waiting, I'd finally gotten my reward.

I knew at fourteen how Colt didn't look at me as anything but a little girl, almost a sister. For years, our relationship stayed platonic. I was too young for him to see romantically, and I knew it would be years until things changed. But I always kept the faith. I always believed in him.

In a way, I'd molded myself into Colt's ideal woman, watching and learning about what he valued in the opposite sex. It was apparent he liked intelligence first and foremost. He usually went for naturally pretty girls, though he also liked a woman who could dress up and turn heads.

God only knew how Lucy had snared him. Over time, she came across as more and more fake, not just in her appearance but also in her personality.

I stepped into the shower, trying to ignore the ache in my chest that expanded every time Lucy's name was mentioned. Colt chose her almost a year ago and left me out in the cold. He preferred her over me back then, and it hurt so much that I stopped visiting home. Although my heart swelled with everything Colt offered, I couldn't help wondering why he'd changed his mind.

He'd told me he'd end things with Lucy—thank God—but I didn't want us to do anything sexual until he'd told her it was over. Even us kissing was a mistake, but he took me by surprise.

I jumped as the shower door opened, and there stood Colt, completely naked.

My heart lurched at the sight of him, all tall and muscular. He was so damned beautiful he took my breath away.

I'd seen him without a shirt on at the compound in summer around the pool. There was always a barbeque or a party going on, and the man candy was out in force. Not that I noticed anyone but Colt. Nobody else compared.

His skin was a golden honey color. It almost gleamed as rivulets of water ran down his chest, darkening the smattering of blond hair there. Colt's muscles—although not overly large like Atlas's—were defined. His stomach had all the bumps and ridges of a six-pack and a happy trail of hair leading to the perfectly curved cock jutting from his body.

Colt looked like a sun god, tall, broad, golden, and beautiful. His face seemed like it had been carved by a higher power as he gazed down at me with his mesmerizing blue eyes.

"Fuckin' knew I'd see you like this and know you were made for me. You, here, lookin' the way you look is worth everythin', even my place in the club. One minute, I can't work out how the fuck I've managed to resist you. The next, I ask myself: how am I meant to look your dad and brothers in the eye, knowing I've been inside you?"

I reached up, cupped his jaw, and murmured, "Do you want to take a step back?"

"No, baby," he assured me gently. "I dunno how it happened, but you've crashed through every barrier I put up to keep you out. All it took was one dance to make me realize you're mine."

I smiled, my heart skipping with delight. "We've danced together before."

"We haven't danced since you were nineteen," he corrected. "I think that was when I knew things were changing. I'm glad you moved away and got your own life. It's the best thing you could've done. It gave you time to grow up, and it gave me a chance to miss you." He leaned down to kiss me, but I pressed a hand to his chest.

"I can't, Colt. You're still with her. I don't want to cheat."

"She's not my girlfriend," he protested. "I'd never do that."

"I'm sorry. I know it's not serious with you two, but she's still between us. Lucy's not my favorite person. She's been nothing but a bitch to me, but I still don't want to be *that* girl." My eyes lowered, and I bit my lip.

His head reared back slightly. "What do ya mean, she's been a bitch to you?"

"I tried so hard to like her," I whispered. "I tried for you, Colt, but I think she's jealous of our friendship. Lucy used to imply that you told her I was annoying. She said my crush was embarrassing, and you wanted me to leave you alone. It's why I stopped visiting home."

The air around us instantly cooled. Colt's lip curled slightly, his eyes darting between mine as he thought about what I'd just told him. Eventually, he tipped my chin up with a finger. "Wait here."

He turned and disappeared from the shower stall, leaving the door open as he went.

I poked my head out. "What are you doing?" I called after him.

Colt strode back from the bedroom with just a towel wrapped around his waist, holding his cell. "Fuckin' bitch," he muttered, stabbing on his phone.

My head reared back slightly. "Colt. The shower's still on. What are—"

He held a hand up to silence me, clicking the speaker button so I could listen.

The quizzical look I gave him dropped as the person he called picked up the phone, and a seductive, breathy voice greeted him. "Hi, love bucket."

Shit.

Lucy?

Chapter Nine

Colt

My eyes swept down Freya's body which was partially obscured by the reinforced glass pattern of the shower door.

A muscle ticked in my jaw as I thought about what she'd just told me. What the fuck had Lucy been sayin' to her? And why the fuck did the bitch think she'd get away with speaking to Freya like an asshole.

Maybe I should've gone about this a different way, but my girl needed to understand how little Lucy factored into my life. Still, the instant she heard Lucy's voice, her face fell.

I could've kicked my own ass, but it was too late to go back and do things differently.

"I miss you," Lucy whined, oblivious to the fact Freya was listening in. "When are you coming home?"

My jaw tightened. When the fuck did she become so clingy? And how hadn't I noticed?

"None of your business," I retorted. "Told ya, you're not my keeper. We're not official, so my whereabouts will always be a mystery as far as you're concerned. Been talkin' to Prez, he said you turned up at the clubhouse lookin' for me."

Freya's eyebrows hit her hairline. Even she knew it was a bad move.

Silence filled the room briefly before Lucy murmured, "I only wanted to know where you were. You never even said you were going away on club business. You should've told me; I'd have got my dad to look after the shop and come with you."

A growl escaped my chest, and I snapped, "No, you wouldn't. Told ya before, we don't got that type of relationship. That's why I'm callin'. Think it's time we called it quits. We're not goin' anywhere, so there's no point beatin' a dead horse."

Freya's eyes rounded.

"What?" Lucy snapped.

I looked to the heavens, muttering obscenities. Lucy was about to start drama in three... two—

"Ten months," she shrieked. "Ten fucking months I've wasted on you!"

Freya raised a hand to cover her laugh.

"Stop with the dramatics," I muttered, lips twitching at Freya. "We're not even official. You must've seen it comin'. If I was gonna wife you up, I'd have done it a month in. All that time with no commitment, babe. Says it all."

"Oh my God," she screamed. "You're such an asshole. I can't believe you're dumping me over the phone. I got asked out on a date last night at the Lucky Shamrock. I turned him down. For *you!*" She sniffed haughtily. "I should've known you only wanted me for sex."

I cocked my head. "Nah, babe. If I just wanted sex, I'd have picked a bitch who was good at it."

Freya clapped a hand over her mouth.

"Excuse me?" Lucy said, tone deathly quiet.

"I've been *excusing* your shitty blow jobs for ten months, babe," I announced. "Too much teeth is a bitch."

"Too much teeth?" Lucy whispered.

"Yeah. Too much teeth. Thought my poor Johnson was gettin' mauled by a goddamned pit bull every time I went near your fuckin' gnashers."

Freya's shoulders shook.

"Oh my God," Lucy yelled. "You're such an asshole!"

"Shame it took you ten months to work it out." I studied Freya, thinking about what she'd just told me about Lucy's bitchy behavior. "And I may be an asshole, but at least I'm not an evil, stuck-up bitch. Heard you've been a cunt to Freya behind my goddamned back. That shit don't stand. The minute you opened your mouth to her, you showed me who you were. Now, I repeat, we're done, it's over, and in about eight seconds, I'll be movin' on. It'd be good if you did the same."

"Should've known *she'd* be involved," Lucy snapped. "You won't hear a word against her." She scoffed. "I can't believe she's gone running to you telling lies when in reality, she's the one who's mean to *me*! You always take her side over mine."

I emitted a growl. "Yeah, 'cause I know Freya better than anyone. She hasn't got a mean bone in her body. I trust her more than anyone in this world. She's my best friend."

Lucy sniffed.

"Lose my number," I muttered, ending the call with a stab of my finger. I turned to Freya, face deadpan. "You happy now, Princess?"

She nodded.

My heart dropped when I noticed her glistening eyes. "So what's with the tears?"

"I'm your best friend?" she asked disbelievingly.

My expression softened. "Yeah, Freya. You're my everything. You're the first thing I think of when I wake up, and you're with me all day until I go to sleep.

You're the brightest light in the room, and sometimes it's fuckin' blindin', but I can't look away. Jesus, I don't ever want to."

One tear fell down her face, but she beamed.

I ignored the warm feeling spreading through my chest. "Hurry up and shower. I'll dry off and wait for you in the livin' room." I turned and left my girl to finish up, going back into her bedroom and pulling my jeans back on.

I'd had every intention of making out with Freya in that fuckin' shower, but after the Lucy incident, it seemed wrong somehow. Bad timing.

It didn't feel right to get down and dirty after essentially talkin' about blow jobs with Lucy. I'd effectively killed the mood with that phone call. Maybe I shouldn't have done it in front of Freya, but I needed her to understand that Lucy meant nothing to me, especially when compared to her.

I meant what I said, my princess really was my best friend. We understood each other. When I was with her, I could be myself. I wasn't the nerd or the know-it-all. I was just me, and I loved that she looked deeper than everybody else.

It worked both ways. I recognized how hard Freya worked and how she tried to make everybody around her happy. I knew she loved training to be a doctor, but I also suspected she did it as much for her dad as for herself. I knew she felt less important than her brothers because her dad's focus was on the club, though I knew he worshipped her.

Doing what made her pop happy was Freya's way of making herself feel worthy.

I'd known her since she was a kid. Even then, something about her called to me. I'd always loved and admired her spirit and her deep-rooted desire to care about everybody around her. As she grew up, the love grew too, until it mutated into the kind of love I'd never dared to wish for myself.

She was always meant to be mine. I didn't want to hurt my prez or my brothers, so I sacrificed my own needs for theirs. But very soon, Dagger wouldn't be my prez; Breaker, Cash, and Bowie would no longer be my brothers, and it bothered me, but strangely, not as much as it should.

Where one door closed, another opened, and behind this particular door stood Freya.

I'd wasted so much damned time; however, it was becoming clear that we would've ended up together regardless.

All the meeting with Shep had done was open my eyes and, in a roundabout way, make the inevitable happen sooner. Even if I hadn't been recruited, I would've woken up and eventually claimed Freya, and I'd have had to leave the club, anyway.

I was so deep in my thoughts I hadn't heard the shower turn off, so when Freya walked into the lounge wearing her robe, it startled me.

"I can't believe you just did that," she said huskily. "Are you okay ending things with Lucy?"

I froze, head rearing back as I looked for signs she was yanking my chain. When I saw she meant it seriously, I threw my head back and laughed.

"Hey!" she admonished. "It's not funny. You were together for nearly a year. She must've had some qualities you liked, or else why be with her for so long?"

I knew Freya was right. Ten months was a long time to be around a woman I didn't want. But there were reasons for it.

"She seemed sweet when I met her." I patted the space beside me, gesturing for her to sit. "Her personality changed so slowly I didn't notice at first, then a few weeks ago, I turned around, and it hit me that she wasn't who I thought she was." Freya sat down next to me, and I slid an arm across her shoulders, pulling her close. "I was lazy, baby. I kept her around because it was convenient, but also because it forced me to stay away from you. I think subconsciously, I used her as a buffer."

"You did," she whispered. "And it hurt me because I thought you were my friend."

"I know," I replied, voice thick with self-reproach. "But we stopped being friends the day you hit twenty-one. After that, it became more. I knew being with you would change every aspect of my life, and I needed time to come to terms with what that meant. You did too, Frey. Bein' an old lady isn't an easy life."

She let out a soft snort. "I know the life, Colt. I've lived it longer than you, remember?"

My jaw ticked. "I know, Frey, but I can understand why your dad worries."

She laughed softly. "Dad doesn't usually remember I exist."

"He thinks the world of you," I argued.

"I know he loves me," she replied. "But my brothers are more important to him."

"Not the impression I get." I played with a lock of her wet hair. "Why does he warn all the club members off you if he doesn't care?"

"He doesn't do that for me. He does it because he's got an idea of who I should be and the life I should lead. Any other dad would just want their daughter to be happy. My dad wants me to be happy but only on *his* terms."

Her words stopped me in my tracks.

Freya was right when she said Prez had specific ideas of what and who he wanted for her, but was his controlling behavior out of hand?

The Sinners were dangerous. They'd taken Breaker's daughter, Kady, and had something to do with Robbie Henderson kidnapping Layla. I could understand Dagger's desire to keep her away from the club so she wasn't constantly looking over her shoulder. But was it becoming detrimental to what Freya wanted for herself?

It was her life, not his, and if anyone could look after her, it was a Speed Demon. She was already in the life and had no doubt been marked from birth. Was he pushing Freya away for her own good but, at the same time, taking it too far and making her feel unwanted?

"Look at me," I ordered gently.

She sighed.

"Princess, look at me," I demanded.

Slowly, she turned until her glistening eyes hit mine.

"When it comes out about us, you gotta know we're gonna get shit. Are you ready for that, Frey? Do you understand how much it will hurt to have your family turn on you?" I asked. "I'll always have your back. But we'll be cast out. I'll be seen as a traitor. Do you know what the consequences will be? If Dagger turned up here I'd be fucked."

She rolled her eyes. "Do you know how often my dad's visited me while I've been in Denver?"

I shook my head.

"Zero times. He doesn't come here. The club's more important. Trust me, Colt. It won't come out yet because it would mean somebody would have to visit." She sat up, twisted her body, and swung a leg over my lap, straddling me.

"Jesus, fuck." I groaned as heat from her pussy hit my cock.

She curled a hand around my nape, leaned forward, and crushed her mouth against mine.

A flame ignited in my stomach as the scent of Coco Chanel hit me in the dick.

She sighed and pressed her pussy against my hardening cock. Her soft tits skimmed my chest, and I raised a hand to cup one gently.

With a strangled grunt, my tongue licked along the seam of her lips, a silent demand to open. My fingers dug deeper into her skin, her hips circling against me.

I pressed my tongue against Freya's, desperate to taste her after years of fantasizing. She was the girl I dreamed of, and finally, we were here together, the way it should've always been.

One hand slid against my chest, and she whimpered into my mouth as her crotch circled mine again.

I pulled back slightly, and my mouth latched onto her bottom lip, gently sucking.

I felt her thighs tremble. Throwing her head back, she moaned at the sensations I evoked, my lips traveled down her neck, kissing the soft skin of her throat before nipping her collarbone gently.

She seemed too far away from me. I needed her taste back, needed her warmth.

"Mouth," I rasped. "Now." I pulled back to look into her eyes again. "Gimme that fuckin' mouth, Princess."

Freya leaned forward again and sucked my top lip, mimicking my earlier action. My hand moved from her hip to dig into the cheeks of her ass so I could pull her hot pussy against my cock. I took her mouth again and fucked it with my tongue, in and out, while I pulled her sweet, weeping pussy against my cock.

I nearly came then and there.

Men went crazy for the beautiful woman in my arms. I'd seen their fevered looks, their slackening jaws, and their wolfish grins following her whenever she walked into a room. She looked like a fucking siren, but underneath, she was a girl next door, sweet, caring, and kind.

My throat heated when I thought about everything I had in my arms. Freya wasn't a girl anymore. Finally, she was ripe and ready for me. She looked, tasted, and smelled like she was all fucking woman. The Chanel scent I'd associated with her for so long had become ingrained in my psyche.

With a soft moan, she broke our kiss. "I feel so empty," Freya whispered. "Please come to my bedroom. I need you, Colt."

My cock wept at the thought of being inside Freya, but I wanted it to be special for her. It seemed wrong to fuck her the same night I'd dumped another woman. I wanted her more than anything, but it just didn't feel right.

However, it didn't mean I couldn't make her feel good in other ways.

"Hold on," I ordered gently, moving her arms until they were secure around my neck. With Freya still on my lap, I slowly stood. Her legs snaked around my waist, and I began to carry her toward the bedroom.

"I know I'm askin' a lot," I murmured. "And I know you don't like my rules, but tell me you want this, and I'll give you everything I can."

Freya's eyes bored into mine like she was searching for something.

"I won't let you down," I assured her as we hit her room. "You can trust me."

A small smile parted Freya's lips, and she nodded. "I know." Her eyes sparkled with emotion. "I do trust you. I'm just worried what will happen if we crash and burn."

I set her ass on the foot of the bed, sank to my knees, and framed her face with my hands. "I'll make you a promise, Princess. If we crash and burn, we'll do it together, okay?"

Her eyes darted between mine. "Are you sure this is what you want, Colt? I know how much you're giving up for me, but do you?"

I grinned because giving up the club didn't seem so bad. The FBI may be good for me, and I could still help the Demons from behind the scenes, except I'd have my girl by my side.

"Baby," I rasped, nuzzling her nose with mine. "Ain't giving up anything compared to what I'm gettin'. As long as you're with me, I can take the world on."

Her eyes welled with tears, and she gave a decisive nod as she said the words that made my heart soar.

"Let's do this."

Chapter Ten

Freya

All my life, I'd been pushed aside.

My dad was so busy with the club that he sometimes made me feel as if I was in the way. It was obvious Pop chose my brothers and the Speed Demons over me. I knew he did it for the right reasons; he had responsibilities to keep the men safe and their families fed. I got it, but a part of me felt pushed aside.

My mom was great, and I knew she loved me, but she left me at the club when she moved to be close to Tim. Again, I understood why. I had school and my SATs and college to prepare for, but still, she chose to be with Tim over me.

It had been a pattern all my life. So, when Colt came to the club and made time for me when nobody else did, I knew he was special. He helped me prepare for tests, making sure I was okay and not overwhelmed with how fast things happened for me at such a young age. He generally had my back.

As I grew older, I found myself studying him from afar. I'd take in the way his eyes would crinkle at the edges when he laughed. How he'd thrust a hand through his thick hair when he tried to solve a problem.

I even studied how his features would darken when he saw a woman who appealed to his baser instincts.

The first time I saw his arousal, I was fifteen.

I walked through the bar one night—later than I was allowed—and there he was, in a dark corner, sitting on a table, legs apart with a woman standing between them.

I watched, mesmerized, as he traced a finger down her cheek and neck until it rested on her collarbone. There, his fingertip traced circles as he nuzzled her neck, murmuring words into her skin.

That night, I experienced my first flush of possessiveness. I didn't like seeing him that way or with a woman who wasn't me. I knew about sex—Jesus. I grew up in a biker compound—but I felt sick when I imagined his body connected to hers in the most primal of ways.

I went home that night, and not for the first time, I slid between cool sheets and touched myself to the thought of him being that way with me. In my fantasies, it was me standing between his legs, and the slick moisture coating my fingers, in my dreams, coated his.

So, you see, Colt Van Der Cleeve awakened me in every way. He was my first and only sexual experience. A part of me never believed I'd be the one he chose, but he'd proven me wrong.

I realized now that Colt had been there every step of the way.

Now, watching how he kneeled before me, worshipping me, I knew I wanted him to be my first in every way. I'd always known he was it for me. I'd saved myself for him, after all.

His lips were soft but firm. He coaxed my mouth open with his and tangled his tongue with mine. His moan was full of need, making my knees turn to jelly as he strengthened the kiss, moving his lips like he was half-starved.

My arm slid around his neck, tangling in his hair to pull him closer, sighing contentedly at the feel of his touch and the urgency of his kiss.

Colt's hand went to my hip and tugged me until my ass rested on the edge of the bed. The belt of my robe unraveled, parting the material, leaving me exposed to his gaze.

His ocean-blues ate me up, and his mouth twisted into a smirk. "Look at you. I knew you'd be fuckin' incredible."

Something fluttered deep inside my stomach, and a shiver of desire went through me.

I was screwed when it came to Colt. The thought of everything going wrong already made my throat burn with the feeling of missing out on something vital. But the here and now was better than nothing; at least I'd get to have a part of him, even if it turned out we were on borrowed time.

The control thing I kinda understood, but also didn't. I'd never been in the position to know if I'd like it but I couldn't help admitting I was curious. It didn't seem particularly kinky to let Colt have total control, but I had no point of reference to compare it to. He'd been open and honest, though. That had to count for something.

Colt nipped my bottom lip. "Is this what you want, Freya? You want me to touch you?"

I took in the face that had haunted my dreams since I was fifteen, and a smile curved my lips, probably the first genuine one I'd felt in years. "Yes."

His shoulders slumped with what appeared to be relief. "Has any man been here with his mouth or fingers?" he demanded, looking into my eyes.

Cheeks on fire, I shook my head.

"Look at you blushin' like a good girl," he said thickly. "You know the minute I touch this pussy, I'm breakin' all the rules?"

My thighs clenched at the mere thought of the forbidden shit we were about to do. Biting my lip, I nodded.

"It's worth it 'cause you saved all it for me, Freya," he said huskily. "Now, spread your legs. Let me see what a virgin pussy looks like."

My eyes flicked over his muscular shoulders, then lower, taking in his broad, firm chest containing a smattering of hair slightly darker than I expected. Slowly, I spread my legs apart.

"Lean back on the bed, Freya," he ordered.

I obeyed.

He sat up and tugged my ass off the bed, hoisting my left leg over his shoulder. His eyes lifted to hit mine, and he grinned devilishly, repeating the action with my right leg until it was just his shoulders holding my lower body up.

I grabbed his arm and yelped.

"Trust me," he said, tone thick with need. His eyes lowered, resting on my pussy which by then was inches from his face. "You're everythin', baby. So fuckin' beautiful." He nuzzled closer, making me moan as moisture flooded my core.

Eyes still on mine, he slid his hand to my pussy and parted my folds with two fingers, holding me open, he tongued my clit, rumbling deep in his chest.

I moaned as a jolt of electricity rushed through my body, the vibrations sending a delicious shudder through me. My back arched higher as Colt's tongue flicked harder, lashing at my clit.

"Jesus." I whimpered.

"He ain't gonna help you now, baby girl. Gonna make this little cunt weep for me." With another growl, Colt's eyes darkened to the color of twilight as he stared up at me, seemingly mesmerized. "Always reckoned you were beautiful, Freya, with that gorgeous hair and exquisite body. But the sight of you like this, all glowing skin, pert little nipples, and tight, wet pussy..." his voice trailed off, face softening. "Baby, you're spectacular."

His tongue came out again and laved at my clit, eyes still holding mine hostage. His mouth covered my pussy, and his tongue flicked inside me in short, dense, fucking motions.

"Colt," I moaned.

His eyes were like magnets, drawing me in with untold promises deep within their depths. "Sweetest cunt I've ever tasted," he muttered in a voice almost demonic with need. "Can't wait to give you my cock." He pulled back and blew a hard breath over my clit, making me cry out at the sensation.

His thumbs pulled me apart until I was totally exposed to him. He leaned forward, seeming to take my entire core into his mouth, and sucked hard.

My hips bucked, and I groaned when he changed tactics and speared his tongue inside my clenching pussy, fucking me with it as deeply as possible while his thumb circled my clit. He kept alternating between tonguing me and sucking on my clit, making me climb higher.

I'd read about sex and even watched porn on occasion, but it seemed like Colt knew my body better than I did. I'd climaxed countless times in my darkened bedroom while I touched myself to thoughts of him and all the ways I could make him mine, but I'd never experienced anything like this.

He released a growl, and the vibration hit my core. The stimulation was too much. With a loud wail, I arched against his face, circling my hips and forcing his tongue deeper as my orgasm hit from nowhere.

Everything pulsed, even my nerve endings burned, and I cried out again and again as my orgasm pounded through me.

"Fuck yeah," he muttered, lashing my clit again. "Fuckin' beautiful."

I whimpered as his thick tongue fucked me through my climax. He moaned into my pussy while his tongue laved my clit. My thighs started to shake, my core still pulsing with aftershocks from the force of the orgasm he'd given me.

Colt hummed with pleasure before pulling back, kissing my mound, and placing my feet back on the floor.

"Jesus, Colt," I whispered, limbs heavy with exhaustion as I scooched back onto my bed. "My legs don't work."

He chuckled. "I've got ya, Princess. You'll be okay in a minute." He stood, blue eyes burning into mine as he popped his buttons, pulled his jeans down his legs, and kicked them off.

Everything about Colt's cock was as beautiful as the rest of him. His length jutted up his muscular stomach, long, thick, and perfectly curved. I could see he looked after himself by the light hair around the base, which was neatly trimmed.

My pussy pulsed again, and my heart leaped as I watched him climb onto the bed and pull the comforter over us before pulling me into the crook of his shoulder.

I rested my face against his chest, sighing as his fingers threaded through my hair. "Are you gonna fuck me now?" I asked softly, eyes half-mast with satisfaction after my powerful orgasm.

"Not tonight, baby," he murmured. "Gotta do some housekeepin' first. You still takin' birth control pills?"

I looked into his face and nodded.

"Up-to-date?" he asked.

"Never miss one," I confirmed. "Babies don't mix with internships."

"I get tested all the time. Not fucked a woman for a while, certainly not since I got my last results back, which were negative." Colt's eyes narrowed. "Do you trust me, Freya?"

"Yes," I said without hesitation.

"Good." He nodded slowly. "I'll never hurt you, baby. Anything we do will be what we both want. I'm not here to make you feel uncomfortable." He leaned across and softly kissed me before taking my hand. "Do you want kids?" He let out a quiet snort. "It's probably the only thing I don't know about you."

I brought a hand up to cup his cheek. "When the time's right, I'd like one, maybe two, but I want to get my residency out the way before I worry about kids."

"Never thought it would happen to me," he murmured. "But you, here, in my arms, makes me think it would be nice to have a kid one day." He rubbed the pad of his thumb over my bottom lip. "Sometime soon, I'm gonna come right there and watch you lick it away."

My hand slid down to cup his burgeoning cock, but he moved it away. "Not tonight, Freya. It's late. You need sleep."

"But what about you?" I asked frantically. "I want to please you too."

"I'm good. You were awake half the night and had a busy day. Tomorrow's a new day, baby. Tonight's been a taster of what's to come. I'm gonna make you feel so fucking good, you won't know what's hit you."

"Are you sure?" I asked. "Because I want to."

He unhooked his arm from my shoulders and shifted onto his side to face me. He motioned for me to do the same, so I turned until we both lay staring into each other's eyes.

"I don't want our first time screwed up by outside shit, baby," he whispered. "We've got time."

"But we have to go back to Hambleton soon," I argued softly. "I don't want to waste a minute of this. I want to make the most of every second we have here because soon, we'll have to hide, Colt."

"We've waited years, Freya. Another night won't hurt." He smiled. "We won't hide for long. Let's get the holidays outta the way, and I'll approach Prez."

My throat instantly heated. "But he'll throw you out, and I won't have you at all."

He trailed his finger down my nose. "We'll make it work," he vowed. "One thing at a time, okay? Let's make sure we want this first."

I nodded my agreement, but I knew there wasn't a world that existed where I wouldn't want Colt. He was everything to me. He always had been.

I just hoped he felt the same way. Even now, when we were at the beginning of whatever we were meant to be, I knew that now I had him, I never wanted to let him go.

At last, he'd chosen me, and now I'd choose him right back every time.

Chapter Eleven

Colt

The following day, we decided to go to Grand Junction to sort the Ed business. On the way, Freya asked if we could call into Christian's auto shop to check on her car. She said she'd tried to speak to him the day before, but he was out on a mobile repair.

After last night, everything had changed.

I was protective of Freya, so I didn't like the idea of my girl being around a man who obviously wanted her. Therefore, when she went to get out of the car, I stopped her.

"Wait," I said, throwing the driver's door open and jumping out. After jogging around the hood, I opened her door and held her hand to help her out of the SUV.

"Thanks," she said, beaming up at me. "But there's no need. I won't be a jiffy."

I barked a laugh. "It's cute you think I'll let you go in there and deal with those horny assholes. And what the fuck's a jiffy?"

She smiled. "The English doctor at the hospital says it all the time. I think it's cool, don't you?"

I slung my arm around her shoulder and guided her toward a sign over a door labeled 'reception'. "Yeah, it's cool as fuck if you're an English doctor, but imagine Atlas coming out with it?"

She slid an arm around my back, still smiling up at me. "Point taken."

I was still chuckling when we walked through the door and into a big square room with a huge reception desk along the entire back wall and chairs down one side. It looked pretty clean for an auto shop.

The guy sitting at the desk looked up from his computer. "How can I help?" His eyes went to Freya, and he did a double take.

My arm around Freya tightened. Standing to my full height, I squared my shoulders and barked, "Christian around?"

The guy looked between us and nodded before scurrying out a side door behind the desk that led to the workshop.

"You okay?" Freya whispered, looking up at me with her eyebrows drawn.

"Hmm." I tamped down the burn and smiled down at her. "Didn't like the way he looked at you, is all."

Frey's lips twitched. "I never realized you were so jealous."

My mouth tightened. "I'm not—usually. You bring it out in me, Princess."

She twisted toward me and walked into my chest. "No need to be jealous, Colt. Now I've got you I don't want any other guys."

My heart bounced at her words. I tipped my girl's chin up with my finger and gave her a soft peck on the lips. "It's not you, Frey. It's the other assholes I don't trust. Don't you see how men look at you?"

Her eyes widened, and she blinked owlishly. "No."

I couldn't help smiling ruefully.

Freya didn't have a fucking clue how beautiful she was. I loved the fact she wasn't vain or up her own asshole, but I also wished she was more aware sometimes.

I heard the door leading to the workshop open and close before somebody cleared their throat. Turning, I saw Christian leaning both elbows on the desk, studying Freya closely. "Hey," he greeted her without sparing me a glance.

My eyes narrowed.

"Hey, Christian," she said brightly. "I've come to check on the car. How's she doing?"

His lips parted in a huge smile. "You've got excellent timing. She's my next job. Hope to have her done by the end of the day. She'll be all ready for you in the morning." His eyes swept down her and up again. "How about I drop her off to you and bring coffee and breakfast? We all know how much you love your Starbucks."

I let out a low growl.

"That's a great idea," my princess replied breezily. "But bring enough for Colt; he'll be at my place too."

I nearly busted out laughing.

Christian's smile faltered, and his eyes finally slid toward me. "Is he your boyfriend?"

I smirked. "Hardly a boy, Chris. I'm all fuckin' man. Ask Freya."

A squeak left her throat.

The other man's eyes narrowed at her. "When I asked you out, you said you weren't looking for a relationship. Said you wanted to concentrate on med school."

My jaw went tight.

I fucking knew it.

My arm slid across my girl's shoulders again, pulling her close. Christian the fucknut needed to know who she belonged to.

"Thing is, Chris," I bit out. "My Freya's as sweet as they come. She's the kinda woman who'd rather let you down gently than make you feel rejected. It's why I've locked her down. You snooze, you lose, and the fuckery of all is, you were years too late."

Freya's face jerked up to stare at me wondrously.

Christian heaved out a defeated breath. "Fair enough."

I leveled him with a stare. "I'll come in tomorrow and get Freya's car. What time?"

He glanced at my girl and then back to me. "About ten. I'll do the work this afternoon and test it in the morning. Is that okay with you?"

"Yup," I told him. "See ya then." I turned and marched Freya out of the auto shop, heading back toward the car. Glancing down, I saw Freya still had a massive smile on her face. "Lose the self-satisfied grin, baby. It doesn't become you."

She giggled. "You know, when my brothers act like cavemen, I want to bang their heads together, but when you do it, it's kinda hot."

I sighed audibly, grabbing her door, and helping her into the passenger seat. "You're driving me fuckin' crazy." Grabbing her seat belt, I pulled it across her lap and clicked it in place.

"Now you know how I've felt for the last six years," she murmured. "It's shitty, right?"

I grimaced. "You have to understand the position I was in at the time. I was twelve years older than you. Me at thirty and you at eighteen wouldn't have been right. You weren't mature enough then. You hadn't lived. At least now you've gone through college and med school, you're more confident and comfortable in yourself." Checking her seat belt was secure, I gently cupped her cheek, turning her face to look into her eyes. "It's happened the way it was meant to. You needed time to find yourself before you saddled your cute ass with me. You were too young, Princess."

Her eyes softened. "I know. It just hurt when you pulled away."

I ran my thumb over her bottom lip. "I had to."

Her forehead furrowed. "Why?"

I popped a kiss on the end of her nose. "It's gonna take us a few hours to get to Grand Junction. We'll talk it out, yeah?"

"Yeah," she breathed.

I stood to my full height and closed the passenger door before making my way around the hood to the driver's seat.

It was becoming clear that Freya had some pent-up frustration with me. I could understand it; her seeing me with other women must've hit hard.

Pulling my door open, I slid into the car and pulled my safety belt on. "Do you know how I met your dad?" I asked, starting the vehicle.

Her face turned toward me. "Yeah. It's club folklore. You'd never met him before but still had his back when he ran into trouble with the Sinners."

I nodded as I pulled out of the parking lot, joining the flow of traffic. "I'd just left the military. Didn't wanna go home, so I decided to buy an old motorcycle and bum around the country. Wyoming was my first stop."

She shifted onto her side to face me, curling her knees up into her chest. "Why didn't you wanna go home?"

I shot her a glance before turning back to the road. "You know my background?"

Without pause, she murmured, "Colter Van Der Cleeve, only son of Conrad and Caroline. Two sisters, Cordelia, twenty-seven, and Grace, twenty-four. Your ancestors were among the first settlers, and now they own most of New York."

My spine stiffened. "You never said you knew all that."

"Why would I?" she asked. "It's your business, not mine. It's no skin off my nose if you're as rich as a king."

"It's not just about wealth," I responded carefully. "It's about status and background. My family is one of the wealthiest in the USA. The Van Der Cleeves helped the Dutch colonize New Amsterdam—now New York—in 1620, but we can trace our name back centuries before that to the rulers of an area in medieval Germany. My ancestor, a gazillion times removed, was Anne of Cleeves, Henry VIII of England's fourth wife, the second one he divorced."

Freya blinked. "You're English royalty?"

"No, my ancestor is," I corrected gently, "Though there is a familial link there, albeit tenuous. Anne and Henry never had children; ours is through marriage, not blood. When it comes to the British royal family, it's only blood links that count for anything."

"That's true to a point," she countered. "But there's always been a question mark over the legitimacy of Edward IV. Apparently, his parents were over a hundred miles apart when he was conceived."

I barked a laugh.

There she went again, challenging me. Was it any wonder Freya caught my attention? She was a bit of a history lover, so I wasn't shocked she knew about British royal ancestry. I fucking loved how brilliant and knowledgeable Freya was. Loved how deeply she thought and how eloquently she put those thoughts into words.

Not many people impressed me, but she got the job done without even trying.

She was goddamned perfect.

My prez and the club weren't interested in where I came from. That was the beauty of being a Demon; I could be myself without all the bullshit that came along with my family name. I wasn't shocked Freya knew about me. I also wasn't surprised she hadn't breathed a word to anyone. She'd been raised with a code of honor ingrained into her. A code I hadn't discovered until I joined the military and later, the club.

"You asked me why I never wanted to go home," I reminded her.

Freya nodded.

"I was engaged," I admitted. "I called off the wedding and enlisted."

"You jilted your fiancée?" she breathed, shock lacing her tone.

"No," Freya," I muttered. "The weddin' was still a month away when I walked in on her in bed with my father."

I could almost feel the shock swirling through the SUV as I concentrated on the road.

"Your father?" she croaked. "But your family's part of New York's high society. How could he do it to you? How could *she* do it to you?"

"You think rich people are decent, Princess?" I asked, shooting her a glance.

"Not necessarily," she denied. "But I never imagined it would be like living in an upscale version of the Jerry Springer show."

I snorted humorlessly. "You'd be shocked if you knew half the shit that goes on. The corruption alone is disgustin'. That's without the lyin', cheatin', and the fucked-up business deals. My father's had mistresses since before my mom married him. He stopped hiding it when I was a teenager. No need to; it's not like she'll leave him. Mom can only get through the day by swallowing copious amounts of booze and pills, but at least she's got the pool boy and her yoga instructor to take the edge off." I barked a staid laugh. "Can't really blame her. My father doesn't give a shit about her wellbeing."

"Maybe everyone's got damage caused by their parents, me included," Freya murmured. "But your dad carried out the most heinous act possible, aided and abetted by the woman whose job was to love you above all others. Of course it left a deep mark on you."

"The betrayal was all my father's," I explained. "I don't blame Victoria. Our marriage was arranged before we were born. I didn't love her, and she probably didn't love me either. I liked her, but only because growin' up, I knew we'd marry. It made things easier if I made a conscious effort. My sister Cordelia's wedding was arranged on the day she was born too. She went ahead with it, but her life turned ugly fast. Now she's stuck with a man just like our father, who cheats and lies. Eventually, he'll wear her down to be the same sad, bitter woman my mom is."

She cocked her head questioningly. "Do you have any contact with them at all?"

My heart squeezed. "I speak to Mom and my sisters occasionally," I admitted. "Told 'em they don't have to stay in New York. They've all got personal money in trust funds and shares from our grandparents. It's not finances keepin' 'em tied to him. They're scared to leave the lifestyle. It's all they've ever known."

My skin warmed at the soothing hand Freya laid on my arm. "I'm sorry he did that to you. It makes me kinda grateful for my dad."

"Your dad's the shit," I agreed. "Doin' this with you brings up a lotta guilt. I don't like goin' behind his or my brothers' backs, but I can live without them. Not sure now if I can live without you."

I heard her sharp intake of breath.

It was probably too much too soon, but now I had her, everything had fallen into place. What was the point in playing games when me and Freya were meant to be together? I was beginning to feel gratitude for

Shep. He'd spurred me to claim my girl. The course of my life was changing drastically, but as long as Freya was by my side, I didn't care.

"How do you know already?" she whispered. "You've only been getting to know me properly for a few days."

I reached over and clasped her thigh. "No, baby. I've been gettin' to know you for twelve years. I think I've always known deep down that you'd be mine one day, but you were too young for me." I smiled. "You probably still are."

"Is that why you pulled away?" she inquired, biting her lip nervously.

"No," I replied, voice thick with emotion. "I pulled away because you were a choice I wasn't ready to make. I couldn't see past the club. I knew I couldn't have you and stay."

"And now you're ready to leave?" she asked. "Are you sure?"

I thought about Shep and all the changes that were about to happen in my life.

It didn't escape me that I still hadn't told Freya. It was hard for me to open up though. I held my cards close to my chest because I'd always been alone in the world. Freya would be a part of my life, and I'd factor her into my future decisions, but it would take time to get used to it.

"I'm ready," I assured her. "I love the club, but it was never meant to be a long-term plan for me. I told Prez I wouldn't be there forever, but I got complacent. The time's right to branch out, especially if it means we can be together." I shot her a questioning look. "Have you thought about what's next? There's no way you're fuckin' enlisting. You need to look for a stateside internship."

She nodded. "I've applied for six positions. They all start their intake next summer, so it's just a matter of waiting to see where I'm accepted and then making my choice."

I nodded along, ignoring the twisting inside my chest.

It would be a while before we could settle. I didn't know where I'd be sent. It was dependent on what role appealed to me. It would be a couple of years before Freya finished her training, and even then, we weren't guaranteed to be offered work in the same city.

I could compromise and find something as close to her as possible, but who knew where she'd end up? I didn't want her to take a job she didn't want just so she could be close to me. Freya deserved to go where she wanted, and to learn the surgeries she was passionate about.

I decided to keep my mouth shut for the time being. I didn't want to influence Freya's decisions. We'd make it—I had no doubt—but it would probably take a while. We could do long-distance until we had more control over our futures.

An empty feeling stabbed through my gut, and I could've kicked myself for wasting so much time. Now, the thought of being without Freya made me wanna punch a wall.

It was crazy how, just days ago, I been able to ignore my need for her and discount all the feelings that we'd built over the years. It was like a light switch had gone off in my head because I'd done a complete one-eighty.

Or had I? Mine and Freya's relationship had been brewing since she was eighteen. Even before that, she'd fulfilled me more than women twice her age. There wasn't another person on the planet who understood me like she did.

A dark feeling crept through my chest.

This wouldn't be as cut-and-dried as I'd assumed. Obstacles were hitting us from all corners. Freya's dad and brothers, the club. My work and hers.

I was already half in love with her, and I suspected she felt the same way, but I was conscious of the fact we were very new. All the bullshit we had to face hadn't tested us yet, but it was looming on the horizon. Once we left our Colorado bubble and returned to Wyoming, everything would change.

I just hoped to God we could get over all the obstructions in one piece, because one thing was for sure: life was about to throw us some challenges, and we needed to be prepared.

Chapter Twelve

Freya

Grand Junction was a pretty town in Northwestern Colorado. It was surrounded by sweeping mountain ranges and lush countryside. It seemed the perfect place to position a Vet hospital. Waking up to such beauty every day would heal the most broken of souls.

My breath caught at the scenery as we approached the town.

"It's pretty, right?" Colt said quietly.

"Yeah," I agreed. "It reminds me of Wyoming."

"Same terrain," he said, glancing out of the windshield. "We're not too far from Hambleton..." His voice trailed off like a thought interrupted what he was about to say.

The journey had started off great. Colt had been playful. We'd laughed and gone deep about his family and where things were going between us. Then, the atmosphere changed.

"Are you okay?" I asked. "You seem distracted."

He sighed. "It kinda hit me that we've got some tough times ahead, Princess." I caught him grimacing slightly before he squared his shoulders and continued. "Think we've gotta be practical in our plans. We dunno where we're gonna be in six months. We've gotta accept that fate might not be on our side."

Uneasiness stirred in my stomach.

"I assumed you'd build a business," I responded tightly. "Do freelance work."

"I've no doubt I'll find work, Freya," he muttered. "But who knows where it'll be. Maybe you shouldn't assume shit about me."

My eyes slashed toward him. "Don't speak to me like that." I turned to face the windshield and crossed my arms across my chest.

He heaved out a sigh.

Silence fell over us, so thick and biting it was almost tangible.

The need to speak and fill the awkwardness with my ramblings hit me hard, but I always did that, always trying to put the other person at ease. I was a people pleaser, and I hated it. Maybe I was a by-product of my childhood. Some kids did terrible things to get their dad's attention. I went the other way. I was quiet and agreeable because my dad puffed out his chest whenever somebody told him what a perfect daughter he had.

It was the only time he ever smiled at me.

As I got older, I began to challenge him. When I pointed out his misogyny, he'd sigh and look to the heavens, cursing under his breath.

Eventually, I stopped being his little girl altogether. Instead, I became his worst nightmare—a woman with a mouth who had no issue using it.

I didn't care though. Being good didn't get me anywhere, and why shouldn't I voice my opinions? Cara did, and Kennedy too. Sophie and Layla were less vocal but quietly assertive. Dad married my mom, who wouldn't take shit, and Iris, although loving, had a will of steel.

Dad respected them, so why couldn't he respect me?

We drove through town, the awkward silence heavy and oppressive. I breathed a sigh of relief when, eventually, we approached the hospital.

It was square in shape, with additional annexes added on. It hadn't changed since I was here last. It looked clean and clinical, much like any other hospital.

Colt stopped at a barrier and told security who we were visiting. After a few seconds, the barrier lifted, and we drove into a parking lot, and he turned the engine off.

"You ready, Princess? he asked, looking up at the building.

I nodded, unclipping my seat belt before leaning down to grab my purse. "Let's get this done."

His eyes narrowed at me for a second. Then he sighed, throwing the door open.

I exited the car too, making sure not to look at him. After having time to think things through, my mood had dipped. Loving Colt didn't give him an automatic pass to talk down to me.

The air was cool and crisp. I loved fall and how nature began preparing for the long winter sleep. Hitching my purse over my shoulder, I followed the signs for the reception.

"Hey," Colt muttered, taking my arm roughly. "Wait for me, Princess."

I shook him off. "Stop calling me that. I'm not a princess. You all seem to think I live in some ivory tower, but I see and do things on the daily that would make men puke. I'm no fucking princess, okay?"

Colt held his hands up defensively. "What the hell's the matter with you?"

I rolled up on my toes, getting in his face. "Your mood swings piss me off."

Colt leaned closer. "You live in a dream world. I'm trying to make you see that things won't always be easy." He raised a hand to cup my cheek. "Drop the attitude."

"Ugh!" I bit out. "You drive me crazy." I wrenched myself away from him, turned on my fabulous heels, and sashayed toward reception, making sure to put a little extra swing into my ass.

We approached the building, heading toward the glass double doors that housed the veteran we'd come here to see. Colt sauntered past me, grabbed the handle, and opened the door with a flourish of his arm. "Ladies first."

I stuck my nose in the air and strutted past him, smiling prettily at the male receptionist whose eyes fell on me and widened slightly.

"Hey!" I approached the desk and leaned on it. "We're here to see—"

"Edward Matthews," Colt said, effectively cutting me off.

The receptionist gaped at me.

Colt clicked his fingers a few times in the receptionist's face. "Earth to asshole. Come in, asshole."

I turned and slapped him hard across the chest. "Hey! Don't be rude!"

The receptionist cocked an eyebrow at Colt, nodding toward me. "Yeah," he muttered. "What she said."

The air in the room cooled.

I looked up at Colt; his expression hadn't changed, but his eyes had frozen to chips of blue ice. His hard stare promised retribution.

The receptionist's shoulders sagged. "Names?"

"Colt Van Der Cleeve and Freya Stone." His tone was rigid and unbending, like steel.

"Ed's popular today. You're the second couple here for him. Some big dude with a buzz cut and a guy with ink on his neck." He pointed behind us, "Through that door, turn right, walk around the side of the building, and you're there."

Shit.

It sounded like Atlas and Cash were here.

Colt and I shot each other a nervous glance before he gave the receptionist a chin lift, grabbed my elbow, and tugged me toward the door.

I wanted to pull away, argue, bite, scratch, and show him he wasn't my keeper, but I knew I'd already pissed him off. Colt's pet peeve was people berating him in public. Maybe I'd just crossed a line, but I was so sick of his mood swings.

I was being bratty, but I couldn't help myself. This was the second time in as many days Colt had blown hot and cold on me. I needed to set boundaries, or he'd think he could get away with it all the time.

We exited the door, but instead of turning right, Colt pulled me left, back toward the parking lot.

"What are you doing?" I demanded, my voice pitchy. Colt didn't often lose his shit, but on the rare occasions he did, he blew like Vesuvius. The last thing I wanted was to be the object of his wrath.

He grabbed my shoulders and backed me into the wall. "What the fuck's wrong with you?" he gritted out.

Our eyes locked, and my heart fluttered, but I didn't want it to. My head was all over the place, and so were my emotions.

"I don't know where I stand with you," I whispered. "Earlier, we were having fun. Then, you get inside your own head, and your mood changes. You don't communicate."

His hands framed my face, and the heat of his body hit mine. "I'll work on it."

I searched his eyes for signs of duplicity. "I love being around you, but sometimes it feels like I have to walk on eggshells, and I don't know how to get through to you."

He leaned down, touching my forehead with his. "I just overthink things sometimes."

"You can't plan everything," I whispered, my shoulders slumping. "Things will come at us from left field sometimes. I know we're gonna get shit from the club, but I'm willing to deal with it because being with you is worth it. If my dad never spoke to me again, I'd understand. It won't be easy, but I'll cope as long as I've got you."

Colt's brow furrowed. "Sometimes, I think you'll deal better than me. I'm gonna miss the club. They're the only people who've ever been a family to me."

My heart cracked inside my chest, but I jutted my chin up. I wouldn't make him choose me, even after our time together. I only wanted him to be happy, "You don't have to leave. We can stop this now if it's too much."

"No!" He stepped back. "That's not what I want. I just don't want you to lose your family. I know from experience how fucking cool they are."

"My dad will come around. Maybe my brothers will be shocked, but I think they'll be okay. The ol' ladies will support us. I know some of the older members won't like it, but I don't live my life for them."

He scraped a hand down his face. "I hate the sneaking around too. My father's a fuckin' liar and a cheat. Always swore I wouldn't be like him, and here I am, lying to the man who's been a better father to me than my own."

A lump formed in my throat.

I'd never truly thought how us being together would affect Colt. After he told me about his family, I got it. He'd tried to be honorable all his life, except now it was all for nothing because he felt he was betraying the club.

"Do you want to stop?" I asked, pain twisting my chest. "We can pick it up later if you decide to leave the MC."

He shook his head. "I am leaving, and no, we're not stopping this. We'll get Thanksgiving and the holidays outta the way and come clean."

My eyes darted between his. "Are you sure?"

He jerked a nod. "Atlas and Cash are here. We'll have to be careful. That big fucker doesn't miss a trick."

I winced. "We better get used to it."

"Yeah," he muttered, pulling me off the wall and turning back the way we came.

"Tell me about Ed," I asked gently as we walked toward the garden. "Is his diagnosis similar to Kit's?"

"His PTSD was caused by combat, same as Breaker's, but Ed's been living on the streets for about fourteen years too. He's been the victim of some terrible shit. He also lost his family years back. The hospital contacted his ex-wife and kids, but she remarried, and his boys don't wanna know. Apparently, Ed was a mess when he came outta the Special Forces, and they saw him at his worst."

I nodded, trying to understand Ed's situation.

It took a complete breakdown for Kit to get help, so Ed must've been strong to survive worse. Colt had let slip in the car that Ed was thinking of relocating to Hambleton when he finished treatment. I knew he'd be okay there. As much as I resented my dad for his dismissive attitude toward me, I couldn't help feeling proud about how he provided a family for those who needed one the most.

"There they are," Colt muttered, nodding toward a bench where Atlas and Cash were sitting alongside a man with buzzed dark hair. I could see the guy was tall. His frame was too thin, probably from malnourishment.

My heart immediately went out to him. Although Ed had company, he seemed so solitary that I could almost feel his disillusionment.

Atlas looked up and saw us approach. He said something to Cash, who stood and made his way toward us.

"Yo," Colt called out. "How's tricks?"

Cash gave Colt a clap on the shoulder and turned to me. "Sight for sore eyes, Sis. You get prettier every day."

Reaching up, I gave him a hug. "How's Cara and Wilder?"

"Fuckin' perfect." He pulled away and puffed his chest out proudly. "My boy's growin' like a weed. Can't wait for ya to get home. He misses his auntie."

Turning toward the bench, I gave Ed a smile and a low wave. "Hi."

"Who's this?" he asked Atlas, who'd stood to greet Colt.

I walked toward him and held my hand out. "Freya."

Ed stood to shake my hand, but I gently batted it away, slid my arms around his back, and hugged him. "Nice to meet you."

He froze.

I pulled back slightly, searching his face for a sign he felt uncomfortable. "I'm sorry. Was that too much? I'm a hugger."

He looked dazed. "No. Not at all. It just shocked me a little. It's not every day a beautiful woman comes to visit and gives me that."

I went to Atlas and kissed his cheek. "You okay?"

"Yip," he replied. "Glad you're here. My Stitch has been threatenin' to come down and get those notes she needs. Told her, while she's knocked up, she ain't steppin' foot outside Hambleton." He gestured for me to sit. "How ya doin', Princess?"

"Good." I smiled, taking the spot next to Ed, who turned to me.

"You're this one's sister?" he said incredulously, looking between me and Cash.

My brother laughed. "She sure is. Freya's trainin' to be a doctor in Denver."

"Is she yours?" Ed asked, looking at Colt.

My heart dropped into my ass, and I felt my cheeks heat.

"Not in the sense you mean," Colt replied calmly. "But I look out for her." He glanced at Atlas, who stared back, lips set in a thin line. "We all do."

I swallowed a gulp, desperately thinking of how I could change the subject. This was way too close for comfort. "How's your treatment going?" I asked Ed.

"Okay," he replied thoughtfully. "I'm still finding it hard to make friends, but I'm more social than I was. I had a couple of buddies on the streets, but they both died. It seemed easier to stay solo after a while. Less heartbreak that way."

"I'm sorry, Ed," I murmured. "People need to do more. I volunteer at a drop-in clinic in Denver to help with minor ailments. I see so many cases like yours. I wish I could help more."

Cash looked at me with soft eyes. "My sister's a fuckin' angel."

Ed's forehead furrowed. "What clinic?"

"The St. Francis Centre," I stated softly.

He nodded. "I know it. It's a good place. They treat you like a human there. They fed me a few times and got me a warm coat." He smiled at me. "It's great that you help. Not many do."

"It must be a huge change for you." I smiled sadly.

"Sometimes I miss the streets," he said wistfully. "Nina said I'd been out there for so long I'd been conditioned to it. At the time, I hated it. I would've done anything for a safe, warm bed. But it's hard to retrain your subconscious after years of the same old thing. Even sleeping on a soft mattress was hard in the beginning. I had to get up through the night and move to the floor."

"I think it's quite normal to feel that way," I assured him. "When Kit came home from the military, he told me how he roamed the country. I know he found settling difficult. He said in combat, he used to sleep sitting up. It's what he'd been trained to do. When he came home, he slept in a chair to keep watch and woke up at the slightest noise."

"That's what Nina said too," he stated. "Are you specializing in mental health? Is that part of your training?"

"No." I smiled. "I'm going the surgery route."

Ed smiled thinly. "You're a very calming influence, Freya. You'd be a great shrink."

Cash held his hand out. "Come on, Sis. Let's get you a caffeine fix. You'll be gettin' withdrawal symptoms soon."

I laughed and threaded my arm through his. "You know me so well, Xan."

We began to make our way toward the building. "How've you been? Pop said you're takin' a year out?"

My shoulder lifted nonchalantly. "It won't be as long as a year. I graduated from med school early, but I've missed this year's intake for interns. I've applied to the programs I like. Hopefully, I should get in somewhere for next summer."

"Can't you stay and intern at Baines Memorial?" my brother asked. "You've been away for so long. We miss ya."

"Aww, thanks, Cash." I laughed as we approached the building. "Who'd have thought you'd actually miss my ass, especially after the holidays last year when I ripped you a new one for stealthing Cara."

He barked a laugh, grabbing the door open for me and gesturing me through. "You went fuckin' loco. Though I deserved it."

I walked past him, clutching a hand to my heart dramatically. "At last. The prince of the kingdom admits he's wrong. Therapy must be working."

He followed me through the door, his forehead furrowing. "Yeah, it is, but it's also Wilder. I gotta do better for my boy. Can't have him growing up like me."

My heart contracted painfully.

Cash was a hard, brash man, but he also had a softer side he didn't let many see.

People forgot how much pressure he was under to take Dad's place as Prez one day. It was no wonder he acted the dick sometimes, though getting your ex-girlfriend pregnant without her knowing wasn't the brightest idea, even though his son, Wilder, was doted on in spite of the circumstances he was born into.

We entered a room resembling a diner. Going to the counter, we ordered coffees before taking them to an empty table and sitting.

"You're a good man, Xander," I murmured. "You just have to teach Wilder it's okay to have emotions."

He barked a laugh. "He'll be okay. His mom shows enough emotion for the whole club."

"How is she?" I asked.

"Amazin," He replied quietly, studying me closely. "How's things with you and Colt?"

My skin prickled uneasily.

"What do you mean?" I rasped, my throat suddenly dry.

He grinned. "I may be an asshole, but I'm not stupid, Sis."

"I don't know what you—" I began.

Cash held his hand up to stop me. "Don't lie, especially to me. You think I haven't seen this comin'. Saw things had changed between you two the day I got outta jail. I'm not Dad, Freya, I'm not against it. In fact, I think you could do a lot worse. If someone told me I couldn't be with Cara, I'd fight tooth and nail for her. The problem is, Dad's laid down the law. It's you or the club. He can't have both."

I stared at him, throat burning and tears glimmering in my eyes. "We know."

Cash's eyebrows snapped together as his eyes examined my expression. I saw the second the truth dawned on him. "Colt's leavin'?"

I gave one nod. "And I'll follow."

He heaved out a frustrated sigh. "Shit's gonna hit the fan, but I'll back you up, so will Cara. Kit and Kennedy will too. Bowie could go either way, and Layla will follow his cue. Atlas won't like the rule break, but deep down, he'll back ya, especially after Sophie makes him see the light."

My eyes widened at his words.

Cash had obviously mulled it over for a while. People thought he didn't care, but he was wiser than they knew. He'd make a good president one day.

I took a sip of coffee. "You've thought this through?"

My brother cocked an eyebrow. "Before he came down, he launched his cell against the wall 'cause he saw the messages between you and some rando. Ain't the actions of a man who doesn't give a fuck, Freya. Kit saw it too. Colt jumped at the chance to come down here and see to Ed. Didn't take a rocket scientist to work out he was gonna claim ya." Cash grinned. "Me and Kit worked it out before the dumb fuck knew himself."

I ran a hand through my hair, wondering if I'd woken up in an alternative universe.

Colt and I being together broke a cardinal club rule. I knew Cara and the ol' ladies would be okay with it. I even believed they'd talk their men around, but I never expected so much support from my brothers. It made me warm inside because I recognized something else.

By having my back, they were going against the club.

They were putting me first.

I took Cash's hand in mine and squeezed. "Thank you."

"Been without my girl before, Freya, and so has Kit. We know what it's like to have a piece of ourselves missin'. Wouldn't wish it on you or him. Colt must have caught big feels if he's givin' up the club for ya. That tells me all I need to know. I'd feel better if he came clean to Pop, though."

"He is," I assured him. "He wants a last Thanksgiving and Christmas at the club, and we'll tell Dad in the New Year. We just need to get through until then."

"If you get caught, it'll be a hundred times worse," Cash advised me.

My brother was right, but Colt needed time at the club to say goodbye, and if I was honest, so did I. It had been my home all my life, and I knew once we came clean, I'd lose my place there.

I mean, it was only two months, and we'd be careful not to get caught.

What could possibly go wrong?

Chapter Thirteen

Colt

The drive home from Grand Junction was uneventful, though it didn't stop me feeling unsettled.

Atlas, on the surface, had been his same old bantering self. But, occasionally, I'd glance at him and find his eyes narrowed on me like he was trying to see inside my head.

Admittedly, it freaked me out.

The SAA saw every—fuckin'—thing. He lumbered around cracking jokes—usually at everyone else's expense—and acted like a dumb fuck. But nobody realized what a sneaky bastard he was until it was too late. Part of the asshole's MO was to make people underestimate him.

But I knew better.

My stare slid to the passenger seat, and my lips thinned.

Freya had been distracted since we drove away from the vet hospital. After her coffee trip with Cash, she'd withdrawn slightly, like she was deep in thought.

It was glaringly obvious something had been discussed that had put her on the back foot. A part of me wanted to show patience and let her work it out before talking about it, but I wasn't that man.

I reached out and clasped her thigh. "What's up, baby? Somethin's botherin' you."

Her head swiveled to face me, and she bit her lip nervously. "Promise you won't lose your mind."

My chest panged. "Can't promise shit, baby, but I'll try."

Freya's hand covered mine. "Cash worked it out."

I frowned. "Come again?"

"Cash knows about us," she reiterated.

My gut plummeted. This was all we needed. "How?"

"He's observant, I guess." She shrugged. "You raised suspicion when you destroyed a cell phone the morning before you came down. He put two and two together, and he's not the only one."

I scrubbed a hand over my face with a tremoring hand. "Fuck!"

"Kit's in on it too," she added. "The good news is, they're going to keep quiet and let us do things at our own pace, though Cash thinks we should go to Dad immediately."

"I need to call him," I muttered. "Find out if anyone else has got the bead on us."

"Good idea," she agreed.

I rubbed a sweaty palm down my jeans.

If my brothers got chatty, we'd be fucked. "It'll get out if too many people know, baby. You prepared for that?"

"I know that whatever happens, we'll be okay." Freya's eyes washed with tears. "But I'm beginning to understand how you feel about the whole lying thing. If Dad finds out my brothers knew before him, it'll make things a gazillion times worse. He'll be hurt."

I'll be hurt too, I thought. *Though physically, not emotionally.*

"Do you want me to talk to your dad when we get back?" I asked, ignoring the warning bells in my head.

"I'll drive up tonight and tell him now if you want me to."

"No," she said thickly. "You'll get beaten and kicked out. We need to sort out where we're going and what we're going to do first. We're not ready, Colt."

"I've got plenty of scratch," I argued. "We can go wherever we want."

"And what about work?" she asked. "I know you won't be happy unless you're using that big brain of yours, and I need to interview for my internships."

Freya was right; it wasn't the right time to leave the club, but not for the reasons she stated.

There was a lot of work to do before I abandoned them. The Speed Demons needed me, and I wouldn't let them down more than I already had. I was well aware of the consequences, but I could try and make up for what I'd done over the next few months by tying up as many loose ends as possible. The least I could do was leave the club in a strong position.

My heart tugged with the thought of saying goodbye, but at the same time, I couldn't help the thrill of anticipation when I thought about the things I could achieve working for the Feds. The icing on the cake was that I'd get a life with Freya, something I hadn't dared to dream of until now.

It was the thought of all the lies we'd have to weave over the next few months that made my chest ache. After everything that had happened with my family, I swore I'd never turn into my father.

But maybe it had always been on the cards.

Maybe I never stood a chance of being decent.

Betrayal was in my blood, after all.

When we got back to Freya's apartment, I showered and then waited for her to do the same before lying back on her bed. I picked up my cell phone and scrolled until I found Cash's number.

My heart felt like it was about to thud out of my chest, but I took a breath, shoved down my nerves, and hit the call button.

It rang a few times before the connection kicked in, and Cash said, "Yo."

My gut leaped. "Can you talk?"

"Hang tight."

I listened as a chair scraped, and Cash murmured to someone that he wouldn't be long. After a few seconds, he said. "Shoot."

"You know why I'm callin'?" I said. "Not gonna lie, this convo's makin' my ass nip, Veep."

Cash barked a laugh. "I bet," he mused. "But you don't gotta worry about me, Colt. It's your prez who's gonna kick the fuck outta ya."

I looked at the ceiling and closed my eyes. "Yeah."

"Look," Cash went on. "I don't gotta problem with you and Freya. Like I told her, I went without Wildcat for years, and it fucked us both up. Don't want that for you, and there's no way I want it for my sister. I'll keep my mouth shut, and so will Breaker, unless it starts affectin' Freya. If I see her hurt by it, you gotta come clean."

My shoulders slumped, the relief palpable.

"Got every intention of tellin' Prez," I muttered. "I'm leavin' the club, but I need to put some things in place before I jet. I can help the Demons from where I'm goin', though I don't think it's gonna go down well with the originals."

"Law enforcement?" Cash asked.

"Yeah," I confirmed. "I don't gotta choice, Veep. They'll come after the club if I don't join the ranks. They've been diggin' up info on Henderson Junior's suicide. My recruiter told me they've got evidence. Even if they're bluffing, they'll plant somethin' to bring the club down. I can protect you better from the inside."

"Jesus," he breathed after a pause. "What a fuckin' shit show."

"Yeah," I agreed. "But it's time too, Veep. Stayed away from Freya until she grew up and did the right thing for her and everyone else. Now I'm doin' what's right for me."

"And you're sure that's Freya?" he asked.

"Not a doubt in my mind," I assured him. "Always felt our connection but in a brotherly way. Started wakin' up a couple of years ago. Took me that long to get my head around it."

"What about Lucy Bloom?" he asked.

I let out a snort. "She was a final attempt to keep our girl at arm's length, brother, and a stupid one to boot. But it's done. Freya's mine, and I'm Freya's. End of."

Cash paused again briefly before clearing his throat and declaring, "Remember when I came outta the joint. Layla had been taken, and the clubhouse was in war mode. Me, you, and Atlas were talkin' in the bar, and Freya burst in. I've never seen a man light up like you did. You were on your feet and comfortin' her within seconds. It was like if she hurt, you hurt. I knew then that this would happen. It's no surprise to me, and Breaker called it too. He's more concerned about the fallout than me. I know Dad's gonna lose his mind, but he'll come around eventually. You've just gotta hang in there."

"I can do that," I replied.

"Then you're set 'cause my sister's the most stubborn person I know. She'll die before she lets Pop win. Mark my words: if she was born a boy, she'd be in line for the top seat, and I'd be left out in the cold.

Freya's smart, and she's got courage and determination. When she sets her mind on somethin', Dad doesn't stand a fuckin' chance."

My chest warmed.

"Thanks, brother," I murmured. "Gotta say, it makes me feel better to have you onside."

Cash chuckled. "Just wanna see my sister happy, Colt, and you're the poor bastard she's set her sights on. I'm all for love and roses, moonlight, and poetry. I'm a fuckin' romantic at heart, doncha know."

My eyes rolled so far in my head that I could almost see the back of my skull.

Cash was a dick. But one thing was certain in my mind. He loved Cara and Wilder, and he loved his sister. Therapy had helped him in ways I couldn't comprehend sometimes. It had taken time, but he was chill these days. I hardly recognized him from the crazy, aggressive, mouthy son of a bitch he was just mere months ago. He'd finally grown up.

"I'm goin' back to my woman," Cash muttered. "Brought her and my boy to the coffee shop for a family outin'."

"Wilder's two months old," I protested.

Cash barked a laugh. "He fuckin' loves it, and it tires him out, so he may let us catch a few z's tonight."

I grinned, trying to work out when Cash turned into a family man? "'Kay, brother. I'll let you go. Thanks again."

"It's not a thing. And tell my sister, me and Cara have her back. She's gotta do what makes her happy. Fuck the club. She's not even a member, so why Dad's making her live under club rules is beyond me." I heard Cara talk to him in the background. "Gotta go, dude. Wildcat needs me. Take care of my sister," Cash ordered before the line went dead.

I clicked my phone off, staring at the screen deep in thought.

Talking to Cash had made me feel better, but above all else, it was a relief that Freya had people fighting her corner. My girl was strong, but everyone needed someone, even if that someone was the person you least expected.

I shouldn't have been surprised, really.

Cash had managed to turn his life around in less than a year. The ex-con who wound everybody up like clockwork toys was turning into a good man who I respected. It was clear he loved his sister, and I knew Cara would break balls to protect Freya.

He'd always been the heir to the throne and treated people like his subjects. It had taken time, but he finally saw the bigger picture, and I had no doubt Cara and the birth of Wilder were behind it.

A shadow appeared in the doorway to the bathroom, and Freya walked in wearing that silky fucking robe, rubbing her hair with a towel.

"How did it go?" she asked, walking around to her side of the bed.

I patted the space next to me and watched her sit down. "The Veep's on our side."

She grinned. "Feel better?"

Gently, I pulled her down and tucked her under my arm. "Relieved. More for you than anything. Don't want you to feel isolated when shit hits the fan. Cash and Cara's support will go a long way with the club. He's gonna be the next prez, so the brothers will look to him for guidance. They love Breaker too. He's turnin' out to be the wise man of the club, alongside Abe. That's gonna stand us in good stead. It'll be a bumpy road, but we'll be okay."

She snaked across my chest and snuggled in tighter. "Who recruited you? FBI or CIA?"

I pulled back slightly, peering down at her. "You heard that?"

Her eyebrows drew together. "Why didn't you tell me?"

I threaded my fingers through her damp hair. "Still tryin' to wrap my head around it myself. I'm gonna be a fuckin' Fed, can you believe it?"

"It could work out," she whispered. "You'll have avenues open that you can only dream of at the club. I've been worried about you missing the work, Colt. It will be good for you."

I popped a kiss on her head. "I dunno where I'll get sent or what I'll be doin', baby. We may be separated for a while."

A mournful sound escaped her throat, and she sniffed quietly.

My heart sank. "Hey." I gently pulled her up by her underarms and turned her face toward me. "Why you gettin' upset?"

Freya swiped at her cheeks. "Do you even know where you'll be working?"

My lips thinned, and I shook my head.

"What if my internship's across the country?" she asked in a small voice. "What if we go through all the stress of being together, and after everything, we're still apart?"

I motioned for her to get on her side so we could lie down and face each other. She needed to look into my eyes and see the truth of what I was about to say.

"We *will* be together, Freya," I murmured, cupping her face and angling her eyes up to meet mine. "Maybe not immediately, but you're my priority, and you need to understand that everything I do from now on is with you in mind. I'll compromise, and you will too, but what I won't let you do is allow your career to suffer for me. There's such a thing as planes, Frey. I'll get on one every goddamned weekend if it means seeing you. It took us years to get here, and I'm not lettin' you go at the first fuckin' hurdle. I've got more fuckin' money than I know what to do with. I'll build you a fuckin' hospital in my backyard if that's what it takes for us to be together. D'ya get me?"

Tears sprang to her eyes again, but she smiled through them and nodded.

My fingers caught on her robe, and I pulled it back. "You're mine, Freya, body and soul." I trailed a finger down her nose and neck, finally resting on her chest. "We're doin' this, baby,, so stop thinkin' of all the things that can go wrong." I curled my hand around the back of her neck and brought her in for a kiss.

Sighing into my mouth, Freya plastered her body to mine. My cock thickened as her heated pussy settled against the crotch of my jeans. My chest almost exploded with pleasure that this woman was mine. At that moment, all I wanted to do was brand her so anyone who wanted to take her away would know she belonged to me.

There was nothing sweet about the touch of my lips to hers or the way my fingers trailed down her back to grab her ass and grind her little cunt against my cock. Everything about our embrace was hot and demanding.

She pulled away slightly. "Please, Colt," she murmured. "I don't want to wait anymore."

My cock kicked at the thought of burying myself inside her tight virgin pussy. "Are you sure? Once we do this, there won't be any going back. Once I take you, I'll never let you go."

She smiled. "I don't want you to let me go." Her fingers went to the buttons of my jeans, and she began to pop them open. "I want you to fuck me, Colt."

I pulled the belt of her robe open and slipped the silky material off her shoulders until she was naked and bared to me.

I'd unknowingly been waiting for this moment for twelve goddamned years. At last, Freya Stone was ready to be mine in all ways.

Chapter Fourteen

Freya

Colt's kisses and touches made my skin burn with need. I sighed, the heat from his body warming mine as he pressed himself closer, allowing his beautiful, long fingers to stroke my nipples into hardened peaks.

"Please don't stop," I begged, voice a whisper as warm lips hit my neck, gently pulling at my skin. My pussy clenched with need. I'd dreamed of this moment for years. I could hardly believe we'd finally gotten here.

Goose bumps covered my skin, following the trail of his fingers as he moved them up to gently fist my hair at the root before rolling me onto my back.

"You make me feel so good," I breathed.

Fingers traced over my pussy, finding my clit, and pressing down gently, making me spread my legs further, a silent request for more. "Gonna make you feel even better soon, baby," Colt rasped, his deep voice filling the room. "You're so fuckin' beautiful."

I smiled, loving the words and the way they curled around my heart.

The ache in my pussy intensified as his fingers dipped inside me. "So fuckin' wet for me," Colt breathed against my lips, his ocean-blues darkening with desire. He nuzzled my nose, and then I shivered as his lips trailed down my cheek and neck.

Colt wriggled down the bed until he maneuvered himself between my legs. Getting to his knees, he looked up at my body. His stare heated everywhere it touched, and I shivered in anticipation.

His hands slid up his thighs, and he lifted one, slinging it over his shoulder before he lowered himself down.

Desperate for his touch, I rocked my hips as he lowered his mouth to my pussy, latched onto my clit, and sucked hard. I let out a loud moan as I felt his lips tug me into his hot mouth, his tongue pressing hard.

I cried out loud.

"Fuck, yeah," he muttered against me, the vibration of his voice almost making me pass out with pleasure before his thumb hit my clit and his tongue speared my core.

I moaned over and over, thighs trembling as every nerve ending set alight. Arching my back, my body took over, and I rolled my hips, chasing the build of pleasure from the sensations coursing through me.

"I'm gonna come," I cried.

Still licking me, he looked up, and our eyes locked. "In my fuckin' mouth, Freya. Give it to me." His eyes slid back to my pussy, and he went back to work, sucking and pulling on my clit.

His finger slid gently inside me, and it all became too much. My pussy clamped down with the building pressure, and I let out a scream as a blazing orgasm ripped through my body.

Strong fingers dug into my ass, pulling me closer like he wanted to drink from me. He hummed on my clit as my climax reached its peak.

My hips jerked into the air uncontrollably. I whimpered as I kept coming. I felt a strong arm fall across my stomach, pinning me in place as Colt ate me through my climax.

I whined with the intensity caused by his growl as he sucked my pulsing clit into his mouth, prolonging the pinnacle of my orgasm for what seemed like hours. "You taste like Chanel," he muttered, releasing me, and sliding up my body. The leg previously placed over his shoulder fell, and he hooked it around his hip before positioning his cock and sliding inside.

I cried out as a sharp, burning pain seared through me.

My eyes flew open as I cried out, mid-arch, shocked and confused by the deep ache.

Colt's hands drove into my hair, and he angled my face to look into my eyes. "Sshh, baby. It's done now." He dipped his head and dropped a kiss on my lips before letting out a groan. "So fuckin' hot and tight, Princess."

I blinked, my shocked stare darting around the room as I battled my disorientation to get my bearings. Finally, my rounded eyes rested on Colt's face, and my skin prickled with realization.

"You ready for more?" Colt whispered against my mouth. "Has the pain gone?"

I concentrated, reaching for an answer. It burned slightly, but it wasn't painful. "I'm ready."

Colt's mouth curved before slowly sliding his cock deeper into my pussy. It still burned, but the ache began to turn almost pleasurable. He ground into me, sliding a hand down and pressing on my clit while circling his hips and moving inside me. A hand went under my thigh and wrapped one leg around his ass. "Hold on, baby, gonna go a little harder now."

With a moan, he slid even further inside and seated himself deep.

My pussy clenched around his cock, and he cursed under his breath. I needed this badly, but I couldn't help biting my lip at the sharp stab of pain jolting through me every time he moved. It seared my insides. Still, underneath the burning sensation, I could feel my pleasure building.

Colt began to move his cock inside me with hard, rhythmic strokes. I hissed as his strong thrusts stretched me out, creating an ache that took my breath away. Finally, I understand the phrase 'hurts so good'. His presence was larger than life, so it didn't shock me that his cock was too.

I couldn't believe it was finally happening. I'd prayed for Colt all these years but never imagined we'd ever be here, doing this.

Colt pushed up, arms locked, palms to the bed, fucking me harder while grinding into me. "I can feel your pussy clenchin' me, Princess." He groaned, bucking into me with increasing force, his hand cupping my ass. "Move your hips up to meet mine. Take it all, baby."

I started to move, meeting him halfway, gasping at how deep he went. "Colt," I whispered. "It's too much."

"You wanna stop?" he asked through gritted teeth.

"No." I moaned. "I just feel so full."

"You're gettin' everythin'," Colt rasped. His hand left my ass and snaked up toward the headboard. He gripped it hard, using it as leverage as he rhythmically thrust inside me.

I let out a keening cry, and my eyes rolled into the back of my head from the burning ache of pleasure pulsing through me.

Wet hit my breast as Colt sucked my nipple, pulling it into his mouth before releasing me. "Jesus, fuck." He groaned, driving into me even harder.

I shrieked as my pussy contracted hard, and my orgasm hit me like a tornado. Blood rushed through my ears, and I called out his name. I nearly came off the bed when Colt circled my clit with a firm press. My entire body bowed, and my world tilted.

"Fuck, yeah," he moaned, watching me as I climaxed. "Goddamned beautiful."

I shuddered, pleasure gripping every nerve. I felt like I'd been catapulted into the damned ozone layer, the high was so intense.

I smiled as I floated back to Earth, feeling hot and feverish but strangely satiated. Finally, it had happened, I wasn't a virgin anymore. I couldn't help a soft purr of satisfaction rumbling through my throat.

Colt's hand disappeared from my clit. Suddenly, it was in my hair, angling my face to plant a kiss on my mouth. "You're fuckin' spectacular," he whispered, circling his hips, and taking my mouth again.

It hit me then. If life separated us, I'd lose this and him.

My heart cracked, the pain forcing tears into my eyes. He buried his face in my throat, groaning into my neck, and I sent up a prayer of thanks. The last thing I wanted was for him to see me cry.

Trying to take my mind off my thoughts, I met him thrust for thrust, matching his rhythm.

A low moan escaped Colt's throat, his hips jerking uncontrollably. "Jesus, fuck!" he shouted, planting deep as a rush of heat filled my pussy. He bucked against me, groaning for what seemed like forever until, eventually, his thrusts gentled, and he slid in and out of me slowly, finally stopping and releasing a deep sigh of satisfaction.

I held my breath, waiting for my heart to stop racing and the burn in my veins to cool.

My fingers trailed up and down his spine, feeling his skin. I couldn't help wondering how many times I'd get this. We had an expiration date, and it wasn't far away. We'd be going back to Hambleton in a matter of days. I'd never felt closer to anyone. How the hell could I pretend he meant nothing when in fact, he was already my world?

The mere thought already made my breath catch in my throat.

Colt's head slowly lifted, and my eyes hit ocean-blue. "You okay, baby? Did I hurt you?"

I took stock of myself, feeling aches and pains. "I'm sore down below," I whispered, cheeks heating. "But that's to be expected, right?"

He pecked my nose and rolled off me onto his back with an arm resting above his head. "Yeah, baby. It's to be expected."

I took in his lean, compact, muscular stomach. Paying particular attention to the ridges and indents that made up his six-pack, as well as the smattering of dark blond hair across his chest with a happy trail running down the center of his abdomen. Without thinking, I reached out and rested my fingers on his chest.

I wasn't a virgin anymore.

My mind went over the events of the night. A blush heated my face, and my nipples pebbled at remembering what had just happened. My heart unfurled, and my lips curved into a satisfied smile. I couldn't have wished for a better first time.

He shifted onto his side, gesturing for me to do the same. When I settled, he entwined my fingers with his, brought them to his lips, and rasped, "Mine."

Tears filled my eyes.

Colt gently pushed my hair back. "It's gonna be okay, Freya."

I tried to blink the tears away, but one tracked down my cheek. "I'm worried about what will happen when we get back to the club."

Colt grinned. "I'll rent a place in town. We can meet there and spend time together."

I rolled my eyes. "Trust you to arrange a sex den."

He barked a laugh.

I slapped his arm. "It's not funny."

"Well, I think it's cute how you think I'm sex mad for you when I waited fuckin' years to get inside that sweet pussy of yours." His eyes turned languid.

I couldn't help giggling. "Hope I was worth all the sexual frustration."

Colt's eyes softened. "You're worth everythin'. Never been into virgins before, but knowin' it's you and you saved yourself for me makes me wanna punch the fuckin' air. You're mine and only mine; you always will be, and I can't say I'm mad about it."

"It's always been you." I smiled. "I knew it the moment you walked into the clubhouse with Dad. You looked straight at me, and it felt like I'd been punched in the chest."

He stroked my cheek with his thumb, ocean-blues bright with emotion. "I was drawn to you from day one. I told myself it was a meetin' of minds, someone I could actually talk to without feelin' like a freak. But Frey, deep down, I knew you were mine. I'm sorry I fought it, but I'm also glad because you grew up to be you and made it so I couldn't imagine a life without you in it. It was knowing I had to leave the club—and you—that spurred me into action. Knew I couldn't walk away without my princess."

My heart bounced in my chest.

"I know it's been fast, and I've gone at light speed, but we already know each other inside out. I'm sure about you and us."

"I'm sure too," I murmured. "It feels like I've been waiting for you to catch up for what seems like forever."

He leaned down and softly kissed me. "Go to sleep, it's been a long day."

His arm went around me, and I snuggled into his chest, smiling when I thought about how I loved it when he called me baby. For a while, I could forget we had to hide and that we may be parted.

So, I closed my eyes, cleared my mind, and just held on, committing the feel of Colt's arms around me to memory, and tried not to think about the fact that one day soon, I may not have him.

⁘

"Morning, gorgeous. Are you ready for our last day?" Abi called through the car window.

I pulled the door open, slid inside, pulled my seatbelt across, and clicked it into place. "Morning, babe."

My friend's eyes fixated on my face.

My head reared back slightly. "What?"

"He popped your cherry!" she announced loudly.

My skull fell back onto the headrest. "Oh my God. How did you even know?"

Her mouth curved into a huge grin. "Woo hoo!!!" She smacked the steering wheel excitedly before turning back to me. "I can smell it. I'm like a vampire or something... No! I'm a hybrid like Klaus Michaelson. An extra powerful, uber vamp slash wolf with a supernatural sense of smell, and you, Freya Stone, do *not* pass the sniff test."

"It's too early for this shit," I whined.

"So," my friend breathed excitedly. "How was it? Did it hurt? Did he make you come? How big is his dickadoodah?"

I laughed. "You're the only med student I know who calls a penis a dickadoodah."

Abigail checked her mirrors and pulled away. "Don't change the subject. You're a woman now. You've been deflowered, so pull up your big girl panties and tell Auntie Abi how it was."

My lips twitched. "You sound like a Regency spinster."

She laughed softly. "I just want to know that Colt treated you right."

I thought back to the night before, and my heart fluttered. "He was amazing. It hurt, but only at first."

My friend glanced at me. "He went easy on you, right?"

"He was perfect," I replied.

She waggled her eyebrows. "Sounds hot."

I couldn't seem to wipe the smile off my face. "It was."

"Lucky bitch," she said under her breath. "I need to meet a hot biker."

"Your Prince Charming will come along one day," I assured her.

"Fuck that," she murmured. "Life isn't a fairy tale. The men we think are our Prince Charming usually end up being assholes. And believe it or not, villains aren't so bad. At least you know where you stand with a villain."

I snorted. "True, Gaston was hot."

"Babe," she retorted. "Gaston was a fuckboy, but at least he had a job, and no doubt knew how to use his dick. For that, I could settle."

We'd been rushed off our feet all day. We'd both been sent to the ER to assist with the victims of a multi-vehicle RTA just after lunchtime.

I'd been checking, examining, arranging scans, and assisting doctors with administering pain relief for hours, so when the rush died down and we were sent on a break, I didn't say no.

I loved my work, but it involved long-ass hours and a lot of study. Some nights, I snatched a few hours of sleep before hitting the books or going to work. It was only going to be for a few years. Once I passed my residency, my crazy hours would calm down.

The cafeteria was quiet, so I was served my coffee quickly before I sat at a window seat and pulled my phone to catch up on my emails and messages.

I replied to a few emails before clicking on my Whatsapp. Cara had sent me a couple of funny biker memes, Soph, her latest ultrasound picture, and Kennedy, a picture of the twins. I smiled, closing the chat thread, heart thudding as I clicked on the last notification—Colt's.

I read the message, and every muscle froze.

Colt: Heard u gave ur digits 2 a certain auto mechanic. Why doesn't it match with the ones I've got?

A cold shiver ran down my spine. Colt said he'd pick up my car. I thought I'd put him off, but knowing him, he'd have gone anyway. How did they even get into talking about me and my phone number? Surely they weren't comparing notes about me?

I brought a hand up to rub my temple, sending up a prayer of thanks that I had the foresight to delete all the message strings on my other phone. Somehow, Christian had let my secret number slip to Colt, and he'd probably hacked into it already.

Fuck.

I stood, suddenly desperate to get back to the ER. We volunteered there doing the grunt work to gain work experience, which would look good on my Intern applications.

I placed my cup on the counter and hurried back down the hallway. As I approached the Emergency Room, my cell buzzed in my pocket. Grabbing it, I clicked on the notification.

Colt: Incoming—The next asshole will need an overnight stay.

A deep frown creased my forehead.

Incoming?

Puzzled, I switched my phone to silent and continued on my way to ER, mind still on the weird message. A feeling of impending doom started to spread through me.

Colt had done something, and I knew I wouldn't like it.

I'd always known he had an edge to him. I'd seen him take out some big guys. My dad had brought him to the club because of a bar fight they got into that fateful night.

I walked past reception, turning as a shout went up, ready to help. But as soon as I saw the patient, my muscles paralyzed.

Christian stumbled through the door, being helped by another guy in overalls.

I fixated on Christian's face, and my hand flew straight to my mouth.

His face was covered in blood.

I watched a nurse guide the men toward the ER with my heart in my mouth.

What the fuck was going on?

One word floated through my head, and my heart plummeted.

Incoming...

I rushed into the Emergency Room, eyes wide, probably from the shock bolting through my system. "What the hell happened?" I demanded, approaching Christian, who had been taken to a cubicle.

"He went for a smoke out back and got jumped," his friend spluttered. "He didn't know who did it, and the cameras are down." He ran a hand over his head, staring at Christian. "It's crazy. They were working this morning."

I closed my eyes, willing my hands to stop shaking. This was one of those times my teachers told me about, where I had to compartmentalize.

But it wasn't the fact Christian's face was mangled that made my chest clench.

Pushing my unease down, I smiled at Christian's colleague. "Thanks for bringing him in." I motioned to a door. "The waiting room's through there. I'll keep you posted."

Christian winced as the nurse gently examined his nose. "I'm in good hands, Dylan. Go back to work. It's too busy for us both to be out. We have three big jobs and can't get behind with them. It's just a broken nose. I'll get an Uber back when they're done."

Dylan's eyes slid to me. "Will he be okay?"

I nodded reassuringly. "Facial injuries bleed more than average, so it always looks worse than it is. I'll get Christian right and send him on his way. Don't worry."

His eyes darted between me and his friend, looking torn, before his shoulders slumped in defeat. "Okay. I'll go back to work. I'll call Jonesy to see if he can cover. When you're done here, go straight home and rest. We'll cope until tomorrow." He rested a hand on Christian's shoulder and gave me a nod before he turned and stalked out.

"Who did this to you?" I asked, watching the nurse clean his wound.

He watched as the nurse excused herself to get some sutures before turning to me. "I think we both know who did it, Freya."

My throat burned with unshed tears. I knew what I had to say, but that didn't make it easy. "I'm sorry. Do you want me to call the cops so you can report him?"

Christian heaved out a huge sigh. "No."

I tamped down the nausea threatening to rise. "Why?"

Christian grimaced. "First, I don't do cops. Had a shitty dad and ended up in juvie when I was fourteen. Second, I kinda deserved it. When your boyfriend came in to collect your car, he made it crystal clear where I stood in your life, and it made me jealous."

My face fell. "It didn't give him the right to hurt you, Christ—"

"Actually, it did," he said, cutting me off. "I said things on purpose to rile him up. Told him you weren't so averse to me when you gave me your number and that he shouldn't worry 'cause the second he left town, I'd take real good care of you."

I rolled my eyes.

"Yeah," Christian added. "I know, but I like you, Freya, and his attitude made me pissed."

I kept my mouth shut.

I didn't condone what had happened to him, but I understood it.

By society's standards, Colt's behavior was over the top. Normal men didn't go around beating on each other for talking about their women.

However, Colt was a biker, and they lived by a different code. Atlas smashed Iceman's bike and truck up just for joking about taking Sophie out. For them, it all boiled down to respect.

"I'm really sorry, Christian," I murmured, gently wiping antiseptic fluid over his cuts.

His eyebrows drew together. "Are you two together, together?"

"Yeah." I glanced at Christian before going back to his cuts. "I'll talk to him. I'll make sure he doesn't come near you again."

Christian nodded. "Probably for the best. Though I wanna reiterate something. I like you, Freya. I think you're special. I'd love to get to know you better."

I let out a humorless laugh. "I'm going back home in a few days, and anyway, I'm surprised you ever want to see me again after what Colt did."

"You'll be shocked at how resilient I am," Christian muttered.

"The doctor will be with you soon," I assured him. "I'm going to order a CT scan. It's a precaution we carry out with any head injury. Will you be okay here?"

"Yeah." He caught my hand gently. "You need to have a talk with him, Freya. I'm no rat, but if that nutcase comes to my place of work again, I'll have to call the cops. It's bad for business."

I nodded, lips pursing.

What Colt had done was ridiculous. We weren't at the club now, and he was lucky Christian wasn't pressing charges. It felt like I was in a dream. I'd never seen Colt fight over a woman before, and his behavior had seriously riled me up.

"Oh, don't worry, Christian," I responded. "By the time I've finished with Colt, he'll never darken your door again. I may come across like Doris fucking Day, but don't be fooled. There's more biker babe in me than you think."

Chapter Fifteen

Colt

My jaw clenched as for the twentieth time that hour. I checked my watch, and my thoughts began to race.

Freya had finished work twenty minutes ago and still hadn't come out. Maybe she'd gotten caught up with a patient or even an emergency. I knew it was customary for a volunteer to get held up with the shitty jobs, even though she'd been at work since the crack of dawn.

But even as I tried to justify her absence in my head, I knew exactly what she was playing at. Freya was punishing me for punching Christian.

For the hundredth time that day, I wished I'd rinsed his bank account and fucked up his credit instead of going all Rocky Balboa on his ass.

I'd made an error in judgment and let him get to me. Though after the shit he told me he was gonna do to Freya when I left, he was lucky I didn't end his sorry life.

My heart jumped as I finally caught Freya walking out of the hospital with Abigail. I opened the door and jumped outta the car. "Yo!" I shouted over in case she hadn't seen me waiting. "Here, baby."

Freya and her friend both slowed down, both looking straight at me.

Waving again, I shot her the sexy smile that usually made panties drop from ten paces. "Your chariot awaits," I shouted.

I swear I saw my princess's eyes turn to slits, even thirty feet away. My heart sank as I watched her pop a hip and jam one hand to it before raising her other arm high in the air and sticking out her middle finger.

My head reared back.

Freya dropped her hand and with her eyes flashing, she shrieked, "You, Colter Van Der Cleeve can fuck right off!"

A snarl escaped my throat.

"You can go back to Wyoming now for all I care. God knows why you thought I'd put up with your bullshit shenanigans, but you've lost your damned mind. I don't like bullies. Fuck off back to playing Counter-Strike 2 and jacking off to those weird ass anime porn sites you're so fond of. I'm done with you."

My cock hardened, and it wasn't at the thought of some weird ass anime porn site.

Fuck me, Freya looked hot standing there with stormy eyes, giving me shit. I mean, she was gonna get her ass tanned for bein' so fuckin' lippy, but I'd have been lying through my teeth if I said I didn't like it.

As much as aggressive women turned me off, an angry Freya was a sexy Freya.

All my good intentions to give her pussy a rest after the previous night flew away with all my fucks. If I had more time, I'd have edged her for hours as her punishment, but I had work to do, and she had to pack her shit.

I walked closer. "Freya. Get your ass in my car." I lowered my voice, leaving her in no doubt about how serious I was. "We need to talk about it."

Her cheeks flamed, indicating that she read my undertone just fine. I watched her body stiffen. "No. I'm catching a ride with Abigail."

My eyes slid to Freya's friend, whose gaze darted between us with interest. I gave her a chin lift. "Hey, Abigail."

A huge smile spread over her face. "Well haven't you been a naughty boy?" She glanced at Freya again, and her smile grew even wider. "Think you better go home with Colt, babe."

I cocked an eyebrow. "Do as your friend says."

Freya huffed. "I'm sick of you and your damned fists. You embarrassed me."

"Baby," I crooned, cock twitching at the challenge in her eyes. "I only defended your honor. Now, get in the car."

She let out a huff.

"Either you come of your own free will, or I'll make ya," I rumbled.

She glared and went to turn away, but I wouldn't allow her to leave before we hashed our shit out. I grabbed her wrist, tugged her into me, stooped, and tipped her over my shoulder.

"Oh my God. Put me down!" she yelled from my back, trying to kick me.

I turned toward Abigail. "You're welcome to follow us back to make sure I don't hurt her" —I swatted Freya's ass— "much."

Freya gave a frustrated shriek.

"You remind me of someone," Abigail said, lips thinning. "He's a chest-beating, me Tarzan, you Jane kind of asshole too." She sighed exasperatedly. "I'll follow you. Good luck." She turned on her heel and walked toward a silver Ford Focus, beeping the locks.

"You've got your way," Freya seethed. "Put me down."

Ignoring her, I started for the SUV. She could whine all she wanted. I just needed to explain what happened with the asshole from earlier.

I opened the passenger door and dumped Freya in the seat before reaching across her chest to grab the seat belt and secure her. "Stay!" I barked, slamming the door, and jogged around the hood to the driver's side.

"You're unbelievable," Freya snarled, eyes throwing daggers at me as I slid onto the driver's seat and clicked my safety belt into place.

"Thanks, baby. You're pretty unbelievable yourself." I started the car and drove out of the parking lot, checking Abigail was behind me before pulling out and joining the traffic. "What's unbelievable is that you didn't tell me you had another number. You let me discover that little gem when asshole mechanic bragged he had your digits."

"It didn't come up," she murmured snippily, tossing her hair.

A kernel of heat crept through my chest. "Well, that cellphone's now dead and buried, and I've changed your real number."

She stilled briefly before slowly turning her head to face me. "You did *what*?"

"Did I fuckin' stutter, Princess? An hour ago, you got new digits. I messaged everybody who I think should have 'em. Any dude on your contact list, whose name I didn't recognize, didn't make the cut."

"How fucking dare you?" she shrieked. "It's taken me a year to memorize that number, and you go and change it!"

"Bullshit!" I bandied back. "You've got a photographic memory."

Her spine snapped straight. "Yeah! For everything except new cell numbers. I can't get my old numbers out of my head, so I mix them up." She shook her head. "You're a fucking psychopath."

I snorted a laugh. "Ain't no psychopath, baby, though admittedly, I've got a touch of the narcissisms." I grinned. "Don't worry, nothin' too controlling."

Freya's eyes rounded. "Nothing too controlling? Colt, you hacked a cellphone network and changed my number so other men can't have it. It's hardly fucking normal."

"Could'a been worse." I shrugged. "Could've blacklisted you with all the telecommunication networks, so you couldn't have a cell phone at all."

My princess slumped back in her seat. "You're crazy."

"Maybe," I retorted. "But I'm not havin' little pissants like your *Christian* talkin' shit about ya. End of."

Freya's eyebrows furrowed. "What do you mean, talking shit?"

My chest tightened. "Told all his Neanderthal cronies that next time he saw you, he intended on giving you his dick."

Her mouth fell open. "He said what?"

"Ain't repeatin' myself, Princess. I gave you the tame version. He got lucky that I only broke his nose and not his legs to boot."

"Oh my God. Why would he say that?" she wailed, cheeks pinkening.

My fingers tightened on the steering wheel. "Ain't lyin'."

Freya turned her head, staring out of her window. "I know. You've always given it to me straight, even when you think the truth hurts."

She was right. I never lied.

Maybe it was because I was related to a man who lied and cheated on his wife and business associates. I'd watched my father screw his circle over for years and even become revered for it. Eventually, he also screwed me over without a thought because brutality and deviousness were respected in that world. It was why I wanted no part of it.

Silence filled the car until we pulled up to her apartment block.

I pulled into a space, cut the engine, and jogged around the hood to help Freya out. Just as I grabbed her hand, Abigail pulled up and parked a few spaces away.

Pulling Freya to me, I waited for Abi to park and get out before I laced Freya's fingers with mine, and we all walked toward the block.

"You two made up then," Abi murmured, glancing at our connected hands before her lips twitched. "You sure showed him, Freya."

"There was more to the story than Christian told me," Freya explained as I opened the door and ushered them inside the building. "He'd been selective with the truth."

"Right," Abi drawled, eyes twinkling at me. "So, he deserved a broken nose after all. Gotcha."

I smirked.

Freya's teeth sunk into her bottom lip. "It's a biker thing," she muttered as we ascended the stairs. "You wouldn't understand. It doesn't end well if a man disrespects a woman from the club."

My lips twitched. Punching Christian had nothing to do with club values and everything to do with him sniffing around Freya. It was probably best to keep that on the lowdown, though.

We got to Freya's floor and said our goodbyes to her friend before unlocking the door to her apartment and going inside.

Freya stretched her arms in the air and gave a little yawn. "I'm showering and going to bed," she told me before heading down the hallway to her bedroom.

I grabbed some water before following her and getting the bag of goodies that I bought for us out of the closet.

Freya thought our fight was over, and it was to a point. Except she needed to be punished for the way she spoke to me outside the hospital. Pulling out the thin black leather bindings, butt plug, and vibrator, I smiled. My princess wouldn't know what had hit her.

All too soon, the shower went silent, and the sounds of Freya brushing her teeth and drying off sounded from the bathroom. I dropped the bag down the side of the bed, stripped down, and put my clothes in the laundry basket before lying back on the bed, waiting.

I didn't have to wait long.

Freya wandered into the bedroom, brushing her damp hair and wearing a short towel.

My hard stare traveled down her bare legs. "Get on the bed."

She halted, her eyes widening as she looked at my nakedness. "I thought we weren't going to—"

"That was before you mouthed off at me, Princess," I said, cutting her off. "You made your mind up without even talkin' to me. When will you start realizing that everything I do is for your benefit? Do you think I want assholes like Christian goin' around town talkin' shit about you? You're no slut Freya, you're intelligent and sweet. All he sees when he looks at you is another notch on his bedpost, whereas all I see is beauty." I threw my legs over the bed, stood, and stalked toward her.

Freya backed up slightly until she hit the wall. "I'm sorry," she whispered, eyes going huge as I approached.

My body hit hers, hand immediately cuffing her throat. "You will be," I, murmured into her hair, breathing its clean scent.

She let out a tiny whimper. "What are you gonna do?"

My gaze lowered to see her nipples beading tightly, and my cock stiffened. At that moment, I bet if I stroked her tight little pussy it'd be fucking soaked for me. Her chest began to flush red, and I knew my fingers secured around her dainty little throat turned her on. "I'm gonna make you cry pretty for me, Princess." My hand left her throat and fisted her hair at the base of her neck. "Get on the bed, face down, ass up, and spread your legs wide for me."

Her pink lips parted in shock, but she nodded and started for the bed. I watched as she put a knee on the mattress and climbed on carefully, with her peachy little ass giving a little wobble.

My hand snaked down to fist my cock, desperate for relief. The sight of Freya's smooth olive-toned skin was enough to make me wanna nut where I stood, but then she opened her legs and showed me a flash of glistening, pink pussy, and I could've howled at the goddamned moon.

She was so fuckin' exquisite; so fucking mine that the inside of my goddamned throat caught alight every time the thought of leaving her flashed through my mind. It was almost sad how many years I'd been searching for exactly this feeling, and crazy that I'd found it with Freya Stone.

She was mine now, and I'd make it so she'd never forget, just like I wouldn't.

Approaching the bed, I palmed her ass, squeezing her skin softly before pulling back and swatting it hard. The imprint of my hand bloomed pink across her flesh, and I smiled.

"Do you know how much I love leaving my marks on you?" I asked, bending to grab the bag I'd dropped earlier. I put a knee on the mattress, moving behind her, running a finger through her sopping wet slit until she jumped as if electrified, moaning.

"Sweetest little cunt in the world, Freya," I muttered, fingers leaving her to rummage in the bag. I pulled out the small, pink, glass butt plug, shaped into a small heart at the end, and a small bottle of lube.

I tapped her ass cheek. "Anythin' been up here before?"

She whimpered and slowly looked over her shoulder, her pink lips slightly parted. She shook her head. "No."

My smile was devilish as I squeezed some lube onto the butt plug and held it against her puckered little hole.

She jumped again. "Cold," she murmured, craning her neck trying to see what I was doing to her ass.

I squeezed more lube onto the smooth, pink glass, covering it completely. Ass play could be good, but care was needed, and I didn't wanna hurt her... much.

Holding the tiny, pointed end against her little virgin hole, I twisted the plug slightly, easing it past the ring of tight muscle.

Freya moaned, wriggling her ass a little.

"Does it hurt?" I asked, not pushing any further until she'd gotten used to the sensations.

Freya stilled. "Not exactly. It feels weird but not painful."

I pushed the plug further inside, closely watching her response in case she tried to pull away. The plug was small, perfect for beginners, so it didn't take long to ease it all inside her until just the glass heart stopper could be seen.

"Does it feel okay, baby?" I asked huskily, eyes glued to the smooth glass glinting in the lamplight. She looked so raw and exposed to me. My cock was hard as iron with pre-cum weeping from the slit, my balls already drawn up, desperate for relief.

"I wish you could see what I see, Freya," I murmured hoarsely, my hands squeezing the globes of her ass. "You look so fuckin beautiful with your ass high, wearin' that pretty plug for me. One day I will make you fuck yourself on a dildo, wearing that plug, while you suck my cock. I wanna fill every fuckin' hole."

She moaned, her pussy clenching so hard, I could see it contracting.

I slid two fingers inside and fucked her gently with them. Her walls tried to suck me deeper, desperate to be filled up. I looked to the ceiling, eyes closed as I fisted my cock again and held the tip at the notch of her pussy. "Are you sore?" I asked, running a hand from the top of her spine to the bottom.

"Yes," she moaned, trying to push back onto my dick. "But I don't care. Please fuck me."

I gave her ass a light swat. "Wait!"

She cried out but stopped moving.

"This is my cunt, Freya," I rasped, sliding my cock through her wet folds, taking care not to penetrate, "I decide when. Not you. Now, be a good girl."

I gritted my teeth; I'd never needed to ram my cock into anyone so much in my life. I looked down, noticing the head, purple and engorged from the rush of blood flowing into it.

She sobbed. "Please, Colt."

My jaw clenched as my fingers skated over the globes of her ass one last time before I took my cock in hand slid it through her wet folds. "Gonna fuck you raw," I muttered, unable to hold back any longer.

With one hard thrust of my hips, I slammed inside her, eyes rolling back at how wet and tight she felt.

Freya sobbed again. "More," she cried.

I pulled back and thrust inside her cunt again, moaning at the sensation of her walls clenching around me already. She felt like she was about to come, and I hadn't even fucked her properly yet. My hips snapped forward, filling her up, trying to give her every inch.

"Yes. Yes. Yes," Freya chanted. "You feel so good, Colt."

My fingers inched up to the pink, glass heart at her ass and gently twisted it while pumping my cock hard inside her.

Freya threw her head back, crying out for God.

My gaze fell on the bag beside me on the bed. I grinned, reaching inside, and pulling out a small pink vibrator. I fumbled for the controls and waited for the buzz to start. Turning it onto the highest setting, I seated myself deep, reached around Freya's legs, and held it to her clit.

Freya let out a loud scream, threw her head back again, and came fast and hard.

I groaned as her pussy contracted around my cock, her inner muscles gripping me so tight it hurt as I fucked her through her climax. One hand held the powerful buzzing vibrator to her clit, while the other spun the butt plug gently inside her ass.

Her pussy gripped me like a vise, making me groan as her orgasm peaked.

I pounded into her harder, marveling at her tight wetness. "That's it, baby," I panted. "Give it to me. I want everything."

After a while, Freya's hips began to jerk, her climax fading. She sobbed, trying to angle her clit away from the vibrator. "No more. Please, it's too much."

I thrust hard, close to coming. My balls were rock hard, every nerve ending on fire. I wanted us to come together, wanted to experience it together. I needed to feel close.

"Gimme another, Freya. Come over my cock again," I heaved, sliding in and out.

She let out a cry. "I can't."

I pressed the vibrator flush against her clit, making her wail. "One more. Please, baby. Let's do it together."

"I can't," she cried, almost on a sob.

"Yes, you can." I moved the vibrator away slightly, taking some pressure from her clit. I growled when she gave an involuntary clench again. "That's it, baby. You're such a good girl." I moved the vibrator closer to her clit again, sensing she could take more. "Your pussy feels so good, Freya. I love the way you grip me. Never known a more beautiful cunt. Made for me, Freya."

She sighed, slowly beginning to fuck back onto me, spurred on by my encouragement. "Oh my God," she whispered. "You feel so good."

"Tell me how bad you want me to fuck you, Princess," I ground out.

"I need you so much," she wailed, crying as I grabbed a hip and pounded harder.

Her pussy contracted again, gripping me tight. "That's it, baby," I ground out. "I can feel it again." Pressing the vibrator flush against her clit, I finally started to let go.

Every clench of her cunt pulled me closer. Every cry and moan made my balls draw higher and higher until suddenly, she screamed and started to writhe, her second climax hitting her out of nowhere.

My fingers pressed into her hip as I came. I could feel every rope of cum as I offloaded inside her. My skin tingled as I emptied my balls with a groan, hips jerking uncontrollably as my eyes rolled into the back of my head.

My heart pounded hard in my chest, pleasure taking over as her cunt gripped me hard one last time, and I grunted my completion. My hips slowed, and I dropped the vibrator, sliding gently in and out of her.

Satisfied whimpers filled my ears, making a lazy smile curve my mouth until finally, I stopped, gently easing the butt plug out of her ass.

Freya collapsed onto the bed, and I followed her down, stretching over her body and giving her all my weight. I kissed the side of her neck. "You're fuckin' amazin', Freya Stone."

A satisfied noise escaped her throat.

Without warning, I got to my knees, and turned her around. Then, crawling to her back, I hauled her against me until we spooned on our sides.

"I've never come like that in my life, baby." I swept her hair away and kissed her nape gently, heart swelling with emotion.

"I can't move," she murmured. "My legs won't work. If you want me to shower, you'll have to carry me."

I kissed her nape again. She must've noticed my OCD. I couldn't touch anyone unless they were freshly showered, but at that moment, curling up to Freya's back, I couldn't summon the will to care. "I want your scent on me while we sleep." I trailed my fingertips up and down her back soothingly.

The more time I spent with her, the more it sunk in that she was it for me.

I waited for her breathing to even out and gave her shoulder one last kiss, murmuring softly into her skin...

"Made for me, Freya."

Chapter Sixteen

Freya

My last week in Denver went by in a flurry of packing and saying goodbye to all the people I'd met over the years I'd been here.

It was the end of an era. School was done, and now the learning really began.

I'd loved my time here. It was where I'd learned to stand on my own two feet, where I'd matured. Denver would always be a special place to me, but I knew in my heart it was time to move on.

I jumped slightly as I heard the front door slam. "Honey, I'm home," my favorite voice called out.

"In here." I craned my neck and watched Colt saunter into the lounge carrying a Starbucks coffee holder containing two takeout cups. "You know how to make a girl happy." I did a grabby hands gesture, sighing with pleasure as Colt handed me a cup.

"You're a fuckin dream," he said, watching me with a smirk as I took a sip, eyes rolling back in pleasure. "I won't need to buy you diamonds if I ever need to get my ass outta the doghouse. A trip to Starbucks will sweeten you up. Easy—fuckin'—peezy."

I lifted my shoulder in a shrug. "The odd diamond would be nice. I mean, a girl's gotta have some sparkle."

"Oh, you've got sparkle, baby. You already shine bright." Colt sank down next to me, nodding toward the bureau I was going through. "Whatcha doin'?"

"Just going through my stuff." I held up a photograph of Abi and me on the first day of school. "It seems so long ago."

He took the image and studied it closely. "It's been no time in the great scheme of things. You've bossed med school like you boss everything else. So fuckin' proud of ya."

My blood warmed. "You're my inspiration."

His eyes lifted to mine. "Huh?"

My lips hitched. "The first day you sat down and went through my algebra homework, it made me want to be smart. I remember thinking, will he be my friend if I'm clever like him?"

Colt's eyes glazed over as he thought back. "You were special, Freya. Not long after I joined the club, your dad told me how the principal at school called him and your mom in to tell them how smart you were. You know they were thinkin' about sending you away to a school for gifted kids?"

"Yeah." A stab of pain shot through my chest. "I begged my mom not to do it. I told her I'd stop studying altogether if they did."

"I remember feelin' sick at the thought of you leavin'. Told your dad I'd help you along. It was crazy; you were a kid, but I was more comfortable with you than the brothers. The thought of you leaving was unbearable. You brightened my world. I was still reeling from what had happened in New York. When I met your dad, I was jaded and didn't trust easy at all. Then I met a young girl with an old soul, and everythin' slotted into place again." His gaze slid to me. "Should've known you were mine."

My heart fluttered.

Colt had a brain like a computer and the heart of a poet. He loved Byron, Keats, and Poe. Never before had I known a man who was so tough, capable, and strong but also so romantic.

He was a puzzle I never wanted to complete because while he kept surprising me, he kept enthralling me too. There was nobody else for me, but him, and I'd have followed him to the ends of the Earth.

I knew we'd have to fight for each other eventually, knew we'd be tested in ways I couldn't comprehend.

And it didn't faze me one bit.

"Come here," Colt muttered, holding out his hand.

I took it, smiling at the tingle I always felt when we were skin-to-skin as I shuffled toward him.

He lifted my leg under the knee and pulled it across his lap until I straddled him, sliding his arms around my lower back. "What you thinkin' about?"

My gaze lowered to his lips. "Just wondering how I got by without you for so long."

He smiled so big his eyes crinkled at the edges. "Been askin' myself the same thing. I tell myself I had to wait for you to grow up, and it happened when it was meant to."

"I know," I whispered. "But sometimes it feels too good to be true and that you'll get taken away."

He brought his hands up to frame my face. "No, Freya. Whatever happens next, we'll get through. As long as we fight for each other, we'll be okay."

Blood raced through my veins, and every inch of skin he touched tingled.

My emotions ebbed and flowed through my chest, surging like the tides until I couldn't hold it in anymore. Tears welled in my eyes. "I love you."

Colt paused briefly before leaning forward, gently pecking my lips and muttering, "Same."

Tears began to burn the back of my throat.

He hadn't said the words, but the sentiment was there. The practical part of my brain told me it was still early days. He'd say it when he was ready. But I wanted to curl up with embarrassment. No girl wanted to be left hanging, but at the same time, I knew I couldn't force it.

"You still goin' out tonight?" he asked, cleverly changing the subject.

I swallowed down the sting from my wounded pride and nodded. "Yeah. It'll be weird saying goodbye to my friends. We've studied together for so long that they almost feel like family. If Abi hadn't promised to follow me when she graduates, I'm not sure I could leave."

"She's fuckin' crazy mad," he said good-naturedly. "But she also runs deep."

I ran my fingers over his cheek and whispered, "Mad isn't necessarily a bad thing. Here, you should embrace a side of you that is quirky and unpredictable, and maybe when you get back to reality, you'll want to take a little of that with you."

"Look at you, quoting Alice in Wonderland," he breathed. "Is it any wonder you knock me off-kilter?"

I smiled, looked into his eyes, cocked an eyebrow, and threw his word back at him, "*Same*."

Colt tipped his head back and laughed.

I noted his sparkling eyes, white teeth, and happy expression and giggled from the infectiousness of his hearty chuckle.

It was hard not to get sucked in by him. Colt had a smolder that I'd loved since I was a young girl. He had something about him, a natural magnetism that held my interest and made other men fall by the wayside.

Of course, I'd waited so long and saved everything for him. Nobody affected me like he did. Nobody else measured up.

I loved Colter Van Der Cleeve so much that sometimes it hurt to look at him.

I always had.

But I couldn't ignore the sliver of uneasiness weaving through my belly because of the one word he threw at me when I made myself vulnerable and told him my truth.

Same.

Colt

Two A.M. and I sat in the darkened lounge, waiting with my hands clenched into fists.

I'd been calling Freya for hours, but she'd ghosted my ass.

She was subconsciously punishing me for not saying the words back to her, and it pissed me off.

There was no doubt I had strong feelings for her that would only grow over time, but was it love? If I was honest with myself, then yeah, it probably was, but soon we'd be back in Wyoming, and in six months, I'd be gone.

I wasn't a stranger to heartbreak. I'd had a fiancé who'd fucked me over and a father who reveled in the destruction he'd caused. The reasons I left New York had stained my soul. The day I walked, my chest felt like it'd been skewered with a pitchfork, but I got over the betrayal by enlisting and learning to compartmentalize.

I'd always been what Prez called a lone wolf, but somehow, I'd gotten used to being around my pack, which was a testament to them. They were the best of people. What I felt for the club couldn't be put in a box and locked away. They were part of me now, but I'd have to leave them soon, which was the reason I'd shied away from saying it back to her.

Good old self-preservation.

A noise sounded from the hallway, and my fingers twitched.

I looked up to see Freya illuminated in the doorway, and my cock thickened. "Where have you been? I've been calling for hours. I was worried."

She sighed. "I'm sorry."

Our eyes locked, mine hardening as they bored into hers.

"Don't do it again," I said, tone firm. "Go in the bedroom. There's a bag on the bed. Put it all on and come straight back to me."

Her eyebrows pulled together, but instead of challenging me, she nodded, turned, and disappeared.

My cock was already half hard at the thought of what was in the bag and what it would look like on Freya, so minutes later, when she appeared at the doorway again dressed in a black, sheer bra and lace topped thigh highs, I hardened to steel.

"I've never seen anyone as beautiful as you," I said, voice thick with desire as my eyes raked down her body. "You're no Princess, Freya Stone. You're a queen."

A smile curved her lips.

"Now, be a good girl and get on your knees."

Confusion flashed behind her eyes, and she hesitated briefly before sinking into the rug.

"Crawl to me," I ordered, tone low and rasping.

Freya lifted her gaze to meet mine head-on. She didn't cower, but why should she? Even half naked and on her knees, she held all the power.

My girl began to move, eyes never leaving mine as she crawled seductively toward me, her heart-shaped ass in the air. Freya looked fucking magnificent. Her skin gleamed in the moonlight streaming through the window. Her hair fell like a mane around her face and shoulders, making her look almost otherworldly.

She kept crawling, gaze holding mine until she knelt before me.

I leaned forward and ran my thumb over her pouty pink lips. "Have you ever taken a cock in your mouth?"

Her eyes clouded over, and she shook her head.

My dick kicked hard. "Do you wanna take mine?"

Freya nodded. "Yes."

Leaning back, I slid down the chair, eyes never leaving hers. "Take it out, Princess."

Her hands came to my crotch, delicate fingers unbuttoning my fly before I lifted my ass to help her pull my jeans down my thighs.

My cock sprang free, rigid, and thick. I grabbed it, fisting the base. "Take the tip in your mouth and suck it gently."

She eyed it, licking her lips, almost making me moan at the sight of her little pink tongue wetting her mouth. She leaned forward, took the tip, and sucked lightly, her soulful, golden eyes rising to meet mine.

My spine tingled at the sight before me. I'd never seen anything as pretty as Freya Stone sucking the head of my cock. Her mouth felt warm and wet, and my balls tightened at the sensations she evoked. Knowing my cock was the first one in her mouth made the moment all the more erotic.

"Wrap your hand around the base and squeeze," I rasped. "Then, go lower and take more of me."

Freya obeyed, her hand moving from my thighs to brush against my balls to hold the bottom. She straightened her back and lowered her head until her mouth butted against her fist. She moaned on my cock; the vibrations making my hips buck upwards.

My princess gagged slightly.

I pulled back a little to alleviate the reflex action of her throat. "I want you to go lower, baby. Ease into it and swallow when it hits the back of your throat."

Without hesitation, she pulled me in deep. I felt her working her throat against the tip, and my eyes rolled back with pleasure.

"That's it, baby." I circled my hips gently, not wanting to overpower her. Take me nice and deep."

She moaned again before she slid me out of her mouth and then sucked me back down.

My hips jumped again. "Best fuckin' mouth I ever had," I crooned. "You look so fuckin' beautiful swallowing my cock."

She whimpered, grinding her pussy against my leg, seeking relief. Her other hand gently stroked my balls, her wet mouth gliding up and down my rigid length.

The tingle in my lower spine grew more intense, and I felt my balls tighten. Freya's mouth was amazing, too fucking amazing. I wasn't gonna last much longer. The temptation to come down her throat was so powerful that even the control freak in me almost threw caution to the wind and spurted inside her mouth.

The thing was, I was nearer forty than thirty. I couldn't stay hard after coming like I used to, and I wanted more than anything for her pussy to pulse all over my cock the way it had done the night before. I wanted to take her and hold nothing back. To stretch her out until her cunt molded to me perfectly.

I wrapped her hair in my fist and slid her mouth up and off me.

She made a hissing sound and pouted. "I want more."

My heart swelled inside my chest. This girl was perfect for me. I wished I'd seen it sooner. I'd have done anything for us to have more time.

"I'll let you do it again tomorrow," I promised. "Now, I want you to stand up and open your legs."

Freya sat back on her haunches, rested both hands on my thighs, and slowly pulled herself up until she stood.

My eyes traveled from her hair down to the lacy tops of her thigh highs, and my cock wept. Her natural sexiness juxtaposed with her innocence, and I fucking loved it.

Freya's face was bare of makeup, but she didn't need it. Her skin glowed with health, her eyes shone brightly, and her pretty pink lips were swollen from sucking my cock.

My gaze traveled down to her heaving tits, encased in black, see-through lace, then lower to her smooth, flat stomach.

I leaned forward, resting my nose on her belly, and sniffed. Her skin held a hint of Coco Chanel from her shower gel and perfume. I loved it on her. It was everything she embodied. Classiness, sexiness, and timeless beauty.

My eyes lowered to her smooth pussy, smiling at the sexy trimmed, thin line of hair running from top to bottom. "Did you shave for me, baby?"

She shook her head. "I get waxed."

A curl of heat wrapped around my gut. "Don't want anyone but me near your cunt."

"I go to a woman," she replied softly, eyes wide.

My fingers reached out and trailed from her navel to her opening, marveling at her soft, perfumed skin. Lowering my head, I slid a finger inside her slit, groaning at how soaked she was. This was the first time I'd touched her tonight, so she'd gotten that way purely from pleasing me. That thought alone made me feel twenty feet tall.

My finger slid up to her clit and pressed down.

Freya's hips jerked, and she whimpered.

I lowered my hand, thrusting my fingers inside her, urging her to circle her hips slightly, trying to find purchase. "Fuck my hand, baby. Take what you need, but don't come," I rasped.

"Please, Colt. I'm so close," she said with a whimper, grinding against my palm.

"No!" I brought a hand up and swatted her ass, smiling to myself as her pussy flooded a little at the sharp sting. "Come here," I ordered quietly, watching as she leaned down.

Shifting forward, I smeared my fingers across her lips. "Taste yourself."

Her tongue darted to lick her lip. Her eyes widened, and a pink flush erupted across her chest.

I stood slowly from the chair, easing my jeans back up my ass. "Walk to the bedroom," I ordered.

She turned and began to glide through the room, shooting a smile at me over her shoulder.

My eyes fell to her naked ass. It was tight, high, and round, a perfect peach. My cock jerked at its slight wobble as she strutted into her room and I wondered if she'd let me take her there.

Introducing her to a butt plug was one thing, but my dick would be a whole different experience. I'd make it good for her, I wasn't really into anal, but Freya's magnificent ass made me second-guess everything.

Catching her fingers, I turned her to face me, tugging her body into mine. My hand cupped her cheek, angling her face upward and lightly touching my mouth to hers.

Freya's lashes fluttered, and she pressed her body into mine, swaying gently as her arms went around my neck.

I lowered my face and took her mouth, firmer than before. My lips parted hers, and I slid my tongue inside to tangle with hers.

Freya groaned at the feel of my hands skating down to cup her breasts in my palms, kneading them softly.

"You're fuckin' beautiful," I murmured against her lips.

She whimpered inside my mouth, her skin breaking out in goose bumps in reaction to the way the pads of my thumbs swept over her nipples, still encased in the black lace.

Reaching behind her, I unclipped her bra, tracing my fingertips up and down her spine, making her body tremor. My lips traveled from her mouth to her flaming cheeks before leaving open-mouthed kisses down her neck. I marveled at the taste of her satin-soft skin that held a hint of Chanel, my new favorite addiction.

"Mine," I whispered, cock aching so hard, I almost went dizzy.

Freya pulled back slightly, eyes shining like gold dust. "Always." She shrugged the bra I'd just unclipped down her arms and let it fall to the floor, her gaze never leaving my face.

My hand went to her sternum and gently shoved, watching as she fell back on the bed before putting one knee on it and crawling over her. "Do you want me?" I demanded.

"Yes." She leaned up and took my mouth hard.

I pulled back, allowing my eyes to travel down her perfect little body, taking in the curve of her breasts, swollen with need. They lowered to the concave of her smooth stomach, created to carry my babies, and the lacy tops of her thigh highs.

My cock swelled, burgeoning at the sight of my woman, and I wondered how I'd ever ignored the beauty I held in my hands. Leaving our bubble would be hard.

We still had the here and now though; we had this week, and I'd store every second of us away in my mind for later when I'd be half a man without her.

Freya's hand cupped my cheek. "Hey. You okay?"

I nodded my reply, pushing all the bad shit away. My princess deserved for me to be present.

Relaxing my knees, I dropped onto her body and stretched over her. My hands went to her face, and I nuzzled her nose. "Gonna fuck you hard," I rasped. "Gonna pound into your cunt until you beg me to stop."

She smiled, and I kissed her lips gently, using my knee to open her legs wider and wriggling my hips into place. Reaching down, I grabbed my dick, holding the tip at the notch of her pussy, and drove inside.

The pleasure was so intense my eyes rolled back in my head.

Freya's pussy was still as tight as a velvet glove, two sizes too small. Her grasping, wet cunt strangled my dick. "Fuck, Freya. You feel so fuckin' good." My words must've hit a sweet spot because her walls clenched around my cock.

She leaned up and pecked my lips. "I want more."

I grunted. My woman's pussy gripped my cock so snugly that my balls were already tightening with pleasure. She felt so fucking tight and slick that I couldn't hold back anymore. I gripped each side of her face and smashed my mouth to hers, sucking her tongue whilst simultaneously thrusting my hips forward.

Freya cried out into my mouth, her back arching off the bed as I ripped through her, golden eyes widening with surprise.

I kept my cock seated deep, my lips still moving over hers, swallowing her cries and moans. Sliding one hand between our bodies, I stayed seated, grinding into her while my finger circled her clit. "Tell me what you want, Princess?"

"Do that again with your hips," she whimpered.

I used my thigh muscles to grind into her again while sliding in and out of her little pussy. "You like that?" I rumbled, my own pleasure making me move instinctually.

"Yeah." A slow smile curved her lips, her eyes glazing over a little. "Do it more."

Circling again, I pressed my finger harder against her swollen clit. My teeth gritted at how hot she burned and how her pussy strangled my cock. "Fuck. You're so goddammed tight, baby. It's killin' me not to come."

I snaked both hands under Freya's ass, tilted her slightly, and thrust rhythmically, catching her soft whimpers as I retook her mouth with mine. Every few minutes, I changed it up. Grinding and circling until eventually, Freya's hips began to thrust up to meet mine.

"Fuck, Freya. You fit my cock perfectly," I muttered, hips snapping harder. My finger never left her clit, so when it hardened even more, swelling under my finger, I knew she was getting close. Every time I talked a little dirty, her pussy flooded. The tingle in my lower back told me I wouldn't last much longer, so I gave her more.

"Love this tight little pussy." I rasped. "Love the way it strangles me."

"Oh my God," Freya whispered as her pussy clenched me like a motherfucker.

"Who's fuckin' you!" I circled her clit harder, pressing down on the sensitive skin. "Say my name when you come, Freya."

Her hips bucked, and her walls clenched me hard as her orgasm exploded. She let out a keening cry, almost screaming with the force of her climax. Her hands flew to my ass, pulling me deeper into her, moaning my name repeatedly.

"Good girl." I pressed down on her clit, kissing her neck as I fingered and fucked her simultaneously through her climax. Her pussy contracted hard around my cock, and I knew I couldn't hold off.

My hands came back to her face, the fingers of one of them still soaked from her pussy. I pushed two into her mouth. "Suck!" I ordered.

She moaned.

"That's my girl." I leaned down and took her lips, my fingers still in her mouth, giving us both a taste of her. My body stretched over hers, and I began to fuck her hard and deep into the bed, relishing the pleasure that settled into every nerve ending.

My balls were so tight they hurt. I removed my fingers from Frey's mouth and reached up with both hands, grabbing the black wrought iron headboard for leverage.

She let out a loud cry as she came, soaking my cock while her body writhed in ecstasy.

Burying my face in her neck, I pounded deep inside her. I gritted my teeth, hips snapping harder against hers, and I let out a deep, long moan as my balls drew up into my body, and I came hard.

I almost blacked out. The strength of my climax was so forceful that my hips jerked uncontrollably, my cum coating Freya's insides. Planting deep, I seated myself within her for a whole minute before my balls finally emptied.

I lay there, spent, giving Freya my weight and panting as she trailed her fingers up and down my spine. My chest heaved, my breath ragged and heavy, my heart racing with the intensity of my orgasm.

It was a goddamned revelation.

I pulled up onto my elbows, looking into her eyes. "You okay?"

Freya looked shell-shocked, but she nodded. "It was amazing."

My head reared back a little further. "Did I hurt you?"

Freya's cheeks pinkened. "Not like the first time; it was another kind of pain. Like a good one." Her nose scrunched up. "Is that normal?"

I threw my head back and laughed.

"Hey!" she admonished, swatting my arm lightly. "It's not funny."

I chuckled. "Baby, I ain't gonna yuck your yum. You like what you like, and a little pleasure-pain can be good with the right person. We can explore it if you want, but I'm not into hardcore shit."

She smiled. "I think I'll like everything you do to me. Every time I needed something, you seemed to give it instinctively. If we only ever did what we just did, I wouldn't care."

My heart tugged. "It was fuckin' amazin', Frey. You were fuckin' amazin'."

Freya's hand came up to my cheek, and her golden-brown gaze bored into me.

I leaned down and claimed her mouth. My chest felt tight at how she made me feel everything I'd tried to suppress over the years.

After being fucked over by the people who were meant to love me the most, it seemed easier to avoid connections. That was why I lost myself in technology. I was dreading going back to the club and our bubble bursting, but a part of me was looking forward to getting to the next stage.

I was ready.

I'd lived in darkness for so long her light was almost blinding. Freya had already given me more than

I deserved, and when the time was right, I'd tell her I loved her because I did with all my heart and soul.

I always had.

Two Days Later

I banged the side of the truck and watched quietly as it pulled away.

This was it; Freya's stuff was on its way back to Hambleton, and we were about to follow. Our time here, getting to know each other, was over.

Deep in thought, I turned and froze on the spot when I saw Freya and Abigail hugging each other so tightly I was surprised they could breathe. My girl's body shook with tears as she said goodbye to her best friend.

Leaning back against Freya's car, I folded my arms across my chest and watched, heart-in-mouth, as Freya let out a little sob.

She'd never had an Abi before. At school, the other girls avoided her because she was so smart. They wanted to talk about boys and make-up, whereas Freya loved to talk about literature and history. I used to feel bad because she didn't have typical teenage experiences, but selfishly, a part of me loved that it was me she turned to instead. Soulmates wasn't a term I'd ever really thought about—my beliefs were more scientific. But if there was ever one for me, hands down, it would be Freya Stone.

I liked that Abigail had adopted her, though. Freya had always been confident in herself, but Abi brought a more relaxed side out that she'd never shown before. Abi made Freya more social and gave her confidence in her femininity, not just her mental ability.

Finally, the girls broke apart. Holding hands, they started to walk toward me.

I noted how different Freya's dark, edgy beauty was when juxtaposed with Abi's blonde, pretty feminine style. They were so different in so many ways, but they connected on a level where their differences complemented each other.

Freya would miss her.

"Hey," I murmured, pulling her into me and sliding my arms around her. "It's only goodbye for now. You'll see each other soon."

"That's what I said," Abigail replied ruefully. "She's gonna put in a good word for me at whatever hospital she ends up working at. We'll never be torn apart again."

Freya laughed, turning until her back was plastered against my front. "Take care. I'll call you when I get home."

Abi reached out to squeeze Freya's hand before patting my arm, turning, and strutting away. I could tell she was doing her best to hold her shit together.

"I'm gonna miss her," my princess said, sighing as she watched Abigail's ass sway through the door to her apartment block.

"I know." I moved forward so I could reach behind and open her door. "But you heard her. It won't be forever. You two are partners in crime."

She looked up at me. "I can't believe this is it. Like I said before, it's the end of an era."

I framed her face with my hands, leaned down, and dropped a gentle kiss on her mouth. "Time to get back to reality."

"It's weird," she murmured. "I'm ready to move on, but at the same time, I'm scared everything's changing."

"It's unsettling for me too," I agreed. "But if we keep our eyes on the prize, it won't seem so daunting.

The sooner we get back and sort out our next move, the sooner we can be together."

Freya touched my hand. "Yeah."

I took her hand, guided her around the car, and helped her into the driver's seat. "Wait for me, I'll follow. Remember where we're stopping off?" Reaching up, I pulled the seat belt across her lap and fastened it securely. "Don't drive too fast."

Our eyes locked. "It's gonna be okay, right? Please promise me we'll get through this."

Reaching up, I cupped her cheek. "We've gotta go through the hard stuff to get to the easy. We just gotta have faith everything will work out how it's meant to. How could it not when you were made for me?"

We smiled at each other like lovestruck teens.

It had taken years for me to get my head out of my ass and claim my woman. We still had a long road ahead, but I was confident in us.

Freya was mine now, and in a couple of months, we could leave the club and start our lives together.

And I couldn't fucking wait.

Chapter Seventeen

Freya

Six hours later, I pulled through the gate of the Speed Demons' compound.

The parking lot was full of bikes. We were nearing the end of October, and snow could fall at any time, so the guys were making the most of riding before they put their bikes away for winter.

I pulled into a parking space, turned my engine off, and stared at the building that had been my home for most of my life.

I was seventeen when I left for college with all the hopes, dreams, and aspirations of a young girl who knew what she wanted but didn't quite know how to get it. Growing up was a part of life, but I was a different person now, compared to the young girl I was then.

In the seven years I'd been gone, I'd gotten older, a little wiser, and a whole lot more confident. I'd earned two degrees and had all the relevant paperwork that told the world I could take an internship in a surgery program in any hospital in the country.

Now I was home, and as I gazed over at the familiar warehouse, I realized I'd missed it.

I grabbed my purse from the footwell of the passenger side, threw my door open, and slid out. The place looked quiet. A couple of old-timers talking by the open garage doors gave me chin lifts, which I reciprocated with a low wave.

I made for the main doors of the clubhouse, noting how the nights were drawing in earlier and already held a nip of winter in the air. I reached out to open the door when a loud scream went up, followed by bellows and shouts.

I halted for a split second before squaring my shoulders and gritting my teeth. Then, hauling the door open, my eyes rounded when I saw people running and pure bedlam erupting.

"Bites his butthole, Jolly Batman," Sunny shrieked, cowering behind a table. "Assless shots me!"

A little growl went up, and Kai leaped through the air, landed on a couch, and did a Mission Impossible roll before aiming a huge Nerf gun and firing at Atlas, who hovered in a doorway, glaring. "It's okay, Sunshine," he yelled. "I got him for ya."

"Go on, Son. Show the asshole what us Stones are made of," Dad bellowed, wielding a foam blaster as he chased after Gage.

Jolly Batman let out a loud bark before jumping up and baring his teeth at the SAA, who bared his teeth right back at the ugly dog. The huge SAA leaned down and barked, then let out a howl.

"Kai!" Kennedy shouted from the bar. "Quick! JB's got him on the back foot."

My nephew lifted his blue and orange Nerf rifle, aimed, and fired off a shot that bounced off Atlas's head. "Bullseye!" he yelled and jumped down to the floor with a loud whoop.

"Good job, Son," Kennedy crowed, ducking to avoid the foam bullet that Atlas fired off toward her. "Next time, aim for his danglies."

Kit popped up next to her, glowering, jumped over the bar, and ran for the SAA. "Leave my Kitten alone," he roared, leaping onto him, and bringing him down with a crash.

"Atlas!" Sophie called from a corner where she cowered with Layla. "Be careful."

"S'okay, Stitch," Atlas hollered, getting to his knees. "I'll show the little scrotum sac who his daddy is." He squealed as Breaker leaped from the floor at his back and tried to throttle him from behind.

"Kai!" Dad yelled as he got Bowie in a headlock. "Shoot the asswipe in the head."

Gage somehow got himself free and ran for the main doors, with Dad sprinting after him.

"Oh my God," Layla shrieked. "Stop! Someone's gonna get hurt."

"Yeah," Atlas bellowed, flipping Kit over his shoulder. "And it's gonna be Breaker."

My brother landed flat on his back with a moan.

"I'll save ya, Dad!" Kai shouted as he took aim and fired another shot at Atlas's head.

My eyes widened as the opening bars to Rihanna's 'Rude Boy' blasted through the speakers, and Kady appeared in the doorway from the kitchen.

"I loves this song!" Sunny shrieked, grabbing Kady's hand, and running for the bar.

My jaw dropped as I watched them climb up and start pulling out stripper moves. Sunny raised both arms in the air and did a slut drop.

I gaped, my eyebrows hitting my hairline.

What the actual fuck?

"Go on, Sunshine," Dad called out, shoving Bowie's head down by the back of his neck until my brother was bent over double. "Show your grandaddy what a gorgeous little dancer you are."

Xan sauntered into the room with Wilder tucked into a baby carrier tied around his neck. He looked around and barked a laugh. "Fuckin' idiots," he muttered before turning back and sauntering off the way he came.

Jolly Batman pranced around Atlas and Kit, who by then were rolling around on the floor.

"For fuck's sake," a voice snapped from behind me.

I whirled around to see Abe and Iris standing in the doorway.

Iris rolled her eyes, gave her man a peck on the cheek, patted my shoulder, and made her way toward the kitchen.

"Stoooop!" Abe bellowed.

Everyone stopped, all eyes turning to me.

"She's back!" Sophie yelled.

Atlas lumbered to his feet and opened his mouth to say something, just as another foam bullet sailed through the air and bounced off his head. "Motherfucker!"

"Woo hoo!" Kai yelled, leaping and punching the air.

I gulped as bodies surged toward me.

"Freya!"

"You look beautiful."

"We've been waiting for you."

Layla, Kennedy, and Sophie smothered me in cuddles and kisses.

"Hey!" I laughed. "What's going on?"

Sophie grabbed my hand. "We've been waiting for you all afternoon, and you know how they get when they're bored."

Greetings rang out from the men, and I caught Sunny and Kady scrambling down from the bar top. Jolly Batman barked loudly, tail wagging and dancing around their legs as they ran toward me.

"Auntie Freyaaaaaaa!" Sunny screamed excitedly. "Dids you sees my sexy dances?"

Bowie's face paled.

"Sunny!" Layla snapped. "What have I told you about saying sexy?"

Sunshine waved her arms in the air, made a pouty face, and started grinding her hips. "Look at me being sexyyyyyy."

Every eye turned to Kennedy.

She put her hands up defensively. "Don't blame me."

"But you taught her how to grind," Layla cried.

Kennedy laughed. "Well, it's not like you can help the kid out. You dance like you've got a stick rammed up your ass."

Layla let out a huff.

Sophie raised her hand to cover a laugh.

I swallowed down my giggle.

An arm slid around my shoulder. I looked up to see Abe shaking his head at everybody. "It's like a goddamned madhouse, Freya. Good to see ya back, girly. We've missed ya."

Dad walked over, his eyes never leaving my face. His thick fingers curled around my nape and he tugged me into his massive, hard chest. The scent of motor oil and spicy cologne swirled all around me. I loved that smell. It hadn't changed for as long as I could remember.

"Good to see ya, sweetheart," Dad muttered in his deep, gravelly voice.

I smiled into his tee. "Hey, Pop."

He pulled back slightly, a hand gripping each arm. "My daughter, the doctor," Dad said proudly.

My heart bloomed. "Not yet, but I'm on my way."

Pop glanced around the room. "Party tonight!" he bellowed. "My daughter's home from med school! It's time for a celebration."

I looked up to study my dad's face, smiling at the proud look he wore.

John Stone was stubborn and immovable. If he said jump, he expected you to ask how high. The club was a fun place to be until he went on the warpath. Our relationship was fraught because I had a lot of that in me too. We clashed, and when it happened, it wasn't pretty.

He was also more intelligent than he let on; he was streetwise and could read a man like a book. His family meant everything to him, and that extended to his club brothers too. He'd give a stranger his last dollar if they needed it more, and he'd do it gladly.

Smiling, I glanced around at all my friends and family, and warmth filled my chest.

It was good to be home.

'Modern Love' by David Bowie blasted from the speakers in the bar. The party was in full swing. Iris and Abe were jiving up a storm while Kady and Sunshine danced around them with Jolly Batman prancing around their legs. Sunny held a pretend saxophone to her mouth, bending up and down; her fingers played imaginary notes. Kadence played an imaginary piano, moving her hands from side to side, fingers flickering on pretend keys.

My heart swelled, a huge grin spreading across my face at the cuteness overload. The way they goofed off and enjoyed themselves with no inhibitions or embarrassment was a joy to watch.

Abe laughed, bending down and egging Sunny on to bust some more moves with her sax.

Movement caught my eye a few yards away. Mason was teaching Kai how to body pop. Suddenly, he dropped to his ass and started spinning on his hips and shoulders.

Sunny shrieked, dropped to her ass, and tried to copy; her saxophone quickly forgotten.

"Can't imagine Wilder being like that," Cara said from beside me with her son slung over her shoulder as she burped him.

I busted out laughing. "If my nephew's anything like his father, he'll be a handful."

Cara's eyes bugged out. "Let's call it like it is. He'll be Beelzebub reincarnated. It's fucking typical that Layla ends up with Pollyanna over there while I'm frantically searching for three sixes somewhere on my kid's body."

"Is he still not sleeping?" I asked.

Cara replied with a grimace.

"Oh dear," I breathed. "Have you had him checked out?"

"The pediatrician says he's perfectly normal," Cara replied with an eye roll. "Which automatically makes me think she doesn't know her ass from her elbow. I mean, it's the son of Xander Stone we're talking about here. Normal doesn't factor."

I glanced over at my eldest brother, who sat at the bar with Gage, Kit, Dad, and Atlas. "True. He does break the mold. Though I wouldn't call Kit or Gage exactly run-of-the-mill, either."

"Kit definitely isn't run-of-the-mill," Kennedy piped up from somewhere behind me. "But his monster's hot, and it's all mine."

I craned my neck to see the beautiful blonde woman who had joined us alongside Sophie, Atlas's gorgeous little brunette wife. Kennedy helped a pregnant Sophie into a chair before sinking down into the seat beside her. "Now, what's all this I hear about you and a certain computer whiz kid?"

A stab of unease cut through me. "Jesus, how many of you know?"

All three women raised their hands.

My eyes rounded at Sophie. "Does Atlas know?"

"No way." She laughed. "Does he have an idea? Well, yeah, he's suspected for a while, but I don't think he wants to know, because having it confirmed means he has to do something about it. Am I going to tell him? Nope. He's got his club business, and I've got my friend's business. What he doesn't know won't hurt him."

"Shit," I muttered.

Cara bumped my shoulder. "Why the long face? You've wanted this for years."

Out of all the ol' ladies, Cara was the one I was closest to. When she first met Xander, she became the sister I always dreamed of having, so confiding in her about my crush was a no-brainer.

"I *have* wanted it for years," I confirmed. "But now we're together, I've realized how delicate the situation is."

Kennedy nodded thoughtfully. "Kit told me not to say anything to Layla or Bowie."

Cara grimaced slightly. "Layla's my best friend, and I love her to pieces, but she'd tell Bowie. Cash reckons he'd tell John."

Kennedy rolled her eyes.

"Ned," Sophie said warningly.

The blonde woman huffed out a deep breath. "Look, I like Layla. She's adorable and kind, blah blah blah, but why has she got to run everything past Bowie? Hasn't she got a mind of her own? Freya needs us. Why can't Layla put her first?"

Cara smiled indulgently. "She waited a long time for Bowie. He changed her and Sunny's lives. When shit hits the fan, she's loyal to him."

"And I'm loyal to Kit," Kennedy replied. "I've stuck by him when I wasn't sure I even wanted to. You can be supportive of your partner without letting a friend down. If I thought Kit had an issue with Freya and Colt, I'd keep my mouth shut."

Sophie nodded her agreement.

"Layla's a good friend," Cara insisted. "She stuck by me when I was a bitch. She's just different from us. It doesn't make her a bad person though."

I squeezed Cara's arm.

The split between the ol' ladies was indicative of how news of our relationship would probably divide the club. Layla wasn't doing anything wrong, but still, it would've been nice to have her support. The proverbial shit would hit the fan when I left with Colt. Having all the women on my side would've been a boost.

"Fair enough," Kennedy acquiesced. "I've gotta remember that not everyone's like me. It would have been good for Freya to have a united front in the officer's ol' ladies thou—"

She was interrupted by the main doors flying open with a crash.

I turned to see who it was. My heart leaped when I watched Colt saunter into the bar, twirling the car keys around his finger. His eyes swept the bar, landed on me, and shot me a sexy wink.

My nipples felt like they'd been set alight, and I almost swooned off my seat.

"That boy's got some swagger," Cara murmured, her voice tinged with admiration.

Kennedy's eyes were glued to Colt's ass as he made his way straight toward the bar. "He's certainly got a certain *je ne sais quoi* about him."

"I remember the first time I ever saw that man." Sophie glanced at me and then back to Colt. "Do you remember the night we took the bullet out of Atlas's shoulder?"

I grinned. "Yeah."

She nodded toward Colt who, by then, was partaking in a shoulder-clapping contest with the other men. "He stood at the doors there looking like Jax Teller's hot, mysterious, leather-clad older brother. I remember asking myself what the hell they put in the water around here."

"There's no question of what you see in him," Cara breathed, eyes raking down Colt's body. "He's got the goods."

I watched as Dad stood from his bar stool, grabbed Colt by the shoulders, and gave him a man hug. He pulled back, still holding my man by his shoulders, and beamed.

My throat went dry, and something painful stabbed through my chest.

I turned away and took a fortifying breath. I'd never really thought about how all of this would affect my dad's friendship with Colt before. He was a favorite. Dad made it obvious. Whenever he spoke of Colt, it was with pride because Pop knew how unique his abilities were.

Seeing them together with their tight bond made me sit up, and for the first time, realize how deep mine and Colt's betrayal would cut him. Dad's best bud was Abe, without a doubt, but Colt came a close second. How would he feel when he left and took me with him?

I couldn't put into words how proud I was to be with Colt, but at that moment, watching my dad greet him like he would a son, I wasn't feeling particularly proud of myself.

Love was all very well and good, but was I being selfish?

"Hey," Cara murmured quietly, looking between me and the bar. "Stop second-guessing yourself. You've got a right to be happy too."

My stomach settled a little at her words. She was right, to a point, but I had to ask myself, was my happiness more important than my dad's?

She took my hand and slipped something in my palm, closing my fingers over it. "There are stairs at the back of the gallery leading up to a small, contained room with a bed, TV, and a fridge. You've also got a small bathroom attached. It's all yours."

My jaw dropped at her understanding and generosity. If anyone ever found out what she'd done, she'd be given a hard time. "Are you sure?"

She made a meh gesture. "I disagree with John. I understand, but I disagree. We all deserve to be with the one we love, and I want you to be happy."

My throat heated at the emotion in her tone.

It was only recently that Cara had given Xander another chance after he cheated on her years ago. She'd left town and got engaged to the man who, not only put my brother in prison, but also secretly terrorized the women of Hambleton.

Their relationship—which was highly toxic—had settled into something so much better for them. Losing Cara entirely had made Cash turn himself around, and seeing them so happy together almost brought me to tears after everything they'd been through.

My eyes automatically slid toward Colt, the same way they had since I was a girl. He sat on a stool at the bar surrounded by Dad, Atlas, and my brothers. He laughed at something on his phone and held it up for the others to see, before his ocean-blues flickered to mine and softened.

My heart wrenched toward him, and my breath caught inside my throat because although I had doubts about lying, I knew it would be worth it just to be his.

We had to get through the next few months as best we could.

Like Colt said, we just had to keep the faith.

Chapter Eighteen

Colt

I loved being back at the club, but I yearned for the freedom Freya and I had back in Denver.

I missed touching her, missed kissing her soft lips, and the craving I had for her intensified. Therefore, when she messaged and told me about the key she had to Cara's gallery, I breathed a sigh of relief.

Now I just had to get outta the fucking place, 'cause since I'd been back, Prez hadn't let me out of his sight. He was driving me nuts. Every day, seeing Freya and having to hold back was frustrating me.

"I miss you," Freya murmured down the phone. "I'm so sick of this."

I swiveled my chair around to face the door so I could watch for somebody coming in. Living in a perpetual state of nervousness disagreed with me too, but what else could we do?

"Your dad's keeping me busy, baby. Go to the gallery tonight. I'll do my best to get over there," I rasped, tone thick with emotion. "Last night, Prez sat in my office until midnight shooting the shit, so if he does it again, I won't make it, but I promise I'll try."

The sound of her deep sigh wrapped around my lungs and squeezed tight. The day I admitted my feelings for Freya, my heart settled. Not being able to pull her into my arms was killing me, especially when she was so close. My body felt deprived of her like it was starved. I needed my girl fix to allow my brain and body to function.

"Hiding us hurts," Freya sniffed.

Her words sunk into my already heavy chest.

What did she want me to do? I couldn't exactly walk into the bar, fling her over my shoulder, and take her to my room for a good fuck. "You know we gotta be careful. It feels wrong sneaking off together while we're under your dad's roof. There's nothin' I can do, so why give me shit?"

She paused briefly. "I never meant it that way—"

"So why d'you keep harping on 'bout somethin' I can't change?" I snapped impatiently. "This is what happens when you do shit on the sly. Betrayal ain't all hearts and roses. Get used to it, 'cause now I'm back, I need to make the club my priority."

Another pause, then, "Right."

My chest unraveled, and I felt like a cunt.

I heaved a breath out, scrubbing a hand down my face. "Fuck. I'm sorr—," but before I could get my apology out, the line went dead.

I leaned forward onto my desk and buried my head in my hands. "Fuck!"

My ringtone pealed through the air. Heart-in-mouth, I grabbed my phone and glanced at the screen, thinking it would be Freya calling back to apologize for hanging up on me. My gut sank when I read the name.

Letting out another curse, I accepted the call and held it to my ear. "What you got for me, Shepherd?"

"Afternoon, Agent Van Der Cleeve," Shep crowed good-naturedly.

"Not yet," I muttered. "Still got more than five months to go."

"Well, maybe I shouldn't tell you about what I've found on your vehicle," he said knowingly.

I perked up slightly at that, especially since I should've been in Church with the officers at that very moment with info on the damned car. Plus, my own curiosity was starting to get outta hand. Loose ends aggravated me.

"It's a long story," Shep continued. "It's top secret. What you tell your Prez is up to you, but you need to know there are lives on the line. What happens next could mean life or death for some.

A bad feeling slid through me, but it didn't stop me from sitting back on my chair and getting comfortable. At last, I was getting somewhere.

A thread of satisfaction weaved through my stomach, and my nerves suddenly settled.

"Shoot."

Taking a deep breath, I knocked on the door to Church. I waited for a loud buzz to fill the air before I pushed on the door and walked inside. My mind was reeling from my conversation with Shepherd. Suddenly, I'd been placed in the middle of a tug-of-war, and I didn't quite know what to do about it.

I gave all the guys chin lifts before my stare rested on Prez, who held Wilder. "We gotta problem."

Dagger stood and placed Cash's boy gently back in his arms. Retaking his seat, he regarded me thoughtfully. "Out with it then."

Shepherd's warnings floated through my brain. *The investigation has been going on for years. Undercover men and women on the inside. Agents' and informants' lives will be at risk if anything gets out.*

Your club cannot get involved until the leading players are exposed.

Placing three grainy images on the table, I lifted my eyes to Prez. "These are the pictures of the car that chased Atlas and Kit." I pointed to the image of the license plate. "See that?"

Cash's brow furrowed. "Yeah. What about it?"

I kept my breathing even and pulse steady. I had to be careful. The Demons' officers weren't idiots. Abe especially could pick out a lie from twenty meters. I had to tread carefully and give enough information to make them happy but not enough to make them suspicious.

"The chase happened weeks ago," I reminded him. "Since then, I've been tracking that plate down and getting nowhere fast. After getting nothin' but dead ends, I decided to take a peek inside a few top-secret databases."

Prez's eyes bugged out. "Don't tell me, the Men in Black are on their way here to arrest you for getting' caught hackin' into their fuckin' computers."

Too late, brother, my inner voice whispered, but I twisted my features into a boastful smirk and cocked a brow. "Those ballsacks couldn't catch me on my worst day, Prez." I tapped one of the photos and looked at the officers in turn. "The way that license plate's laid out reminded me of somethin', so I did a bit of digging and just got a hit." I paused, resting my gaze on Prez. "It's a government plate, Dagger. FBI, to be exact."

A few seconds of shocked silence settled over the room. The officers cursed and shouted as the severity of the situation sunk in.

Prez held his hand up for silence. "Quiet! I need to think." His hand went to his beard, and he rubbed it thoughtfully for a minute.

My stomach felt like a heavy weight had settled inside it. There was no going back now; I'd just lied to my club. Didn't matter that I was protecting them. I wouldn't be forgiven.

"What the fuck's goin' on?" Bowie breathed. "Why were the FBI tryin' to traffic women?"

Prez closed his eyes. "God knows."

"I've thought about it," I said, trying to hint at what I knew without giving it away. "Every agency from the local PDs to the President's Office is filled with people with an agenda. Believe me, boys; when it comes to extreme wealth, the rich are so fuckin' terrified of losin' everythin', they'd sell their sons and daughters to stay on top. The social elite is a club that's impossible to infiltrate but also impossible to turn your back on if you're one of 'em."

Prez rested his elbows on the table and held his head in his hands. "This could be bad. If the FBI's involved, we've gotta watch our backs, not only with the Sinners, but with the law too."

Cash ran a hand through his hair. "They could storm this place and get rid of us with no comeback what so—fuckin'—ever."

An uneasy feeling washed over me.

How could I try and alleviate their worry? Nobody would storm the club, but if I gave the game away and told them too much, the FBI wouldn't hesitate to pull every man, woman, and child in on trumped-up charges. The agency had spent years and a whack of money on their investigation. There was no way they'd let anyone compromise it.

The Demons were a well-respected club, but even if every ally stepped in, they'd still be no match for the FBI. I'd have to be very fucking careful and set some things in place during the rest of my time here if I was going to protect them how I wanted to.

If I let the cat out of the bag and the Demons stepped in, they'd get annihilated.

"Let's all calm our tits for a minute," Abe said, leaning forward. "Why are we jumping to the goddamned conclusion that the authorities are dirty? A much more likely scenario is that they could be investigatin' the trafficking ring."

"I dunno," Atlas rumbled. "Don't fuckin' trust any pigs. Don't care what fancy letters they go by."

Prez pursed his lips, shaking his head at the SAA. "The only reason you don't trust 'em is 'cause you're always breakin' the goddamned law and gettin' fines."

Atlas curled his lip. "I'm a biker. Live by my own fuckin' laws. I do what I want, when I want."

"Yeah, until Sophie tells you to do somethin' else," Cash said under his breath.

"Dunno how you fuckin' dare," Atlas muttered. "You're so pussy whipped you walk around in a daze half the damned time."

Cash gestured to his chest. "I gotta fuckin' newborn. Sleep's just a memory these days. Of course, I'm fuckin' dazed. Give Soph a few months to pop, and you won't be such a judgy cunt."

Just then, Wilder opened his eyes, scrunched his face up, and let out a loud cry.

Cash cursed. "You've woke the baby up, ya fuckin' prick." He shot Atlas a withering look. "Can't wait until Sophie delivers. I'm gonna hire a marchin' band to play show tunes outside your house day and night. See how you fuckin' like it." He laid Wilder gently on the thick wooden table, went into a large blue diaper bag, and grabbed a bottle before scooping his son up again and gently pushing the nipple in his mouth. "There ya go, Son," he crooned. "Ignore Uncle Fat Ass. He's simple, but he's harmless."

Wilder stared up at his dad knowingly, sucking gently before kicking his legs like a frog while letting out a huge fart.

Chuckles rose through the room.

My lips twisted. I'd never worked out what it was about expelling shitty-smelling air from one's intestine that made grown men revert to teenagers.

These particular assholes didn't disappoint.

"That's my boy," Prez said proudly.

Cash cocked an eyebrow. "If he's followed through, you can change his ass. Sometimes, it's like he's got rats livin' up there." He wrinkled his nose. "He gets it from his mother's side."

"Your ass was worse. Many a time, I told your ma to take ya to the doctor." Prez's mouth pursed in apparent disgust. "It wasn't fuckin' normal."

My mouth hitched for the first time in weeks as laughter filled the air.

Prez's stare fell on me. "Any other business?"

Silence.

Eyes still on me, Dagger picked up the gavel and banged it into the sound block. "Fuck off, everybody except Colt and Abe."

My stomach gave a jerk as question after question stabbed through my mind.

Did I fuck up? Did Prez suspect something? Could he tell I'd lied to him? Did he suspect something with me or Freya?

It was obvious I hadn't been myself since I got back.

Sleep had become illusive at best. Food tasted like cardboard, and my attitude had been disgraceful. Freya was in my head constantly. I couldn't stop thinking about her and us. It didn't help that I couldn't get a fix of my girl.

Freya Stone was my cocaine, and I'd gone cold—fucking—turkey. My hands shook constantly, and my gut swirled with nausea. I craved her so much that I'd opened the bottle of Coco Chanel I'd brought and hadn't given her yet and had taken to sniffing it to get my fill.

The sound of boots shuffling toward the exit registered somewhere in the back of my brain before the door to Church closed, leaving me with Prez and Abe.

"Sit down, Colt," Dagger ordered quietly.

I parked my ass in Atlas's seat and inspected my nails, anything to avoid looking my Prez in the eye. The sickness inside wasn't just about Freya; lying to the people around me ate away at my conscience.

"What's goin' on, Son?" Dagger asked gently. "Are you sick?"

I shook my head, unable to trust myself to speak.

Abe's hand clasped my shoulder reassuringly. "Colt, we can't help you if you don't give us something to work with."

"I'm okay," I blurted out. "It's nothin'."

The two men exchanged looks.

"Is it 'cause you dumped Lucy?" Abe inquired tentatively. "Are you havin' second thoughts? You wouldn't be the first man not to appreciate a woman until the relationship's over. Though I gotta say, you didn't seem that struck on her when you were together."

I scrubbed a hand over my face. "Nah. Gettin' rid of that troublemaker was the best thing I've done in months." My stare went to Prez's, but I lowered my eyes. It hurt to look at him knowing what I'd done, not only with Freya but with Shep too.

I swallowed down the bile rising through my gullet.

Fuck.

"I'll be okay," I croaked. "I'm just feelin' unsettled at the moment. It'll pass."

"You sure nobody's fuckin' with ya?" Abe asked. "'Cause you know you're one of us, and we stick together, always."

"The old fart's right." Prez grinned. "If someone fucks with one of us, they fuck with all of us. We're family."

I nodded blindly. "I'll be okay." My voice conveyed way more conviction than I felt.

"Good man," Prez said, meeting Abe's stare before his eyes slid back to me. "Wanna run somethin' past ya on the downlow."

I looked at him expectantly. "Okay."

Prez leaned forward, elbows to table. "Remember we caught Brett Stafford at the mayor's mansion the night we got chased?"

I nodded. "Told ya then somethin' didn't feel right about it."

Prez frowned. "Yeah. Me and Abe agree."

My eyes darted between the two men. "You think Henderson's involved?"

"We think it's likely," Abe confirmed. "Me and Dagger have been thinkin' about a few things. First, who's got enough influence in town to allow our clubhouse to be attacked with no investigation?"

"Second, there's the Sinners burning our rentals down," Prez interjected. "You could see those flames for miles, but no fire trucks and no pigs sniffed around."

"I came to the same conclusion," I said, lips thinning angrily. "Robbie Junior was into all kinds of heinous shit. What if it's in the family?"

Prez brought a hand up to pinch the bridge of his nose. "Stafford drove his van to the Henderson mansion that night we found the girls. We reckon he picked 'em up from there."

Slowly, I closed my eyes. "Fuck!"

"That seems to be the general reaction," Abe rasped under his breath.

I sucked air in through my nose to settle my swirling gut. "We said the Sinners must have friends in low places. Knew Henderson was a dick, never once thought he was a skin trader." My eyes met Prez's again. "Why aren't you tellin' the boys?"

"And have Atlas wanna do recon?" Prez challenged. "The boys would ride down there all guns blazin'. We need a more subtle plan."

"Fair point." My eyes narrowed as a thought came to me. "What if I recon the place?"

"That's not what we want," Prez told me, rubbing his beard thoughtfully. "Me and Abe have been thinkin'. What if we can get cameras in his office?"

"It's a good idea," I replied. "I can do it, but I'll need access and someone to look out for me."

Dagger's face blanked. "I know someone who may help. Thing is, if we get caught, it won't be good for her."

"It wouldn't be fuckin' great for me either," I responded. "So it's good for her that I'm invested in gettin' in, doin' the job, then gettin' the fuck outta dodge ASAP." I noted Prez had paled slightly under his weathered tan. "Who's your contact? And are you sure they can be trusted?"

He lowered his gaze. "Elise Henderson."

An angry sound escaped my throat. "His *wife*? Are you touched?"

His mouth set in a thin line. "Elise helped us before, brother. She saved Layla's life."

My eyebrows shot up.

Prez's eyes lifted to meet mine. "I'd like to think she can be trusted; I feel it in my gut. She betrayed me when we were young, but still, she's one of the best women I know."

I studied Prez's pained expression.

He was highly protective of the club. He wouldn't put any of us in danger. He'd rather die himself than send any of us to our destruction.

"I trust you more than anyone in this world, Dagger," I muttered. "If you think she'll help, we'll go with it."

Prez's eyes darted over my face, and he grinned. "We fuckin' lucked out when we got you, Colt. Don't mind sayin' I look at you as another son. Never known a man smarter or more loyal, not only to me, but to my boys and my girl too. I know you came here off the back of a betrayal, and I know what you had to overcome to be the man you are. Proud of ya, Son."

My gut sank down to my ass.

If Prez knew his so-called loyal brother was his biggest betrayer, he'd shoot me. Every word that came out of his mouth stabbed like a tiny blade. I was treating John like my father treated me, and the realization sickened me.

"I'll message her and arrange a meet," Prez continued. "Gotta test the waters first."

"What if she's in on it?" I asked.

Prez rubbed his temple contemplatively. "Then we're fucked."

Abe sat forward. "The Elise Bell I knew would never be involved in that shit. She was always a good girl, kind, sweet, and she cared about everyone."

I dipped my chin, staring at Prez. "Didn't she fuck you over and marry the mayor?"

Prez tilted his chin proudly. "There were extenuating circumstances, but yeah. We were together before I went away on a mission and got captured by the enemy. By the time I got back, she'd married Henderson and had a kid."

I closed my eyes, my heart hardening at what Prez had endured. "Did she Dear John you?"

"Nah." He sat forward again to study me. "She thought I was dead. Married him on the rebound, from what I can gather. Asked her to divorce him, told her it didn't matter to me and that I got how she must've felt when the military told her they'd presumed I'd been killed. Leesy told me there was no goin' back and that it was over. Three days later, I met Adele in a bar, got drunk, knocked her up, and the rest is history."

"Fuck!" I muttered.

"Yeah. That's about the long and short of it." Prez said quietly. "Throughout all that, she remained kind and caring. Does a lot for charity, especially for kids in need. When we were young and together, she told me how she wanted to be a social worker and have a house full of rugrats." He smiled at the memory.

"Crazy how she only had one, and he turned out to be a menace to society," Abe said thoughtfully. "She was a born mother, but he was a born pervert."

"It's lookin' like he got his proclivities from his dad," I mused. "Maybe Elise saw deep down what her boy was and closed shop."

Prez shrugged. "In the words of Cara; it's not my circus and definitely not my monkeys. All I want is to get you access to the mansion, set up what we need, then it's just a case of sitting back and watchin'."

A thought flickered through my mind.

What if putting cameras in the house affected the investigation? Shep had told me they had FBI on the inside, though he didn't say who. I assumed it would be guys who worked for the mayor or someone on his security detail, maybe.

Fuck!

Spying pissed me off.

I responded to facts, not whodunnits.

And now I had to navigate the club's needs while keeping them safe and away from the Fed's scrutiny, along with working for the FBI and keeping their informants and undercover agents out of shit.

Plus, I had to keep Freya happy.

What a shit show.

I rose from my chair. "Gonna get the equipment I need together and see if I can find a floorplan of the mayor's mansion. The sooner we can organize everything, the more prepared we'll be."

"Thanks, brother." Prez smiled.

We all exchanged chin lifts, and I made my way to the door, then out into the hallway toward my office, getting deeper into my thoughts as I walked.

This shit was delicate, and I couldn't help wondering if I should call Shepherd and fill him in. After what he'd told me before I hit Church, I knew interfering with the Fed's investigation could cause problems.

But I wasn't FBI, and I wouldn't be for months. Even when I had my badge, I'd still show the Demons loyalty, even if they turned their noses up at it. For now, I'd do my job, get into the mayor's mansion, and get eyes on the place. My club needed info; I could deal with any fallout later.

A burst of women's laughter floated from the bar, and my mind went to Freya.

It didn't look like I'd be able to get away anytime soon, which meant Freya would keep nagging. For a fleeting second, I thought about ending it. Now we were back, I had so much to prepare for. We could pick it up later when I'd left and started my new career.

I rubbed at my aching heart.

The thought of Freya not being mine made my chest pang. Though after the way I spoke to her earlier, I wouldn't blame her if she told me to fuck off anyway. Things were getting on top of me, and not having her in my bed wasn't helping my state of mind.

Maybe I needed to make more of an effort to carve some time out for her. As things stood, neither of us were happy with the new normal. I had to work something out to make things better, or else we'd crash and burn.

The memory of our nights together flashed through my brain, and I almost groaned out loud as my cock thickened. I missed sex, of course. Our week together had gotten me used to it. But what I missed more was the closeness, the feel of Freya's lips on mine, and how she looked at me like I hung the moon.

I wasn't a man who enjoyed kissing or cuddling in the afterglow of sex, but with her, it was everything; because the cold, hard truth was Freya Stone made me feel like a king.

Losing her wasn't an option, but if I wanted to keep her, I needed to start showing her that she was special, and I was worth the sacrifices she'd no doubt have to make.

Chapter Nineteen

Freya

I walked into my room at the clubhouse, feeling exhausted after several nights of restless sleep through missing Colt so much. As I closed the door behind me, I turned on the light and almost jumped out of my skin when I saw the man himself sitting on my bed.

"Jesus," I whisper-shouted. "What the fuck are you doing? Trying to kill me off?"

"Sorry," he said softly, looking up at me with his ocean-blues. "Can we talk?"

My heart sank as memories flooded back to our last telephone conversation—the one ending in anger, dismissiveness, and hurt feelings. "Do I have a choice?" I asked snippily, leaning back against the door.

"Baby, I'm sorry for how things went down between us," Colt began earnestly. "I know I was out of line and acted like an asshole."

"You think?" My voice dripped with sarcasm, but inside, a part of me was relieved he'd acknowledged his dickish behavior.

Colt chuckled ruefully as he got to his feet and slowly walked toward me. "I dunno what's got into me, Freya. I feel so fuckin' antsy all the time. I've got your dad on my back wantin' me to deal with the club business I missed when I was in Denver, and on top of that, he won't leave me the fuck alone." He took my hand, brought it to his mouth, and gently kissed my knuckles, sincerity shining in his beautiful eyes.

My heart fluttered.

I opened my mouth, about to automatically let him off the hook, but the memory of the dismissiveness in his tone stopped me.

It wasn't the first time he'd lashed out and hurt me, and what worried me was the dawning knowledge that there was a pattern to Colt's attitude. Every time he turned on me, he apologized and said he'd work on it, but he was obviously just paying me lip service.

I pulled my hand away from his, steeled my spine, and tilted my chin proudly.

His hands came up and framed my face. "Fuckin' hate it when you pull away from me, Freya. And what really fucks me up is that the reason you do it is 'cause I've fuckin' pushed ya. I've been single a long time, baby. All I've done for twelve years is please myself. I'm still gettin' used to thinking of me as an us. Add on the crippling guilt I feel every time your dad so much as looks at me, and I feel like a cornered animal. Maybe I need more time to adjust. A lot's happened, and it's all gone at light speed."

My throat thickened. "Do you want to take a step back?" The thought of us pulling away from each other made me feel sick, but if it was affecting him to the point where he was a dick to me, it was for the best.

"No." He shook his head vehemently. "That's the last thing I want. I need you, Freya. You're the only one who keeps my head straight half the time. I just need you to bear with me while I adjust and work things out. It won't happen overnight, but when it concerns us, I promise I'll do better."

The sincerity in his oath warmed my skin. Honesty flashed behind his expressive blue eyes. I could tell he meant every word from the steely tone of his voice.

Colt's blond hair, good looks and his rugged edge made my heart race whenever we were in each other's vicinity. I'd been drawn to him since I was a girl and understood he was a complicated man. I was there for the taking, ready and waiting to start our life together, but a part of me wondered if he was still catching up.

"Don't do it again," I murmured, holding his gaze. "I won't let anyone treat me like shit, Colt. You included."

He smiled softly, then leaned forward and kissed me gently on my lips.

Shivers ran through every inch of my body, but I still pulled away. I'd forgiven, but I hadn't forgotten. The fact he kept doing this shit to me was something I still had to think hard about. I wasn't the girl who'd put up with it. Constantly walking on eggshells wasn't my idea of a loving relationship.

"I'll do my best to get to the gallery," he told me quietly, resting his forehead against mine. "Stay there tonight. Wait for me."

I nodded, eyes flitting over every millimeter of the face I'd adored for so long. I'd wait forever for my man, but after our argument, he didn't need to know that.

Colt cursed under his breath as his cell phone buzzed in his pocket. He fished it out before looking at the screen and rolling his eyes. "I gotta go. Sorry, baby. Your pa's drivin' me batty." He slipped his phone away again and cupped my jaw. "There're some bags in the bottom of your closet. Got 'em for ya in Denver. My way of tryin' to show you how much I care." Our eyes locked. "And I do care. I feel everythin' for you, baby."

My insides melted at his words.

This was why I loved him. Colt may have been one percent asshole, but the other ninety-nine percent was perfect. The way he looked, thought, moved, and spoke did it for me.

The air swirling around us felt alive. Silence hung thick and heavy until Colt's eyes softened. Clearing his throat, he rasped, "I gotta go."

"Okay." I nodded in agreement, not trusting myself to say anything more.

Colt gave me one last look before turning and heading towards the door.

As he walked away, I couldn't help asking myself if we'd ever find a way to make things work, or whether we were just two people who were meant for each other but just weren't destined to be together.

For the first time since we'd gotten together, doubt circled like a noose around my neck, and every day, it pulled tighter and tighter. It wasn't that I didn't love Colt; I did, heart and soul. I even believed he loved me in his own way.

But I couldn't ignore the question whispering through my mind. A question that made my stomach clench with pain.

Is love enough?

"Nice boots," Cara called out enviously from the couches when I strutted out to the bar a half-hour later. "That bag's hot as fuck too," she added, peering at the black tote slung over my shoulder. "John's gonna shit his shorts when he sees your credit card bill."

"Colt bought them for me." I looked around to check nobody was listening before looking down and almost preening at my sexy new footwear. "They're a 'sorry I was an asshole' apology."

She whistled through her teeth. "I'll need to lay some hints for Xander. His idea of an apology is offering me a drag of his smoke after a quick fuck."

I giggled and grimaced at the same time. "That was funny as hell, but also way too much fucking information, Cara. He's my brother. There are some things I don't need to know."

"Fair enough." She waggled her eyebrows suggestively. "But I wanna know everything that happens between you and Colt, including width and girth. Mama needs to live her life vicariously through you now she's an ol' lady again with a kid who doesn't know what sleep is." She glanced over the rest of my outfit. "Are you going out?"

"Yeah." I glanced around the bar. "I was gonna go to the salon. My hair needs trimming, plus Tris and Anna know I'm back. They'll start to think I'm ignoring them if I don't go and see them."

"Can I tag along?" Cara asked. "Cash has got Wilder and won't give him back. I've expressed plenty, so he won't even notice I'm gone." Her lips pursed. "That's all I'm needed for these days, titty milk. My cute little boobies have turned into fucking cow's udders."

"Oh my God!" a voice shrieked from behind, "How are you wearing the Kate Botta 85 leather knee boots?! Say it isn't so!"

I turned to see Kennedy floating toward me on air, staring down at my boots with stars in her eyes. As she approached, she fell to her knees as if in worship. "They're so beautiful." Her eyes caught on my calfskin bag, and she squealed. "Pretty!"

I held out a hand to help her up, grinning.

"Colt bought them for her," Cara whispered from behind her hand. "Sorry for being an asshole gifts."

A slow grin spread over Kennedy's face. "I think I'd be encouraging Kit to be an asshole if his way of making things right was a pair of Kate Botta boots."

I made a mental note to send Kit a few pictures of what Kennedy liked. My brother had arranged to take Kai and Kady to the mall to pick out gifts for her birthday. Obviously, a pair of Louboutins would earn him some brownie points.

"Freya's going to the salon," Cara told her. "Thought I'd tag along too. Cash and John have spirited Wilder away. Xan said I should catch up on some sleep, but nanna naps make me feel worse. A pamper session would be good. You coming?"

"Definitely," Kennedy said with a decisive nod. "Let me get my stuff." She turned and strutted in the direction of Kit's room, ass swaying as she went.

My eyes slid to Cara. "You seem to get on well with her."

"She's a fucking riot," Cara said with an evil grin. "Love Layla and Sophie, but that chick's turned the clubhouse into a fun place to be. You weren't here, but not long ago, she put bitch Cherry in her place. Dunno if you heard, but Cherry started getting mouthy with Soph, so Kennedy challenged her to a strip off. I joined in, which was hilarious, seeing as I was days away from having Wilder. You can imagine the looks on everyone's faces when I climbed up onto the bar, heavily pregnant, and busted some moves. Cash loved it, even though he had to stand in front of me at the bar, ready to catch me if I tripped."

I busted out a laugh. "I heard Cherry got kicked out. Is that why?"

"Yeah," Cara replied. "She got too big for her skanky boots. After the whole April thing, John's coming down hard on the club girls."

"It's been a long time coming. The guys have definitely gotten complacent. They should've taken them all to task after what April did to you years ago."

Cara smiled. "Thank you. I'm glad I've got your and the other ladies' support. I felt a lot of resentment toward your dad and the other guys. I talked to him about it, and he apologized. We're on track now, and Wilder's helped bring us all close again."

I reached out and squeezed her arm. "I missed you. When you and Cash split, I lost a sister. I'm glad you're back and better than ever."

Cara took my hand and pulled me in for a hug. "Me too. Freya. I'm sorry I upped and left you. I was so fucking heartbroken and depressed, but I should've realized you were caught in the middle too. If it's any consolation, I missed you all terribly. I remember lying in bed the Christmas after it happened, crying because I knew you'd all be having fun here without me."

I pulled back slightly and looked into her eyes, noting how they glistened. "That's just it, Cara. Nothing was the same without you."

She beamed. "Good. If I had a shit time, you should've had one too."

I rolled my eyes. "Same old Cara."

"You better believe it," she grinned. "Some things never change."

"You three together are trouble," the prospect muttered as he reversed into a parking space a hundred yards away from the salon. "Your men must be fuckin' sadists."

"Aww, Billy," Cara said in a baby voice. "You nervous of us itty bitty girls?"

"Scared fuckin' shitless more like," he muttered, switching off the engine. "I'll wait here for ya. Take your time. I'm gettin' out of cleaning duty bein' here." He settled back in the driver's seat and pulled out his phone.

We opened the car doors and stepped onto the street, shouting our goodbyes to Billy as we slammed them closed and headed toward the salon.

A high-pitched and loud *"ladieeeees"* filled the crisp fall air.

I looked to see Tristan standing at the doors of the salon, clasping his hands together. "Oh, my laaawdy!" he drawled excitedly. "It's like watching a Vogue fashion spread materialize before my very eyes."

"Hey Tristan," Kennedy called out.

"Afternoon, Farrah," he called back. "Hair's lookin' *stunning*. I gotta new keratin treatment in if you want Uncle Trissy to give you the goods. Your mane's amazin', but I can get those locks feelin' as smooth as a baby's ass."

"Farrah?" I whispered to Cara in a confused tone.

"Fawcett," she murmured back. "As you can tell, he's a little bit in love with Kennedy."

"I thought he had a crush on Hendrix and Atlas?" I questioned.

Cara grinned. "He fell out of love with Hendrix when he started being a dick to Anna. Atlas, he still loves, except he says he can't get his head around getting fucked by him in his fantasies anymore."

"Huh?" I asked, even more confused.

Cara's lips twitched. "Tris accidentally on purpose, fell in Atlas's lap, felt how big his dick was, and ran scared. He said Dan's hung like a donkey, and he's not into beasties."

"Oh my God," I breathed, eyes wide.

Cara laughed as we approached the salon doors. "Sophie's confirmed the fact."

Tristan held the door open for us, kissing our cheeks as we filed inside. "Are you back for good, biker princess?" he asked as I walked past.

"Just for now. I'm looking for an internship starting next summer." I looked around the salon, cursing under my breath, when I saw two blonde women at the reception desk with Anna handing over their credit cards.

Seeing Serena Stafford was bad enough, but running into the woman with her was my worst nightmare, seeing as the last time I heard her voice was when Colt dumped her over the phone just before he ate me out for the first time.

Awkward.

Anna handed Lucy's card back with a smile before the girls turned toward us and halted.

"Hi," Lucy said begrudgingly to Cara, eyes sweeping down me and stopping on my boots. "I'm surprised you can afford those boots, being a student and all." She pouted.

"What I can and can't afford isn't really your business," I responded with a toss of my hair.

"Daddy probably bought them for you." She sniffed.

I grinned knowingly. "You'd be shocked if you knew who really bought them, Lucy."

Cara covered her smile with her hand as Kennedy barked a laugh.

Lucy's eyes narrowed.

She knew what I was getting at. Honestly, at that point, even if Colt hadn't gifted them to me, I would've hinted he did. Anything to wipe the smug look off her face.

Lucy Bloom was lovely to everyone around her, even me, when we were in company. But as soon as we were alone, she turned bitchy. It told me that she wasn't only a nasty person, but she was sneaky too. Mean girls usually had a dangerous streak, but then so did biker princesses.

Lucy stormed past me, bumping my shoulder with hers. "Hey!" I turned, ready to cuss her out, but she was already out the door, Serena hot on her heels.

"I think you got flower girl mad," Tristan murmured, craning his neck to watch the girls walk down the street.

"She deserved it." Cara turned to me. "I've never seen her act that way before."

My lips pursed. "That's because she's sly and usually only does it when nobody else is around. I guess now Colt's dumped her, she doesn't have to put her Miss Congeniality act on anymore."

"Colt dumped her?" Anna asked me from behind the reception desk.

"About a week ago," I confirmed.

"I bet she didn't take that well," Anna mused. "On her last appointment, she was in here boasting about how much he loved her and wanted to take things to the next level."

A laugh escaped me. "Didn't sound that way to me when he called her and told her he was done."

Tristan's jaw dropped. "You were there?"

I swallowed to ease the dryness in my throat.

What the fuck was I thinking? As much as I'd have loved to tell Tristan and Anna about me and Colt, they were good friends with Layla. I didn't want to put them in a position where they had to lie to her for me or even keep secrets.

Also, more and more people were becoming aware of mine and Colt's so-called secret relationship. If we weren't careful, it would get back to Dad. We had to be more cautious.

"Don't be silly." Kennedy gave a dismissive wave of her hand. "He told us about it when he got home." She nudged Cara. "Didn't he?"

"Yeah!" Cara confirmed brightly. "Freya was there too."

My shoulders slumped with relief. Making sure nobody was looking, I mouthed, *thank you*.

Kennedy sent me a conspiratorial wink.

"It was only a matter of time," Anna said, walking from behind the reception desk. "I could tell his heart wasn't in it."

I took a sharp intake of breath.

Anna had lost at least fifteen pounds in weight. It was a lot, seeing as she was already slim before, and didn't need to lose a pound. I looked at her face and hair as if seeing her for the first time. Anna had long, curly red hair that usually shone with health, but now hung lank and dull. Her smooth, creamy complexion was now pale and drawn.

"Are you okay?" I asked, tone shocked. "Has something happened? You've lost so much weight."

Tears sprang to her eyes.

"Honey," I breathed, taking her hand. "What's going on?"

"She's heartbroken," Tristan said flatly.

Anna forced a smile on her face. "Oh, it's not that bad. I'm fine."

Tears heated the back of my throat.

My friend was in obvious pain. Who the hell had hurt her so badly that she couldn't eat? I wracked my brains, trying to think of who she'd been seeing, and almost groaned out loud.

"Was it Hendrix?" I asked, tone shocked.

Anna blinked her tears away and smiled blankly at me. "Yeah, but I'm okay."

"What happened between you two?" Kennedy asked gently. "Last time I was here, you and Hendrix were out in the back room smooching. Now you look like your heart's been ripped out." She took Anna's hand and led her over to the salon chairs, looking back and gesturing for us to follow.

Anna took a seat on a small sofa under the window with Kennedy and Cara while me and Tristan pulled a couple of chairs over.

"We started seeing each other casually just before Layla and Bowie's wedding," Anna told us, wringing her hands nervously. "It was going fine, and I thought we were getting closer, then I saw him out on a date with another woman."

Cara shook her head. "Ugh. Fucking men."

Anna let out a quiet snort. "We'd never said we were exclusive, but it hurt, so I told him unless he dropped the others, I'd end it." She sighed. "I'm too old to navigate the dating scene. I want a man who wants me and only me."

"Fair enough," Kennedy agreed. "What did he say?"

"Drix asked me for some time, which I agreed to, but then things started to change. He became distant, almost aloof. We stopped going out, and after a while, I realized I'd turned into a booty call."

"I told her he was stringing her along," Tristan interjected. "One night, I went over to Mapletree to meet a friend, and there he was in the bar, almost dry-humping some skank. The asshole saw me and walked out. Ten minutes later, I went out to my car, and there he was, getting head in the goddamned parking lot up against one of the club's SUVs."

"He cheated?" Cara asked angrily.

"That's just it," Anna murmured. "He didn't. We never had the conversation. After that, I walked away, but Hendrix started pursuing me again. He told me things would change, so I gave him another chance. Then, his dad fell ill, and he started visiting Virginia. I called him one night, and a woman answered his phone and said he was in the shower."

My heart hurt for her. "Oh, Anna. I'm so sorry."

"I tried to understand what was happening, but he ghosted me," Anna recounted. "Blocked me on his phone, even started avoiding me in town. Then I heard he'd left."

"Didn't he tell you?" Kennedy demanded.

"Oh my God. What an asshole," Cara snapped.

Anna shrugged. "He is an asshole and a rotten pig, but I fell hard for him. Now I'm trying to pick up the pieces. I know I'm gonna be okay, but it's gonna take some time to get there."

Tristan nodded in agreement. "He's like a pixie haircut, Anna. At first, it seems like a good idea, but then you realize it's just... not."

Anna laughed through her tears. Kennedy reached across the table to hold Anna's hand. "I'm glad he's gone. We don't have to stand by and watch you settle for someone who treats you like second best when you should be his priority."

Tristan nodded. "You're the best boss bitch ever. If he can't see your fabulousness, he doesn't deserve it." He looked at each of us in turn. "Now. I've had a genius idea. We've got no more appointments today. Why don't I crack open the prosecco we've been saving for a rainy day and get fuckin' shit-faced." He rose from his chair and walked toward the kitchen out back.

Kennedy grinned. "I've heard worse ideas."

The other women started talking about Hendrix again, and I couldn't help drawing similarities between mine and Anna's situation.

Secret relationships were not only tricky to navigate but also heart-wrenching at times. It had been days since I'd touched Colt, apart from earlier when he'd gone to my room. I'd feel him looking at me across the bar and know I couldn't even go over and talk to him in case somebody noticed we were too close.

At least we had tonight. Colt wouldn't send me to the gallery by myself unless he thought he could make it. My mind went to the other bags he'd given me, full of lingerie, and I smiled. I couldn't wait to touch him. We'd only been back days, but it felt like years since we were together.

I'd make tonight so memorable that Colt would never want to leave.

Chapter Twenty

Dagger

I'd been holed up in my office, staring at my goddamned cell phone for thirty minutes straight.

It was always hard when I knew I had to talk to her. The last time I called—when Layla was snatched—time was of the essence, so I didn't have time to procrastinate over a mere fuckin' telephone conversation. I'd messaged her in case *he* was there—her sick fuck of a husband—and waitin' was torture. Rippin' off the band-aid was somethin' I'd been doin' since I'd put an end to my marriage. That was the day I stopped trying to paper over the cracks 'cause it never worked, and honestly, I'd never truly felt whole again after her.

The peal of my ringtone ripped through the room, and I jumped like I'd seen the ghost of Bandit streaking naked across my office. With a curse, I scooped up my cell and looked at the screen, which showed one letter, 'Z.' I clicked the green button and said one word. "Leesy."

"Our place, one hour," she breathed, her sweet voice wrapping around my lungs and squeezing. She'd always robbed me of breath, though I'd gotten used to it a long time ago.

"'Kay," I rumbled from my chest, tone thick with emotion before barking, "Leesy!"

The sigh she expelled was sad and full of pain. "What?"

"Be careful," I told her. "If it's too risky, don't come."

"It's okay," she assured me quietly. "He's going to a meeting soon, but thanks for caring." A brief silence fell over the line before another sigh escaped her, and the line went dead.

My eyes went to the cell phone screen, and I stared sightlessly at it as my mind conjured up images of my beautiful girl in my arms, back before everything got so damned complicated. Back when it was me and her and nothing penetrated our little world unless we wanted to let it in.

The ache inside that had crippled me for years was everyday life now. I'd lived with it for so long it was part of me.

I hadn't been able to shrug Elise Bell off since the moment I met her; she was as much part of me as my kids were, and as much as the notion made the ache living inside me intensify, I knew she would always be inside me, making me yearn for what could've been.

The creek had changed.

It wasn't our place anymore. Maybe my subconscious loved the fact that whenever I came down here now, all I saw were the new houses under construction and a building site, instead of her.

But sitting astride my bike, looking down at the rush of clear water, I was still taken back to lazy summer days when we didn't have a care in the world.

This place was where I noticed she'd turned into a woman, where that first flush of young love pumped through my veins and made me feel like I could take on the world.

Me and the other club brats used to hang here, bein' little shits. Leesy and her friends used to sunbathe on the banks, dangling their legs in the water when the sun got too hot.

All our firsts still lingered in the air, swirling and rustling around me like the orange fall leaves floating in the cool breeze, carrying the promise of winter in the air.

I heard the hum of her electric car and watched her park and turn off the power. The driver's door flew open, her feet hit the ground, and she walked toward me.

My heart raced like it always did when I caught sight of her, and for the hundredth time, I wished it wasn't like that with us.

My eyes roamed hungrily over her, taking my fix of her thick mane of blonde hair, the feel of it etched in my memory as I ran my fingers through its silky, long lengths. I could almost pick up her scent, which I knew would be clean and fresh, like strawberry wine, mixed with summer fruits.

Our gazes locked and held, and a ghost of a smile played around her full, butter-glossed lips that I already knew would taste of cherry Chapstick. Elise was a little thicker than before, the confidence that came with age making her even more beautiful than when she was mine.

I often felt cheated that I'd missed the best part. Watching her grow as a person would've been extraordinary, but it wasn't in God's plan for us.

It wasn't meant to be.

"Hey, John," she said, approaching until she stopped about a foot away. "You look well."

"You too, Elise." I grinned reassuringly. "Were you careful?"

She nodded. "He went to a meeting, it's all good." She looked around at all the construction going on. "This place has changed."

"Yeah," I agreed.

Leesy's gaze rested on me again. "You always said you wanted to build a community for the brothers and their families. You did it, John."

I nodded, suddenly unable to speak 'cause originally, the dream was that she'd be by my side when it happened. Funny how life turned out.

"What did you want to meet for?" she asked softly.

I held her eyes briefly, wondering if I should go in gently or just say it like it was. But I didn't have to think too hard. I wasn't a beat-around-the-bush kinda man.

"Your ol' man's up to some gnarly shit," I grated out. "Gonna put a stop to it, and I need to get cameras in your house."

I saw the flash of temper ignite behind her eyes, and momentarily, it shocked me.

When she was mine, Elise had fire, but whenever I'd seen her since, she was as docile as a lamb. It was like the fire had been extinguished, leaving a dark, empty shell.

"Don't you ever say that again," she snarled. "I get what I did and what you thought happened, John, but through it all, I only ever had one *ol' man,* and it wasn't *him.*"

My jaw clenched with the pain shooting through my heart because, shamefully, I couldn't say the same. I'd replaced her like I thought at the time she'd replaced me.

"What do you need cameras in my house for?" she asked, tilting her chin up.

I covered my grin with my hand because I'd always loved her the most when she gave me attitude. "We think your *husband's* involved in somethin' very fuckin' dark, Leesy."

Something else flashed behind her eyes, which looked a lot like panic. "What do you know?"

I cocked my head, takin' in the flush of her cheeks and the shutters falling over her eyes so as to not give anythin' away.

Interesting.

"You know all about it, doncha?" I muttered.

She cocked an eyebrow. "You think I can be surrounded by monsters for this long and not see them for what they are?" She let out a humorless laugh. "You always did underestimate me."

"Nah, Leesy," I responded. "I didn't. You're the one who underestimated me. You thought I wouldn't come home to you when you should'a realized I'd always find my way back."

Tears welled in her eyes. "One day, I'll be able to tell you."

"Tell me what?" I demanded.

She stared at me in silence.

I scrubbed a frustrated hand over my face. "Look, we're goin' around in circles. I didn't ask you here to talk about the past. I need your help. There's bad stuff happenin' in town, and all roads are leading back to your husband and his lackey."

She stared at me for what seemed like an eon, thoughts whirring behind her eyes. There was more going on than she was admitting. Weirdly though, I still trusted her.

"I'll work something out and message you," she said finally. "It may be short notice. I don't always know his schedule until the last minute, and there are usually people around. If I get you in, you'll have to pretend to be workmen or something."

"Anythin'," I agreed, a thread of relief lacing my tone. "My brother will be ready to mobilize whenever you can swing it."

"Good," she nodded thoughtfully, her gaze raking over me. "You look well, John. How are your kids? I saw Kit with his twins in the coffee house last week. They're beautiful."

I smiled indulgently, the same way I did whenever anybody mentioned any of my grandchildren. "They are. And a chip off the old block too."

She beamed. "I'm happy for you. It was what you always wanted."

Yeah, Leesy, my inner voice whispered, *but I wanted it with you.*

We stood there for a while, drinking each other in, trying to get enough of each other to commit to memory until the next time. God only knew when it would be; the times we saw each other like this were few and far between. But then, I guess it had to be that way 'cause we weren't us anymore.

The look of longing on her features gradually faded until she smiled. "I'll be in touch."

I jerked a nod, watching her turn and head for her car.

"Leesy," I called out.

Her steps faltered, and she craned her neck. "What?"

"Keep your eyes open at all times," I pleaded. "If he's involved in what I think he is, you could be in more danger than you know. Watch your back, and if anything happens, get your ass to the clubhouse, stat. He won't be able to get to you there."

Her eyebrows drew together. "That means a lot, John. Thank you." Then, with a smile, she turned and walked back to her car, slid in, and drove away without a backward glance, taking my soul with her...

Yet again.

Elise

All I ever seemed to do was walk away from John Stone, which was crazy considering he was the one person existing who I yearned to hold on tight to and never let go.

My heart beat solely for him. It always had and would until my last breath.

Our years together were my happiest by far. Every time things got too rough, I'd lie down in my darkened bedroom and regress back to the time when I was his, and he was mine, and not a soul could come between us.

Until they did.

Every step I took in the opposite direction from him felt like I was being torn in two, but what choice did I have? My decisions were taken from me a long time ago, along with everything else that meant anything to me.

I drove for ten minutes, keeping my shit together, then, when it was safe, I pulled the car over, leaned back in my seat, and wept. Seeing him always got me like this. Even catching glimpses of him in the street broke my heart, so a full-blown conversation was torture.

My chest felt heavy like a ton of weight had been dropped on it.

John knew too much, but it didn't shock me. His club's involvement was becoming a problem. My Stone always was too curious for his own good. He had an avenging angel complex, and that wouldn't do at all, not in my line of work.

Leaning down, I pulled my purse from the footwell and rummaged inside for my cell. I scrolled to my most recent call and clicked before holding the phone to my ear.

"Where are you, Elise? There's an issue with the latest shipment. The boss is trying to contact you."

I let out an audible sigh. "Can't I take an hour? Jesus. The incompetence is astounding." I paused briefly. "We have a problem. John Stone is sniffing around. He wants me to let his men into the house so they can install cameras." I rolled my eyes at the string of curses floating down the line. "There's no point cussing God out. It's not his fault."

He waited a beat before muttering, "We'll have to give them access, or Stone will be suspicious. At least we can control what information goes out."

"That's what I thought," I agreed. "Is Robert still out tonight?"

"Yeah. He has a meeting, then he's arranged to see one of his women. He won't return until tomorrow."

I rolled my eyes. "Poor girl. Hope he's compensating her well." I shrugged. "So, tonight's the night?"

"Tonight's the night. Make the call."

My lips pursed. "Okay Brett. I'll make the call."

Chapter Twenty-One

Colt

"I'm tellin' ya," Atlas boomed. "Kyle's turned to the dark side. Mauricio's fucked."

"It's for TV," Cash interjected. "Andy probably asked her to play it up for ratings. Kyle and her man are fine. It's all for show."

Atlas shrugged. "Don't care if she's turned gay. I'd still let her sip from my Coke can." He lifted his hip from the couch in a circling motion.

Bowie barked a laugh. "If Kyle's really into women now, that's doubtful."

The SAA dropped his ass and puffed his chest out. "I'll put her on my 'shouldn't but would' list. That way, she'd have no choice. Every fucker knows those lists are sacred."

"What about Vanderpump?" Breaker inquired. "Thought she was on your list?"

"I got eight bitches on there," Atlas explained. "Kyle will be number nine." He brought a hand up to tap his lip thoughtfully. "I'll put the country singer girlfriend on there too. Want Kyle to be comfortable with the whole scene." He jerked a decisive nod. "There you go. There's my ten. My list is officially filled."

"Go ahead and put Kyle on your list, honey," a voice floated over from the bar. "I'll put Mauricio on mine. He's handsome as hell and as rich as the devil with his successful real estate business."

Atlas froze.

A roar of laughter went up.

I grinned, scrolling through my phone.

"Who's on your list, Soph?" Cash called over.

Sophie turned on the bar stool, her pregnant belly protruding. "Well, Mauricio now," she began before beginning to reel names off. "Gerard Butler, Idris Elba, Jensen Ackles, Shemar Moore, Jamie Frazer, John Wick, Clooney—"

"Nice choice," Layla added. "Clooney's a classic. He'll never go out of style."

Bowie narrowed his eyes at his wife.

Sophie nodded her agreement before continuing. "Jimmy Garoppolo, Jacob, the werewolf from Twilight, and in my number one spot, Massimo Torricelli."

Layla smirked and fanned her face.

"Doe!" Bowie barked, obviously pissed.

Atlas's head reared back. "Who the fuck's Massimo Torti—fuckin'—whatever? I'll kick his ass."

I barked a laugh, eyes still on my cell. "It's the dude from the 365 Days movie. His real name's Michele Morrone."

"Stop!" Sophie held a hand up. "I don't want to fuck Michele Morrone. I wanna fuck the character, the Mafia Don." Her eyes turned dreamy. "He's hotter than a solar flare."

Atlas's face turned purple. I was sure I could see steam coming from his ears.

The door to the bar flew open, and in walked Cara and Kennedy with my princess, bringing up the rear.

Fingers twitching, my stare roamed hungrily down her tight little body, landing on the sexy as fuck knee-high boots with red soles that I'd bought her. I decided there and then that one day soon, I'd fuck in her those boots and only those boots.

My cock kicked in my jeans.

Fuck yeah.

"Yo, Wildcat," Cash called out, eyes softening as his woman walked toward him. "Whose number one on your 'shouldn't but would' list?"

"Massimo Torricelli," she announced, sinking down onto his lap and sliding her arms around his neck. "No contest."

"What about you, Kitten?" Breaker asked thoughtfully.

"Same," she told him, taking the seat next to Sophie. "I had a dream once that he came into my office because he'd killed a rival Mafia Don and needed legal counsel. Let's just say he fucks like a God. My desk needed a good disinfecting by the time he left."

"Jesus," Atlas muttered, lip curling at Breaker. "Can't you keep your woman under control?"

"He can try." Kennedy retorted.

"What 'bout you, Frey?" Cash asked.

My eyes slid to my girl, who opened her mouth to reply but was cut off by Bowie. "No! That's my sister. She's a virgin until she marries."

Cash busted a gut as everyone else's stares slid straight to me.

My gut jerked when Atlas looked around before his eyes narrowed on my face.

I went back to my cell phone, mentally cursing every fucker around me who was intent on giving the game away.

"Who's on your list, Bowie?" Sophie asked.

He smirked. "Doe, Doe, and Doe."

Layla beamed.

"What about you, Colt?" she inquired curiously.

"I know." Freya laughed.

I smiled because she did. I'd made her watch all my favorite sci-fi movies growing up. Freya knew me better than I knew myself.

"Okay," she began. "Natalie Portman as Princess Amidala, she's number one, seeing as he named his bike after her. Then, Princess Leia in the gold bikini, Kelly Le Brock in Weird Science, Sarah Connor, Carrie-Anne Moss from the Matrix, Jane Fonda from Barbarella, Zoe Saldana from Guardians of the Galaxy and the Star Trek reboots, Tricia Helfer who played Number Six in Battlestar Galactica, Captain Janeway, and last but not least, every schoolboy's dream... Seven of Nine."

I tipped my cell phone toward my girl with a smirk. "What she said."

"Fuckin' weirdo," Cash muttered. "Who the hell has Captain Janeway in the same 'shouldn't but would' list as Seven of Nine?"

"It's the authority factor," I told him. "And Janeway's hot in a Karen kinda way."

Cash shrugged. "Fair enough."

"What about Freya, Colt?" Cara called over. "Do you know her as well as she knows you?"

Bowie looked to the ceiling and shook his head.

Atlas dipped his chin and stared at me.

My heart stabbed inside my chest.

I was caught in a classic case of 'fucked if I did and fucked if I didn't.' Everybody knew we were friends. Of course I fucking knew who her crushes were.

It would've looked more suspicious if I'd shied away from the question than if I hadn't, so I put my cell to one side, leaned forward, elbows to knees, and stared at Freya. "There isn't ten; our Princess is picky as fuck, but let's start with Clooney, but only since he married Amal and founded the Clooney Foundation for Justice. Doctor McDreamy from Grey's Anatomy. She cried for days after they killed him off." I grinned. "Daryl Dixon from The Walkin' Dead, she likes that he fights for the community. Han Solo, because he was all man, and last..." My eyes narrowed on my girl as she blushed prettily. Her eyes slid to Sophie, and I barked a laugh. "Massimo—fuckin'—Torricelli."

Freya shrugged. "He knows me well."

Breaker let out a hoot.

Cash chuckled.

Cara high-fived Kennedy.

Sophie giggled.

Atlas almost burned a laser beam hole into my forehead with his beady black eyes.

Sitting back, I turned my head toward the corridor as a voice yelled, "Officers! Church! Now!"

"Jesus, Abe," Breaker rumbled. "We gotta get the kids from school soon. We just had Church this mornin'. Is Pop on steroids?"

"The women will have to get the kids today. Iris has got Wilder and Willow in the kitchen with her. You're sorted." His stare rested on me, and his eyes hardened. "You too, Colt."

My gut sank, my first thought going to Freya.

Grumbles went up as we all rose from our seats and made our way toward Abe, who stood in the hallway with his arms folded across his chest. "There's been developments," he murmured. "Your prez has got shit to relay." He turned on his heel and marched down the corridor toward Church.

We all followed. Cash fell into step beside me and murmured, "Thought Dad had rumbled you there for a minute."

"Rumbled him for what?" Atlas barked from behind us.

I glanced back toward the SAA and shrugged. "You know me, always gettin' into places I shouldn't."

His lips drew into a thin line.

The SAA suspected something. People assumed he was as stupid as he looked, but he was Sergeant at Arms for a reason. I needed to have a word with the boys and tell them to dial it down a notch.

I'd have come clean if I could, but there was work to do before I could leave. Plus, Freya wasn't ready. My girl was still waiting to hear about the internships she'd applied for and as yet, had no clue where she'd end up.

For all my bravado, actually not being able to touch Freya since we'd returned from Denver had given me a new understanding of what life would be like without her in it. Had I caught up entirely? No, but I was learning fast.

Abe lifted his hand to the scanner and pressed his thumb to the pad. A loud buzzing sound filled the air before he pushed the door to Church open. We followed him inside, sat down, and faced our Prez.

Dagger sat forward in his chair and rubbed his beard. His eyes were glazed, deep in thought. "We're sendin' Colt up to the mayor's mansion to plant surveillance equipment."

Silence fell over the room before Cash sat back and folded his arms across his chest. "About fuckin' time. Been tellin' you for months, there's somethin' not right about Henderson. I wondered how long it would take for you to dig deeper."

Atlas grinned. "I'll go with techno boy."

Prez's head reared back. "No, you fuckin' won't."

Atlas looked taken aback for a second before his face hardened. "I'm SAA. I need to make sure Colt's backed up. I assume he's sneaking in?"

The dim light in the office flickered behind Prez, who sat at the head of the table, his face a stoic mask as he regarded Atlas. "Listen up and listen good," he began, his voice low and gravelly. "This shit's delicate. You walk around town like the big man. Everyone knows you at a glance, brother. Your size alone raises eyebrows. We need to do this incognito."

Mutters and grunts echoed through the room, but I remained silent, my mind already racing with the thought of what we were about to do.

"Colt," Dagger continued, his gaze landing on me. "At four-thirty, you're gonna rock up to the mayor's house under the pretense of carrying out some upgrades to their internet. Elise Henderson will let you in, take you to where you need to be, and make sure nobody questions ya."

For a second, the weight of the task settled heavily on my shoulders. I couldn't let Prez down. I had a lot of shit to make up for. "Understood."

Prez's eyes slid along the table and rested on his youngest son. "Breaker, you're goin' too. You've got the most experience gettin' in and out of places silently and fast. You'll both be in overalls and baseball caps pulled low. Get in, do the job, then you get the fuck outta dodge. Any trouble, both of ya, shoot before you're shot. Just get outta there in one piece. I hope it doesn't come to that, but if it does, you're the right man for the job."

Darkness swirled in Kit's eyes at the mere thought of morphing into soldier mode. "Copy."

Dagger turned to Atlas. "You can take 'em if you want but wait in the van. I want you to wear a baseball cap pulled over your eyes and listen out. You hear or see anythin' untoward you get in there and shoot every fucker you can see."

"We should take one more person," Atlas muttered, looking around the table. "Two inside, two outside."

"Bowie," Prez ordered. "He outdrives everyone else. He'll be good in case you wanna get away fast."

Bowie jerked a nod.

Prez turned to Cash. "You're the most technical one after Colt. Hole up in his office. We can watch what's goin' on in real-time. I don't fuckin' know how to work all the computer stuff. It goes over my head." He checked his watch. "You've got an hour and thirty. You gonna be ready?"

"I'm ready now," I confirmed. "We just need to sort the overalls and load the van."

Prez grinned. "Knew you wouldn't let me down."

My throat thickened, and I felt my face pale because I had let him down in the worst way. I was fucking his daughter, and even though she deserved better than a hidden life, I couldn't let her go. It was a melancholic thought, the realization that our love couldn't exist in the open, but still, right then, I clung to it like a lifeline.

"You take the lead, Colt. Breaker, you take his back," Prez ordered. "Elise will take you to the mayor's study and his bedroom. I want cameras and audio set up in both."

My eyes rounded. "I won't set up a camera in a woman's bedroom, Prez."

"She said it's not her room," he murmured. "They sleep separately."

"I've heard rumors around town he fucks around," Bowie said with a lip curl. "Apparently, he's always gotta mistress on the go somewhere. He fucks 'em off after a while and moves on to the next."

Dagger's gaze dropped.

"Don't blame her for not fuckin' him then," Breaker interjected. "No woman wants to suck a dick that's just nutted in other women."

Prez's fingers twitched, and he closed his eyes as if blocking out the words. After a minute, he pulled in a deep breath and looked up again. "We need someone on the cameras twenty-four-seven. Trafficking women isn't exactly a nine-to-five."

I shifted in my seat.

Leaving the club had thrown up the issue of who would do my job when I'd jetted.

Two men came to mind. The first was Arrow. He was very technologically minded. As an ex-marine, he dealt with their tech gear and radios and headcams when out on missions. I knew that shit wasn't easy. Often, the conditions he had to work under would be difficult.

The other was our new prospect, Billy the Kid. That little fucker could do all kinds of shit, like coding. He was a typical Gen Z, glued to his cell phone and useless without technology. Though I guess the same could've been said about me, and I was a Millennial. The problem was that until he got patched in, he couldn't get access to any club business or its secrets.

"I reckon we could give Arrow a shot," I suggested. "Billy's pretty technical too, so when he patches in, we can get him to help out. I need backup, so can we look at giving them somethin' more permanent depending on who works out better?"

"Done," Prez agreed. "I'll talk to them both. Billy's workin' out well, so I don't think it'll be too long before he gets his patch." He looked around the table. "Has anyone got shit to add?"

Silence.

"We're done," he announced with a bang of the gavel.

As the meeting adjourned, I couldn't help the sense of dread filling my chest, not for the mission but for what came after.

My eyes slid left to study Breaker, who wore the same grey overalls and baseball cap as I did. We both carried holdalls filled with sensors, microscopic cameras, and bugs.

"You ready?" he asked.

"As I'll ever be." I raised my hand and rapped three times on the massive oak double doors that led into the mayor's mansion.

Craning my neck, I turned toward the black van where Bowie sat in the driver's seat wearing an identical cap to me and Break. The letters on the side of the vehicle had been stuck on by Bo, who, thank fuck, was an awesome designer and could copy the logo of the telecommunications company like a boss.

The door opened to reveal a beautiful blonde woman wearing yoga pants and an oversized sweater that had slipped off one shoulder. Her face was make-up-free, and her thick blonde hair hung loose.

"Come in," Elise Henderson said with a gentle smile. "The mayor's out and won't be back for a while, and his assistant isn't due back for another hour."

"Assistant?" Breaker inquired.

Elise smiled wanly. "Brett Stafford."

Me and my brother exchanged glances before stepping over the threshold and following Elise into the vast hallway, which boasted a massive staircase running up one side of the wall to a balcony on the floor above. To most people, it would've been impressive, but I was a man who'd been raised in the lap of luxury, so I wasn't intimidated.

"Can I get you anything?" she asked, smile still in place as she gestured for us to follow her through the vast hallway into a room, which, going by the computer equipment and filing cabinets, was obviously an office.

"No thanks," I replied, hauling my massive bag onto the antique desk near the window.

"We need to get on, Ma'am, but thank you," Breaker said politely.

Elise took the hint and gave us a nod. "I'll leave you to it then, gentlemen." As she turned, her gaze landed on Breaker. "You look so much like John. So handsome."

He studied her briefly. "Thank you, Ma'am."

Her eyes filled up. "Your mother instilled beautiful manners in you." She laughed. "Your father wasn't so polite when he was young, but still a good man in every way. The one most like him though, is Gage. Your father and he were identical. Sometimes I see Gage in the street and do a double take, and then I remember..." Her voice trailed off, brow creasing. "Anyway, I'll stop bothering you." She gave us both a polite nod and swept out of the room.

Breaker's eyes slid to me, bugging out. "I just officially met the woman my ma and pa ended their marriage over. My world's weird enough without shootin' the shit with the love of my pop's life." He shuddered.

I went into my bag, pulled out the equipment, and laid it out on the desk. "Elise Henderson's club folklore."

Breaker's lips set into a line. "Yeah, and my ma never lived up to her."

The steely thread in Breaker's tone made me turn. "She did. Adele's well thought of. Your ma was the perfect ol' lady. The men would've died for her."

"Maybe the men would've." Breaker shrugged. "But not my dad." He nodded toward the door where Elise had just exited. "She's Pop's. Always was."

I went back to the devices on the desk and started to do my last-minute tests. "It was over years ago. They both moved on. I get your dad probably wonders what could've been, but I'm sure he's happy with his lot."

Breaker let out a snort. "You don't get it, Colt. My Gramma Constance told me once that Stone men fall hard, fast, and forever. Later, Bandit told me the same, then my dad. It happened to me, Cash and Bowie. I know Bo loved Samantha, but he was young at the time and thought with his dick. Now he's found Layla, he knows she's his one." His stare rested on me. "I don't think it's just Stone men it relates to either, also reckon it applies to Stone women."

My chest tightened. I busied myself with the electronics, switching them on and checking the signals. "What are you gettin' at?"

He stuck his head out the door, checking around before walking toward me. "It started with Bandit and my gramma. He set his sights on Connie Forrester when she was fourteen. He was eighteen, and he knew she was his the second he saw her. In those days, it was normal for women to wed at fifteen and sixteen." Breaker grinned. "He sat me down when I was nine and told me he waited two years before going to her dad to ask for his blessing. Poor fucker got turned away."

"What did he do?" I asked curiously.

Breaker barked a laugh. "On the day she turned sixteen, he kidnapped her, whisked her away on his bike up to Cheyenne, and went straight to the courthouse." His eyes took on a faraway look. "I think she was the only person who Bandit ever truly loved. I remember him tellin' me how the second he laid eyes on her, she took his breath away and never gave it back. He told me Gramma was fuckin' beautiful. Long, dark hair, big brown eyes, and dusky golden skin. I remember her so clearly, even though I was a kid when she died. She looked like a fifties pin-up girl until the day she passed." Breaker's stare met mine again. "Gramps reckoned men used to go crazy for her. They'd go out, and he'd always end up in a fight 'cause some chancer tried his hand with her." He smirked. "Did you ever see a picture of her?"

I shook my head.

Breaker went into his inside pocket and pulled his wallet out. "She was in her mid-twenties here, probably around the same age as my sister is now. Look."

I took the tiny black and white photograph he held out and stilled.

"Uncanny, ain't it," Breaker murmured. "Her and Freya could be identical twins."

I handed the image back, throat suddenly dry. My brother obviously had some words for me, but to my chagrin, he was beating around the bush. "You got somethin' to say, Break?"

"Yeah," he muttered. "I disagree with Dad's rule. You're one of the best men I know, Colt. Freya loves you. I went a long time without Kennedy and my kids. I wouldn't wish that shit on my worst enemy."

My gut twisted at the steely thread in his tone. "But?"

He folded his arms across his chest. "But, Colt. You're not doin' the right thing by her. Freya's puttin' on a brave face, but it's obvious all this secrecy is eatin' away at her."

I ran a hand through my hair. "What am I meant to do?"

Kit skewered me with a look. "You shit or get off the pot."

My heart crumbled in my chest. "I'm not ready yet. I gotta get the club into a strong position before I jet."

He shook his head, pursing his lips. "My sister needs a man who'll put her first. You're too fucked-up to see past your insecurities to be what she deserves. Until you can acknowledge she's your endgame, stay away from her. Don't need some weak piece'a shit sniffing around my sister."

My hands balled into fists. "Watch it, Breaker."

"What ya gonna do? Punch me?" He barked a laugh. "Takes a man to do that shit, and you're distinctly lacking a pair of balls right now. We both know you won't start zilch, seein' as you have to explain to Dad why, and don't think I'll lie for your dumb ass." He shook his head. "I want Freya's man to fight tooth and nail for her. Someone who'll risk everything. Thought it would be you, Colt. It's a shame I was wrong. I would've liked you for her."

"It's gonna happen, Break," I assured him. "She's mine."

"She's not yours until you claim her, and you're nowhere near ready. If you're not careful, some lucky bastard will look at my sister and see the same beauty we do. He'll make her his wife and give her babies, and she'll love him for seeing everything she is and be so fuckin' loyal that she'll never look at another man, including you. That's when you'll look back and wish you'd taken a risk for her. Except you'll also see it was never really a risk. Loving Freya and being loved back would be a privilege."

The thought of her with somebody else made my blood boil. No fucker would ever love her like I did. "Shut your fuckin' mouth," I bit out.

My brother rolled his eyes, turned, and walked back to the door, shaking his head. "Stupid fucker." He stuck his head out just as the sound of the front door slamming ricocheted through the place. He pulled back into the room, slipped behind the door, and hissed, "Pull your cap down. It's Stafford. He knows me."

I did as I was told and shoved my equipment back inside before going over to the router and quickly unscrewing the back panel, fingers tremoring with the rush of adrenalin coursing through me.

The tapping of footsteps echoed from the hallway, getting louder as Stafford got closer, and I couldn't help but swallow down an anxious gulp.

Stafford didn't know me, but if he got too close, there was a chance he could still recognize me from town and from wearing the Speed Demons' patch.

However, Breaker knew him from when they were kids. Stafford only needed to get a glimpse of him, and he'd know we'd infiltrated.

My heart pounded inside my chest as the footsteps stopped outside the door to the study. I glanced at Breaker, my heart dropping when I caught a glimpse of metal glinting in the light.

The fucker had a knife, which was all very well, but I'd been told about Breaker's fixation with slitting throats and throwing blades at scrotums. If Stafford walked in here, he'd be dead within seconds, and the last thing I needed on top of everything else I had to do was to cover up a murder.

Heart-in-mouth, my eyes slid to the doorway that Stafford filled, and I pulled my cap down to cover my eyes.

His eyes were lowered, reading something on the cell phone in his hand. Slowly, his eyes lifted, resting directly on me, and he barked, "Who the fuck are you?"

I nodded toward the router in my hands. "I've been asked to speed up your internet connection."

His eyes narrowed, and he opened his mouth to say something just as a voice floated through the hallway. "Brett? Is that you, darling?"

He turned on his heel just as more footsteps tapped on the tiles, and Elise appeared. "Oh, you're early, fabulous. I was wondering if you'd take a look at some legal letters your father sent me. I'm a little confused by the jargon, and I know you're familiar with it, being a law graduate and all." She threaded her arm through Stafford's, turned him away, and led him across the hallway, chatting innately as they went.

My shoulders slumped with relief as their voices faded.

"Close call," Breaker rasped, stepping out of the shadows. His dark eyes blanked as they met mine.

"Best you get on with your shit. The sooner we get outta here, the better."

Within thirty minutes, we were on our way home.

Elise had even taken me upstairs on the pretense of using the washroom, allowing me to plant bugs in the master bedroom. I'd also managed to get into the kitchen and dining room without anyone knowing to place some cameras in those rooms too.

"We shit bricks when Stafford pulled up in his pussy car," Atlas rumbled from the back. "Almost charged in there after him."

"Had to remind Stallone here that Dad would take his fuckin' patch if he did his usual trick of goin' in all guns blazin'," Bowie said tightly.

"Not my idea of a good time," Atlas muttered. "But I reckon Prez would stop me doin' recon if I lost my shit. Life without recon would just about fuckin' end me. A man needs some excitement in his life."

Breaker grinned. "As soon as Sophie's pushed your kid out, you'll be begging for a quiet life."

"Nah." Atlas grinned. "I'll strap my boy on my back in one'a those contraption things your brothers' used and take my Thor up the woods to teach him how to shoot."

Every eye slashed to Atlas. "Thor?" Breaker inquired.

Atlas puffed his chest out. "Yeah. Gonna name all my boys after gods and keep it in the family."

"Your name's Daniel," I said sarcastically.

The SAA puffed his chest out. "My road name's not."

Bowie barked a laugh.

Atlas's head reared back. "Better than your nature names, asshole. I mean fuckin' Willow." His lips thinned. "No, you wouldn't dare."

Bowie grinned, eyes still on the road. "Got all my names picked out. Eight altogether."

I turned to him. "Eight?"

He jerked a nod. "Yep. Thought if I can knock Layla up with twins a few times, we'll be set. We know twins run in the family now, so I've given my balls a good talkin' to and told 'em to start performing. Love my little Willow, but I want twins, and I want 'em fast." He nodded his head toward his brother. "Not lettin' this little scrotum take all the glory."

"Jesus, Bo." Break laughed. "Don't think it works like that."

"Easy for you to say." Bowie retorted. "You've got your twins. Reckon I can overtake ya within two years. You've got two, I've got two, so even if your woman gets knocked up next year and you have another dynamic duo with her career, she'll be dunzo. If Doe's carryin' twins now and I can get her knocked up again next year, I'll have you beat, no problemo."

Breaker looked to the heavens, shaking his head.

Settling back in my seat, I smiled at the thought of a mini-me running around the place. I wasn't like the boys; one or two would do me, but I'd never met the woman I wanted to be their mother until now. Well, technically, I met her twelve years ago, but I had to wait for her.

I'd never really thought about being a dad before. The shit I went through with mine put me off, because what if my kid inherited his fucked-up genes? These days, the idea appealed, but I had to get a move on. I wanted to be young enough to get down on the ground and play without putting my back out.

An uneasy feeling stabbed through my gut when I thought about how Freya was only twenty-four with the world at her feet. Kids were way off for her. Our timing was terrible. She had to get through a year of interning and her residency before she could even think about having children. I'd probably be in my forties by the time she was ready to slow down.

My feelings for Freya had been building for years, so why was I not claiming my girl? Something was holding me back from going all in and making her officially mine.

The conversation I'd had with Breaker floated through my mind, and an icy chill went down my spine because he was right when he said I wouldn't meet another Freya. Letting her go would leave me empty, but the thought of holding onto her was making my chest tight with panic. Since we'd been back, I'd pulled away, and deep down, she'd probably realized it too.

So, one question remained.

What the fuck was I gonna do about it?

Chapter Twenty-Two

Freya

The waning sun cast a shadow across my room at the clubhouse as I stood in front of my open dresser. My fingers grazed over the silk and lace garments inside, trying to decide what to wear for my date with Colt later.

My stomach fizzed and popped at the thought of meeting him. It had been so long since we'd touched each other, and I couldn't wait to feel close to him again. My skin tingled with anticipation. The thought of us spending time with him after days apart ignited a warmth inside me that I hadn't felt since we were last together in Denver.

Having to hide from everybody was starting to take its toll. I hated that all our moments were snatched, but it only made them all the more precious. The only thing I could do was hold on to the fact it wouldn't be forever and that we were working toward a future, but it was tough.

Pulling out a red lacy set, I held it against my body, examining my reflection in the full-length mirror. The ruby color contrasted with my olive skin and accentuated my curves. I just hoped he would appreciate it.

My eyes sparkled with excitement as I imagined the way Colt's blue eyes would light up at the sight of me wearing them. There was a hardness about him that had developed over the years, but he was different with me. A lightheartedness lingered under the surface when we were together, and I loved that I could bring that out in him.

Shoving the red lingerie inside my travel bag, I zipped it closed and hauled it over my shoulder before making my way through the door and down the corridor.

My heart fluttered, and I smiled as I hit the bar, heading to the main doors. A few of the men sat down and were shooting the shit. I gave them smiles and pushed the door open, stepping into the parking lot and turning for the spot where my car was parked.

"Hey!" a voice called.

I craned my neck to see Sophie making her way toward me, stopped, and walked over to meet her. Taking in her pregnant belly, I smiled. Soph was so tiny that even at five months pregnant, she looked like she was about to pop. "You okay?"

She huffed and puffed, red-faced, as he waddled toward me. "Jesus," she heaved out. "Is it March yet?"

I laughed. "Just a few months to go."

"I feel like I'm carrying triplets already," Soph huffed, eyes resting on my bag. "Where you going?"

"I'm staying at the gallery tonight," I explained before lowering my voice. "Colt's meeting me there."

"Ahh," she said knowingly. "A lovers rendezvous. I bet you're looking forward to some privacy."

"You could say that." I waggled my eyebrows and laughed.

Soph smiled. "Have a good night. I just wanted to let you know Cash is going down to Grand Junction to get Ed tomorrow. We're going to settle him in and then let Kennedy loose on him."

My heart warmed. "How's his recovery going?"

"Okay," she replied. "The vet center's happy with his progress. He's a lot more nervous than Kit was when he came home, but Ed's never been here before. It's all new for him. Even the thought of having his own apartment is stressing him out,"

"Is he okay for money and support?" I asked.

"Yeah," she told me. "Ed's claimed his military pension and Nina's helped him apply for a grant. Kit's hired him to protect Kennedy, so he's got work already, and you know your dad will find him something if it doesn't work out. Kit's taking him up to Rock Springs, and he's got Nina on speed dial. We're all set."

"We're one of the richest nations in the world," I grumbled. "Why do so many people struggle to afford healthcare? And there are millions of people on the streets. What's going on?"

Sophie shrugged. "Budget cuts and a general attitude of not giving a shit. We send men and women to war, break them, and then forget about them. Look at what Kit suffered. Thank God for places like Grand Junction."

"We'll look after him too," I said determinedly. "He can't go wrong with the club and the ol' ladies behind him."

Sophie made a sound of agreement. "I wanted to ask you about your internships. Have you settled on a specialty yet?"

"Definitely trauma surgery," I confirmed. "I loved working in the ER."

"Did you take my advice about applying to smaller hospitals?" she asked.

I nodded. "Yeah. I've applied to programs with small intakes."

"Good." She said, sounding relieved. "You're ready to carry out simple surgeries now. A smaller hospital will be glad to have you. You need training, of course, but you've already got the basics down. You'll be an asset." She cocked her head. "What's Colt said about it? Is he following you?"

I opened my mouth to reply but stopped when I realized I didn't actually know the answer. I wracked my brain, trying to recall conversations about it, but nothing sprang to mind. My blood ran cold when it hit me that nothing had been set in stone. Never once had Colt said he'd find work close to where I took a placement. I'd just assumed he would.

Sophie knew about mine and Colt's relationship, but I hadn't told the ol' ladies he was joining the FBI. He'd only told me about it because I'd overheard his conversation with Cash, but he'd changed the subject before going into any meaningful detail.

A heavy feeling settled in my stomach.

"We haven't spoken about it yet," I whispered, throat hot with emotion.

"Oh," she exclaimed.

Biting my lip, I wondered how one solitary word could be filled with so much pity.

Sophie squeezed my arm. "Are you okay?"

Tears flooded my eyes. "I don't know. You just made me realize that he hasn't made any plans with me. He said we'll be together, but we've not discussed details. I don't know how I missed it."

"It's not like you," Soph murmured. "Since you've been back, I've noticed how quiet and subdued you've been. You're not loud at all, but you make your presence known. It's like you've shrunk into yourself. You're the first one to give the guys shit, but you seem so distracted that all their shit goes over your head."

My brow furrowed.

Sophie was right. Since I'd gotten back, I'd been unsettled. A feeling of impending doom had weighed down on me. If I was honest with myself, Colt had been a little offhand with me, like I was an irritating child he had to tolerate. It made me nervous about what we were doing.

My eyes lifted to Sophie's. "I need to pin him down, don't I?"

"I think so, Freya. You should be making plans for the future. You've only got a couple of months left here. You should at least have an idea of where you're moving to." She winced.

"I'm such an idiot." I shook my head at my own stupidity.

"No, you're not," Sophie told me. "You've not been in many relationships, and believe me, if anyone knows how these asshole bikers can screw with your head, it's me. There was no asshole bigger than Atlas when he was courting me. He said one thing but meant another. Maybe Colt's just confused with all the changes."

My stomach dragged so heavily that I felt sick. "Maybe," I agreed, but deep down, I knew the truth. Being back at the club had spooked him. Colt spent a lot of time with my dad, and it was bound to make him feel shitty about what we were doing.

The problem was, I could reassure him all day long, but he had to come to terms with everything himself. Whether he meant to or not, Colt was playing games with me, and I had to put my foot down, or else he'd think he could walk all over me.

I felt nauseous, and my insides were shaky, but I was also pissed that he was acting like a child.

Again.

Ugh.

Did Colt think he had the monopoly on guilt? I could already imagine the shock in his eyes and the weight of his disappointment bearing down on me.

An audible sigh escaped my lungs because here we were again. Same shit, different day.

The ruby underwear may have been a waste of time because, even though I wanted us to use the night to reconnect, Colt and I obviously needed to have a serious talk.

The coffee shop was busy when I got there.

It was only five o'clock, and Colt wouldn't get to the gallery anytime soon, so I stopped to grab a coffee and something to eat on the way.

"Hey!" Martha, the new owner called over as I walked inside. "It's Freya, right? Kit's sister?"

"It certainly fuckin' is Marth, darlin'," a deep, gravelly voice with a trace of an Irish lilt said from behind. "Whatever she wants, put on my tab."

I whirled around and looked up into bright blue eyes, except those particular ones didn't belong to Colt; they belonged to a dark-haired, muscled, extremely good-looking guy.

"Tadhg," I murmured. "When did you get back in town?"

A wide, sexy smirk pulled across his face. "A few days ago. Ma decreed that we all needed to get our asses back to Hambleton for the holidays. Me Da's not well."

"I'm sorry to hear that." I smiled sadly. "It's good to see you though."

Tadhg O'Shea was a year older than me, so I knew him pretty well from school because I'd skipped a grade. He was confident, intelligent, and so curious that he'd left town at nineteen to travel the world. Somehow, he'd fallen into the stock car racing scene and over time, had become pretty successful.

"I'm meetin' Donovan, but he's late as feckin' usual." Tadhg rolled his eyes. "Tell me what you want, then go sit."

With a broad smile, I relayed my order, turned, and made my way to a table at the back of the room, where a coat hung over the back of one of the chairs. Tadhg had left his phone and a newspaper sitting there without a care in the world. But then I guessed the O'Shea's didn't have to worry about anybody stealing their shit. The brothers were notorious around town for their boxing and fighting skills, and their dad, Lorcan, was rumored to have connections to organized crime.

Nobody messed with the O'Shea's unless they were crackpots.

I took the seat next to the chair with the coat hanging on it, facing the counter. As I sat, the door flew open, and in walked Donny O'Shea.

Me and every other person with a vagina stared at the man who walked in and sighed. On top of that, my nipples got hot.

I'd crushed on Colt all my life. He was it for me; there was no question about that. But, if Colt had left town, or if he'd gotten run over and killed by a stampede of wild horses, I was certain I would've turned to Donovan O'Shea for comfort.

Tall, dark, handsome, muscled, cocky, lady killer and lady fucker, notorious giver of orgasms, Donny O'Shea, was a town legend. He fucked anything that moved. Tall, short, thick, thin, white, black, Asian, Donovan loved them all, and to be fair, they all loved Donny right back.

I hadn't fucked Donovan, though once—on one of the many occasions Colt got himself a new girlfriend, and I swore I was moving on—I fucked him in my fantasies.

Just once you understand.

When I was seventeen.

And as much as I felt like I'd cheated on Colt that night, by God, he made me come so hard.

Maybe it was the guilt factor.

Since then, on the rare occasion he was home from the military, and I caught a glimpse, I blushed as red as a raspberry martini, just like now for instance.

I watched as Donovan clapped his brother's back, listening as Tadhg said something in his ear. Slowly, Donny's head swiveled around the room, landed on me, kept going, and then immediately flicked back to rest on my face.

He grinned. All white teeth and gleaming blue eyes.

Immediately, Donovan O'Shea put me in mind of the big bad wolf, whereas I was innocent little Red Riding Hood with ruby underwear in my overnight bag to prove it.

My nipples tingled.

I think Donny knew this from ten paces away because he grinned bigger.

Then my pussy tingled.

Fuck!

Tadhg turned, holding a tray laden with coffee and snacks, and both brothers approached in perfect step with each other. The younger O'Shea was a beautiful man, tall, dark, and muscular but in a lean, sinewy way.

However, Donovan had the muscle, the swagger, and the burning eyes that disintegrated my panties from ten feet away. He was hot in a confident, almost uncaring way.

God only knew how I did it, but I held Donovan's stare until he stopped next to the table, towering above me.

"Gorgeous," he rumbled, eyes sweeping down my legs. "Help Daddy out and move chairs for me."

Instead of pulling my top off and waving it around my head while singing 'Come and get me Donovan O'Shea,' my forehead furrowed. "Why?"

His lips tipped up. "I need to watch the door. What if a mad gunman bursts in and starts shootin'? I need to protect you."

I sighed again before getting to my feet and parking my ass in the chair he held for me. I'd grown up around military men and, therefore, was privy to their obsessions about being able to observe the room.

Once he had me settled, Donny took a seat, leaned back, stretched his legs out, and manspread his ass, making sure he positioned himself where I couldn't help noticing the big bulge of his cock.

I cocked an eyebrow.

He smirked. "So, Freya Stone. Tell me somethin'. How the fuck did you grow up to look like that, and I didn't notice? Did that pa of yours lock you in an ivory tower so no man could bring his cock close?"

Tadhg pushed my coffee across the table, leaning forward to hear my reply.

I swirled my index finger around the rim of the mug. "By the time I graduated high school, you'd already left for the military. Then, I went to college and med school. Maybe we kept missing each other."

"Med school," he murmured, looking distinctly impressed. "Beauty and brains. How's that goin' for ya?"

I shrugged. "Pretty well, seeing as I just graduated."

His impressed expression turned to shock. "You're too young."

"I'm twenty-four," I confirmed. "And I studied hard."

His sexy, slow grin spread across his face again. "Don't tell me. You graduated top of your class."

I grinned back. "In the top two percent in the country and fourteen months early."

"Damn!" he muttered, eye-fucking me into next week. "Go out with me."

"Can't," I murmured. "I'm seeing someone."

Donovan's eyes slid to his brother, who was looking between us interestedly. "Did you know little Freya Stone grew up to look like this?"

"Not exactly," Tadhg replied. "I've been away as much as you. But I saw her at seventeen, I suspected then."

"Damn!" Donny repeated, before addressing me once more. "You goin' to the big birthday party at the club next weekend?"

"Of course," I told him. Smiling at how well my brother had done to arrange all of Kennedy's Vegas friends to be flown over for the thirtieth birthday. "It's gonna be a great night."

"It's the hottest invite in town," he agreed. "Me and T are helpin' Cal out in the bar and going down the clubhouse later. Can you believe Kit's got DJ Raven on the decks? We saw her in Ibiza. She'll have the crowd rockin' out." Donny cocked his head, his eyes roaming over my face. "You gonna save me a dance?"

My lips twitched. "You wanna fill in my dance card, your Grace?"

He barked a laugh. "I'd rather be the sexy, dark pirate than the Duke."

I looked up at him over the rim of my coffee cup and took a sip, studying him.

Donovan was handsome and had that thing about him that drew women in like magnets. Tall, built, cocky men with swagger seemed to be the women of this town's catnip, as evidenced by how well all the other younger bikers did getting the girls when they came out on the prowl. Hell, Kit, Bowie, and even Cash, back in the day, went through the town like walking STDs.

Obviously, I'd been a little more sheltered. It was no wonder I'd fallen in love with a biker. They were all I'd ever really known.

Draining my cup, I placed it back on the table and twisted around to retrieve my purse from the back of the chair where I'd hung it. "Thanks for the coffee, Tadhg." I sent him a bright smile and went to stand.

Donny got to his feet. "You goin' already?"

I nodded. "I've got plans later."

"With the dude you're," he raised his hands and bent his fingers into speech marks, "seein'."

Ignoring him, I smiled to myself and gathered my things together. "See you soon, guys." I hooked my bag over my shoulder and walked to the counter to pick up sandwiches, pastries, and water for later.

As I walked out into the now-dark Main Street, I felt a presence behind me. "Hey, Freya."

I turned to see Donovan zipping his jacket up and following me outside. "Don't run off. I wanna talk to ya." He approached, collar up and his hands in his pockets to brace from the cold. "Who ya seeing? Is it serious?"

The question made me wince internally, though the fifteen-year-old who crushed on Donny, along with every woman in town under the age of eighty, could've squealed. Colt was screwing me around for sure, but no part of me was tempted. Now I'd got my man. I wouldn't let go without a fight.

"It's heading toward serious," I explained. "I'm falling for him."

His face dropped, and he looked downcast. "Fair enough."

I laughed. "You'll be fine, Donny. I'm sure you can go to your little black book, make one call, and get a date."

"Maybe, but it wouldn't be with you." He studied my face. "Tell ya what. If things don't work out with your mystery guy, come to the bar, and I'll buy you a drink. I'm on leave until New Year."

"I'll keep it in mind," I promised. "I'm sorry, I have to go. I'll see you around."

"Yeah." Without warning, he leaned forward, tucked my hair behind my ear, and kissed my cheek. "You better."

Squeezing my eyes closed, I tried to build a wall between Donovan and my senses. His cologne smelled like summer rain mixed with sage and citrus, which, combined with the leather scent of his jacket, was manly and I had to admit, incredibly appealing.

Donny pulled back, flashed me a grin, and sauntered back into the coffee shop. "See ya around, Freya Stone." The bell tinkled above the door, and he disappeared.

I stood there for a moment, still feeling the warmth of the kiss on my cheek, wondering how Donovan could be so affectionate when the man I loved didn't seem to be making any effort at all to spend time with me.

I shook my head to clear my thoughts and walked to my car. As I opened the door and slid in, my mind filled with my conversation with Sophie back in the club's parking lot.

My heart beat erratically in my chest when it dawned on me how vague Colt had been. I hadn't noticed at the time how he'd managed to change the subject pretty skillfully whenever we talked about the future.

It made my stomach unsettled, to say the least.

Starting the car, I checked my mirrors and carefully pulled out of my spot toward Monument Street, which was just the next street over. Within three minutes, I'd driven around the back of the gallery and parked in a spot that wasn't visible from the road.

I got out of the car, grabbed my overnight bag, and made my way up the metal stairs to the first-floor apartment. Unlocking the door, I turned on the light, looked around, and beamed a smile.

The tiny apartment was cozy and welcoming. The walls had been painted a soft off-white, and Cara had accessorized the place with dark mulberry-colored cushions, rugs, and throws.

The space wasn't big, about twenty square meters in all, but Cara had made the most of the room. A bed had been pushed into one corner with a nightstand facing a modern TV attached to the wall. The opposite side contained a small kitchenette with a hob, fridge, and cupboards on the wall. An open door revealed a small bathroom with a toilet, sink, and shower.

My fingers tremored, and my stomach fizzed. I settled down on the bed and pulled my underwear from the bag along with my Chanel spray.

Time to get ready. Colt would be here soon.

Two Hours Later

I held my cell phone to my ear and waited.

An automated voice came on saying '*the person you are trying to reach is not available. Please try later.*'

My throat heated, and my mind began to war with itself.

It's still early yet. Colt went out on a job earlier. Give him a chance.

But why is his cell phone switched off?

He's probably in with Dad and the officers debriefing.

But they went out hours ago.

My eyes swept down my body, noting how good the red lacy bra and panties looked against my olive skin. I'd gone to a lot of effort, but Colt wasn't here to see it, even though he told me he'd be here by now.

A cold feeling slid through my chest, and my lungs tightened. That feeling of impending doom was back, and stronger than ever.

I lay back on the bed for a moment, staring at my phone in my hand, trying to control my rising discomfort. It had started to rain outside a while ago, and I wondered if it had somehow held him up. Excuses floated through my head, but underneath, I couldn't shake the bad feeling in the pit of my stomach.

Taking a deep breath, I tried calling Colt once more, but again, my call went straight to voicemail.

Hot fury began to bubble up inside me.

Was he playing me for a fool?

My lips pursed. Stabbing at my cell phone again, I held it to my ear and waited.

"Hey, babe," my best friend breathed. "How's things back in cowboy country?"

Hearing her voice made my eyes well up with tears because it brought home how much I missed her. "Hey Abs."

She paused briefly before crying out, "What the fuck's going on? Why are you calling me crying down the fucking phone?"

"Everything's been going wrong since I've been home," I whispered. "I wish I was back there with you. I miss you so much. Hearing your voice set me off."

"I miss you too," she replied firmly. "But you've not even been home a week yet. What the fuck's upset you already?"

"It's Colt," I admitted. "I'm feeling neglected."

She huffed down the line. "He seemed fine when you both left. What fuckery has he managed to pile on you now?"

"I've hardly seen him," I explained. "Eventually, we agreed to meet somewhere tonight and he's late.

I'm laying here in red lacy lingerie, waiting on a man who I'm worried won't show. I wanted to speak to him about a few things and try to get close again, but he's not here yet and his cell's turned off."

I could hear the sound of my best friend gritting her teeth on the other end of the line. "So why are you still there?"

"We need to talk," I relayed, biting my lip. "I need to put him on the spot and demand a few answers."

"Ya think?" she snapped. "Look. I get you've caught feels. I get it's taken years for him to make a move, but what the actual fuck, Freya? Why are you letting him screw you around?"

My friend's words started to sink in until the clouds in my head suddenly parted, allowing my common sense to shine through.

Abi was right. I'd turned into one of those women I swore I wouldn't be. A year ago, I was kicking ass and taking names, Now, I was holed up, dressed in sexy lingerie all for a man who couldn't be bothered to appreciate it.

I thought back to all our conversation, at how he's kept me dangling on a string and in a way, playing with my emotions. I'd been so desperate to get him, that when I finally did, I'd stopped speaking out because I wanted to keep the peace, and deep down I was scared of losing him.

The problem was, by allowing him to walk all over me, I'd lost myself.

It started in Denver when he spoke to me like shit and acted like a prick. I made allowances for him because I knew he was ravaged by guilt. I wanted to support him, but by trying to help, I'd somehow turned a blind eye to his assholery. Even Sophie had noticed the change in me, she told me earlier I wasn't myself and I knew she was right because I hadn't felt myself since Colt declared I was his.

I'd gotten him but I was scared of it all going wrong. I'd made excuses for his behavior, and I wasn't acting like myself. God, no wonder I'd been feeling so unsettled.

It was Colt's job to reassure me and make me feel safe, but he hadn't even tried.

"I can hear you thinking, babe," Abigail murmured. "Are you seeing the light?"

"Yeah, Abs," I responded quietly, mind still racing. "And it's bright as fuck."

"There's my girl," she whispered. "What you gonna do now?"

My jaw set tightly as I pulled the blinds slightly to one side to see the weather had worsened. Rain bounced off the sidewalk, hard and heavy. "I'm staying here," I decided. "I'll give him tonight. If he turns up and has an explanation, I'll give him a chance to talk it out with me. If he stands me up, I'll turn biker chick on him."

"Why don't you come down for a few days and stay with me?" she asked. "It wouldn't hurt to get some space."

My heart ached at the thought of leaving him, but Abi was right. I was in too deep. Getting away for a few days would help me see things clearer.

"I'll see what tonight brings and take it from there," I said quietly. "Thank you, Abi. I fucking love you."

She let out a snort. "Love you too. Give him hell." The line clicked and went dead.

I glanced at the display on my cell, hoping so fucking much that I was wrong and Colt had sent me a message while I'd been talking.

Nothing.

Grabbing the remote control, I switched on the TV, anything to fill the deafening silence in the room.

A part of me held out hope that Colt would knock on the door, soaked through, saying the weather held him up, or he'd been delayed at the club, but deep down I knew he wouldn't show. It was what my feeling of impending doom had been about.

I stood, went to my bag, and grabbed a tee, slipping it over my head before grabbing my toothbrush and heading into the bathroom, all the while feeling the weight of my sinking heart.

My throat burned with unshed tears, but I didn't want to break down. I wanted to be strong because on so many occasions recently, I'd been his doormat.

It was time to face facts.

What hurt me the most was that I would've given up everything for him, my family, my life in Hambleton and even my career if it was what kept us apart, all because I thought what we had was worth it.

I was a fool, because when the chips were down, Colt wouldn't even give up one night for me.

When I'd finished brushing my teeth, I wandered back into the main room and slid under the comforter, laying down on my side to watch the TV. Except I didn't take in a word, I stared blankly at the screen still deep in thought.

Why wasn't I worth making an effort for? Our relationship was already on thin ice, and the icing on the shitty-assed cake was that Colt was pulling away from me.

For hours, I lay there thinking and working things out in my head and as dawn eventually broke, reality stared me in the face.

I looked at the door willing it to fly open and for Colt to run in and apologize but my heart weighed heavy with disappointment when it remained closed.

With a breath, I threw the comforter off and got out of bed, grabbing my washbag, and heading for the bathroom again. I wasn't going to stay here wallowing in self-pity. I need to get the fuck out of here, and away from *him.*

This was the last time he'd treat me like an afterthought. I could do better; I *was* better. My chest burned, and my stomach swirled with emotions.

How fucking dare he treat me like an asshole? How fucking dare he think I'd put up with this goddamned bullshit? Anger razed through me, most of it aimed at Colt, but a small part at myself.

I wasn't this girl. I wasn't about to take the scraps he threw at me.

Stomping around, I got dressed, shoved my stuff in my bag, and made the bed. Then, as I walked out the door without a backward glance, I felt a small sense of freedom, because at least I could be me again and not have to feel like I was merely being tolerated; a nuisance who got in the way of the shit Colt really wanted to deal with.

If this was Colt's attempt at love, he could keep it stick up his ass.

Chapter Twenty-Three

Colt

Footsteps startled me awake.

My eyes flew open before settling on the TV screen on the wall of my office. I blinked, confused, lifting my head, trying to work out what the fuck I was doing and why I wasn't tucked up in bed.

Sitting up straight, I groaned at the pain shooting through my back.

I was too fucking old for this shit. I needed a comfortable, warm bed to spend my nights in, not my office chair. Rolling my shoulders, I worked out the seized-up muscles in my back before stretching my arms up high and yawning.

A piss, coffee, and Iris's scrambled eggs were needed, and in that order. As if on cue my stomach rumbled loudly and I rubbed my gut, thinking that maybe I could get Ris to throw some bacon on my plate too. I was fucking starving.

Leaning back, I checked in my pocket for my cell phone and fished it out. I looked at the screen and cursed under my breath when I saw it was switched off.

I'd forgotten to turn it on again after I got back from the mission. It was eight P.M. by the time we'd debriefed in Church, so I'd kept it off while we talked, and forgotten about it afterwards.

It wasn't like me at all, but I was so hell-bent on watching the cameras to see if I could pick something up and then I must've nodded off.

The glow from my cell phone lit the room up and the time flashed four minutes past six, before messages and notifications began beeping. Scraping a hand down my face, I cursed under my breath. Jesus, couldn't I have a night off without people fucking harassing me?

I clicked on the first message when I noticed it was from my sister. Holding my breath, my eyes scanned the text, and I smiled when I saw she was telling me she was pregnant. After making a mental note to call her later, I clicked onto the next one, grinning when I saw it was from Freya.

Within seconds my smile died. A sinking feeling dragged my stomach down to the cold ground before I looked to the heavens and muttered one solitary word.

"Fuck!"

I was meant to meet her last night at the gallery, but I'd fucking forgotten. It had been a crazy day infiltrating Henderson's office, almost getting rumbled by Stafford, then getting back, reporting to Prez and getting the feeds up and running.

As I clicked through the messages she'd sent throughout the night, my gut sank lower and lower. Freya wasn't fucking happy with me at all. I couldn't blame her. I'd literally stood her up, which was fucked up in itself, but when I also took into account how we'd not had much time together since we'd been home, I felt like even more of an asshole.

Clicking the cell phone, I pressed the call icon and got Freya's voicemail. I looked up again, praying for divine intervention because my girl was gonna chew my ass for this and rightly so.

I went to stand, all thoughts of coffee and fucking bacon forgotten, when the sound of footsteps echoed through the hall, jolting me out of my funk. Something told me it was her. The steps were too light to belong to a man, so that ruled out a brother, and the only other people conscious at this time of day were usually Iris, and Sophie if she was working, and neither of them would be coming to see me for a morning chat.

As if conjured by my thoughts, she appeared at my door, beautiful, sexy as all fuck, and going by the clench of her jaw, also damned furious.

I closed my eyes, straightened my back, and opened my mouth to apologize. "I'm so fuckin' sorry, baby—" I was cut off by something whizzing past my ear, glancing off my head with a smack. "What the fuck!" I jumped up and froze as I looked down and saw one of the new boots I'd brought her on the floor just behind me. My eyes lifted, rounding as I noted how red her face burned and how tightly her teeth were clenched as she went into the bag she held and pulled the other boot out.

"You can shove your shit up your asshole!" she shrieked, drawing her arm back and launching the other boot at my head.

"Motherfucker!" I snapped; ducking left to avoid the spiked heel stabbing me in the eye. "What the hell are you doin'?"

Growling, she heaved the bag off her shoulder, kneeled to the floor and tipped everything I'd ever bought for her out of it. "You're a fucking asshole," she grated out, standing tall again. "I waited hours for you, and you couldn't even be bothered to fucking call me." She stomped toward me and swung the leather purse. "You can take your shit and stick it all. Fuck you and fuck your shitty ass promises."

I swerved left to avoid the bag hitting me in the face. "Calm the fuck down, Freya," I grunted, grabbing her hands.

A frustrated angry noise escaped her throat, and she threw me off before rolling up on her toes, getting in my face and screaming. "Fuck you!"

My stomach dropped, and I cursed myself for forgetting about her. "Freya, stop. I'm sorry, okay?" I pleaded, ducking again to avoid another swing at my head. "I must have lost track of time and fallen asleep at my desk."

"Lost track of time?" she screeched, tossing her long dark hair so it cascaded down her back like a waterfall. "Do you know how long I waited for you? Or how many lies I had to tell Dad so I could sneak out for the night just to see your sorry ass?"

"Jesus, woman, listen to me," I demanded as my hands went up defensively as if I was trying to calm a wild animal. I took a breath, mind whirring over how the fuck I was gonna get out of this latest dick move. "Baby, I know I messed up, and I'm sorry, but I can't go back and change it. What I can do is apologize and promise it won't happen again. I'll do everythin' I can to make it right."

"You mean buy me more clothes? Or shut me up with promising more dates you don't keep?" She let out a humorless snort. "I don't fucking think so. I'm done with being pushed to the side. You're the one who wanted this. *You* asked *me*. You promised nothing would change when we got home. You said we'd make time for each other. Jesus, Colt. You'd rather fall asleep at your desk than make the effort to spend time with me." She shook her head exasperatedly. "I fucking lay there for hours in lingerie, like an idiot, waiting for you to walk through the door. I would never treat you that way." Freya's tone was sharp, hurt flashing behind her golden-brown eyes.

I could feel my face growing hotter as her words sliced into me, the weight of her disappointment landing like a physical blow. My eyes darted between hers trying to convey how sorry I was.

"All I can do is apologize," I muttered, running my fingers through my hair frustratedly. "I just forgot."

"You forgot?" she snarled; her beautiful face contorted in disbelief. "You knew how important last night was to me. Jesus, we'd arranged it hours before. You promised, and you still let me down."

My chest tightened, heat flaring in my lungs. "Jesus, woman. I've been workin' my ass off to get the club set for when I leave. I've got a lotta shit to take care of, why can't you gimme a fuckin' break? Ya think I like bein' glued to my desk? You think I enjoy not even havin' the time to take a long shit? Why can't you be more understanding?"

Her head reared back, all color draining from her face. "I'll tell you why I'm not more understanding. I don't trust you anymore because all I heard you say in your little speech just then was when *I leave*, you didn't say *we* or *us*." Her mouth went slack. "So, tell me, what are the plans for when *we* leave? What about *us,* Colt?"

Chest twisting, I looked to the heavens shaking my head. Suddenly, I felt more pissed off than apologetic. Why was she pushing me for answers I didn't have? "I don't fuckin know yet."

She just stared at me, and I watched her gorgeous eyes fill with pain.

I heaved out a breath. "Give me time."

One side of her mouth hitched, as if I'd said something funny.

"What's your fuckin' problem?" I demanded, grabbing her shoulder. "What do you want from me, Freya?"

"I want the same thing I thought you wanted, for us to leave, together. You've changed your mind, haven't you?" she croaked.

I scrubbed a hand over my face.

It wasn't that I'd changed my mind per se, everything just seemed to be going at a hundred miles an hour. One minute we were friends, the next we were talking about spending our lives together. It was overwhelming and, quite frankly, daunting as fuck. I wasn't used to going fast, I liked having time to think things through, but with everything else I had to deal with, I felt like I was fighting a losing battle, and it was wearing me down.

She must've taken my silence as confirmation because her eyes filled with tears, and she nodded. "I see."

"No, baby, listen," I begged. "I just need some space to concentrate on the club. I love you."

Freya swiped furiously at her cheeks. "You can have all the space you want."

"What the fuck are you talkin' about?" I demanded.

She stared up at me, eyes sliding over my face like she was drinking me in. "You're not ready for me."

My gut clenched. "What do you mean I'm not ready?"

She pointed to me then to her. "This. Us. *Me.* You're not ready. You need more time."

My heart ached at the pain slashing across her face. "I'll be okay, baby. I'll catch up. I promise."

"Please don't," she whispered. "Stop making promises you can't keep. Ever since we've been back you've done all you can to avoid me. I have to get angry with you to get any attention and even then, you say the right thing but it's just to placate me."

I rubbed at the pain shooting through my chest. "I love you, baby."

She let out a sob before pulling her shoulders back and taking a deep breath to get her hurt under control. "I know. I love you too, but it's not working. The timing's all wrong."

I opened my mouth to deny every word and admit I'd been an asshole, but nothing came out. There was so much pressure on my shoulders already with the Sinners, the mayor, and the FB—fucking—I. Adding Freya into the mix and the fallout we'd cause when everything came out was too much. Maybe she was better off out of it. I needed to deal with one problem at a time.

I'd claim her, but I needed to let her go, at least until I left Wyoming. We could see where we were at after I'd gone and regroup then.

"I'm sorry," I murmured, tucking a stray lock of hair behind her ear. "You're right, the timing's shit. I never thought of the bigger picture. It was selfish of me to keep you around when I couldn't do the right thing by you. If there's one thing I know above everythin' else, Freya, it's that you deserve the world. Problem is, right now I'm not in a position to give it to ya."

Freya squeezed her eyes closed and lowered her head. It was as if my words physically wounded her. Her small frame trembled, like the bottom had just fallen out of her world.

"I'm an asshole," I went on. "I shouldn't have started this up."

She flinched and my gut dropped because I knew I'd just delivered the final blow. I expected her to start ranting, to lose her shit and slap me, God knew I deserved it.

But she didn't. Instead, Freya took a deep shuddering breath, her slender shoulders rising and falling beneath her tee. Her eyes opened again, and I saw they were brimming with hurt and despair, but also resignation and even acceptance.

She lifted her fingers, cupped my jaw, and stroked her thumb over my stubble. "I hope you find it someday, Colt," she murmured. "When you do, I hope I'm there to see it."

My head reared back, her words striking a chord deep inside me. "Find what?" I snarled, trying to mask the stab of vulnerability threatening to surface. I wasn't that man anymore, weak and trusting; I'd learned a long time ago the only person I could depend on was me.

Freya smiled sadly as a lone tear tracked down her cheek. "Take care." With a final, lingering glance, she turned on her heel and walked out the door, leaving me alone with my heart cracking inside my chest.

I stared after her, marveling at how her inner strength put mine to shame.

Freya had always been the person who propped me up. Nobody else brought so much light to my dark fucked-up world, but what we had was too much, too soon. Even after a few days of being home I could see her light fading and I knew I was the one snuffing it out. If I wasn't careful, she'd consume me; I couldn't risk it, not after last time. There was a reason I didn't get too close to people, the thought of showing her who I was underneath made my throat constrict.

Freya needed a man who could pay her attention and give her what she needed, not a screwed up, jaded old hacker who'd been walking around dealing with Daddy issues for the last twenty years.

It was crazy how it took me twelve years to get her, and then I'd gone and fucked everything up in one night.

For someone so smart, sometimes, I was a fucking idiot.

The reason I didn't ever make snap decisions came to light within hours, because by the afternoon, I was already deeply regretting my decision.

My concentration was shot to pieces. Every time I sat back and closed my eyes, all I could see were my princess's tear-filled golden-browns looking pleadingly up at me. It had been days since I'd held her, but I could still feel the warmth of her body pressed against mine, taste the bittersweet memory of her lips, and it drove me fucking crazy knowing I'd given it all up on a whim.

I leaned forward, holding my head in my hands.

For days, a voice in the back of my mind had been telling me to end things with Freya, for her sake. My feelings for her were so immense and consuming that I didn't want to subject her to all the bullshit affecting my life. But now I'd backed off, something wasn't sitting right with me.

My head told me I'd done the right thing, but my heart was dying at the thought of her not being mine. At first, I'd felt noble and righteous for letting her go, but as time wore on, my skin began to feel tight and itchy, like it was too snug to contain all my emotions.

Maybe I'd been a little hasty.

And also a bit of a prick.

I closed my eyes and cursed under my breath, asking what the fuck was wrong with me?

Back in Denver, I'd been happier than I had for years, and one hundred percent committed to building a future with Freya, but since we'd been home, all I'd done was self-sabotage and push her away.

I wondered why that would be when Freya was everything to me. Deep down I knew there wouldn't be another woman in my life, only her. If I lost my woman, I'd lose my future, so why had I been so intent on pushing her away?

Jeez, I needed more therapy than shit-for-brains Cash, and that was saying something.

Suddenly, my throat went dry as a bone and my fingers tremored as the weight of my decision hit me like Thor's goddamned hammer.

"You're such a fuckin' idiot," I muttered to myself, the words weaving around my soul like a curse. My heart contracted painfully at the notion that I'd really gone and fucked-up this time.

Rising to my feet, I pocketed my cell, intending to sneak down to Freya's room, apologize, and hope I hadn't screwed everything up too much, but I was stopped by the sound of heavy footsteps.

After a few seconds, Bowie appeared at the door. "Yo. Gotta go into town to meet Callum and Donovan O'Shea. Wanna come?"

My mouth twisted. "Why?"

"Callum asked me to go to the bar for a little chat but not to let Dad know. Don't mind admittin' Colt, sounds ominous as fuck. Can't take Pop, for obvious reasons. Cash is nowhere to be found which means he's probably fucking Cara somewhere. Break's at Kennedy's office 'cause he can't go five minutes without seeing her, and Atlas took Soph to work."

I barked a laugh. "So that leaves me, bottom of the pile."

"Don't be a fuckin' asshole. I'd rather you come than most of them anyway. Cash would end up in a pissing contest with Cal just because he can't help himself, and At would stand there glowering like a motherfucker."

Mouth thinning in frustration, I stood again and grabbed my leather jacket from the back of my chair.

I didn't have much choice but to go. Bowie could see I was just sitting here watching an empty room on the cameras. I'd have loved to go see Freya and make my apologies, but I guessed it could wait. She'd waited twelve damned years for me so another afternoon wouldn't make much difference.

I fell into step behind and followed him down the corridor to the bar. "What does Callum want a secret meet about?"

Bowie shrugged, "Said it's somethin' to do with Donovan."

My eyebrows darted together. "You think he wants to prospect?"

"Doubtful," Bowie mused. "Can't see him takin' even one of Dad's orders or cleanin' the clubhouse after a party."

"Is he still enlisted?" I inquired, opening the main door, and waving Bowie through.

"Yeah," Bowie replied as we walked into the parking lot. "But he's requested to pop smoke next year. Cal told me he's at home until early January then he's got six months left." He headed for his bike.

"I'm not riding, Bo," I told him.

"Why?" he asked, spinning around to face me. "The snow's comin' in soon. Make the most of it."

I winced. "It's colder than Santa's ballsack."

"You pissy little kid," he muttered. "You wanna take the SUV?"

I shrugged. "You can ride. I'm fuckin' not."

Bowie shook his head as he headed for one of the club's vehicles. "Fuckin' rich boy pussy ass."

I rolled my eyes, pulling the door to the passenger side open and sliding in.

"Sometimes I wonder why you're even a biker," Bowie muttered, settling into the driver's seat, grabbing the keys from the drink's holder, and starting the engine.

"So do I, brother," I snipped back, pulling my seat belt on.

Bowie laughed, following suit as he pulled out of the compound and joined the road to make the short drive into town.

Even though Bowie was an asshole for implying I didn't belong, he was right. I wasn't a born biker like he and his brothers were. Honestly, I only liked riding when we went on club runs, and that wasn't for being on a bike, I just loved the camaraderie and sense of belonging.

It was just one more thing I didn't have in common with the brothers.

One more thing that set me apart.

One more thing that made me realize I needed more than club life.

My heart panged because another realization hit me.

I wanted more than club life but only with Freya by my side, and I was fucking it all up. It had taken me time to adjust back into the MC knowing what was going to happen and also knowing Freya was mine. Guilt had held me back, but I was beginning to see things differently. Being with Freya wasn't a betrayal, when in our hearts, I was hers and she was mine. The only betrayal that I could fathom was us staying apart.

Okay, so I hadn't exactly been honest about our relationship, but I also only allowed something to happen when I knew I was leaving, when truth be told, I'd been tempted by the club's princess for a long-assed time.

Suddenly I felt thirty pounds lighter.

Loving someone and wanting to spend a life making them happy was a beautiful thing. Why should we let anyone influence us into passing up opportunities that made life worth living? I loved Freya and if I had to choose any woman to have my sons it would be her, 'cause my genes may have been faulty, but her perfect ones would more than make up for it.

Throughout the drive I began to understand how lucky I was to have my girl. She loved me to the point where she'd put up with my shit and had proven she was in it for the long haul.

I was a very fortunate man and I needed to stop taking her love for granted, because although Freya had the biggest heart in the world, she was no idiot. There was only so much she'd take before she blew her top, like this morning.

"Why you grinnin' like a loony?" Bowie asked, tugging me away from my thoughts,

"Just thinkin'," I said defensively, watching as he pulled into a parking space just outside the Lucky Shamrock.

"Well, stop it," he ordered. "Need your head in the game. Cal's one'a my closest boys but he's wily as fuck. If he wants a favor or he's got some shit to say, we gotta be ready. He won't blindside us, but he's asked us here for a reason, probably a favor."

We both exited the SUV and Bowie clicked the key fob to lock it before we turned and approached the bar.

As we got to the door, it opened. "Top'a the fuckin' morning to ya, boys." Callum O'Shea waved us through to the dimly lit bar where his brother Donovan already sat at a table with a beer bottle in front of him.

"Yo," he called over, getting to his feet.

Bowie greeted him with a chin lift while fist bumping Callum. "Looking well, Donny O'Shea. The military agrees with ya."

Donovan returned his chin lift and clapped me on the back. "Thanks for comin' boys."

Bowie glanced at me before turning back to Calum. "Why the fuck are we here? Not like you to go for all this cloak-and-dagger bullshit. If you've got something to ask the club, you know Dad will hear you out."

My eyes narrowed as I watched Donny's cheeks redden slightly, and a sinking sensation swept through my stomach. Something was about to go down that I wasn't gonna like, one bit.

"It's nothing important or even cloak-and-dagger," Callum interjected, going to the bar to collect a coffee pot and some mugs. "We just wanna run somethin' past ya and if possible, ask if you'll put a word in." He brought the cups of coffee over, gesturing for us to sit. "It's nothin' to do with business and everythin' personal."

Bowie sent me a slight nod and we took our seats around the table. "What do ya need, Cal?"

A wide smile spread across his face. "It's not for me. Our Donovan here needs you to approach your pa and put in a good word in for him."

"What for?" Bowie asked with a tone tight with confusion. He turned to Donny. "You wanna prospect, bro? You gotta see Dad, Cash, and Atlas. They deal with recruiting, not me."

Donny cocked his head. "It's nothin' like that. Callum called you 'ere 'cause I need a good word puttin' in with your da. Thing is, I wanna get to know your sister and Cal told me I gotta go through John first."

All air whooshed from my lungs until I was almost winded by the irrational surge of jealousy coursing through me. He'd called Bowie here because he wanted to fuck his sister?

My woman?

Over my dead fucking body.

Stunned, I watched as Bowie regarded Donovan carefully. "How serious are you about her?"

"I met her in the coffee shop last night," Don replied. "And I gotta say, she blew me away. Had a lotta women, Bo, but never a serious one. Didn't wanna leave some poor cailín keepin' the home fires burnin' while I went and played soldier, didn't think it was fair. But now I'm leaving the army and thinking about buying the gym, getting all new equipment, and growing the business. I'm in a good position to settle down."

My lip curled.

"He's also helping me run the bar," Callum added. "He's a fuckin' eejit but he's got some brains too and he's loyal to a fault."

My hand under the table clenched into fists and I used the movement to try and stop myself from picking up a damned chair and launching it at the glass wall of spirits lining the back of the bar.

Bowie nodded, deep in thought. "You serious about my sister?"

Donny glanced at Callum before nodding. "Only met her last night but I could see how special she was the second I laid eyes on her. Then we got talkin' and I knew I was right. Brains, beauty, and she's sweet as cherry pie, as well as funny and cute. I wouldn't mind shootin' my shot."

I rubbed at the ache flaring through my chest.

The thought of Donny fucking O'Shea trying his luck with *my* woman was akin to some fucker stabbing me in the heart, then twisting the knife for good measure. She must've ran into him on her way to Cara's gallery. My molars ground together as I thought of my girl getting hit on by a manwhore O'Shea brother and me not being there to defend her honor.

"I asked her out, but she said she's seein' somebody," Donny added. "Any idea who the fuckwit is?"

I bristled as it hit me how Freya had blown Donovan out the water for me, and to show my thanks, I'd left her in a strange apartment alone all night. She was loyal to me, even after I'd been distant and then, to top it off, I stood her up for her trouble.

I closed my eyes, trying to ignore the nausea clutching at my stomach.

Asshole was too good a word for me. How could I be so dismissive toward a girl who was so fucking perfect? In trying so hard to not be like my father and push her away, I'd done the exact opposite and started treating Freya the same way that asshole treated my mom. The realization hit me like another knife to the chest, and I had to stop myself from groaning out loud.

Bowie shrugged. "She either said it 'cause she's not interested and wants to let you down gently and not hurt your feelings, or she's been seeing some pimply-nosed med student down in Denver." He turned to me. "You were down there with her recently. Do you know anythin'?"

My mouth twisted. "She's single, but she wouldn't give him," I nodded toward Donovan, "the time of day."

Donny's had reared back. "What the fuck did I do?"

"You're a slut," I confirmed. "Freya don't like that shit, she's a decent girl. You're not good enough to shovel her shit."

Callum barked a laugh.

Bowie grinned.

"I was only sowing my wild oats." Donnie said in an affronted tone. "Didn't wanna settle down is all."

I curled my lip at him in disgust. "Like I said. Not. Good. Enough."

Donny's eyes narrowed on me.

"What do you think your da will say to it?" Callum asked Bowie.

Bowie shrugged. "He'll probably tell your brother to fuck off. He wants my sister with a doctor or lawyer, not a hoe-bag, ex-military ladies' man who part runs a bar, and a gym, and who also has tentative links to the Irish fuckin' Mafia."

I nodded my agreement, lips twitching at the crestfallen look on Donny's face.

"But if you're serious and you promise to treat her like the princess she is," he continued. "I'll have a word. Just remember, my sister's a good girl. She deserves someone who'll look after her."

My smile faded.

Donovan smirked. "Daddy likes a good girl."

Brain almost combusting, I let out a loud growl.

"Motherfucker," Bowie sneered.

"Not fuckin' helpin', ya muppet," Callum snapped. "Haven't even got her da on side yet and you're sending it all arseways."

Bowie's eyes darted between the brothers before resting on me. "What the fuck language is that?"

"Irish dialect," I explained. "Muppet is idiot, and if somethings goin' arseways, it means it's gettin' fucked-up."

"Right," Bowie said, eyes sliding back to Donovan. "I'll talk to Dad, but chances are he'll hunt you down and dick punch ya for even suggesting taking my sister out. Sure, you still want me to open my mouth?"

Donny shot Bowie a wink. "Yeah. She's worth a dick punch."

My chest tightened. It didn't matter that Freya loved me and wouldn't touch Donovan O'Shea with someone else's dick, he should speak more highly about her. "That's the wrong way to go about it for a start, asshole. Freya's a lady and deserves respect. You're not fit to lace her goddamned sneakers."

Callum chuckled. "Someone's jealous."

My throat went dry. "She's my best friend and I respect her."

Cal nodded slowly, mouth hitching. "Riiiight."

Bowie stood from his chair and nodded for me to do the same. "We gotta get back to the clubhouse."

Me, Callum, and Donny got to our feet.

"Appreciate ya, Bowie," Cal said, clapping him on the back. "Talk to Dagger, see what you can do."

Me and Bo made our way toward the door. "Catch you on the flip side," he called back as we left the bar, closing the door behind us with a thud and heading back to the SUV in silence.

"Well, that was fuckin' surreal," Bowie muttered, unlocking the car, and sliding into the driver's seat.

"Donovan O'Shea fucks everythin' that moves," I told him, climbing in next to him, fastening my seat belt, and watching as my brother did the same. "Freya's too good for him."

He started the car, checked his mirrors, and pulled away. "Ya think?"

"I know," I responded. "She won't go for him anyway."

Bowie lifted one shoulder in a shrug. "I dunno. She crushed on him when she was younger."

My body locked. "Huh?"

"Yeah." He chuckled, giving me some side-eye. "You weren't the only one she had hearts in her eyes for."

My head swiveled left. "Don't you fuckin' start too."

"Well, it's no surprise," Bowie scoffed. "And Cal was right, you did sound jealous back there."

"What if I am?" I asked, testing the water.

He glanced at me. "Then you better watch your back, 'cause Pop and half the club will cave your skull in. You'll need Freya the doctor in your life 'cause you'll probably be eating through a damned straw for the rest of it."

"What about you?" I inquired. "Would you give me your blessing?"

"Nope," he admitted. "Not 'cause I don't like ya, Colt. I'm as close to you as I am to Cash and Kit. I just don't want Freya with a biker. It'll hold her back."

I nodded because that I could agree with.

"When Freya meets her man and has her babies, she'll do anything for them," he went on. "I don't want her to have to. Plus, being with a Demon would tie her to Hambleton. I want her to be able to see places, even work abroad if she wants to."

My chest burned even hotter at his words. He was wrong because I wouldn't tie her to anywhere. I'd travel with her and see the world if it was what she wanted. However, Bowie didn't know that yet.

"Don't you want that for Layla too?" I asked.

Bowie shook his head. "Layla loves the simple life. As you know, things weren't good for her when we met. At least me and the club can protect her, Sunny, Willow and all the other babies I'm gonna plant inside her. She could hardly afford to eat when I met her, now, if she wants somethin', I'll give it to her."

I sat back contemplating what Bowie said and I got it. Being with a biker would hold Freya back, but I wouldn't be a biker for much longer, so it was immaterial. Though even a brother would be better than Donovan—scabby dick—O'Shea.

The whole encounter had made me think.

I had been an asshole to her, though it wasn't something I'd done intentionally. I didn't like change and I hated lying, so being back at the club while dealing with lots of shit had made me realize I'd actually needed a transition period to get my head around the changes, if nothing else.

The good thing about it was that Freya knew me so well, she'd get it.

I was lucky to have her, and knowing Donny was on the prowl, it was apparent I needed to lock her down. This had changed everything. No more screwing around, no more taking her for granted.

From here on in, it was me and Freya together. I needed to see which states she was applying to intern in and see what type of work I could do there. I could compromise and I knew Freya would too if it meant we could be together.

By the time we pulled back into the compound I'd worked everything out in my head.

Me and Freya would sort our bullshit, I'd make damn sure of it. She was everythin' to me and the thought of her not being by my side made my heart shrivel up. What the fuck had I been pulling away for? Jesus, sometimes I was an asshole, and I knew she deserved a better man than me, except I was determined to start being more supportive and put her before me, every time.

However, first I had to find my girl, apologize, and beg her to give me another chance.

Bowie clicked on his turn signal before pulling around to drive through the gates, which were already opening for us.

"Home sweet home," Bowie muttered, driving through them, and heading for a parking space just outside the main doors. "What you doin' today?"

"Watching the mayor's mansion and workin'." I told him, eyebrows furrowing when I saw the clubhouse doors fly open and Cara come stomping outside, followed by Cash.

"What the fuck's goin' on there?" Bowie murmured, stopping the engine, and nodding toward them.

"God knows," I replied, throwing my door open. "They're always arguing about somethin'."

"Not getting' involved," Bowie said, climbing out of the car and giving Cash a chin lift before walking past the couple toward the clubhouse.

Sliding out of the passenger seat, I closed the door behind me and headed the same way as Bowie. My stomach felt jittery and my fingers tremored slightly as I ran a hand through my hair.

As I approached Cara, she spun around to face me.

"What did you do to Freya?" she demanded in a whisper-shout.

My head reared back slightly. "What do you mean?"

Cash shook his head, his mouth tightening into a thin line. "She took off about a half hour ago. Said she's goin' away for a few days. We assumed you'd pissed her off again."

My steps faltered.

"You're an asshole," Cara snapped. "She was upset when she left so I know it's because of you." She shook her head. "Fucking biker shits. You're all fuckers."

"Hey!" Cash said, voice affronted.

Cara turned on him. "You're the fucking worst of them all, though this one comes a close second." She jerked her thumb at me. "One minute he's all loved up, then next she's running out of here like a bat out of hell, all upset. Jesus, Xan, we only just got her back."

Cash's eyes slid to me and he got up in my face, bumping my chest with his. "What the fuck did you do to my sister?"

I pushed him away from me. "I was an asshole, but I was just coming to apologize."

"Fix it!" he snarled. "Or I'll see ya in the fuckin' ring. I told ya, treat her right and then you go and piss her off. What the fuck's wrong with you?"

In that moment everything got to me. My love, fear, and guilt. Donovan, and how I had an overwhelming desire to take a baseball bat to his thick fucking head for even looking at my girl.

I bent over at the waist and let out a roar.

"At last, he gets it," Cash muttered, looking me up and down.

Almost blindly, I stood to my full height again. "How long ago did she leave?"

"Not long before you got here," Cara snapped accusingly.

Cursing under my breath, I turned on my heel and stalked to the garage, trying to keep my head and my mind focused despite the turmoil swirling through me. My gut felt tight, like it was cramping, and my chest ached from the painful pounding of my heart.

I couldn't think straight, the fact she'd left me screwed with my head. Freya wasn't a quitter; she stood her ground and fought her corner.

Going to the counter, I grabbed my helmet and put it on before unhooking my keys from the wall full of 'em and putting on some leather gloves. Then, I went straight to my brand-new customized British racing green, Harley Davidson Nightster and began to walk it to the doors.

If Freya Stone thought she was leaving me, she was about to get a big ole shock.

Chapter Twenty-Four

Freya

"Fucking asshole," I muttered under my breath as my car flew past the huge town sign telling me goodbye and to come back soon. I stuck my tongue out at it like a five-year-old. "Not fucking likely."

I blinked back the moisture welling in my eyes, trying to keep my anger high and my sorrow at bay, because I knew once I let them out, I'd cry a river, and I didn't have time to stop at the side of the road and wait for the tears to dissipate, there'd be too many.

Instead, I focused on the road and how the trees and fields on either side were bathed in silver from the grey clouds and snowy air. I counted down the seconds as the wheels ate up the asphalt and the miles. Eventually, my chest began to loosen, and the air slowly expelled from my lungs, leaving my insides barren but my mind full of a plethora of self-destructive thoughts.

I wished he could've loved me more than the club.

I wished he could've chosen me.

Why was I never enough?

Jutting my chin up, I shook my head slightly, trying to loosen the confidence-draining vulnerabilities that had plagued me since I was a little girl who needed her daddy so badly, but always found he was too busy to be there. It was the story of my life.

Freya never made the cut.

I'd done everything to try and elevate myself to their standards, done everything they'd asked and demanded of me, but nothing was ever good enough for them. It was time to stop trying to be everything to everyone and just be me. God only knew why I kept setting myself up for a mighty fall.

Fuck Colt, fuck Dad, and fuck the Speed Demons. They could all keep each other warm at night in their old age because I'd be long gone, living my best life, and doing me.

A tear tracked down my cheek.

"Shit!" I whacked the steering wheel with palm of my hand, letting out a cry of frustration just as the roar of a tailpipe filled the air somewhere behind me.

My eyes darted to the rearview to see a flash of dark, metallic green fill the road from way back. Colt's bike stuck out like a sore thumb because unlike all the others in the club, it was new, shiny, and woefully underused.

I let out a frustrated huff, pressing my foot down on the accelerator a little harder. The balance of my car destabilized slightly, the ice on the road making the car skid and threaten to fishtail. I gripped the steering wheel tightly, knuckles white as I drove into it, easily regaining control.

The sight of Colt's stupid shiny bike taunting me in the rearview made my blood boil. I knew he was coming for me, saw he was doing it at breakneck speed too, but I was determined not to make it easy for the Mr. Rich Biker, born with a silver spoon jammed between his entitled ass cheeks.

I gritted my teeth muttering to myself to keep my eyes on the road, forcing my gaze forward. The rearview mirror showed a blur of green metal, then Colt shot past me so fast I may as well have been standing still. His hand came out and he jerked his finger to the side of the road in a command to pull over as he took a fork off the road that led to a lay-by shielded behind the tree-lined route.

A curse left my throat. I applied gentle pressure to the brake and turned the car to follow his bike up the slippery slope.

There was no point ignoring the grumpy asshole and with the mood I was in, I was all too happy to air our shit in public, even if we were on a quiet country road. I maneuvered my car up to the lay-by, taking care not to skid again, until I slowly came to stop just behind his sexy-ass green bike.

By the time I turned my engine off, Colt had dismounted, put his bike on the kickstand and taken his helmet off. I could tell by the tension in his shoulders he was furious, but it wasn't until he turned to face me, and began to stomp toward the car that I realized he was hanging on by a thread.

He looked like an avenging angel. His light features and tanned healthy skin juxtaposed with the black jeans, leather jacket, scarf wound around his neck, and thick leather gloves he wore. He stalked toward me, a feral tiger eyeing his prey, and I couldn't stop the slight tremor scattering through my fingers.

His ocean-blues fell on my face, almost incensed with cold, hard fury. My hand reached for the door handle, but his rage-filled stare pinned me to the seat. A frisson of fear ran down my spine when I saw the curl of distaste on his lips as those beautiful blue orbs promised I was about to be very fucking sorry.

A tiny flicker of regret tightened my chest, but I was determined not to let him see how much he was putting me on edge. I jutted my chin up and cocked an eyebrow, holding his gaze like a brat. He was always so cool and in control and I wanted to shatter it. I wanted him to feel lost at sea without a life preserver, the same way I always did when it came to him.

My door flew open, and I heard him snarl.

A squeak escaped my throat as he hauled me out of the car one-handed and threw me over his shoulder like I weighed ten pounds.

"What are you doing?" I shrieked, pounding his back.

The sharp slap he gave my ass stung my skin to the point it took my breath away. The next thing I knew my bare butt hit the hood of the car and Colt's hand cuffed my throat. My eyes widened fearfully as he leaned down, got in my face, and bellowed, "Why you driving like that in the fucking ice, Freya? You almost skidded! And more to the point why you running away?"

I went to open my mouth and bite out some kind of smart comeback, but nothing came out.

His eyes swirled with hate, love, fear, and plain old fury, as he kicked my knees apart and with one tug, pulled me to the edge of the hood.

My pussy flooded.

I wore a little pleated plaid skirt with knee high boots, so when he shoved the hem up to my waist and looked down at my soaked, white cotton panties I had no doubt he could see the full force of the affect he had on me.

There was no rhyme or reason in the way my body reacted like it needed his touch to function every time he laid a hand on me. He brought me to life. My heart beat a little bit faster, and my blood ran a little more forcefully just from being in the same space as the man who could elicit such a visceral reaction with a single look.

I gulped, then moaned gently as his fingers pushed the cotton material aside and thrust hard inside me. "W—What are you d—doing?" I stammered.

"Showing you the way it's gonna go from now on," he rasped, anger still bleeding from his tone as he roughly fingered my unsuspecting pussy. "You don't run from me, ever. You stay and we talk our shit out."

My jaw set tightly. "You fucking ended it," I yelled. "You told me the timing was wrong!"

"Does it look like I'm ending it, Freya?" he grated out, thrusting another finger deep inside my cunt. "You fucking stay, always, because I need that from you. I need to know you're mine even when I don't act like you are." His breath looked like little puffs of cold air in the breeze as he punctuated each syllable. "I know it's fucked-up, baby, but you need to stay, because if you leave every time I freak out, we won't make it. I'm screwed in the head when it comes to you and me, but I'm gonna sort it."

Tears sprung to my eyes, and I felt my bottom lip wobble with the emotion I was trying to hide from him. "You always say this. It's not fair," I whispered against his lips.

"I know," he sucked on my bottom lip roughly, before releasing it with a soft pop. "I'll work it out, but you need to stay until I do, 'cause I'm not losing you, Freya. My heart won't beat without you giving it life."

The beauty woven through his words made me gasp along with the stinging chill biting into my bare flesh, raising goose bumps along my thighs.

The only warmth on my body was from Colt's strong hand still cuffed around my throat. The heat from the engine under the car hood was quickly fading to give way to the icy coldness in the air swirling around us. Roughly, he pushed me down and covered the length of my body with his. "You wanna fuck Donovan O'Shea, Princess?" he snarled against my cheek. "You wear this little skirt so he could flip it up and give you his cock?"

My heart almost stopped with shock and my mouth made an 'o' shape. "Umm—N—No?"

"Damned fuckin' straight," he growled. "This pussy belongs to me. Not him! Not anyone but fuckin' *me*."

The sound of a zipper floated on the air and my eyes widened in shock. "Not here," I whispered, voice panicked. "People can see..." My voice trailed off when I caught the animalistic glint in his eye.

Colt's lip curled as he looked down at me. "I'll fuck you where I want and how I want." He glanced at the road. "We're hidden by the trees, but if I wanted to take you out on that road and fuck you in front of the folks of Hambleton, I'd do it, and d'ya know why?"

I shook my head, too shocked and suddenly way too turned on to speak.

"'Cause you're mine and if I have to prove to every man in this town—including Donovan fucking O'Shea—what that means, I'll fuck you all day long and sell 'em tickets to the greatest show on Earth." Colt roughly spread my legs until they lay flat on either side of me, getting me opened as wide as he could before maneuvering between my thighs and yanking my panties to one side.

Anticipation thrummed through my veins and our eyes locked.

"Let this be a lesson in ownership," he said flatly, before his hips lunged forward and he drove his cock into me with one hard thrust.

My back arched off the hood and I cried my pleasure into the cold ether.

Colt threw his head back and yelled. "Fuckin' goddamn." His hips bucked roughly into me, and my pussy clenched involuntarily around his beautiful hard cock as he fucked his frustration out of him and into me.

"This is *my* cunt," he gritted through clenched teeth, ramming his cock into me so roughly that I felt the soft skin of my core swell from the force of it. "I'll video myself painting it with my cum and send it to that O'Shea fuck. Asshole needs to understand who owns this shit."

I moaned at the mere thought.

Even though I knew I should have been disgusted by his words, I loved the possession in them, the obvious fury he felt toward another man trying to take me away. God help me, I always thought I was a modern, independent woman, but this man reduced me to my baser instincts.

He turned me inside out and I loved it.

"Fucker think he can touch what's mine," Colt rasped, grinding his cock savagely into me. "I'll break every finger he lays on you. This pretty cunt's mine, you saved it for me. I'll kill him if he tries."

I whimpered, my back writhing on the hood like a snake as I took the pounding from his cock. I'd never felt so packed full before and my pussy wept at the filthiness of his words and the images they conjured in my mind.

A sound rumbled from the road.

My head turned toward a vehicle approaching in the distance and my pussy gushed a little more moisture over his hard length.

Colt cursed. "That's it. Soak my cock," he snarled, fucking me so hard my body moved up the hood. "Show me who owns you, Princess."

I knew we were covered by the trees, but I also knew if someone peered closely enough through their window, they'd see Colt fucking me like an animal. My body seemed to love the idea because despite the biting cold, my skin burned so hot it itched.

He forcibly grabbed my jaw and tugged my face back toward him. "Eyes on me," he ordered roughly.

"Stay with me and take what I fuckin' give you." His hands came to my hips, his strong fingers digging into my skin, enabling him to hold me down and brutally drive into me. "Nobody but me is ever getting into this perfect little cunt, Freya, so you better start liking it 'cause I'm gonna fuck you so hard, and so often, I'll break you."

"I do like it," I cried, meeting his hard thrusts even though my movement was limited. "I love it." I clenched my walls around him, trying to show how much I adored him inside me.

"Fuck yeah. I know you love it." He grabbed my legs again and pulled them together as he bent them at the knees, pushing them up to my chest while his cock thrust into me over and over. The angle made me so tight it almost hurt to take him so deep and rough. The clenching sensation in my core went into overdrive, almost like I was trying to pull his cock deep inside me where he belonged. My pussy felt so heated and so savagely used that it throbbed around his length.

I moaned again, the pleasure intensifying as his thrusts became harder, deeper, and slowly, more erratic. "Love this pussy, Freya. It's mine and I'm gonna train it so it doesn't work for anyone but me. See how it grips my cock like God created it for me to use as I see fit?"

My eyes rolled into the back of his head and my thighs began to shake with my incoming climax. Nobody had ever talked so dirty to me before. I never realized how deliciously erotic it could be.

"Don't stop, please don't stop," I begged, my ass bouncing on the hood as he held my knees up and pushed them further into my chest, snarling every time he ground into me.

"Fuck, gonna come. Get ready, you're gonna take it harder." Suddenly, he released my legs, tipped them all the way back and rutted into me, rooting as deep as humanly possible while simultaneously pressing down hard on my clit with his thumb. "Come on my cock. Now!"

With a scream, I went off like a firework, literally, because lights flashed behind my eyes. My head writhed from side to side as every nerve ending set alight with my orgasm. I whimpered with pleasure as my body arched from the hood until I felt like I was levitating.

Colt's loud grunt, and the swelling of his cock indicated he was there and his cum warmed my insides as he bathed my core with his seed. "Fuck. Fuck. Fuck," he chanted, throwing his head back as his orgasm hit him. His face contorted with pleasure as he released everything he had inside me. "My fuckin' woman," he gritted out, giving my ass a light swat as he emptied himself into me. "Mine!"

Colt's hips continued pumping until eventually they began to circle and slow. His hard grunts turned into a long, satisfied hum and he opened his languid eyes to meet mine and grinned wide.

It was funny how I lay flat on my back on the cold, hard metal hood of my car with my pussy exposed to the icy cold elements, but deep down, I'd never felt warmer in my life.

My hand reached up for his cheek. I still ached for him, still yearned for him to be inside me even after what we'd just done. I had so much fulfillment, so much contentment in my life except when it came to Colt. Sure, he'd filled me with love, but I'd always wanted more.

Years of being deprived of him had made me so hungry that I knew I could never be sated.

Colt leaned down and covered my body with his from chest to hip, caught my lips with his and murmured. "Consider us back together, Freya."

Laughter bubbled up my throat. "You're fucking crazy!" I yelled happily.

"Only for you, baby." He leaned down and kissed me gently again. "Only ever for you." His eyes darted between mine. "You okay? Did I go too hard?"

My eyes held his. "I never imagined it could be like that."

He nuzzled his nose with mine. "You ain't seen nothin' yet, my innocent little sexpot." He pulled up slightly to look into my eyes. "Your car was sliding over the road. Please come home. Don't drive to Denver until the ice clears." He waggled his eyebrows. "I'll let you watch while I warn O'Shea off ya for good, fuck with his phone, and wreck his credit history."

"You're so romantic," I teased gently. "Caveman."

"You drive me fucking crazy," he told me, eyes softening. "Nothing affects me, ever, but you send me outta my goddamned mind. Had a goddamned meet with the O'Shea's; Donovan asked Bowie to put a word in with your dad so he could take you out. It sent me loco."

My mouth dropped open. "Oh my God."

His lips contorted angrily. "Is he who you want?"

Acid burned my stomach at the notion of anyone touching my skin but Colt. "No," I said vehemently. "How could I want anything but this?" I pressed my hand against his chest.

"Tell me you're mine," he whispered against my lips.

I nodded, unable to speak through the emotion clogging my throat.

"Say the words, Freya. I need the words."

"I'm yours," I said huskily.

His hand framed my face. "And I'm yours."

After a beat, he gently moved away, pulling out of me, as he did so. "Exploded harder than a fuckin' asteroid hitting Earth, baby." His hands reached for my panties, and he gently pulled them down my legs and off. "These sexy little fuckers are hot," He muttered, using the panties to clean our mixed cum from my thighs and pussy in soft sweeps, before balling them in his hands and pocketing them with a smirk.

"Hey!" I griped. "All the sexy underwear I own, and you take that plain white pair."

He reached out a hand, pulling me up and settling me back on my feet. "Gonna keep 'em to jerk off with when I can't get a hold'a you, 'cause after that scene I'm feelin' as horny as a fourteen-year-old boy. That shit's in my spank bank now." He tagged my neck and pulled me into his body. "Love you, Freya. I know I'm wobbling and I'm sorry, but you gotta stick by my side and let me work through it. I know I'm bein' an asshole, but the guilt got on top of me."

I peered up into his eyes. "You're a very complicated man, Colter Van Der Cleeve."

He framed my face with his hands and kissed me gently. "Thank God you're so uncomplicatedly perfect for me. We fit, and it makes us stronger together. I'm sorry I keep losing sight of that."

"I know it's hard for us at the moment," I murmured, looking into the eyes I loved so much. "It won't be for much longer. I'm waiting to hear about my internships. We'll know more soon."

He slid his hands around my back and locked them together. "I wanna tell the club. I've been workin' on somethin' that's startin' to come to fruition. I feel better about us leavin' now."

My heart bloomed like a flower in spring. Finally, he said *us*. It was all I wanted. I understood we'd have to play a lot by ear, but we had to remain an us while we worked it out.

I reached up and cupped his cheek. "I'm so happy. I knew it was worrying you. I'll come see you later. I'm freezing and we need to get moving before the roads ice up completely. You're on your bike for God's sake."

He grimaced. "Gotcha."

"Let's go home." I smiled up at him reassuringly, committing the face I loved most to memory.

Colt led me to the driver's side and settled me in, bending down to kiss me one last time. "I'll follow you. High gear, low speed." Colt shook his head, looking at my old Toyota. "Bought you a graduation gift months ago. Should be here in the next couple'a weeks. I'll feel better when it is."

I blinked. "You got me a graduation gift months ago? But we weren't even—"

Colt cut me off, pressing one last quick kiss to my lips. "Loved ya then, love ya now. Simple as that."

Before I could respond, he was striding back to his motorcycle, leather jacket billowing in the breeze behind him. I stared after his retreating figure, open-mouthed and stunned into silence as I watched him swing his leg over his motorcycle. The engine roared to life beneath him, and he looked over his shoulder to send me a roguish wink before putting on his helmet.

Colt captivated me in ways that even a month ago, I'd never thought possible.

I couldn't escape him. The gold hue to his thick, luxurious hair. How his eyes crinkled at the corners when he laughed, and the way they darkened when he whispered sinful words into my skin. I was lost in lust and feelings so big that their invisible chains bound me to him soul deep.

Shaking my head, I smiled in wonderment as I put the car into drive. Trust Colt to throw me so completely and fantastically off-balance. He was an enigma I never wanted to solve because where was the fun in that?

With a squeal of my tires, I slowly inched forward, checking my mirrors before pulling out onto the road in the direction of Hambleton. Colt's tailpipes roared behind me, his single headlight illuminating the road like a comforting kind of companionship.

And even though the sky was grey and the air heavy with the onslaught of winter, I knew this was just the beginning for us, and I couldn't wait to get on with it.

Chapter Twenty-Five

Colt

"This place is the shit," I murmured, looking around the gallery apartment as my hand trailed languidly up and down the soft, supple skin of Freya's naked arm.

My girl sighed and burrowed deeper into my side. "It's perfect. Private. Nobody will find us here." Her fingers teased over the rough hair on my chest and moved lower, curling around me and a low groan rumbled in my throat. "Think I'm all fucked out, Freya."

She smirked and brought her hand back up to my ribs. "It's ok, old man. You've more than exceeded my expectations over the last ten hours."

Being with Freya felt like a new lease of life. Her humor, wit, and playfulness brought things out of me that had been barren for years, that was if they'd ever existed at all. She was fascinating, all-consuming. Even when she wasn't with me physically, she was still there in the back of my mind imprinting on me.

Since that day last week when I'd chased her down the country road everything had finally slotted together. I'd gone hard on her, rougher than ever before and she'd lapped it up, thrived on it even.

It showed me how even though she was younger than me, we still had a meeting of minds. It proved I'd underestimated her, and I knew I had to pull my head outta my ass if I wanted the future I'd dreamed of with her.

It also made me get my backside into gear with an idea I'd had a while back but had been procrastinating over. It would leave the club in a better position when I left, so, in the last week I'd been out and about in town, reappropriating certain equipment and databases which could help the Demons streamline the way they handled things with the Sinners.

But I'd keep that for Church later. In the here and now, I had my woman, naked, next to me and not much time left to appreciate it.

I gathered her close, inhaling her soft, warm skin, and reveling in the feel of her silky hair against my chest. "It's good we've got this, baby. Don't want everyone gettin' suspicious of how much time we spend together."

"I just want to be with you any way I can," she whispered.

My heart swelled with emotion. It was crazy how at thirty-six I was experiencing my first flush of love. It wasn't a thing though, I was happy I saved at least that for her, I mean, she'd saved a lot more for me. Thinking back, I realized Freya had always been my safe place, the one person who got me. She was my home, and the rest of the world could've burned for all I cared.

"Gotta go," I muttered.

"I know." she smiled sadly.

"Your gift will be here any day now." I grinned.

She laughed. "How you gonna explain it away to Dad?"

"I'll tell it like it is. I think the world of you and wanted to get you a graduation gift. They know money's not a concern for me. It's not like I haven't invested a lot more into the club before." Pulling away, I jackknifed to a sitting position and got out of bed.

"I never knew that," she mused.

I shrugged, leaning down to retrieve my jeans from the floor. "It's not a big deal." I slid the denim up my legs before fastening the buttons. "I want the club to have the best equipment, especially when it comes to security." Walking to the tiny bathroom, I grabbed the spare toothbrush Freya had brought for me and loaded it up.

Freya appeared at the doorway. "When are you telling Dad about everything you've been doing on the sly?"

I continued brushing for a few seconds, taking in her tousled hair, perfectly sized, pert breasts, and how the white lace of her panties accentuated the olive tone of her soft, smooth, fragrant skin. Turning back to the sink, I spat and rinsed. "Promise me when we live together, you'll only walk around the house like that. Only ever wanna see you wearing clothes when we go out."

She giggled. "What if we get visitors?"

"I'll send 'em away." Tagging her waist, I tugged her into me, loving how her hands automatically slid up my chest and around my neck. "Couple of months, baby and we can get this thing goin' for real. No hiding, no sneakin' around. Just you, me, work and eventually, babies."

She smiled sadly. "I'll miss the club."

My heart panged because I would too.

Kissing her softly, I pulled her back into the bedroom and grabbed my tee. "How long you gonna stay here?" I asked, slipping the soft cotton over my head.

"About an hour," she murmured. "I'll call Abi and go home. Hopefully, I can time it for when you're all in Church."

I nodded. "Good idea." Sitting on the bed, I pulled on my socks and boots, then grabbed my jacket and scarf, and headed for the door with a wink.

"See you later?" Freya called after me.

"Yeah," I assured her, craning my neck. "Love you."

"Love you too," she replied, her final words lingering sweetly in the air as I closed the door behind me.

I jogged down the iron stairs to my bike that I'd strategically parked, hidden away out of sight from the road. The bleak landscape no longer seemed so cold and dreary. Freya warmed me from the inside out. As long as I had her, I could make it through anything.

I swung my leg over the saddle and pulled on my helmet before starting her up and heading onto the main road outta town toward the clubhouse.

As much as I hated riding, especially in the cold temperatures, I was grateful for it then. I could hide a bike better than an SUV, especially one belonging to the club. To keep meeting Freya, I needed to be discreet to avoid awkward questions.

Not for the first time, I pondered how much I hated all the lies, though I'd settled down considerably since the week before when I'd chased Freya on my bike and fucked her on the side of the road.

The whole Donovan O'Shea thing and the threat of her leaving me had pulled me back to where I needed to be. I'd resigned myself to the belief that what we were doing wasn't wrong when there was so much love involved. How could it be bad when we were so beautiful together?

It didn't take long to ride onto the road leading to the clubhouse. The prospect must've seen me coming because the gates to the compound were already opening when I pulled up. The hinges of the heavy iron gates squealed, piercing the silence.

I gave Billy a nod as I rode past him.

He returned a half-smile, his face unshaven and lines of tiredness around his eyes. The poor guy was run ragged keeping this place secure day and night. But he was loyal, and that was what mattered most.

Parking close to the garage, I killed the engine and sat for a moment, staring at the clubhouse.

I couldn't believe I wouldn't be here much longer. It had been my home for so long, I couldn't imagine being so happy anywhere else. Still, I'd have Freya and that more than made up for it.

Dismounting, I put my kickstand on, squared my shoulders and headed toward the main entrance, smiling as the sound of a lone guitar played through the doors.

Pushing them open, I walked inside the bar to see Prez sat next to Kady who strummed the acoustic guitar like a pro. The place wasn't busy. Weekdays never were because all the brothers were out working in the construction company, or down at the bar we owned.

"Colt!" Kady cried. "You wanna learn the 'From the Vault Tracks' from 1989 Taylor's Version with me?"

"Later, pretty girl." I grinned. "Got work to do then I've got Church." My eyes slid to Dagger. "Right, Prez?"

He jerked a nod. "Waitin' for Kennedy to get back from her office. Kady wasn't well this mornin' so she got the day off school." He puffed his chest out. "I've been looking after her, haven't I, little Kady girl?"

The pretty blonde girl looked up at Prez with her big blue eyes and nodded earnestly. "You've been a good babysitter, Grandpa. You're so much fun and you know all about Taylor and Travis."

Prez nodded seriously. "That's right, Kady girl. That's 'cause your Gramps is down with the kids."

I brought a hand up to cover my smile.

Prez's gaze landed on me, and he cocked his head. "Where have you been?"

"Went out last night," I muttered.

"And you're just getting' in?" he questioned.

I shrugged, deciding the less I said, the better.

Prez leaned forward. "Gotta say, I'm happy you got rid of that Lucy. She's stuck up."

"Yeah," Kady agreed. "She's jealous."

My head reared back slightly as I took in the little girl. "Kady, how do you know when someone's jealous?" I asked, curiosity getting the better of me. Breaker had told me how Kady could feel people's emotions. I just put it down to her being sensitive, but maybe there was more to it.

She looked up from her guitar, her brow furrowing as she tried to find the right words. "It just feels icky." She scrunched up her little button nose. "Like there's a scratchy cat inside them."

I nodded thoughtfully, struck by the raw honesty of her answer.

It made sense that Kady had picked up on Lucy's personality—the envy had always been there, lurking under the surface, even before I fully acknowledged it myself. Lucy's jealousy toward the club, Freya, and my work had driven a wedge between us a long time ago and I couldn't help wondering why I'd let it go on for so long.

"Does it make you feel sick when people around you are jealous, Kady?" I asked, for the first time trying to gauge the impact it must've had on her.

"Sometimes," she admitted. "But Gramps says people just need to figure themselves out."

"Your gramps is a wise man, sweetheart," I said, looking over at Prez with genuine admiration. You could say what you wanted about Dagger, but he loved his family. I'd never known it with my own father, so it was a trait I admired.

"I'm the boss for a reason, right, little Kady girl?" Prez smiled down at his granddaughter who gazed back up at him with shining eyes and nodded her agreement.

The sudden creaking of the heavy doors drew everyone's attention to the main entrance. With a swagger, Atlas sauntered into the room. His eyes scanned the room, settling on Prez. "Need a word, boss."

Kady caught Atlas's pointed stare and must have sensed something heavy was going on. "I'll go and see Iris," she sang, scrambling down from her seat and heading toward the corridor to the kitchen.

As soon as Kady disappeared, Prez fixed his gaze on Atlas. "What's goin' on?"

Atlas's muscles visibly tensed. "Gotta problem, boss," he said in a strangled tone. "Me, Bowie and Reno were patrolling, and we ran into some Sinners heading outta town in a van."

My heart started to race as I watched Dagger's eyes narrow on the SAA.

The mere mention of the Burning Sinners was enough to make his jaw harden and his hands clench into fists. "Go on," Prez said through gritted teeth.

Atlas hesitated for a moment before continuing. "We got 'em to pull over and found a girl in the back. One of the assholes got away, but we managed to detain the other one. We've got him and the van outside."

A feeling of dread settled like a heavyweight in my stomach.

"Damn it," Dagger muttered under his breath, running a hand through his beard.

"The girl's no older than thirteen or fourteen," Atlas went on. "She says she's from Laramie. Those assholes snatched her yesterday on the way home from school."

"Where is she?" Prez demanded.

"Still in the van," Atlas replied.

Prez's forehead furrowed. "Where's the Sinner?"

Atlas grinned big. "Sweating like he's done ten rounds with Tyson. We bound his hands with zip ties, attached him to the back of the van with rope and made him run behind us."

Prez's eyebrows hit his hairline. "Didn't ya get seen?"

"Nope." Atlas's grin widened. "Went the long way around; kept to the back roads."

"Jesus." Prez scrubbed a hand down his face. "Every time we think we've put a dent in their operation something like this happens. We need to go on the offense." His voice sounded strained, betraying his growing frustration.

Atlas's grin stretched from ear to ear. "Fuck yeah."

"Where are Bowie and Reno?" Prez asked.

"Keepin' watch on the van," the SAA replied, his anger evident in the tight set of his jaw. "Not leavin' the kid out there alone."

"Good call," Prez mused. "Get the Sinner down in to the Cell. We'll question him tonight."

Atlas jerked a nod before sauntering to the door, opening it, and whistling shrilly through his teeth. Seconds later Bowie appeared dragging a scruffy looking dude with his hands tied, wearing a Sinners' cut into the bar. "Cell?" he asked, grinning evilly.

Atlas rubbed his hands together gleefully. "Yip. Already made a date with him for tonight. Dinner and wine. The pervert won't be able to speak by the time I've finished with him."

"Especially when I cut his tongue out," Prez snarled. "We've got one hell of a night planned."

The Sinner's eyes went wide as saucers. He visibly gulped as Bowie dragged him toward the stairs leading down to the basement to the Cell, the place where we kept captives, and which also doubled up as a panic room when we needed to get the women and kids safe.

Prez waited for Bowie and the prisoner to disappear before turning to Atlas. "How's the girl?"

The SAA winced slightly. "Scared but okay. She's a feisty one."

Dagger rubbed his beard contemplatively. "Good, she'll need some'a that spunk when it sinks in how close she came to bein' trafficked. We'll get Iris to sort her, see what information she can get from her and then we'll arrange to get her home again."

"What about the cops?" I asked.

"We'll get Iris to have a chat with her, tell her how important it is that we're not brought into it," Prez muttered thoughtfully, raising his eyes to meet mine. "Call the boys in, tell 'em I'm calling Church early. We gotta get this shit sorted once and for all. Sick of waitin' around for the Sinners to make a move."

Atlas gave Prez a one finger salute and made his way toward the kitchen.

"I'll go call the boys in now," I said, turning toward the corridor leading to my office.

"Tell 'em I want 'em here in ten," Prez ordered, standing as he slammed his fist down on the bar. "We're gonna destabilize those motherfuckers before they get the chance to bring it to us."

Fifteen minutes later, I watched as Abe, Cash, and Kit filed into Church and took their seats.

"Iris okay out there with the kid?" Dagger asked through gritted teeth.

Abe nodded. "Yeah. She's made the girl more food than she'll probably be able to eat. Poor kid's scared witless, but she seems to be responding to Iris well enough. They roughed her up a bit when they took her—she's got some gnarly bruises on her back—but she's generally okay."

"It's good we're getting the victims before they get really hurt," Bowie muttered.

"Agreed," Cash said with a nod. "But it makes me worry more for the ones we're not savin'."

"Cash is right," I interjected. "For every one person we save they're probably getting three more through, maybe even more."

"No more!" Prez growled. "I've fuckin' had it with those bastards thinkin' they can continue their business through our town." He turned to Atlas. "Have you got anything out of him yet?"

Atlas smirked. "Nope. I gave him a couple of love taps to see how he took 'em. I reckon he'll crack within minutes. Problem with the Sinners is that they'll take any old idiot in with the lure of money, but these people aren't smart or competent. They're in it for the scratch, which makes 'em disloyal to the club."

Prez stroked his beard thoughtfully. "Wanna know where they're hangin' out these days. All biker clubs have a bar they frequent. We're gonna get it out of the fucker in the Cell and Breaker's gonna blow it sky high, taking every Sinner in there with it."

Atlas rubbed his hands together gleefully. "What about the others?"

"Colt's been compiling a list of properties owned by their club and affiliates. Breaker's gonna rig up bomb after bomb and give you all a lesson in placing and setting them off, then we do a coordinated attack." His eyes narrowed on the SAA. "I want an officer on every property with at least two additional men. We're gonna have to ask the boys for help on this one."

"Easy," Atlas replied. "Arrow, Reno, Shotgun, Fender. Reckon Billy would be an asset too."

"Got another mission Billy may be good at," Prez muttered.

Atlas's eyes lit up.

"We're gonna pick off Sinners in the street, herd 'em up like the animals they are, and take 'em out. We need good shooters." His stare went between me and Cash. "You two can be in charge of that side of the operation. You're two of our best shooters."

Breaker cleared his throat indignantly.

"We need you in charge of explosives, Son," Prez declared. "You can't do it all. Dunno how many times I gotta tell ya, we're a team. No man in this club's an island. Your strength is explosives, and we'll need that if we're gonna take as many Sinners out as we can."

"We need to think about retaliation too," Abe said, leaning forward to address Prez. "We'll need the women and kids on a tight leash. And put extra men on the gate."

Prez nodded. "Draw up a new roster, brother." He looked around the room. "What do you think about callin' the families back in for lockdown? Want the women and kids safe."

I looked around at all the men's faces, trying to gauge their moods. Telling 'em about Freya's gift wasn't high on my list of priorities but now was as good a time as any.

I cleared my throat. "Bought Freya a graduation gift, but I may have gone a bit crazy."

Silence fell over the room and every eye slid to me.

"What sort of graduation gift?" Cash asked, curiosity threading his tone.

I winced. "A car."

Prez's eyes narrowed on me. "Are graduation gifts even a thing?"

"Pop," Bowie said thickly. "Your only daughter's just graduated med school. Why would you not buy her a gift? She's worked her ass off for years."

Prez held his hands up defensively. "Calm the fuck down, Son. I've bought her a plot of land down by the creek to build her house on." He puffed his chest out proudly. "Who else can say they've bought her a house?"

Cash's stare focused on me, and he smirked. "So, tell us, Colt. What car did you buy my beautiful and talented sister? Was it a nice Tesla, maybe a Range?"

Breaker lifted an expectant eyebrow, grinning at me.

Bastards.

Pulling my shoulders back, I sat up straight, opened my mouth and just said it. "Got her a Mercedes G-Class."

Atlas whistled through his teeth.

Bowie sat up a little straighter.

Breaker's lips twitched.

Cash barked a laugh.

"That's one hell of a fuckin' car, Colt." Abe said disbelievingly. "What the fuck made you drop all those G's on a car for Freya?"

I shrugged. "She's always wanted one. Thought she deserved a little treat."

Cash barked another laugh.

Fucker.

"A little treat?" Bowie said, eyebrow cocked. "How much are they?"

A waved a nonchalant hand. "I can afford it. A couple'a hundred G's won't make a dent in what I've got."

Prez's lips tightened. "I don't know what the fuck you boys are talkin' about. If it ain't a motorcycle, it's not on my radar."

"Speakin' of which," Atlas interjected. "We were out on the bikes today and I could feel the ice on the roads. First snow's on its way. Maybe we should start picking the Sinners off sooner rather than later. It'll be easier on bikes than in SUVs."

"It's Kennedy's party tomorrow night," Breaker said thoughtfully. "We can send patrols out starting Sunday. We'll need Saturday to call a full member Church and fill the boys in."

Atlas leaned forward. "We'll have to formulate a plan. Bikes are more maneuverable but we're gonna need vans for the bodies."

"Patrols of three," Prez ordered. "Two on bikes. One driving a van."

"Or we could do three out on their bikes, then send vans in afterward to clean-up," Cash suggested.

"What do you all think?" Dagger asked the room before turning to Abe. "Come on, voice of reason, out with it."

"Prefer Cash's idea," Abe admitted. "Safety in numbers."

"Me too," Bowie added.

"Works for me," Atlas chimed in.

Breaker sat forward, elbows to table. "I'll be blowing shit up wherever I can, so you do you, boo."

Dagger rolled his eyes. "Looks like I'm outvoted."

"The son surpasses the father," Abe crowed. "He's been doin' that a lot lately."

Prez shrugged one shoulder. "Ain't complainin'. Bandit always said, each President should be better than the last."

"Didn't take much to surpass Bandit, Dagger. You lucked out there." Abe smirked.

Chuckles went around the room.

My thoughts raced as I considered the implications of our decision. It wasn't just about pulling off another job; it was about protecting our family and our town. If we failed, everything we worked so hard to build would come crashing down.

Not for the first time, I wished I'd be around. I felt like a rat deserting a sinking ship, but on the other hand, I could help from behind the scenes too.

Atlas scratched his beard. "So back to the little piggy in the Cell. I bagsy first dibs."

"Go for it," Prez said indulgently. "But once you get what we need, get rid of him. Don't want you playing with your food today. We gotta party to get ready for and a girl to return to her home."

"Me and Iris will sort that," Abe told Dagger. "You guys deal with the asshole. I'm gettin' too old for torture, and my Iris needs to put her feet up more, not stand over a sink scrubbin' blood outta my clothes."

"Gotta say," Prez mused. "I'm startin' to feel the same way. It all seems like a lotta effort to me these days. Love the club and love the businesses, but the tough stuff is losin' its appeal more and more. Maybe it's time we took that step back we were talkin' about, Abe."

My eyebrows snapped together. "Huh?"

Cash, Breaker, and Bowie exchanged looks.

Atlas folded his arms across his chest and cocked his head.

"Dunno why you're all lookin' so shocked," Abe muttered. "Me and Prez have been talkin' about lettin' you idiots take more on for a while now. Cash is comin' out with some good strategies which elevate the shit we do, and he's got good men around him in you officers. We were thinkin' that maybe we could concentrate on the business side of things for a while and let you deal with the biker shit."

Prez nodded his agreement. "When all this trafficking business is over, I was thinkin' of goin' on a road trip. Take a year out and visit all the states. You all know it's somethin' I've wanted to do for a long time. I'm in my fifties now and yeah, I keep myself in good shape, but I don't wanna be too old to enjoy it. Dunno if you've noticed but most decisions in the last year have been decided by one of you, not me, and not Abe."

I stared at Prez as stunned silence settled over the room.

He wanted to step down? Retire? Jesus, I couldn't get my head around it, the mere thought made my brain explode. Prez's dad founded the club and kept goin' well into his sixties. Dagger was in his mid-fifties and had plenty of life left in him. The Speed Demons would still be one-percenters, dealing in drugs, women and guns without our Prez, which was something I would have never been involved with. He made the club successful, so him not being around seemed wrong somehow.

But then, I'd been here twelve years and I needed something else, so was it so wrong of Dagger to live his last years doing what he wanted too? He'd sacrificed so much for the club. His peace of mind, his friendships, hell, even his kids and marriage to a point.

Maybe it was time for Prez to take something back for himself.

And maybe I could do something to help him achieve that.

I sat forward in my seat to address the table. "I've been workin' on somethin' for about six months that'll help you trace vehicles."

"What the fuck?" Prez breathed.

I grinned. "It's like a license plate recognition program that'll ping whenever a particular vehicle heads into Hambleton. It'll get clocked on the road leading in, then different cameras will track them to where they're goin'. It's like a network that communicates with itself, then back to us. Governments all over the world have 'em. I adapted the same concept for us. No vehicle, bike or truck will get into, or around Hambleton, without us knowing its every move. It'll help you pick the fuckers off. There won't be any waitin' around or patrolling for Sinners. As soon as we get a ping, our team can mobilize. No wasting time hunting or missing somethin' 'cause we're hunting in the wrong part of town."

Dagger leaned back in his chair, his stare never leaving my face. "What made ya set that up?"

"It came to me back in the summer when the Sinners attacked the clubhouse," I relayed. "When Cara ran in, warning us, I thought how lucky we were that she got to us in time. Then I got to thinking about vehicle recognition and started to build my own program. All the license plates of the Sinners' vehicles are in the file. Even went into Law Enforcement and DMV records with names and addresses to find personal vehicles used by their families. All the cameras we set up feed license numbers back here. Anything in the system will ping from the relevant camera which I can tap into and scan, then send a patrol straight out to the relevant area. They won't get away with shit."

A brief silence fell over the room until Atlas shifted in his seat. "Are you tellin' me that the second a Sinner drives into town, we'll know what, where, and who?"

"Basically," I confirmed.

Atlas grinned, nodding his head at me almost proudly.

"You boys know what the best thing about bein' Prez is?" Dagger asked, voice husky with emotion.

We all looked at him enquiringly.

"This," he stated. "The growth and evolution of not just the club, but you boys too. And the fuckin' brotherhood we stand for." Prez sat forward again, his stare going from one face to the next, taking everyone in. "We've got boys who're takin' us to the next level, and it makes me and Abe proud to see how far you've all come." His golden eyes, just like Freya's, rested on me. "Good fuckin' job, Colt. It's still sinkin' in how much you've just put us forward, and it's appreciated down to my bones."

My throat thickened with emotion.

"So!" Prez waggled his eyebrows. "Tonight, we get busy down the Cell. Tomorrow, we party, after we've held a full-member Church, and Sunday we start picking off any Sinners who think they can sneak in." He rubbed his hands together. "Sounds like a good fuckin' time to me. Any other business?"

Silence.

He picked up the gavel and smashed it into the sound block. "Have fun boys."

Chairs scraped as the brothers rose to their feet.

"Who's up for a couple'a hours down the Cell?" Atlas boomed as he headed for the door.

"Me!" Bowie said, following him keenly.

"Yep," Cash replied, striding to keep up.

"Gotta pick Kennedy up from work," Breaker told us, holding the door for Cash.

"I've got shit to do," I muttered, heading after the boys. Turning, I caught Prez's eye, my gut warming at the look of pride on his face, and something hit me.

Leaving was something I had to do for me and Freya if we were ever gonna have a chance, but at least I'd achieve what I'd set out to do.

Leave them in a better position.

Chapter Twenty-Six

Freya

The clubhouse looked amazing.

Kit and the men had outdone themselves in transforming it into a nightclub of sorts. I mean it was still the clubhouse albeit cleaned up nicely, but the low lights and makeshift wooden dance floor gave it a sleek vibe that impressed the hell out of me.

I'd just gotten back from Giovanni's where the family had a celebratory dinner for Kennedy's birthday. Kit had pulled me aside and asked me if I'd come back early to make sure everything was ready for the big reveal. I'd jumped at the chance, mainly because I wanted to help, but also because I thought I could get a few minutes private time in with Colt before everybody came back.

My stomach leaped as I approached the main doors. The sounds of low music, chatter and laughter already wafting through to the parking lot. Smiling excitedly, I pushed the doors open and was immediately greeted by a familiar face.

He did a double take when he saw me. "Freya!" he yelled, holding his arms out for me. "Look at you."

"Iceman!" I squealed. "What are you doing here? Thought you'd defected to Virginia." I ran toward him and jumped, making him go on the back foot as he caught me in his arms.

"Jesus, girl," he muttered into my hair. "Surprised Prez let you out the door in that dress." He placed me gently back on my feet, looking me up and down.

I smoothed down my short, black leather strapless dress and smiled. "Not even he would dare tell me what to wear." I looked around him to see a handsome, tall, stocky guy. "Hey. I'm Freya Stone."

He looked at Ice. "She the princess?"

"Yeah, Pyro. Off-limits," Ice confirmed.

I rolled by eyes before looking around and noticing a gaggle of women at the bar who I'd never met before. I nodded toward them. "Are they Kennedy's girls?"

"Apparently so," he said, noting how they were laughing and having a good time. "All of 'em ex-strippers and from what I've been told, at the time, the best in the business. Wait until you meet their old boss, Marcus." Ice chuckled. "He's a fuckin' trip."

I looked up at Iceman. "As much of a trip as you?"

He barked a laugh. "Fuckin' doubtful."

Ice was a good-looking guy. Tall, fair, and muscular. His black jeans and tee showed off his nice, large biceps, decorated with cool tribal tattoos, as well as the dips and contours of his large pecs and six-pack, which were much more prominent than before.

Out of all the club members, Ice was the one I was closest to—apart from Colt.

I'd always gotten along well with him. He acted out but did it on purpose half the time because he was bored. He was an extremely intelligent man—he flew jets in the Navy which was a highly sought after profession—and which only went to the smartest and most resilient men and women.

"Have you been working out?" I asked, eying him approvingly.

He lifted his tee to show me the sculpted ridges of his stomach, making me almost swoon. "Yeah, baby," he muttered. "One good thing about the new clubhouse is the new gym Hendrix had installed. I spend a lotta time there."

"The new clubhouse is a hotel, right?"

Ice jerked a nod. "It's fuckin' gorgeous. Built in the nineteen-twenties so it's all art deco. Eighty rooms, a huge basement and land for miles so we can build on later, if we want. The place belonged to Hendrix's dad, and it got too much for him to manage so he signed it over and the rest is history."

"And how's the chapter doing?" I asked. "Someone said Drix had a few teething problems."

Ice's face darkened. "Yeah. Hendrix's Veep decided he could do better startin' his own club. It took its toll on Prez. Still is if I'm honest."

My lips pursed. Anna was my friend, and I was aware of how badly he'd treated her over the last six months. "It's shitty being betrayed by someone you trust, right?"

Ice's lips twitched. "He went to see Anna the minute we rolled into town. She told him to eat shit and die. First thing he did when he got back to the clubhouse was reach for the whisky bottle and pull Candy into a room. He misses her. Knows he fucked-up."

"He left it too late," I explained. "And it didn't help that he ghosted her and left town without a word. He humiliated and hurt her."

"Yeah." He winced. "Told him months ago to contact her, but all the shit was goin' on in Virginia, and he was caught up. Told me he'd leave it until he could take the time to dedicate to her. Personally, I think he knew it wouldn't go down well so he buried his head in the sand."

"And ended up leaving it too long?" I murmured thoughtfully.

Ice shrugged.

"There're not many women like Anna out there. Smart, sweet, good business head, and beautiful," I stated.

"I'm thinkin' Drix knows that seeing as he's actin' the fool now. He had more feelin's for her than he realized at first and lost her through his own actions. Now he needs to chalk it down to experience and move on."

"Agreed." I studied Ice again and shook my head, smiling. "I really miss you, Ice."

He ruffled my hair like I was a kid. "Miss you too, Princess. Miss everythin'."

"Can't you come back?" I asked hopefully.

"Nah. Too late," he replied. "Breaker's taken over my role here, and anyway, Drix needs me. Not gonna abandon my brother when he needs my backup the most."

I patted his arm. "You're a good man."

Ice smirked. "Don't tell anyone." His eyes lifted to look at something over my shoulder and dropped back to my face. "Freya. Why the fuck has Donovan O'Shea been looking at me for the past five minutes like he wants to rip my head off and shit down my neck?"

I closed my eyes. "Shit."

"He's headin' this way," Ice muttered. "Want me to get rid?"

I sighed frustratedly. "He keeps asking me out, but he's not really my type."

Iceman grinned. "I think you're the only woman who ever existed to say Donny O'Shea isn't their type. But it's all good. I'll stay with ya and give him some stink eye. We'll sort it." He took my hand, pulled me to his side, and slid an arm around my shoulders, watching as the other man approached.

Donovan didn't look very happy. His stare fell on Ice's arm around me and narrowed.

My heart gave a jerk.

I didn't like the notion of hurting Donny, but I had turned him down when he'd asked me out. Dad had refused him too, so I didn't know why he was acting possessive all of a sudden. It wasn't like we were a couple. We hadn't even been out.

"Evening," Donny said as he swaggered toward us. "Could I have a word with Freya?"

Ice looked at me, then back at Donovan and his arm tightened around me. "Go ahead."

Donny's face paled slightly when he realized Ice wasn't going anywhere, but to give him his due, he pulled his shoulders back and went for it. "Wondered if you've changed your mind about dinner?"

"I told you I'm already seeing someone. I'm really flattered that you asked, but I'm not the type of woman to string two men along at once."

Donovan's lips twitched. "I know, Freya. It's why I asked in the first place. Thing is, I'm not convinced you are seein' someone. I think you know my reputation and you're runnin' scared, and I get it, I do. But I want you to know the other women knew the score, I was always honest with 'em and told 'em I didn't want anythin' serious."

I placed a gentle hand on Donovan's arm. "I really am seeing someone. I promise."

Donovan's brow furrowed, his cocky grin fading. "Oh." His shoulders slumped in defeat, and he stepped back, shoving his hands deep into his pockets as he cleared his throat.

Ice looked between us, grinning.

An awkward silence fell over us. I dropped my gaze, smoothing the leather of my dress down self-consciously.

"Sorry," I offered, throat thick with the need to escape from the awkward situation. "Well, I better go get ready before the party starts."

Donny nodded absentmindedly, his eyes already scanning the crowd behind me for his next conquest.

I stifled the relieved sigh rising through my throat. Crisis averted, now I just had to get to Colt before anyone else waylaid me.

A sudden chime sounded from my purse.

It was a notification from Colt. I'd set him to a certain ringtone so I could recognize it was him whenever he called or messaged.

I looked up at Ice. "I need to go to my room and freshen up before the party gets going."

His arm slid away from my shoulders, and he clapped Donovan on the back. "Wanna get a beer with me, bro?"

Donny shot me one last lingering look before giving Iceman a chin lift. "Sure, man."

Turning for the corridor, I lowered my eyes so as not to catch anyone's gaze and have to stop and talk. I was desperate to see Colt before everyone else got here but I also had to be careful. I didn't want to raise suspicion.

Somehow, I managed to get to the corridor without being stopped. With my heart racing inside my chest, I strode to my room and let myself in.

Clicking on the light, I looked around the empty space and breathed a sigh of relief before pulling my cell phone from my purse and reading the message Colt sent me.

Colt: I see you. Get the fuck away from that asshole.

I smirked because, let's face it, it didn't hurt Colt to see other men interested in me. I'd put up with that shit for years. Now the boot was on the other foot he could feel a smidgen of what I'd had to witness.

Plus, it made him show me who I belonged to, and I loved it when he got all growly.

I was putting my phone away when the door burst open and Colt stood there, eyes blazing at me.

My heart leaped as he strode across the room in two quick steps and grasped the back of my neck, pulling me close by my nape. His calloused fingers tightened on my skin, igniting sparks. I inhaled his familiar scent of leather and Creed, and my pulse quickened. It was crazy how even after all the years I'd known him, his presence still overwhelmed my senses.

I tilted my chin up, parting my lips in invitation but instead of kissing me, he leaned down and grated out, "I was in my office watching you on the cameras. All I fuckin' do is watch you on those things. Can't tear my goddamned eyes away from you."

"I didn't encourage him," I breathed.

"You encourage him by existing, baby. You only need to look at a man and he's under your spell. I should know, you've bewitched me for years."

"Good," I whispered. "Because you're the only one I want."

He nuzzled my nose with his. "I love you more than anything. I'd lay down my life for you, Freya." His head descended and he caught my mouth with his.

Every nerve ending tingled, and blood began to rush through my veins. It was always like this with us. Whenever Colt touched me, he set me alight. I burned for him.

"You're mine," he said softly. "Nobody else can have you. If I could lock you up to stop men even looking at you, I would."

Before I could respond he crushed his lips to mine again.

I melted into him, my hands tangling in his hair to pull him closer.

Colt groaned, the sound vibrating in his chest, and he walked me backward until I hit the wall behind me. He braced his hands on either side of my head, caging me in. The hard length of his cock pressed against my belly, and I rocked my hips involuntarily in an attempt to soothe the ache between my legs.

One hand slid down to grip my ass so he could grind me against him. "Tell me you're mine," he demanded, kissing down my jaw. "I need the words."

"I'm yours," I said with a moan. "Always."

"Damned straight," he muttered, circling his cock so it hit my sweet spot. "I love you more than anythin', Freya." He pulled back slightly and grinned. "We gotta get outside."

"Oh my God," I whined. "You've gotten me all worked up."

Colt chuckled. "I'll make it up to you." He raised a hand and cupped my chin. "You go out first, I'll follow a few minutes after—"

I jumped slightly as a loud rap sounded from the door. "Freya!" Atlas boomed. "Ya seen Colt?"

Colt's body locked.

My stomach plummeted and my eyes bugged out. "Er—Um—No?"

"You decent?" the SAA called out. "Open the door."

Colt paled and he pointed to the bathroom before turning on his heel and disappearing.

I waited for the bathroom door to click closed before walking to the door to my room and opening it. "Hey!" I said, smiling at Atlas who had his arms crossed over his chest. "You okay?"

One eyebrow lifted. "Why you in here? Thought you'd be out there lettin' your hair down."

"I was just dropping my purse off and putting some lippie on," I lied. "Are you all back now?"

"Yip," he stated, nodding up the corridor. "Best you get out there. You're missin' all the fun." His eyes flicked up and over my shoulder, studying the room behind me. "You alone?"

My brow furrowed. "Yeah. Why?"

"Just feel like there's someone in there," he muttered before shrugging. "But obviously my spidey senses are in overdrive. Must be all the strangers in the bar." His eyes met mine and he grinned. "Come on. I'll walk you up."

Resigned to the fact I'd have to go with him, I went to walk out of the room.

"Aren't you forgettin' somethin'?" he asked knowingly.

I cocked my head. "What?"

"Lock your door," he ordered gently. "Place is full'a people we don't know well. Can't be too careful."

I swept a hand down my outfit. "I'm not taking a purse out. Where would I put my key?"

"Behind the bar," Atlas suggested.

With a sigh, I went back into my room and grabbed my keys before walking out again and locking my door. I bit my lip. I'd have to sneak back and let Colt out as soon as I could.

"Happy now?" I asked the SAA as he held his arm out for me to take.

"Happier," Atlas replied in his deep, rumbling voice. His large hand engulfed mine as he tucked it into the crook of his arm.

We walked together up the corridor, the pulsing beat of dance music getting louder as we neared. My steps faltered as we walked into the bar, and I looked around. The heavy bass pounded through my chest like a second heartbeat as the music flooded my senses. I smiled as I took in the dance floor already packed with people, their arms raised in the air toward the DJ booth where a beautiful woman spun her decks, controlling the crowd with the music.

Lights flashed, bouncing off the walls of the bar, lighting the place up before lunging it back into darkness as the resonating beat seemed to make the walls expand with every thump.

The atmosphere was electric.

Atlas leaned down to my ear. "I'll leave you with the boys." He nodded toward the bar where some of the brothers were shooting the shit. "Gonna go check on Stitch. She was feelin' tired after the meal, so I sent her to lie down. If you see techno boy, tell him I need a word." He saluted me with one finger and walked away.

Heat hit my back. I turned to see Colt behind me. "How did you get out?" I called over the music.

"You think I don't have a key to your room," he replied quietly, leaning down to my ear. "It was a close one." He took my hand and pulled me toward the throng of dancers. "Come on, baby."

It wasn't unusual for me and Colt to dance together at parties. We'd been doing it for years, even when I was a teen, he always danced with me. Years ago, he even taught me how to waltz and tango saying that when I was a rich, successful doctor it was a skill I'd be grateful for.

I didn't care. I just wanted to be close to him and dancing was a good way to achieve it.

Colt nodded toward a group of girls dancing up a storm. A flash of blonde hair caught my eyes, and I recognized Kennedy losing herself in the music. She looked so beautiful and sexy bumping and grinding her hips, watched over by Kit who stood with his back to a wall with a group of guys.

He couldn't take his heat-filled eyes off her.

Colt pulled me close, and we began to move together in time with the pounding beat. Our bodies swayed and pulsed in sync with the crowd. Flashing lights illuminated his handsome face and my heart swelled at our closeness.

I loved being this way with him. Just for a moment I could pretend we were a normal couple, openly together. I could forget all the obstacles in our way and just act like any other girl would with her man.

His hand came to my hips, and he stepped closer until our bodies connected. I slid my hands up his chest and we moved as one in time to the thudding bassline of the song.

He leaned down and whispered into the shell of my ear. "You havin' fun?"

I rolled up on my toes to whisper back, "Always with you."

Colt laughed, the sound resonating through his chest and against mine. In that moment, the noise and all the people around us faded away until it was just me and Colt, lost in the rhythm. His head dipped until it rested on mine, our lips hovering temptingly close. Everything around us blurred until all that remained was us, lost in each other.

"Love you," he murmured, eyes ablaze with need.

I ignored the temptation to lean in and gently kiss him, instead whispering, "I love you too, Colt." Elation snaked through my chest as a loud roar went up from the crowd.

Beams flashed around the room, tiny pinpricks of light turning everything from light, to dark, and back again.

The beat pulsed harder until a chorus of synths came in, carving out a pretty melody, coupled with the echo of bongo drums that added an extra layer of bass.

I stopped dancing and looked up just as every light in the place shone on Raven.

The crowd yelled as she raised one arm high in the air, made a fist, and pumped it in time to the beat, building higher and higher. Harder and harder. Suddenly, she stilled, almost suspended, as the resonating thump hit a crescendo before she crashed her fist down hard and dropped the bassline.

The crowd went crazy. Every person on the dance floor moved just as a man's soulful voice sang over the music.

Colt's fingers squeezed my hips and we moved together, once again in perfect sync. Our eyes locked and my heart swelled so euphorically in my chest that I almost laughed out loud with its effervescence.

It was the perfect night. Me, Colt, and the way he made me feel; like I was his and he was mine and nothing could break us apart. Emotion filled my already overflowing heart as I thought about how far we'd come. How he made me feel like it was okay to be me and that I was good enough.

Colt was the only man who ever put me first and whatever happened when everything came out, I knew we'd be indestructible, because he'd shown me that I was more important than the club.

Suddenly a shout filled the air.

Colt grabbed my arm and pulled me to his back. "Stay behind me." His tone was stern.

Leaning over his shoulder to see what the fuss was about I saw Hendrix barreling toward the spot where Kennedy had been dancing. He pointed his beer bottle and slurred. "I juss wanna birthday dance with Kitten."

"Fuck!" Colt cursed under his breath.

My eyes went to Kit and widened when I saw pure fury flash behind his eyes. His hands clenched into fists, and he snarled. "Fuck off, Drix. You're wasted. Go to bed."

Drix's expression darkened. "You should fuckin' know all about bein' wasted, ya little pissant." He turned in our direction and began waving his arms to get attention and bellowed, "Hey! See this little motherfucker. He was wasted off his ass for ten goddamned years, and now he thinks he can tell *me* what to do." Spittle flew from his mouth, his face reddening angrily. "I'm a goddamned *president*. You motherfuckers need to learn some *respect*."

The music lowered, as whispers and mutters went up from the crowd. Every neck craned to see what was going on.

"What's he doing?" I whispered to Colt. "This isn't like Hendrix."

He turned to look at me over his shoulder. "He's losin' the fuckin' plot. Believe me, Kit's the last fucker he should piss off. He won't take Drix's shit."

I stared at the scene in disbelief.

Hendrix was cool, calm, and collected, even in a crisis. It was like he'd left Wyoming and turned into somebody I didn't recognize.

Kit pointed toward the main doors and ordered, "Get the fuck out."

"Fuck you!" Drix hissed through clenched teeth.

Cash who stood a few feet behind Kit called, "You heard him. Get your drunken ass outta that door before you embarrass yourself even more than you already have."

Hendrix threw his head back and laughed manically. "Here comes the fucknut VP who thinks he's all that." He smirked. "You're a bigger cunt than him." He nodded toward Kit.

"Oh shit," Colt muttered as Kit's body locked in anger. "Drix is fucked. He's just pissed off two officers from the mother chapter. He's gone too far this time. Fucker's gonna get knocked out."

My chest panged.

Colt was right. Biker culture was dependent on respect. When another biker came into our home and disrespected the officers there would be a price to pay.

My heart stopped as Drix and Kit stared each other down, as if they were both waiting for the other to make the first move. It didn't take long because suddenly Hendrix roared like a crazed animal and rushed Kit.

I let out a cry.

"Watch your back," Colt shouted along with warnings from the other Demons, but Kit didn't need help. He bounced on the soles of his feet, waiting for Hendrix to almost reach him before spinning to one side. Drix in his drunken stupor lost his balance. As he fell, Kit grabbed the back of his collar, pulled his head up and landed a jab square on Drix's nose so hard, I heard it crack.

I sighed as Hendrix's nose exploded under the impact. Blood flew everywhere and he hit the floor with a loud thud.

Colt barked a laugh. "Fucker's been askin' for that since the second he walked into the clubhouse. At one point, he was so belligerent, I thought Prez would deck him. The only reason he didn't was because Kai was there." He shook his head. "You okay?"

I shrugged. "It's not the first fight I've seen in here, Colt and it won't be the last."

He grinned. "True."

Iceman and his friend, Pyro, who I'd met earlier, took hold of Hendrix's arms and legs, and carried him through the crowd of people toward the main doors as Bowie bellowed, "Where's the party gone? Let's keep it movin'."

The music started up again and everybody resumed dancing as happy shouts and whoops filled the air.

I tapped Colt's shoulder until he turned toward me. "I better go check on Hendrix. Kit's broken his nose for sure, but I want to check for concussion."

Colt rolled his eyes. "He deserved everythin' he got. Leave him."

"I can't," I replied softly. "It's not in me to turn a blind eye. I have to check. If anything happens it's not just Hendrix I'd worry about, it's Kit too. I know Drix played the fool but they're still brothers."

Colt folded his arms across his chest. "I said no."

My brow furrowed with curiosity. "Why are you being like this?"

He cocked his head. "I've told ya. He deserved it."

"I don't dispute that," I argued gently. "But how would you all feel if something happened to him?"

Colt shrugged nonchalantly.

Out of the corner of my eye I saw a flash of black as Atlas made his way toward the doors, probably to see what was going on with Drix. I turned to follow but was stopped by Colt grabbing my elbow.

"I said no," he muttered angrily.

My mouth twisted as I studied him. "You can't tell me what to do."

His ocean-blues darkened. "Yeah, I fuckin' can if you're mine."

"Colt." I went to try and reason with him, but his eyes flashed furiously.

"I just want us to enjoy the party," he seethed. "If you go out there now, you'll get caught up. It's not the first punch Hendrix has gotten, and with way he's acting, it won't be the last. I just want us to have a nice night without shit gettin' in the way as per fuckin' usual."

"I think you're being unreasonable," I murmured. "This is my job."

"You're not on duty now," Colt snapped.

I sighed.

He studied me for a moment before his shoulders slumped. "Tell you what, Freya. Do what you fuckin' want. Go play doctor and leave me hangin'." He turned and disappeared through the crowd toward the corridor leading to his office.

A part of me was desperate to follow. I got it. We'd both been looking forward to tonight because it gave us an excuse to dance and have fun with no raised eyebrows.

However, he needed to understand that I loved my work and sometimes it would have to take precedence, especially when I was doing my internship and residency programs. I'd be given shitty, long hours and called into the hospital at the drop of a hat, and it was something he'd have to deal with.

The doors flew open again and I turned to see what the commotion was about.

Atlas appeared with Hendrix slung over his shoulder and headed toward the corridor leading to the medical rooms, Ice and Pyro walking behind him.

Atlas's eyes began to search the packed bar before falling on me and jerking his head toward the corridor.

Without a thought, I began to follow, walking fast to catch up. By the time I got to the room, Atlas had already laid Hendrix on the bed. "He threw up outside but didn't wake up. I remember Stitch tellin' me it could be a sign of concussion."

I nodded, moving toward Hendrix who was still asleep. "It could be."

"Should I get Stitch?" the SAA asked.

I shook my head. "I dealt with this a lot in the ER back in Denver. If I get stuck, you can fetch her but I'm sure I'll be okay."

Atlas nodded.

"Will he be alright?" Iceman asked.

I smiled up at him. "Yeah. I'll try and reset his nose while he's passed out. I don't really want to give him pain relief in case he is concussed. But I'll know more once I've examined him."

Over the next thirty minutes, I carefully cleaned the blood from Hendrix's face and set his nose as best I could. His right eye was swollen shut because he bumped it as he fell, his orbital bone likely having a blowout fracture.

I checked his pupils—the left dilated normally to the light I shone into it, but the right—which had the suspected fracture—seemed slow to respond, which indicated a concussion.

After checking Drix's vitals and blood pressure, I felt around for internal fractures and bleeding. His breathing was normal, and his blood pressure wasn't elevated at all.

Ice looked up from the chair where he'd been watching. "Is he okay?"

"He'll live," I said softly, checking his pulse again before I started packing his nose a little to try and set the shape before it started healing. I was just taping across the top when Atlas appeared in the doorway. "How's he doin'?"

"He's got a broken nose and a concussion, but he'll be okay," I advised him.

"You did a good job with his hooter," Atlas grinned. "You may have made it prettier than before."

I laughed. "He won't look pretty for a good week. His eye will swell shut and it'll turn an interesting color along with his nose."

Atlas walked over to the bed, looking down at Drix and shaking his head. "Stupid bastard," he muttered softly. "Should'a known this would happen." He walked toward Iceman and took the seat next to him.

"He's been spiraling ever since Coyote fucked us over," Ice muttered. "This morning he went to see Anna to try and talk things out and she told him to fuck off. I think it was the catalyst."

Atlas gave Iceman a silent look, telling him to shut up about club business.

"It's okay," I said. "I can't do anything more for him. Stay with Drix, check his breathing every half hour. There's a blood pressure machine there. If it's elevated, or you're in anyway concerned come and get me immediately." I busied myself throwing away all the blood-soaked bandages and anti-bac wipes I'd discarded.

"Somebody has to stay here and monitor him at all times," I told Atlas.

"I'll stay," he rumbled.

"Me too," Ice muttered.

"Goodnight," I murmured, throwing them both a smile over my shoulder as I made my way through the door and into the corridor.

The party was still going strong when I hit the bar. Throngs of people were dancing and having a good time. My eyes rested on Donovan who was making out with some girl as they slow-danced to the funky tune blaring through the speakers.

I grinned, shaking my head thinking how quickly he'd gotten over me as I made my way toward the corridor where Colt had disappeared earlier, I assumed to his office.

We'd had a silly argument, and I didn't want to stress about it all night when we could simply talk things through. I did get where Colt was coming from. We didn't get to spend time together publicly so I could understand his frustration at me. But he also had to know this was me. In future if we went out and there was an emergency, I wouldn't think twice about helping. Medicine was my calling and although I loved him more than anything, I had a duty to help too.

Lights blazed from Colt's office as I headed toward it. Usually, it was a hubbub of activity down here but with it being so late and the party raging, it was deserted.

That was why I heard the woman's giggle so clearly.

My heart clenched painfully, and my steps faltered as voices carried through to the hallway.

"I've told ya, Lucy. Get the fuck off me," Colt snapped.

Another giggle before Lucy said cajolingly, "Oh come on. Nobody will know."

"I'll know," Colt muttered angrily. "I told ya to get off."

"Oh, come on," she murmured breathily. "You're not seeing anyone. Let's fuck for old time's sake. Nobody makes me come like you do, Colt."

I closed my eyes, trying to tamp down the sick feeling threatening to overtake my stomach. A bad taste made my mouth water and a lump formed in my throat.

"No, Lucy!" Colt snapped louder. "Get your fuckin' hands off me."

My hand met the wall and I held on for dear life.

Why did he let her in there? Why hadn't he thrown her out? I had no clue Lucy was even at the party unless she'd turned up while I was treating Hendrix.

My feet moved again, my heels tapping against the tiled floor announcing my arrival to Colt and Lucy fucking Bloom. I got to the open door and studied the sight before me with a sneer.

Colt sat on the edge of his desk, one boot planted on the floor, his hands holding Lucy's away from him as she tried to touch his face.

"Aww come on, Colt," she teased. "You used to love me touching you."

A squeak escaped my throat and two sets of eyes slashed toward me.

Colt pushed Lucy away by her wrists. "I told you to leave." His jaw clenched angrily. His eyes flashing retribution.

Lucy pouted. "Oh, come on. Don't act like you didn't want me here in front of your little girlfriend." She shot me a triumphant look. "I was fighting *him* off before you walked in."

I folded my arms across my chest and cocked an eyebrow. "Funny that. I could hear you from the top of the hallway and I distinctly remember you begging and Colt saying no."

"That's just the part you heard. Before you turned up, we were discussing how good we used to be together." She leaned in and brushed a kiss across Colt's jaw.

"Enough!" Colt roared, pushing her away so hard that she teetered on her high heels. "Told you to get the fuck out." He pointed to the door. "Don't ever come back."

Lucy sulked before turning on her heel and sashaying toward me. "Good luck with him," she crowed. "You'll need it seeing as ten minutes ago he was all over me."

I rolled my eyes. "You're so fucking thirsty it's embarrassing. You heard him. Get out."

She gave a little shrug. "Think what you want, but we know the truth, don't we, Colt." She sent him a conspiratorial wink and swept out the door and up the corridor with her parting shot of, "See you around, Colt."

I closed my eyes, trying to ignore my aching chest and the tears gathering behind my eyes. "What the fuck was she doing here?"

"I can explain," Colt said softly.

Shaking my head, I glared at him. "I know nothing happened. I heard everything, but why didn't you throw her out sooner?"

"She showed up outta nowhere and wouldn't leave me alone," he insisted. "I never asked her to come." He stood and grabbed my hand. "I'm sorry."

I pulled my fingers free and stumbled back a step. "But you didn't throw her out either, did you? I had to walk in here and see her pawing at you while you just sat there."

"I was trying to make her leave quietly without causing a scene," he bit out. "I didn't want anyone at the party getting wind of our business. And anyway, if you'd have stayed with me like I fuckin' asked in the first place, it would never have happened."

My lips twisted into a wry smile. "So, it was my fault?"

Colt walked around his desk and sank into his chair. "If the shoe fits."

"Fuck you," I whispered, a tear tracking down my cheek.

"I've said I'm sorry," he muttered. "I dunno what else I can do."

"You don't get it," I breathed, tone quiet with fury. "You fucked me over for her a year ago. You stopped spending time with me, and you stopped being my friend because she made you. All that time you were fucking her even though you profess to not even liking her, but still you put her before me. How do you think that makes me feel?"

His eyes lifted to meet mine until I could see the regret shining in them. "I can't turn back time. I wish I could click my fingers and erase the last year, but I can't."

"I know," I whispered, nausea rising through my stomach. "But then I walk in here and see her touching you..." I shook my head sadly. "How would you like it if you walked in on me and Donovan like that?"

"Freya," he rasped, tone laced with warning. "Don't fuckin' say it."

"Exactly," I retorted. "And nothing ever happened between me and him. You were with her for nearly a fucking year. Is it any wonder that I'm so fucking jealous I want to scratch her eyes out?"

"There's no need to be jealous of her—"

I slashed a hand through the air to cut him off. "The same as there's no need for you to be jealous of Donny."

"I was an asshole," he admitted. "I'm sorry."

"Yeah, you were," I muttered.

Colt rose from his chair, stepped toward me, and pulled me in his arms. "Nothin' happened. Wasn't interested. I'm not interested in anyone except you. If something happened to us tomorrow and we couldn't be together, I wouldn't be interested in anyone else. You're the girl I've waited for, Freya. I wouldn't jeopardize that for the world." He laced our fingers together. "You wanna go back to the party?"

I shook my head.

His eyes swept down my dress. "You look too good to have an early night. Wanna stay in here with me? We'll get some beers and snacks and watch the CCTV. Gotta get the video of Hendrix and Breaker's fight sorted for Prez." He waggled his eyebrows. "We can make a night of it."

I laughed. "Does this shit turn you on?"

He grinned wolfishly. "Almost as much as you do. And guess what else?"

My forehead furrowed. "What?"

"I can watch the cameras to see if someone's coming while you get on your knees under my desk and suck me off."

I busted out a laugh. "You sure know how to show a girl a good time."

"Stick with me, baby." He sent me a sexy wink. "I'll keep you right."

Over the next half hour we got snacks, beer, and blankets and holed up in Colt's office watching the cameras. He showed me how to work the equipment and flick from camera to camera. We kept a watch on the party, and on the mayor's mansion. We even checked the cameras Colt had set up around town and tested the license plate recognition system.

Then I crawled under the desk and gave him head before he crawled under the desk and returned the favor.

And it was one of the best nights of my life.

Chapter Twenty-Seven

Colt

Over the next few weeks, winter set into Hambleton. The snow came down thick and fast, leaving a white blanket over the sidewalks and roads. The bikes were put away and the snow tires went on the trucks that the brothers hauled out of their respective garages, to get around in over the next few months.

Things had been quiet with the Sinners. Too quiet. We'd pulled over a few vans and rescued three more girls, but I couldn't shake the feeling in my bones that something big was on the horizon. Still, we were in the best position we could hope for with the new recognition system set up. It was doing its job.

"Need a progress report on the houses, Colt," Prez demanded.

My eyes veered up to meet Dagger's. He'd kick my ass if he knew I'd zoned out in the middle of Church. He was anal as fuck about that shit.

"Good," I replied, not missing a beat. "The construction crew managed to get fifteen properties watertight before the bad weather hit and were able to start work inside the houses. Plumbing, wiring, putting internal walls up, and general construction's goin' well too. The entire fifteen should be ready for decoration come spring." My eyes flickered over Cash, Bowie, Breaker, and Atlas. "You need to take your women shopping for bathrooms, kitchens and all the fixtures and fittings you want installed. I've ordered your security systems, and your home hubs are in storage, ready to go."

Prez's face screwed up. "What the fuck's a home hub?"

"Home hub controls your security, lights, music, locks, even your stove and laundry facilities," I explained. "Everything's controlled by either your phones, a remote control in each room or it's voice activated. We're sparing no expense. These houses are environmentally friendly buildings for the future. We can upgrade the technology as we go along. There'll be nothing else like 'em."

Prez puffed his chest out. "Fuck yeah. Can you go through it all with me? You know I'm as technologically minded as a gnat."

I grinned. "Of course. Though you shouldn't have a problem, it's pretty straightforward."

Prez nodded thoughtfully. "Yeah, and Kai can help me with it all too. He's good at all that computer shit."

"You'll be fine," I assured him.

"Kitten's already got everythin' on order," Breaker interjected. "The furnishings have cost more than the fuckin' build."

Cash barked a laugh. "You can afford it. I've had to play the stock market for the last ten days to afford everythin' Cara wants. She's rinsed my bank account."

"You've got savings haven't ya?" Prez asked. "You're a rich little cunt."

"Don't tell Cara that, she'll start spendin' again," Cash muttered. "Gotta start savin' for Wilder's college."

"He's three months fuckin' old," Atlas said incredulously. "You got plenty'a time for all that malarky." He shook his head. "Sayin' that you may have a point. Maybe I should start savin' for Zeus's college every month for his college fund."

Prez's mouth twisted. "Who the fuck's Zeus?"

"My boy," Atlas replied defensively.

"Sounds like a fuckin' porn star name." Abe chuckled. "And what if you're havin' a girl?"

Atlas shrugged. "My Stitch chooses the girls' names. I choose the boys'."

"Fuck me," Bowie muttered. "Zeus Woods. Poor little lad's gonna be fucked with a name like that."

"Zeus is king of the Gods," the SAA said, tone menacing. "Nothin' wrong with settin' a fuckin' precedence. And you're a fine one to talk. What kinda name's Willow? Poor baby's named after a tree and the ginger witch in Buffy the Vampire Slayer."

Silence fell over the room briefly before Breaker asked, "You watch Buffy the Vampire Slayer?"

Atlas jerked a nod. "Yip. But that's as geek as I go, except for the Star Trek movies with the Borg in 'em, and the new ones with Chris Pine. Oh, and the first three Star Wars."

"Why just the first three?" Abe asked, confusion lacing his tone."

"'Cause they're men's movies," Atlas told him. "Lots'a shooting and shit. The others are too girlie."

My lips twitched.

Cash sat forward to address Atlas. "I wanna know about Buffy. When did you start watchin' a TV show about a schoolgirl who slays vampires?"

Atlas cocked an eyebrow. "It's a bit more than that, Cashy boy. I mean, Buffy was the chosen one and Sunnydale sat on the Hellmouth. They had Big Bads comin' outta their assholes in that show. And Buffy was a tough little bitch. She had some good moves." His eyes glazed over. "Reminds me of my Stitch. She could'a been the Slayer, the Chosen One. Have you seen her roundhouse kicks?"

The corner of my mouth hitched. "Stitch would've kicked her ass," I assured him.

"Buffy was hot," Bowie mused.

"Not as hot as Faith," Breaker muttered.

"Now see that's a fuckin' disgrace," Atlas rasped. "Faith worked for the evil mayor who turned into a big snake. She was a killer, and alright, I know she came good in the end, but before that she cast a spell and took over Buffy's body and fucked Riley."

I brought a hand up to cover my smile.

Prez turned his stare on Abe and demanded, "Are you hearin' this?"

The secretary shrugged. "I gave up with 'em a long time ago."

"It's like he's speakin' another fuckin' language," Prez continued. "Do you remember the days when we actually discussed club business in Church? This room is fuckin' sacred and all we talk about is dicks, Real Housewives, and teenage girl Vampire Slayers."

Abe held a hand up. "Whoa, whoa, whoa. You're the one who talks about Taylor Swift and Travis Kelce."

"He's got ya there, Pop," Cash muttered.

"That's different." Prez's lips pursed and he sniffed. "Traylor's current affairs and it's 'cause of the kids. I'm their grandpa and I gotta know what the fuck they're talkin' about or I'd be goddamned lost."

"Fuckin' Taylor Swift is all Sunny listens to these days," Bowie said, looking at Breaker accusingly. "I blame your daughter that Sunny's gonna end up with a goddamned concussion from twatting her noggin off a wall 'cause she twirls so fuckin' much."

"Blame my girl all you want," Break retorted. "Kady could be listenin' to worse. Carry on with ya whining, and I'll bust out some gangster rap for Sunny and laugh while she beats along to how they fuck their bitches up."

Bowie paled.

Atlas busted out laughing.

Cash chuckled.

Prez's lips twitched. "Right. Last business I've got is to say that the recognition system's working up a storm. Had a few pings and of course, we got those three girls safe last week." His eyes slid to Atlas. "Good job on the disposal."

The SAA smirked. "Fuck you very much. Ya got a hairy crotch."

Cash barked a laugh.

Breaker's hand clapped over his mouth.

Abe let out a hoot.

Prez's eyes narrowed. "You dirty bastard. Bandit'll be rollin' over in his grave. Why can't you talk like a normal person?"

Atlas's chest rumbled with laughter.

Dagger looked around the room with his nose in the air like Atlas was giving off a bad smell. "Any other fuckin' business."

Silence.

"Church is over." He banged the gavel down hard on the sound block. "Fuck off the lotta ya."

The sound of chairs scraping across the wooden floor went up and we all headed for the door.

"Wait!" Prez called loudly.

We all stopped and turned.

"Someone said Freya fucked off to Denver for the weekend. Do you know about it?" he asked.

Cash cocked his head. "She went to see her friend before the holidays started."

"It's thick fuckin' snow out there," Prez muttered.

"The main roads are clear," Bowie told him. "I taught her how to drive in the bad weather, and I put her snow tires on. She'll be fine. She's been driving in snow for years, including down in Colorado."

Prez raised a hand to rub his beard thoughtfully. "I'll have to have a word with her. I see less of her now than I did when she lived a fuckin' state away. She'll be off to start her internship soon. She needs to spend more time with the family while she's here."

Abe's forehead scrunched up. "She's a young girl with the world at her feet, Dagger. She'll be a qualified surgeon in a few years. Let her have some fun."

Prez ignored him, instead looking at Cash. "When's she coming home?"

"Monday," the VP replied. "She told me she's spending the weekend with Abi."

Prez nodded. "I'll talk to her then." He nodded toward the door. "You can all fuck off now."

Atlas opened the door and held it for us as we all filed through and walked up the corridor toward the bar.

I fell into step next to Cash. "Thanks, brother."

He turned to me and rolled his eyes. "Where is she, Colt?"

A grin spread across my face. It was involuntary, like a kid sneaking a cookie before dinner. I knew my answer would be ambiguous, but I couldn't bring myself to care. "I got her stashed somewhere safe, don't worry."

"That look on your face tells me that I don't wanna fuckin' know the whys and wherefores." Cash heaved out a breath. "Thought any more about comin' clean?"

"I'd go and tell Prez now," I rasped as we headed into the bar. "She doesn't want to yet. I've told her, New Year's Day at the latest and I'll be goin' to his office for a sit down."

"Fair enough." Cash nodded. "I'll make sure I'm around to back you up."

I clapped him on the shoulder. "Appreciated, brother. Goin' out now to reposition some cameras."

"Right. Give Freya my love. Warn her that Dad's on the warpath." Cash's jaw tightened, the muscles in his neck cording. He caught my eye, and I knew he was about to give me a lecture, but instead he shook his head. "You two are playin' with fire."

"I know." I leaned over the bar to grab the coat and scarf I'd left there earlier when I came in from the gallery. Slipping them on, I wound my scarf around my neck, checked my pockets for my keys and headed for the door, whistling happily as I strode through the main doors to the parking lot.

Suddenly, a twinge of doubt twisted my gut.

Cash was right, the longer we held off coming clean, the more chance we had of being caught. Except it was too late for second thoughts. Freya was mine and I wouldn't give her up for anything. I'd made my choice and I'd deal with the consequences later.

For now, I had to go check on my girl.

My footsteps sounded tinny as I ascended the metal steps to the bijou room above the gallery where Freya was waiting. My cock thickened at the mere thought of the sight I'd walk into. I'd left her here for a few hours while I went back to the club, did some work, and went to Church.

The room was in darkness except for the TV which had been turned down low. I stopped, mesmerized by the sight of the lights flickering over Freya's naked body.

My throat went dry as I studied my woman's sleeping form and I knew for as long as I lived, I'd never forget how beautiful she was or the emotions she made me feel.

Her tiny, talented doctor's hands were tied together above her head and attached to the wrought iron headboard of the bed she laid on. Every inch of her body was exposed. From her beautiful thick, tousled hair to her pretty scarlet painted toes.

Freya's chest moved softly, drawing attention to her small, perfectly formed breasts that heaved with every deep breath she took. My mouth, which was dry just a moment before, began to water at the thought of taking her cherry red little nipples in my mouth and nipping them hungrily.

Quietly, so as not to wake my girl, I placed my keys and wallet on the nightstand and pulled at the nape of my shirt to take it off. My boots and socks came off next, followed by my jeans and shorts until I was naked as the day I was born.

Slowly, I crawled up the bed until I lay at Freya's back and slid my hand over her waist. "Baby," I whispered into the shell of her ear.

She awoke with a jerk, moaning out loud, and my cock kicked.

"Do you need the bathroom?" I whispered.

"Yeah," she rasped.

I reached up and untied her hands from the headboard before bringing her arms down and rubbing the feeling back into them. "Do you ache?" I asked gently.

"A little, but it's fine," she replied craning her neck to look me in the eye. "Can I come yet?"

"Maybe." I smirked. "Depends how good you suck me off."

She groaned. "Please."

I shushed her softly. "Go use the bathroom. You can freshen up, but if you touch yourself, I'll edge you all weekend, Freya. Be a good girl for me or I'll make you suffer."

Her cheeks flushed at my words, but she jerked a nod and swung her legs over the bed and stood before disappearing into the bathroom.

"Leave the door open," I ordered.

"So you can hear me pee?" she retorted. "I don't think so."

I chuckled. "Do your business then open the door."

She began to mutter under her breath. "So bossy."

"Freya," I warned. "Keep sassing me and I'll put you over my knee."

A giggle came from the bathroom.

My heart swelled with so much emotion for my girl, it felt double its normal size.

I'd had her holed up here since the night before. I'd fucked her, came but made sure she didn't. Since then, I'd been back twice to do it all over again, except I wouldn't let her climax. The last time I got dressed to leave she was almost crying, begging me to let her come, but I refused and left.

I wanted to get her to a place where she'd have the best orgasm of her life when I finally allowed it. I knew already it would be big for her, but she still had a way to go to get to the pinnacle.

In the meantime, I loved the control she allowed me. Freya was fucking perfect. She understood what I needed and gave it to me without question. I'd looked all my life for a girl like her. I should've known by the connection we'd had historically that my ideal woman was right there under my nose. Should've known she'd eventually mean everything to me.

Over the weeks I'd come to terms with everything. I'd miss the club, but only for the people in it. I'd made my choice, and I was strangely okay with it. Shepherd kept in touch. I'd even spoken to my new boss, who assured me I'd have plenty of intricate work to keep me busy. He'd outlined a few things, and I knew I'd love the work, even if I did have to become a fucking Fed.

I'd see in my last Christmas with the Demons, then in the New Year I'd speak to Prez, explain my feelings for Freya, and leave. I knew I was simplifying it all in my head, but I also knew that whatever happened, me and my girl would be together, even if there was an initial separation while I sorted us somewhere to live. However, I reckoned within the next six months we'd be settled. Me with my work, and Freya with her internship and subsequent residency.

We just had to get through the next few weeks.

My gaze lifted to study my woman as she appeared at the door to the bathroom.

There was a glow about her that hit me square in the chest. I'd never loved like this before, and I knew there was only her for me. Part of me wished it hadn't taken me so long to get there and that I hadn't wasted so much time, but maybe it was just the way it was meant to be for us.

"Come here," I ordered gently, watching the flickering lights travel over her soft, supple skin.

Freya walked toward me with swinging hips and a smile that lit up her gorgeous face.

"Did you touch yourself?" I asked, catching her by the hips as she approached the bed.

She looked me in the eye and shook her head.

"Say it," I told her, landing a soft kiss on my belly, emotion making my voice husky.

Immediately she knew what I needed because she whispered, "I love you."

I nuzzled her stomach. "I love you more than anything," I whispered into her skin. "I'd fuckin' waste away without you."

Her hands cupped my face, and she angled it upward while she looked down into my tender gaze and smiled.

"Lay down," I ordered gently, my cock lengthening as I watched her obey without hesitation. "Flat on your back, head on the pillows."

Freya shuffled up the bed and rested her head back as I instructed.

I swung a leg over her chest and straddled her, knee-walking up until my crotch hovered over her face. "Make me come and I may return the favor."

Freya's eyes met mine and she smirked, before curling her fingers around my hard cock and squeezing gently. She knew exactly how hard to grip me. I'd trained her to know what I liked and how I liked it. It was hard to believe that mere months ago she was untouched and had never had a cock in her mouth. She was a fuckin' natural, a unicorn woman who loved giving pleasure even more than receiving it.

Her hand began to move up and down my length, gently jacking me off.

I groaned out loud and threw my head back, letting my body take over from my mind, concentrating only on the effect she had on me and the way she made me feel.

I'd already come that morning when I fucked her, but knowing how primed I'd gotten her made me harder than a steel pipe, because I knew that when I finally allowed her to come, it'd be big.

A wet sensation on my cock made me hum with pleasure. I peered down to see Freya lick me from top to bottom with the flat of her tongue.

"Fuck yeah," I muttered. "Take that cock."

Her eyes blazed as she licked delicately around the head before taking just the tip in her mouth and sucking gently.

"Love the way you taste me, baby." I groaned as her other hand came up to gently palm my balls. "You suck me like you were born for it, Freya. Never known a better mouth than yours."

She hummed over my cock; the soft vibrations from her throat making my hips jerk and my dick thicken even harder in her mouth.

My spine tingled as if I'd been electrocuted.

I leaned up to grab the headboard and hitched my hips higher so I could get better access to Freya's hot mouth. "Open your throat, baby," I ordered. "I'm gonna stuff it full of my cock."

She sighed around my length which made me jerk again, but the angle allowed me to slide my cock a little deeper until it hit the back of her throat. "Swallow me," I told her, my voice so husky with the pleasure she gave me, it was just a rasp.

Freya moaned and opened her throat for me, allowing me to ease even deeper. My fingers tangled in her hair, pulling her head up slightly so I could gently fuck her mouth. "That's it, beautiful girl," I crooned. "Swallow me all the way." I looked down and groaned at the tears running down her cheek. "Fuck yeah." I moaned. "Cry pretty for me while I fuck your face."

Freya's gaze lifted to meet mine and I almost came, there and then, at the tears welling in her eyes. She let out a satisfied moan before hollowing her cheeks out and sucking me down hard.

I threw my head back and let out a shout, hips circling as I gently pumped my cock in and out of her throat.

With a moan, she sucked me deeper, her hands going around to clutch my ass and force me into her mouth.

Lights began flashing behind my eyes. "Jesus, fuck, Freya," I murmured, my hand trailing down to her neck that almost bulged with being filled by my cock.

She swallowed around me again and I let out another shout as her tight muscles gripped the tip of my dick. I felt my balls draw up into my body and without warning, they released and with a loud curse I spurted down her throat.

My thighs began to shake as streams of cum jetted into her mouth. I held onto the headboard for dear life, my lower back tingling so forcefully, it was almost painful. My hips lost all sense of rhythm as my orgasm took over my body and black spots danced behind my eyes.

The air filled with my moans and Freya's whimpers. She gripped the base of my cock, making me shout out loud again as she jacked me off, milking every drop of cum from me. I fucked her mouth brutally, chanting how much I loved her mouth and how hard she made me come, until my climax began to wane, and I opened my eyes, looking down at my magnificent woman.

A trail of milky cum escaped her mouth and ran down the side of her jaw.

"Swallow me down, baby," I whispered. "Make me part of you."

Her throat worked a couple of times, and I smirked as a little more cum escaped the side of her mouth. Leaning down, I cleaned it up with the flat of my tongue, licking from bottom to top as she sighed.

"Oh my God," she whispered. "That was so fucking hot."

I released the headboard and sat back on my haunches before my knees gave way and I sank down on the bed beside her. "I've never come like that in my goddamned life, Freya. How the fuck can you be so inexperienced but suck my cock like you were made for it?"

She turned and faced me until our bodies aligned so closely, I could feel the heat radiating from her skin.

"I had a good teacher," she murmured, a teasing lilt to her voice.

Reaching up, I covered her hand with mine, marveling at the delicate, fragrant skin. A swell of emotion filled my chest because, in that moment, I felt so profoundly connected to her that it took my breath away.

I'd never felt this close to a living soul before, never felt like I belonged until her.

"We've got years of this to come," I said softly, my tone thick with adoration. I stroked her hair back from her face, my fingertips skimming over her temple. It took in the cut of her cheekbone, the olive tone of her skin, and the elegant line of her throat that just minutes ago gave me more pleasure than I'd ever known. "This is just the beginning for us."

Tears welled in her eyes, but she smiled through them. "I know."

I grinned. "You ready to come now?"

Her cheeks blushed scarlet. "Can you? I mean, after what we just did..."

My fingers trailed downward over the curve of her stomach to meet the juncture between her thighs. "More than one way to skin a pussy, baby."

Her giggle turned into a long, drawn-out moan as my middle finger dipped inside her little wet cunt.

"Jesus, Freya, you're fuckin' soaked for me," I said, leaning forward and nuzzling the dip in her throat. "You want me to make you feel good."

"Yes," she whispered, eyes fluttering closed as my finger worked her core.

"Beg," I whispered.

"Please, Colt. Make me feel good," she pleaded, not missing a beat. "I've been waiting hours."

A satisfied smile spread across my face, and I took her mouth, sucking gently on her top lip before shuffling down, planting soft kisses and tiny sucks across her throat and chest.

Her back arched as I took one little rosy nipple into my mouth and gently nibbled on it the way I'd fantasized earlier. While I kissed and nipped, my finger worked inside her sweet, tight little pussy, making her wetter with each thrust.

"Did you bring it?" I rasped.

Freya's eyes slowly opened, and she nodded toward the big calfskin Louboutin bag I bought her in Denver. "In there."

Sliding off the bed, I grabbed it and searched inside until my fingers curled over hard, cold metal. With a grin, I pulled out the steel, curved dildo just a little bigger than my hand. One end had a big, metal silver ball attached, the other end, a smaller one.

She raised up onto her elbows. "What is it? I've never seen one like that before."

"It's a dildo," I replied. "I held it out and stroked a hand down it. "See this curve? It's designed so this ball here hits your G-spot."

Freya's eyes widened. "It's big."

I pushed her down onto her back. "Back to the headboard, baby."

She shuffled up on her back.

"Open those sweet thighs for me," I demanded. "Show me how wet you are."

Her legs fell open at the knees and I caught a glimpse of glistening pink skin.

"You're so fucking beautiful, Freya," I said huskily, descending until my face drew level with her pretty little pussy. "Every time I look at you it's like a dream come true."

Her eyes dropped to mine, golden irises blazing with need.

A growl rumbled through my chest as I lowered my head, whilst simultaneously sliding my hands up the inside of her thighs, pushing them open wider.

Freya's knees trembled and she shuddered. "Please. Don't tease me."

I inhaled her scent, Chanel, and everything else that made her who she was. Her skin smelled sweet and fresh; the muskiness of her soap mixed with something fruity. "You drive me fuckin' crazy," I muttered, nipping the soft skin on the inside of her thighs.

"Not as crazy as you make me," she retorted. "Jesus, Colt. Just fuck me already."

I smirked, determined to edge her a little more before I let her come. With deliberate slowness, I traced a finger around her clit, all swollen and engorged.

Her hips jerked and she let out a moan.

My lips wrapped around her clit, and I sucked hard, pulling it with my mouth until her pussy gushed, flooding my fingers with her juices. With a groan, I feasted on her, licking, sucking, nipping, and thrusting my tongue so deep inside her that she began to clench.

Even though minutes before, I'd come harder than a freight train, my cock twitched. I ground against the bed, eating Freya until my face was soaked. With my mouth still working her, my eyes raised to meet hers and we stared, lost in each other.

"Love how you taste," I muttered, nipping her clit gently. "Love how you're mine to eat and fuck whenever I want." Raw desire for her clawed at my insides and suddenly, I couldn't get close enough. I grabbed her hips, tipped them, and ate her like she was my last meal.

Her cunt pulsed in my mouth, and she whimpered. "I'm gonna come."

I pulled back.

"No," she whined. "Please, Colt. I need it."

My hand reached for the dildo I'd placed next to her ass, and I positioned the smaller ball at her entrance. "Are you ready?"

She nodded enthusiastically. "Don't stop."

Slowly, I slid the cold metal ball inside her until the toy was about halfway in.

Freya threw her head back and let out a loud, keening cry, and her entire body began to tremble.

Against all odds, my cock thickened until it was almost as hard as the steel bar I was slowly fucking her with. She began to pant, her chest heaving as her breaths sawed in and out. I positioned the ball so it directly hit her G-spot.

The sound she emitted sounded like a sob.

My woman looked beautiful with her feet planted on the bed and her knees spread wide. Her pussy was pink and swollen from the amount of blood rushing into her nerve endings. Her hips canted and she met every thrust of the dildo with a loud moan.

My head lowered again, and I latched onto her clit while I fucked her, making sure to skim the metal ball against her front wall.

Freya's head thrashed from left to right and back again, her hair sexy and tousled as she threw it back and groaned loudly. Her pussy glistened and I lapped at her clit, moaning until the vibrations hit it.

Her cunt clenched so hard it sucked the dildo deeper inside her. "I'm gonna come, baby," she cried. "Please let me come."

"Do it," I rasped. "Come." My lips caught her clit again and I sucked it into my mouth, hard.

Freya's body shook with pleasure. Her hands raised above her head to grab the headboard and she circled her hips, grinding herself onto the dildo as she came with a loud scream.

A gush of liquid filled my mouth and I moaned. Another stream followed and I drank down its sweet taste, not quite believing that I'd made my girl squirt.

I continued to fuck her with the dildo, nipping her clit harder, prolonging her orgasm for as long as I could.

Freya's body convulsed and she screamed, her hips jerking uncontrollably. I'd never felt a cunt clench tighter, she gripped the toy like a vise, her hips jumping and grinding as I kept hitting her G-spot until, after what seemed like an eon, I felt her orgasm finally fade, leaving her wrung out and shaking on the bed.

Gently, I pulled the dildo out of her pussy and climbed on top of her body to smooth her hair back from her face. "You okay?" I asked, kissing her nose.

"I don't k—know what happened," she rasped, her voice catching as she spoke. "I think I left my body for a second there."

"It's because I edged you," I explained softly. "It's always way more intense when you have to wait for it."

"I came so hard it almost hurt," she murmured. "I didn't think it would stop."

I couldn't help grinning. "You squirted, baby. It was the hottest fucking thing I've ever experienced. Thought my cock would explode." I kissed her jaw. "We're definitely using that dildo again."

She laughed softly. "I thought squirting was just in porn."

My eyes narrowed. "What porn have you been watching?"

She giggled, looking up at me innocently. "Abi told me."

"Brat," I muttered, lips twitching as she laughed out loud. My throat thickened as I studied her. My heart filling with love for my amazing girl. "Never known anyone like you, Princess. How did I go so long without this?"

She smiled softly. "We got there, Colt. That's what matters."

"You're exquisite," I said, tone suddenly hoarse with all the emotions hitting me full force.

A faint blush stained her cheeks. "So are you."

I eased my body off hers, laid behind her and tucked her into me. She made me so happy, so content. My mind had always been too active. I'd always found it hard to switch off and center myself, but Freya calmed me.

My fingers slid across her waist and cupped her belly. "I can't wait to plant my baby in here."

Her hand covered mine and squeezed. "Our babies will be so smart it almost scares me."

I leaned across and kissed her neck, smiling as the effects made her shiver. "They'll rule the world and it'll be beautiful."

For hours we lay there, talking, and planning our future. We discussed our wedding, our family, our hopes, and aspirations. We talked about my work and what I wanted to achieve at the FBI, and Freya told me how she wanted to earn enough at a hospital so she could help veterans by carrying out pro bono surgeries.

If I didn't know before that night, I knew it after.

My girl was more than I ever wanted and everything I ever needed. During the night, I fell in love with her a little more, if it was even possible. She made me feel things I'd never dreamed of and want things I'd never dared to before.

I knew she'd be mine one day soon, but I never suspected what we'd have to go through to be together. The pain and the heartbreak and the fight we'd have to put up.

I should've known that nothing good ever came easy.

Chapter Twenty-Eight

Freya

Christmas at the Speed Demons clubhouse was an experience, which this year began at the crack of dawn.

I was startled awake by a bang on the door and Atlas's voice booming, "Rise and fuckin' shine, Freya. The kids are pissin' their goddamned pants with excitement downstairs. I'll leave your coffee here. You've got thirty minutes."

"'Kay. Thanks," I called out, my voice hoarse from sleep.

I patted my nightstand for my cell phone and saw it was six-thirty. Letting out a groan, I sat up, swung my legs over the bed and stood, raising my arms in a loud yawn. After retrieving my coffee from the hall, I padded into my bathroom and brushed my teeth before tying my hair up and jumping in the shower. Within ten minutes, I was brushing on mascara, a touch of blush, and swiping a slick of dark red lip gloss across my mouth, before slipping on a short, oversized blush-colored sweater dress and black, suede thigh-high boots.

Was it a little sexy for Christmas Day? Probably, but I wanted to gorge myself on food and the dress was the most forgiving thing I owned. Plus, it wouldn't hurt to impress Colt a little from afar.

With one last look in the mirror, I grabbed my cell, put it in my purse and headed out into the hallway. My tummy gave an excited leap. I loved Christmas; I knew it was mainly a kid's holiday, but I couldn't help getting swept up in the excitement of it all. It was a magical time of year.

I swept through the bar, grinning when I saw Dad with his back to me in a Santa suit, down on his haunches, arranging gifts under the tree. "Morning. Merry Christmas," I called out.

He craned his neck and sent me a wide smile. "Merry Christmas. Go get your coffee and make sure you bring your old dad one back too. I'm spitting feathers here."

"No problem." I swept through the corridor to the kitchen to find it packed.

Cash and Bowie sat at the countertop with their heads in their hands. Atlas was at the huge table with a very pregnant Sophie on his lap. Layla was helping Iris at the stove and Cara was looking at Cash like she wanted to kill him.

Sunny came rushing up to me, her glossy, red-brown curls bouncing as she barreled into my legs and hugged them. "Merry Christmas, Auntie Freya." She squeezed me so tightly she almost stopped my blood flow. "Did you know Santa came? And guess what?" Her high-pitched voice turned into a screech. "He brought my daddy and Uncle Cash a headaches!"

Bowie groaned in pain.

I blinked in surprise as Sunny giggled, her big, grey eyes, so much like her mom's, sparkling excitedly.

Cara sidled up next to me, her lips pursed tight. "John decided to make the boys join him in a Christmas tipple after Church last night," She rolled her eyes. "It turned into a game of 'Never have I Ever'. Imagine my shock when two hours later, Atlas barges in my room with Cash flung over his shoulder so drunk he couldn't speak." She glared at my brother who looked down at his hands sheepishly.

My confusion was evident on my face as I studied Cash. "But you don't even drink."

"Tell it to Pop," he muttered, rubbing his temple. "I blame him."

"You could've said no!" Cara snapped. "Now I've gotta put up with you and your hangover all day."

Xan held up a hand to quiet Cara. "I'll be fine once the Advil kicks in." He rubbed his temple. "Only took six shots to bring me to my knees. One minute I'm takin' a drink. The next I'm wakin' up in the middle of the night with a mouth tastin' like somethin' died in it."

"Best Christmas ever!" Sunny yelled, punching the air.

Cash and Bowie groaned.

"Mornin'," a voice chirped from the doorway.

I turned to see Kit with his arms slung over Kennedy's shoulders with a wide grin spread across his face.

"Yay!" Sunny punched the air again. "Where's Kai and Kady?"

Kennedy nodded toward the bar. "With your gramps, helping him sort the gifts out."

Sunshine let out a little squeal and skipped toward the door.

"Be good, Sunny," Layla called out. "Help your grandpa and don't get in his way." She put a plate of bacon and scrambled egg, and a cup of coffee down in front of Bowie. "You'll feel better after you eat."

Bowie looked down at the plate and his face turned green.

"Told you both last night you'd regret it," Kit crowed, planting Kennedy down on a seat at the table and going over to the coffee pot. "Ya better not ruin Christmas for the kids."

Cash groaned. "I'll be fine. Just waiting for the pills to start working."

I caught Cara's gaze and grinned as she rolled her eyes again.

I looked toward the doorway as a familiar voice called out, "Good morning my babies! Merry Christmas."

"Mom!" I breathed.

She held her arms out for me to walk into. "Hello, Daughter. You look amazing!"

My hands went around her shoulders and I sighed. "I've missed you."

Mom pulled back slightly. Her eyes flicked over my face before narrowing slightly. "There's something different about you. What's going on?"

My stomach dropped.

Mom knew me inside out. I should've expected her to notice something was going on with me. She was the same with my brothers too. She only had to look at us to know we were up to something. We never got away with anything as kids, and it was the same now.

"Nothing's going on," I insisted, but I knew I'd have to tell Mom about me and Colt. She'd be okay with it, especially as she'd never agreed with Dad's stupid rule. Still, she wouldn't be happy about the lies and the sneaking around. The woman was honest to a fault.

"Right." Her eyes flickered between mine. "We'll chat later."

Mom greeted everybody before moving over to help Iris at the stove.

Layla came to sit down and rubbed her burgeoning stomach with a soft smile. "They're active today. I think they're playing football in there."

Just after Kennedy's birthday party Bowie took Layla for a sonogram where they discovered they were having twins. Bowie hadn't stopped boasting about it, to the point where even I got bored of his attitude.

Needless to say, Dad was over the moon, and now Bowie and Layla were his new favorites.

Abe sauntered into the kitchen and made a beeline straight for Iris. "Get away from that stove, woman," he said good-naturedly. "You prepared everythin' already. These assholes are big enough to look after themselves."

Iris slapped Abe across the chest. "Shush, old man." She retorted. "It's all done, and now Adele's here she'll help."

Abe stuck two fingers in his mouth and let out a piercing whistle. "Merry fuckin' Christmas," he called out. "Prez is ready for you all. Could you make your way into the bar please."

I walked over to the coffee pot and quickly poured a cup for Dad before grabbing my purse from the counter and following everyone through the corridor toward where Dad had set up the room ready for today.

The bar looked amazing.

Dad had put up a huge Christmas tree in the corner by the sofas. Its white lights twinkled in the muted lighting of the room. Underneath it were brightly wrapped gifts sorted into piles and huge Santa sacks full of presents.

Fairy lights lit the countertop of the bar, giving the place an ethereal air that just added to the magical atmosphere. Dad had outdone himself.

Dad stood and turned to face us all with outstretched arms. "Ho, ho, ho. Merry Christmas."

I froze.

Pop wore the same Santa suit he used to put on when we were kids. The problem was, he'd put on a few pounds of muscle since then, which made the suit skintight, especially around the crotch area.

"Jesus, Pop. Not again," Bowie wailed.

Cash turned green and ran for the door.

"Fuck me," Breaker muttered. "I think I just threw up in my mouth a little."

Mom jammed her hands to her hips. "John Stone, what have I told you about that suit? You'll scare the kids."

Kai peered at Dad's dick. "Grandpa," he muttered. "Your nutsack's hangin' out."

Kady's eyes went wide.

Dad pointed at us all in turn. "I let you assholes get to me last year, but not this time. I ain't changing until I've finished playin' Santa. If you don't like it, look somewhere else. Iris put a support down there so there won't be any accidents."

"You need reinforced steel to cover those fuckin' things up," Bowie told him. "Jesus, Dad, it's obscene."

John peered down at his crotch. "You can't see anythin'."

Kennedy barked out a laugh. "You better not turn too quickly. You'll poke someone's eyes out with that thing." She smirked. "Gotta say though, John. I may have picked the wrong Stone man."

Kit growled.

Dad adjusted the Santa pants. "I know they're a bit snug, but it's all part of the fun, right?"

Cara laughed.

Layla blushed.

Adele sighed.

The main door burst open and Billy the prospect came sauntering in carrying a pink and white pet travel cage along with a purple and white one. "Yo, boss," he called out. "Where d'ya want these?"

Dad punched his fists to his hips and looked to the heavens. "Billy, you stupid asshole. I didn't give ya the signal."

"What signal?" Billy asked, tone confused.

"The signal where I call ya and tell ya to bring 'em in!" Dad yelled, stomping over to the prospect, and taking the carry cages from him.

Suddenly, Sunny let out a piercing scream.

Bowie ran over to her, face panicked. "What is it? You okay, Sunny? What happened?"

"Oh my Gods!" she screamed.

"Sunny!" Layla berated. "What have I told you about saying that?"

"But, Mama," Sunny squealed. "It's a pussy cat!"

Dad puffed his chest out. "One kitten's for you and one's for Kady. Pink one belongs to Sunshine, the purple one's little Kady girl's."

"Fuck!" Kennedy said under her breath.

The air filled with piercing screams as Sunny and Kady began to run around the bar.

"Jesus," Bowie muttered, rubbing his temple.

Within seconds, the two kittens were out of their cages and being snuggled by the little girls.

"Oh my Gods, she's so tiny" Sunny shrieked. "She's so pretty, and adorable, and fluffy." The little girl cuddled the pure white kitten, eyes rounding as she pulled it into her neck to snuggle.

"They're Munchkin kittens," Dad said proudly. "They won't grow big."

I took in the cute kittens and smiled at their tiny ears that sat flat to their heads. "What are you going to call them, girls?"

Kady smiled at her white cat with tan paws. "Taylor!" she announced.

Sunny sat on her ass to tickle her kitten's tummy. "I know! I'm calling my kitten Princess Pretty Pussy," she shrieked.

Atlas barked a laugh.

Abe let out a hoot.

Dad's cheeks reddened slightly.

Bowie winced. "Fuckin' great." He stared at Dad. "Cheers for that, Pop."

Dad preened before turning to Kai. "Your gift's outside, Son." He glanced at Billy who gave him a nod before turning for the door. Dad clasped Kai's shoulder and led him out to the parking lot, Kit and Kennedy following behind.

I fell into step behind them, curious about what Dad had been up to. Knowing him he would've gone crazy. This was the first holiday with Kennedy and the twins at the clubhouse, and I knew Dad would want to make it special for them.

An excited shout went up from the parking lot and my steps faltered when I saw Kai jumping up and down in excitement next to a black dirt bike.

"John!" Kennedy shrieked. "What did you do?"

Dad shrugged. "He's only allowed to go on it when someone's with him," he announced. "I'm makin' that rule right now."

Kai's eyes shone. "Please, Mom. Please can I keep it?"

Kennedy sighed exasperatedly. "Do I even have a choice?"

Kit slid his arm around Kennedy's shoulder. "It's okay, Kitten. I'll look after him. We'll make sure he's safe and I'll teach him properly." He studied his mini-me son who'd already thrown his leg over the saddle and was trying the bike out for size. "No fuckin' around on it, Kai. If you wanna ride, you learn properly. Get me?"

Kai looked up at his dad, nodding earnestly. "Yeah, Dad. Thanks."

A huge grin spread across my brother's face as he gazed down, almost awestruck at his son. There was so much love between them that it made my chest swell with emotion. It was so beautiful to see Kit finally at peace after all the trauma he'd experienced.

The door opened and my heart fluttered as Colt came sauntering out. He was dressed my favorite way. Black jeans, long-sleeved top, and leather jacket. He looked like something out of a magazine. Handsome, charismatic, and sexy as hell.

His stare caught mine and he shot me a sexy wink. "Merry Christmas," he called out, his eyes resting on Kai's bike. "Whoa, nice wheels, Kai."

My nephew puffed his chest out, resemblant of my dad. "Grandpa got it for me. Isn't she cool?"

Colt cast an appreciative eye over the dirt bike. "You'll have hours of fun on this, but you make sure you're safe, yeah?"

Kai nodded furiously. "Already talked to Dad. He's gonna teach me."

A strangled sound escaped Kennedy's throat.

Kit laughed and pulled her in closer to him. "Don't worry, woman. I'll look after our boy."

I smiled because I knew he meant it.

"Come on," Dad yelled. "It's freezing out here—" he was cut off by a loud rumbling sound coming from down the road.

Colt smirked, turned to Dad, and muttered something I couldn't quite catch before glancing at me and grinning.

Dad stalked over to the small hut where the prospects did their guard duty and began to open the gates.

I looked on, curious as a huge car hauler turned slowly into the compound. My chest began to squeeze when I noticed the lone vehicle it carried. It was my dream car, a big, beautiful, matt black Mercedes-Benz G-Wagon with a huge, red bow on top.

"What the hell's going on?" I murmured to myself as the car hauler pulled into the parking lot and came to a stop.

The truck driver jumped down from his cabin and called out, "Freya Stone?"

My jaw dropped as something thrilling buzzed through me. I pushed the excitement down, taking a deep breath to stop my heart from pounding. There was no way somebody would buy me my dream car. Jesus, you could buy a house for the same money as a G-Wagon.

"Over here," Kennedy called out, pointing me out to the guy who walked toward me with a clipboard under his arm.

"What's going on?" I asked as he approached.

"Happy new car day." He beamed a smile, handing the clipboard to me with a pen. "Just sign here and here," he asked, pointing to two spots on the paperwork.

I stared at him with my mouth hanging open and my heart racing out of my chest.

"You are Freya Stone?" he checked.

I nodded, lost for words before taking the pen and signing my name twice, almost robotically.

My mind reeled as I stared at the matt black vehicle, parked in the lot, its chunky, thick lines and tinted windows gleaming in the winter sunlight. What the hell was going on? I'd dreamed for years of owning a G-Wagon. I used to tell Colt that when I made my first million, I'd treat myself. Nobody else knew it was a secret wish of mine, just him.

My body locked, my spine straightening as rigid as steel as my eyes lifted to meet his gaze across the parking lot.

A grin stretched across Colt's face as he watched me take in the sight of the luxury car, mischief dancing in his expression.

My eyes widened big as saucers, "What did you do?" I screeched, my voice echoing off the clubhouse.

Colt just shrugged nonchalantly. "Happy graduation," he called back, arms folding across his chest as he shot me a smirk.

My mouth formed a perfect 'o' shape, disbelief filling my head. "It's too extravagant," I told him. "It's too much."

He lifted one shoulder in another casual shrug. "I can afford it. Told ya I was gonna get you a graduation gift. That old banger you drive is as old as the dinosaurs. Figured it was time to upgrade your ride."

I jerked my thumb toward the G-Wagon. "It's a three-hundred-thousand-dollar car, Colt."

Dad head jerked back in surprise. "It's a what now?"

"We talked about it in Church," Colt reminded him. "It's not like this is total shock to ya, Prez."

"Don't remember that part," Dad muttered, rubbing his beard while he eyed the car. "It's a lotta scratch to be throwin' around, Son."

The clubhouse doors flew open, and Atlas came sauntering out, followed by Cash. "She's here." My brother whooped. "She's fuckin' gorgeous."

Dad stared at Atlas skeptically. "Did you know how much scratch this one spent?" He jerked a thumb toward Colt.

"Yeah," Atlas said, eyes darting over the car. "We talked about it in Church. He's a rich little fuck. Pocket change to him."

Dad's lips pursed. "My mind must've been somewhere else. Don't remember talkin' about it." He turned to Colt and clapped him on the shoulder. "Personally, I think it's a waste of green, but it's your money. Your decision." He gave the men chin lifts and headed back into the clubhouse.

I stared at the car, my shock turning into a tide of emotion. Gratitude swirled along with disbelief as I took in my beautiful new car. This gift was beyond anything I could've imagined, and it was just like Colt to remember the small conversations and make my dreams come true.

My heart fluttered as my eyes found Colt's again across the parking lot. He'd risked a lot to get me this car. Dad seemed to have accepted it just fine, but it could've gone a completely different way.

Colt's smile spread slowly across his face, crinkling the corners of his eyes, which were fixated on me. He dipped his chin, a silent affirmation of his feelings.

Tears welled in my eyes, blurring his beautiful face.

There was so much reflected in his ocean-blues—love, adoration, pride. My chest twisted as emotions swirled within. I had to get away, I was so overwhelmed. When I glanced back, Colt still gazed at me steadily, his eyes saying everything his voice couldn't.

"Thank you," I mouthed silently.

"I love you," he mouthed back.

My heart swelled.

We were so lost in each other that we didn't realize somebody was watching our silent conversation. If we had, we would've been more careful, but then again, maybe not. Our feelings were so all-consuming, how could we hide them? They were written all over us, in our faces, in the loving looks we threw at each other, and in our reactions whenever the other half of our soul entered the room.

As much as I wanted to be careful, it was getting harder to hide my feelings. The thing was, I knew we had to do it the right way or else we'd hurt my dad, and I didn't want that.

Except, little did I know that very soon, the choice would be taken away, and it would turn out to be a damned nightmare with repercussions I couldn't even begin to imagine.

Chapter Twenty-Nine

Colt

After Freya took Sunny, Kady, Kennedy, and Layla out for a spin in her new car, we all went back inside to watch the kids tear open their gifts.

I'd never seen so much excitement contained inside one room before. The kids were feral, shouting and yelling whenever they opened a gift, but above all else they were grateful, which was nice.

As soon as everything had been cleared away, Adele stuck two fingers in her mouth and let out a piercing whistle. "Can I have your attention please?" she hollered, eyes going from one person to the other as we lounged together on the couches. "The cursing ban is officially in place. You know the score. Five dollars a cuss, all proceeds go to the kids."

"Fuck!" Atlas muttered.

"Five dollars please, Assless," Sunny yelled, skipping toward the SAA, holding her hand out with Jolly Batman prancing around her ankles.

Kai cocked his head at his grandma. "So, what you're sayin' is, every time someone cusses, they have to give us kids five dollars?"

Adele grinned. "That's exactly what I'm saying, Kai."

The boy punched the air. "Cool!"

Atlas went into the inside pocket of his cut and grabbed a wedge of cash. "I'm sorted for the day. Got five grand, all in fives. Job done." He pulled a bill out and handed it to Sunny.

"I don't think so," Sophie interjected, slapping him across the chest. "All that cash wasted because you've got a dirty mouth. That's money we could be spending on the baby."

Kennedy shrugged. "I'll write you kids a check. One of you will have to tally me up at the end of the day."

Kit chuckled.

My gaze slid to Freya, and I smiled when I saw she was watching me intently.

Kennedy waved a hand. "Any of you ladies want to partake in a glass of wine with me?"

"It's eleven o'clock," Layla argued.

Kennedy squeezed two fingers together. "This is how many fucks I give. I don't often drink. I work like a horse, and I look after my kids. If I want an early drink on Christmas day, that's what I'll have."

"Five dollars please, Mommy," Kady called from the corner of the room where she and Sunny were playing with the kittens.

"Shit," Kennedy said under her breath.

"Ten dollars please," Sunny sang.

Kennedy rolled her eyes. "Write it down."

"You're as bad as Atlas," Sophie told her exasperatedly.

"No I'm not," Kennedy argued. "There's no mouth bluer than his." She nodded toward the SAA.

"I'll have a glass of wine," Cara offered. "Cash had a drink last night so it's my turn. I've expressed enough milk to last Wilder a few days."

"Knew you wouldn't let me down," Kennedy told her. "What about you, Freya?"

She went to nod her agreement when her mouth clamped closed. "What's that?" she asked pointing toward Breaker's woman.

Kennedy glanced behind her. "What?"

"On your finger," Freya said loudly. "Is that a ring?"

Breaker leaned down and kissed the top of Kennedy's head. "Took you all long enough to notice. I asked Kitten to marry me this morning and she said yes."

Kennedy held up her left hand and wiggled her finger. "It's a blue diamond. Kit said it matched my eyes."

"More like ya fuckin' teeth," Atlas muttered.

"Fuck off, Coca Cola boy," Ned retorted. "Go swing a dick."

Sunny's voice filled the air. "Five dollars please, Assless."

"And you, Mommy," Kady added.

"See what you've done now," Kennedy said good-naturedly. "Now I'm gonna torture you all day so you end up spending your five grand on my kids."

"Bring it on, bitch." He chuckled.

"That's another five dollars please, Assless," Sunny called over.

The SAA grumbled under his breath.

"What was that, Atlas?" Kennedy asked, tucking her hair behind her ear, and angling herself toward him. "I'm sure I heard you cuss twice there." She deadpanned at the SAA.

I chuckled.

"Ten dollars please, Assless," Sunny yelled.

"I didn't fuckin do anything," he blustered.

"That's another five," Kady requested.

Cash barked a laugh.

Bowie shook his head, grinning.

"Wait!" Freya interrupted, holding her hand up. "I want to know all about the proposal. How did it happen?"

Kennedy leaned forward to address her. "He woke me up this morning with a cup of coffee and it was already on my finger. He told me we're getting married and not to take too long planning it. He doesn't want to wait."

Freya smiled broadly. "That's so romantic."

Atlas rolled his eyes. "Breaker's a soft cunt. Always has been."

Sunny shrieked. "Assless! The 'c' words is ten dollars."

"Since fuckin' when?" he argued.

Sunny stomped over, jammed a hand to her hip and popped it like the little diva she was. "That's a bad, bad word. My mommy said so. If you keeps sayin's that word I'll make you pay ten dollars. How would you like if we saids 'oohh look at Atlas's bigs penis'?"

Laughter filled the room.

"Oh my God," Layla murmured, cheeks staining red.

Cash started to bust a gut.

Breaker chuckled.

Bowie shrugged. "She's gotta point. It is a nasty ass word."

Sunny turned to Bowie. "Five dollars please, daddy."

He looked up to the heavens. "Great."

Freya giggled. "At least she said it was big, Atlas. It could've been worse."

More laughter rang out and I almost choked.

Kennedy coughed. "Coke can."

"Fuck me," Atlas muttered.

"Five dollars please, Assless," Sunny yelled.

The SAA went into his inside pocket, took out the thick clip of bills and dropped it on the coffee table next to him. "Just take it," he snapped. "There's no point even thinkin' I'll get to keep any." His eyes narrowed on Bowie and Breaker. "Wait until Zeus is older. I'll get him to get it all back for me in future holidays when your kids are grown up."

Sophie's forehead furrowed. "Who's Zeus?" she asked, tone confused.

"Our boy," he told her gleefully.

"It sounds like a porn star name," she argued.

"Told ya," Cash piped up.

I sat back from my position at the bar and got myself comfortable.

This lot were hilarious. I loved their banter, especially when the ol' ladies got involved. My heart squeezed painfully in my chest because next year, chances were, me and Freya wouldn't be here to witness all the love and laughter.

Knowing I'd be with my girl softened the blow though. Who knew, maybe we would be here but as a couple. I glanced down at Freya who was already staring at me.

"It'll be okay," she mouthed.

I nodded my agreement,

My stomach twisted. I really hoped my girl was right because I'd miss this, and I knew she would too. Right at that moment, sitting at the bar taking in all the jokes and banter, something hit me.

There was no Christmas like a Speed Demons' Christmas, I just hoped this one wasn't our last.

Cheers went up around the table as Iris, Adele, John, and Abe walked into the bar loaded up with trays full of ham, potatoes, vegetables, and gravy.

Sliding my hand onto Freya's knee under the table, I squeezed gently.

The day was turning out to be strangely emotional and bittersweet for both of us. Maybe it was the time of year that made us catch all the feels. Christmas had always been family time at the club, and I couldn't stop thinking that our days here were drawing to a close.

As the dishes were passed around the table and we helped ourselves, I was reminded how the new year was only a week away, and the consequences of coming clean and dealing with the fallout were becoming more real every day. Suddenly, the thought of Prez's reaction made my throat dry and my hand tremor slightly.

Prez would beat my ass, that was a given, but I wouldn't fight back.

First and foremost, he was my prez and even though I'd betrayed his trust, it didn't take away the respect I had for him. Also, I knew in his and the club's eyes, I'd done wrong. Maybe Cash and Breaker were on my side, but it didn't take away how I'd lied and gone behind Prez's back.

The thought of a beating didn't scare me, I'd had 'em before and no doubt would again. I was more afraid of the disappointment Prez would throw my way. He trusted me and although I'd broken that trust for what I believed was a good reason, I knew it didn't take my colossal betrayal away.

So, sitting there next to the woman I loved, I took everything in, because it would be the last time.

Everyone's mood seemed melancholy.

Bowie sat the other side of me with Sunny next to him, and I could overhear him talking to her.

"It's been a year today since you became my daughter," he said softly.

Sunny looked up at him and beamed. "I wished for you," she murmured. "Mommy was sad, and she was too thin, and I knew she didn't eats enough 'cause she wanted me to eats all the food. I prayed to Jesus to send me a daddy who'd looks after Mommy."

My throat thickened.

Bowie took his daughter's hand and squeezed it. "I knew you were meant to be mine at our first barbeque. Do you remember?"

She nodded furiously.

"You told me to get your mom flowers and take them to the salon. Said she'd love me if I did." He grinned down at her. "Best advice anyone ever gave me."

By then the table had fallen silent, everyone listening to the conversation.

"Then remember when I brought you your Switch?" he continued. "You ran at me, squealin' and I thought I'd done somethin' wrong. Then you looked up at me with those big, baby doe eyes and it hit me in the chest, Sunny. You were mine, the same as your mom was. I knew I was put on the Earth for you two. Then we had Willow and we've got the twins coming soon and I'm so fuckin' happy, Sunshine. You're the light of my life."

Layla let out a quiet sob.

John gulped.

Even Atlas looked at father and daughter with the softest eyes I'd ever seen on him.

"Daddy?" Sunny said gently. "That's five dollars, please. You swored."

Everyone began to laugh.

I took the bottle of wine Bowie passed to me and poured Freya then myself a glass. I'd chosen it so I knew it was good stuff. It was the wine my mom used to serve at dinner parties. My stomach jerked at the thought of my mom, and I realized I hadn't called her to wish her a merry Christmas. She'd probably be drunk by now anyway, so I decided to call her the next day.

I reached under the table and squeezed Freya's knee again. She looked gorgeous in her baggy sweater dress and high boots. I smiled at the notion that soon, we wouldn't have to hide anymore. I didn't mind admitting it was beginning to wear me down.

"Are you okay?" Freya asked softly.

I took a bite of potato, put my fork down, and twisted my body to face her, chewing thoughtfully. "Just thinkin' about life and where we'll be next year," I told her, voice low to avoid being overheard.

Freya looked around the table, then back to me. "I know. It's hard to imagine. I've never known anything but this."

"Any regrets?" I asked gently.

Her eyes lifted to meet mine and she shook her head. "Not one. I'll miss this but I don't think it'll be long before we can come back. In the meantime, we can have our own Christmas's together."

I gave her knee a supportive squeeze, hoping to instill some confidence. We could do this. We could build our own life, our own family, and traditions.

I turned back to the table, lifting my fork to take another bite, but the motion stilled halfway to my mouth when I caught sight of Atlas watching us. His stare hardened as it flicked between me and Freya, and his lip curled angrily.

My heart plummeted into my ass, and I heaved out a slow breath.

Of course, he knew—Atlas was smarter than he looked. Thoughts and questions raced through my mind but only one stood out.

What was he going to do about it?

I'd have to speak to him, explain the situation and ask him to hold off on telling Dagger. I wanted the chance to tell him myself.

Despite his rough exterior and blind loyalty to the club, Atlas was no troublemaker. If anything, he worked tirelessly to smooth out tension within the club. I doubted he'd run to Dagger telling tales—it wasn't his style at all—Atlas knew Dagger's reaction would be a shitstorm of epic proportions.

With more bravery than I felt, I met Atlas's stare head on.

He tilted his chin slightly toward the hallway leading to my office, a silent command to talk.

I gave him a slight dip of my chin in agreement. Turning to Freya, I muttered. "Be back soon. Just remembered I haven't spoken to my mom today. Gonna go make a quick call."

She looked up at me questioningly. "What about your food?"

I rubbed my stomach, giving her the impression I was full. "I've had enough. Gonna save myself for all the leftovers. You know there's always enough food to feed an army."

She smiled understandingly before turning her attention back to Kennedy who was seated on the other side of her.

By the time I stood and headed for the corridor, Atlas had already disappeared down it. With more confidence than I felt, I sauntered after him all the way down to my office.

The minute walk seemed to take an hour. Every step felt like I was marching toward my execution.

Atlas working everything out wasn't something I'd factored into the situation and if I was a betting man, I'd wager that Atlas's loyalties didn't lie with me. He was a biker through and through and he always did what was best for the club as a whole. I couldn't help hoping he'd understand that telling Prez about me and Freya would be bad for the Speed Demons.

I walked into my office, closing the door behind me, pulled my shoulders back, and braced.

Atlas's eyes scrutinized me before he scraped a hand down his face. "How long?" he asked bluntly. "And don't fuckin' insult my intelligence by lyin', it's as clear as the nose on your pretty boy face."

There was no point pretending and certainly no honor in lying. "A couple of months," I admitted. "It started when I went down to Denver. It's pretty new, but I know she's mine. Been feelin' it for a while, but it took time to catch up."

"So, it's serious?" he asked.

"I wouldn't risk everythin' for somethin' that wasn't," I explained.

Atlas rubbed his beard, deep in thought. "Reckon you should tell, Prez. You know he'll kick you out, right?"

"Yeah," I confirmed.

"When?"

"New Year's Day," I muttered. "I wanted to tell him straightaway, but Freya wanted one last holiday at the club. It's real between us. You don't gotta like it, but I'd appreciate you givin' me time to come clean myself."

Atlas eyed me briefly before dipping his chin in assent. "I'll give you a week, but if Dagger finds out from someone else it'll make him even more pissed."

"I know," I assured him. "I'll tell him. One week."

"What ya gonna do when he throws you out?" Atlas asked. "Join another club?"

I noted his narrowed eyes and it hit me that he was worried about the club's security, especially if I joined another MC. "I've been recruited by the Feds."

He cursed under his breath, viciously.

I held a hand up. "They know Henderson Junior died in questionable circumstances. They've threatened to pin it on the club if I don't give in. On top'a that, they caught me peekin' inside places where I definitely shouldn't have been. If I don't join 'em, they'll lock us all up and throw away the key."

His lip curled into a snarl. "Fuckin' pigs."

I shrugged. "I'll be one of 'em soon, At. Can't escape it. I'm lucky to have gotten away with it for as long as I have." I looked him dead in the eye. "They'll never discover the inner workings of this club from me, brother. I know it's hard to trust me given the circumstances, but I swear on everythin' holy, I'll never talk about it. I'll always be here to help with anythin' you need, no matter if I'm a biker or a Fed."

He shook his head. "Can't work with pigs under any circumstances. I get what you're doin', even think it's noble, to a point, but you know me and the law. We don't mix. Once you leave you cease to be my brother."

A flash of pain jolted through my chest. I expected it, Atlas didn't like law enforcement, he never had, and I couldn't blame him. From what I could ascertain, Atlas had come across more than his fair share of dirty cops, Sophie's ex-husband included.

"I get it," I murmured. "Thanks for givin' me time to approach Dagger. It's much appreciated."

Atlas jerked a nod. "If you don't tell him by midnight on New Year's Day, I'll have a chat with him. I'm doin' this for Freya. You've touched his girl who you knew was off-limits. I can't respect that."

"What if it was Sophie who was off-limits," I asked.

"Nothin' would keep me away from my woman," he retorted. "But the fact remains that she wasn't. I wasn't breaking the rules the second I touched her. You were."

I jerked a nod. "Message received."

"It'll be a blow to the club to lose ya, Colt," he admitted. "We'll feel your loss."

"That's just it though, Atlas." I rubbed at the tension headache forming in my temple. "You don't need to lose me. I'll always help ya if you need me. I won't abandon you."

"Even if I took a leap of faith, Prez wouldn't entertain it after he finds out about you and Freya." He shrugged.

"Yeah." My lips thinned. "I know."

He clapped me on the back. "We better move our asses. Stitch will be wondering where I've gone. Don't need her givin' me shit, especially when she's knocked up."

We turned for the door and walked up the corridor in silence.

Suddenly, it had become even more real. There was no turning back now, even if I wanted to—which I didn't.

We took our seats again and I smiled at Freya as she finished her conversation with Kennedy.

"Everything okay with your mom?" she asked.

"All good," I told her, grabbing my wine glass and draining it. I almost laughed out loud when across from me, I saw Atlas tuck into his food like our powwow had never happened.

I think he understood that I'd never put the club in danger or jeopardize anyone's safety. As much as I'd done shitty things, I still respected, loved, and cared for my brothers.

The table seemed quieter than when I left. I realized the kids had left the room. "Where have Sunny, Kai, and Kady gone?" I asked Freya, filling my wine glass again before I topped hers up.

"They asked to go outside," she explained. "I said it was a bit cold, but Dad said it was okay as long as they wrapped up."

"That's weird," I mused. "New kittens, dirt bikes, and toys comin' outta their assholes and they wanna go out back?"

"You're right," Freya replied softly, craning her neck to see outta the window into the backyard area. "I hope they're not going up on that death trap slide."

I barked a laugh. "Baby. Sunny won't go within ten feet of it after she got stuck at the top with Atlas. She's shit scared of it."

Freya giggled. "It was the funniest thing I've ever seen—"

An ear-splitting scream sounded from outside.

Chairs scraped back as every man—including me—jumped up from the table and checked their cuts for weapons.

Kai's voice bellowed from afar. "Dad! Help!"

My heart began to race as I stood and sprinted after Bowie, Breaker, and Cash who all darted for the corridor leading to the kitchen where we could get to the closest exit leading to the backyard.

"Who's got a weapon?" Breaker called out.

"Me!" Atlas replied from my back.

"Get up front with me," Breaker ordered, his dark eyes blanking. "Be careful and remember the kids are out there. They could cop a stray bullet."

My shoulders tensed at the mere thought of one of the kids getting shot. I kept my head down, following Breaker and Atlas through the kitchen until we all burst out of the door together. I looked up when suddenly, an eerie, high-pitched bugle sound filled the air.

My eyes widened at the scene before me. "What the fuck?"

A big, brown elk raced past us with Sunshine riding low on its back, clinging onto its huge, fanned antlers for dear life.

"Hornnnyyy! Stoooooopppppp!" she shrieked as it galloped toward the parking lot.

"Dad!" Kai yelled. "Save Sunny! She wanted to ride on Horny, but he bolted."

Bowie scraped a hand down his face. "Jesus, fuck!" he bellowed. "What on God's goddamned green Earth is Sunny doin' ridin' a fuckin' elk?"

"It's her horsey," Kady shrieked, wringing her hands. "Horny's her pet horsey."

Atlas roared with laughter. "She kidnapped a fuckin' elk?" He bent over, hands to knees, busting a gut. "Jesus Christ." He hooted another laugh. "A—A—And fuckin' Horny!" He fell to the ground on his ass from laughing so hard.

Prez appeared at my back. "Don't just fuckin' stand there. Somebody go save Sunshine."

Breaker grabbed Atlas's gun and went to aim.

"Noooo, Daddy!" Kady screamed. "Don't shoot Horny. He's our pet!"

"Well how else am I meant to stop him?" Break yelled.

"I'll go get some rope," Cash suggested. "I'll lasso the motherfucker."

"This ain't the wild west," Dagger bellowed.

"Fuckin' is," Cash retorted. "I can rope those antlers no problem."

Sunny let out another piercing scream as the elk changed direction again and sprinted toward the back of the yard. Luckily, we'd mended the fence leading to the woods so it couldn't escape with her on its back.

Dagger jammed his hands to his waist and looked to the heavens. "Get somethin' to make a lasso with," he yelled. "And be quick."

"Here ya go, boss," Billy said, appearing with a length of thick rope. "This'll do the job."

Cash grabbed it, immediately making a noose, and tied it.

"Oh my God!" Layla shrieked as she slowly made her way out of the kitchen, rubbing her pregnant belly.

"Save her, Bowie." She peered closer. "Wait. Is that an elk?" Her eyes widened and she screeched, "What's Sunny doing riding an elk?"

"I—It's her h—horsey," Atlas stuttered through his belly laugh. "She c—called him Horny."

Layla covered her face with her hands. "Oh my God."

"It's okay," Cash shouted. "I'm gonna rope the motherfucker. I'll save her."

"Hurry up, Uncle Cash," Kai called out. "Look, she's scared."

I peered over to see Sunny's face all scrunched up and wet with tears, screaming as the elk ran past us again. "Mommyyyyyy! Heeelp!"

"Hold on, Sunny!" Layla shouted. "Cash is going to save you."

The VP ran toward the elk, circling the lasso above his head like a biker version of John Wayne. He threw the loop toward the elk who sidestepped it and ran the opposite way.

Tears streamed down Atlas's face.

"You were nowhere fuckin' near ropin' it," Prez muttered. "Try again."

"Oh my God, Cash," Cara snapped as she barreled out of the kitchen. "Just throw the fucking rope. Stop pussy-assing around."

Atlas, still on the ground, held his crotch in his hands. "Gonna piss my breeches," he barked through his laughter. "Jesus fuckin' Christ."

Abe's lips twitched so hard it looked like he was having a seizure. "She doesn't fail to amuse us every Christmas, does she?"

"Oh my God," Layla murmured again, her tearful eyes following Sunny who screamed her lungs out.

Finally, the elk began to slow down, obviously exhausted. "I'll grab the left side," I offered.

Bowie pursed his lips. "I'll get the right."

"I've got the rope," Cash shouted, following behind us as we tried to corner the massive elk.

The beast tossed its head and let out another loud trumpeting call.

Sunny wailed.

We approached slowly. "We should hold our hands out, so Horny doesn't think we're a threat," Cash suggested.

"It's an elk, asshole," Bowie muttered. "Not a fuckin' prisoner of war."

"How the fuck does your kid get herself in these messes?" I asked, keeping my voice low as we edged closer.

"God knows," he murmured. "She gets it from her mother's side."

We neared the elk. "Slowly," Bowie said gently. "Get to the side of the fuckin' thing, and grab Sunny."

"On it," Cash replied quietly. "Don't make any sudden movements." He crept up to the side of the elk, and as soon as it tossed its head, he grabbed Sunny off its back. "Got her," he yelled, sprinting for the kitchen, with Sunny tossed over his shoulder.

A loud roar went up as everyone began shouting and clapping.

"Run!" Bowie yelled, turning on his heel and sprinting back toward the kitchen.

"Fucker," I muttered, twisting my body, and following hot on his heels.

The elk let out another loud trumpet from behind us as we raced toward the kitchen.

"Get the kids inside," Bowie bellowed. "It might bolt for 'em."

"Horny won't hurt us," Sunny cried, looking up from Cash's shoulder with a tear-streaked face. "He's a good horsey. He likes carrots."

"Sunshine," Bowie barked. "It's a fuckin' wild elk, not a horse."

"Five dollars please, Daddy," she said, stretching her hand toward Bowie as Cash ran inside the kitchen with her.

Everyone else trailed in behind them from the yard, all talking at once. He handed her over to Layla who bent down, running her hands over Sunny's body to check for injuries. "Are you okay, Sunshine? Are you hurt?"

Sunny shook her head. "Horny didn't mean to scare me," she insisted. "He's a nice horsey and he loves kids."

Layla stood to her full height again, face shocked. "How long have you had him?" she asked, her voice tight with fright.

Sunny's bottom lip wobbled.

"Since the day we got to the club," Kai admitted. "Horny wandered down from the woods, so Sunny took him to the old barn the club used years ago for storage. He's been living there ever since."

Layla's eyes widened. "She's kept a wild elk in a barn for nearly six months?" Her gaze slashed to Sunny who stood there pouting.

Kai's eyes lowered. "Yip. I wanted to tell you, but if I did Sunny wouldn't talk to me and I'm not a rat." He looked up at Breaker and rolled his eyes. "You know what women are like."

Kennedy raised a hand to cover her laugh.

"I just wanted a horsey," Sunny murmured. "And you saids no." Tears filled her eyes and she let out a tiny sob.

Prez's back snapped straight. "Prospect!" he yelled out the kitchen door.

Billy sauntered in from the yard where he and a few of the men were talking, probably about how they were gonna get rid of a fucking elk. "Yeah, Prez?"

"Call around all the ranches in the area. Ask 'em if they've got any ponies for sale," he ordered.

Sunny's eyes rounded. "Oh my Gods," she whispered.

"John! No!" Layla protested.

Atlas began to crack up laughing again.

Dagger turned to Layla and shrugged. "It's just a pony or two."

"I don't want one, Grandpa," Kai told him. "I've got my bike."

Kady kept her mouth shut. The kid wasn't stupid, and she obviously was all over getting a pony.

Kennedy popped a hip. "I hope you're not expecting me to muck out shitty stables, John. I'm far too pretty for manual labor."

Dagger turned to her, rubbing his beard in thought. "God, forbid you get your hands dirty. That's what we've got prospects for."

Billy pursed his lips. "Great."

"Come on, everyone," Abe bellowed. "Excitements all done. Let's get back to the table."

Laughter and chatter filled the air about the elk incident as everyone headed back into the bar. Me and Freya lagged toward the back and walked together.

My pinkie reached out to touch hers. I couldn't stop myself, whenever she was close, I needed to feel her, even if it was only a millimeter of skin. I'd never been drawn to anyone like I was her. Our hearts were magnets, pulling us together and connecting our souls.

Getting through the day knowing what was about to happen made my chest ache but it also strengthened my resolve. The stakes were high, but Freya was worth the risk. I'd choose her every time, no hesitation.

I only hoped that Dagger would go easy on me when the truth finally came out.

Chapter Thirty

Freya

I slicked on some nude lip gloss and smoothed down my long white skirt, making sure my matching crop top was in place and my boobs were contained.

It was New Years Eve, and I was dressed to party.

Christmas day had passed without any more elk incidents, thank God, and the following days that led up to New Year were filled with love, laughter, and family.

I'd soaked everything up. Each joke, every burst of laughter, and every beautiful, heartwarming moment because I knew everything was about to change.

Colt and I snatched fleeting moments together, but it was difficult to get privacy with so many people around. Families were still living at the clubhouse because of the fires the Sinners set earlier in the year. The new houses were being built, but everybody was in limbo until they were finished.

Most of my interactions with Colt were over the phone with him in his room, and me in mine. We were tempted to sneak around and do some bed hopping but Colt didn't feel right about it with my dad under the same roof.

Talking of Dad—he announced the day after Christmas that he wanted to throw a New Year's Eve party. A buzz of excitement spread around the clubhouse and the town. Everybody was invited, Dad said, he wanted it to be the shindig of the year.

My excitement was palpable. Colt planned to go into Dad's office first thing in the morning on New Years Day and tell him all about us. The party was an opportunity for me and him to go out with a bang amongst all our friends and family and say a proper goodbye.

My eyes caught on the boxes and bags stacked up in the corner of my room.

I'd started packing and throwing away all the things I didn't need. I'd already filled two suitcases and had boxes full to the brim ready to go into storage. It was crazy how much stuff I'd accumulated over the years.

Shifting through everything evoked memories that were so beautiful, I couldn't help wishing there was a different way. Leaving everybody I loved made my heart ache and although I knew it was something I had to do, it wasn't easy for me.

However, I had faith in Colt and what we had. Living without him would be akin to all the light in my life being stripped away, and as much as I knew I'd miss home I couldn't help feeling excited for our new beginning.

My cell pinged with a notification. I smiled, knowing who it was before I even picked up the phone.

Colt: Show me!

I stretched my arm upward, pointed my phone downward, and snapped a picture. Then, I sent it to Colt with a love heart emoji.

Within a minute he sent me a GIF back of a cartoon cat with his eyes shooting out on stalks. Giggling, I sent him one back of two love birds kissing before heading for my door and making my way down the hallway, strutting on my strappy sandals, to inject a swing in my hips.

The thumping music and chatter enveloped me as I stepped into the already crowded bar. It took a few seconds for my eyes to adjust to the dim lighting. I spotted Colt's tall figure leaning against the bar. His gaze immediately caught mine and his lips curled into the sexy smirk that made my heart race. With a little wink, he tipped his bottle back, Adam's apple bobbing as he took a swig of beer.

My heart swelled inside my chest watching him joke with Dad, Cash, and Kit. I stared, wondering how his charm could draw me in from so far away, when a familiar voice brought me out of my thoughts.

"Freya!"

I turned to see Kennedy's blonde bouncy curls catch the light as she stood and waved excitedly. Cara, Sophie, Anna, and Tristan were all seated around a table with her, beckoning me over. Weaving through the crowds, the heavy bass of the song pulsed through me, and I couldn't stop a wide smile from splitting my face.

"Hey!" I exclaimed, joining the group and taking the empty seat next to Tristan. "This place is popping."

"It's fucking awesome," Kennedy agreed.

"Did you see who the cat dragged in?" Tristan asked, nodding toward Lucy on the dance floor. "The cat being Serena 'stuck-up' Stafford."

I craned my neck. "Where's her husband?"

Tristan laughed, wriggling his shoulders. "Word on the streets of Hambleton is that he ran off with a young, pretty bartender from the country club."

My eyes widened. "No way!"

He nodded, crossing his index finger over his chest. "Cross my heart, hope to die, stick a big dick in my eye, if I tell a lie."

I giggled. "They've only been married a year."

Cara leaned forward conspiratorially. "Looks like Carl Tucker's looking for an easy lay." She nodded toward the dance floor where the man in question was sliding his arm around Lucy's shoulder, trying to talk to her while she danced.

I laughed, settling comfortably in my seat before stealing another look at Colt. His eyes were on me, blazing with heat as they flicked down my body then back up to my face. He smiled sexily, then turned back to say something to Cash.

"Oh my God!" Tristan exclaimed, his gaze sliding toward Colt. "Are you and the golden god...?" He paused. "You know. Is he filling up your love box?"

"Sshh," I said, looking around, trying not to laugh.

"He certainly is," Kennedy chimed in. "They're both so loved up with each other it can get a bit sickening."

"Amazing!" Tristan clapped his hands together rapidly. "You've lusted after the golden god for years. Oh, Freya, you've given me hope. Dreams really do come true."

Just as we began to laugh, the opening bars to 'Mr. Brightside' by The Killers came on. It was mixed with a dance tune, giving it a cool, electro vibe.

Tristan jumped up. "Come on, Princess Stone. It's about time we lit up the dance floor."

"I'm coming!" Kennedy announced.

Cara got to her feet. "Me too."

Tristan pulled me into the throng of people moving in time to the song. I craned my neck to see Cara and Kennedy following. We found a spot and began to dance, moving in time to the music.

Tristan grabbed my hips and pulled me into him. "Come on, Freya. Show daddy what you've got."

I threw my head back and laughed, snaking my arms around his neck, and grinding on him.

Tristan was so much fun. I loved going out with him. He was my partner in crime and always showed me a good time. He let loose and gave zero fucks, which appealed to me. I loved him like a brother, and we had each other's backs.

I looked around to see Kennedy and Cara dancing next to us. Tristan took my hand and spun me before grabbing Kennedy's fingers and doing the same to her.

Cara went behind Tristan and grabbed his hips, moving with him in perfect synchronicity. Trist let out a whoop, turned, and pulled her in front of him, giving her a kiss on the cheek. Kennedy and I laughed. She grabbed my hand and started grinding her hips like the ex-Vegas stripper she was, showing me how to copy.

One song morphed into another. We carried on dancing, making up funny little dances and laughing raucously. Our group steadily got bigger, Anna joined us, then Reno and Shotgun came over and started screwing around, pretending to ballroom dance with each other.

We were screaming with laughter when I caught a flash of leather and dark blond hair out of the corner of my eye, turning to see Colt and Breaker coming over to join us.

Tristan nudged me, nodding toward Colt. "Didn't take him long."

I grinned as he approached, eyes flashing with desire as they took in my white outfit and sexy heels.

He caught my fingers and pulled me close, rasping, "You look fuckin' edible."

My eyes lifted to meet Colt's. "So do you."

His fingertips dug into my hips, and he began to move with me in time to the music, leaning closer and whispering into the shell of my ear. "Tempted to drag you outta here, pull that sexy skirt up around your waist and fuck your tight little cunt until you beg for mercy."

Heat flared low in my belly, desire rushing through my veins like wildfire. I ground into him with a soft moan, craving the feel of his hands on my skin. "Jesus. You're such a tease."

"So are you in that outfit." Colt nipped the curve of my neck, the sharp sting sending sparks skittering across my shoulder. "I wanna slide that skirt right up over those sexy hips of yours." His hands slid down to cup my ass, pulling me tighter to him. I could feel the hard ridge of his cock pressed against my belly and I sent up a word of thanks that the dance floor was so packed nobody could see where his hands were.

I looked up. "I want you to fuck me so bad," I purred.

Colt growled, the sound vibrating against my cheek. "Be careful what you wish for, Princess. Tomorrow, when we leave, I'm gonna spend a whole month buried inside you."

"Promises, promises," I sassed.

He threw his head back and laughed. "Oh, it's a promise alright."

I looked up into his languid, hooded eyes. The bright blue had darkened, a telltale sign that he was turned on.

He leaned down to whisper. "Are you packed?"

Our eyes locked. "Yeah. Just the essentials."

"You ready for what's to come?" he asked.

I smiled up at the man I'd loved since I was a girl, and who I knew I'd love until the day they put me in the ground. "As long as I'm with you I'm ready for anything."

He grinned down at me with soft eyes, swirling with emotion. "You wanna get a drink?"

"Yeah."

Colt turned me toward the bar, guiding me through the crowd of people dancing. His hand on my back was a steadying presence as his touch directed me through the writhing mass of people on the dance floor, who cleared a path as soon as they saw Colt's broad shoulders trying to get through.

Dad stood at the bar, shooting the shit with Cash and Atlas. He saw us and raised his beer bottle. "Yo. You kids enjoyin' yourselves?"

I smiled broadly. I liked Pop when he was tipsy. He was a big guy and could handle his beer, so he didn't get drunk often, even though he was funny as hell after a few beers.

"Hey, Dad." I approached him, rolled up on my toes and kissed his cheek. "The party's amazing."

He puffed his chest out. "There's no shindig like a Speed Demons' shindig," he said proudly. "Back in the day, Friday nights around here were famous throughout the state."

Atlas angled his beer bottle toward Dad. "Prez is right. We used to have a queue down the block of people tryin'a get in. Bandit used to go out, see who liked the look of and let them in. If they had the wrong hairstyle or shoes, he'd tell 'em to fuck off."

I giggled. "I can't imagine Gramps doing that. I mean, even I knew growing up that he had issues, but he was always so lovely to me. I can't imagine him being an asshole."

Dad smiled indulgently at me. "Your grandpa thought the sun rose and set with you, Freya. The day you were born he wept like a baby. Said you were the most beautiful thing he'd ever seen and that you'd go far. He'd be so fuckin' proud'a ya. Just like I am."

Another thing about a tipsy John Stone was that he got over emotional and extremely loving, which usually I'd be all over, except I knew what the following day would bring. I couldn't stop the ache from ravaging my chest when I realized that in a matter of hours, all that pride he felt toward me would disappear.

Over the next couple of hours, we stood at the bar with Dad, Cash, and Atlas, joking around, chatting, and laughing. Before we knew it, the countdown to the new year was about to begin.

It was Cash who had his eye on the clock. After beckoning Cara, Sophie, Kit, and Kennedy over, he put one hand on the bar and jumped up onto it before sticking two fingers in his mouth and let out a piercing whistle.

The music lowered, and the crowd quietened down.

"Everybody settle," my brother bellowed. "It's time!"

Everyone cheered and roared their approval and then their feet began to stomp.

Cash threw his head back and howled loudly to the moon. "Mess with a Demon..." he yelled. Men who were previously sitting, got to their feet, and joined in as the entire room yelled the rest of the Demons' club motto. "And we'll raise hell!"

An earsplitting cheer almost raised the roof of the clubhouse. The atmosphere was electric, I could feel the charge in the air as everyone raised their glasses.

Colt flashed his phone up at Cash who eyed it and nodded. "Here we go!" he began. "Ten." Voices hollered and hooted, all joining in with Cash as they counted down to see the new year in. Finally, they got to one and an almighty roar went up.

Dad tugged my hand and pulled me into him, his familiar scent of engine oil and Kouros cologne weaving around me as he leaned in close. "Happy New Year, sweetheart," he muttered, his breath warm against my ear.

Before I could respond, Kit grabbed me, planted a kiss on my cheek then passed me onto Cash who did the same. Bowie appeared from nowhere with a tired looking Layla and bellowed "Happy New Year" to more shouts and cheers.

Atlas grabbed me and gave me a sloppy kiss, then another pair of arms wrapped around me, squeezing tight.

Cara, Kennedy, and Sophie suddenly huddled around me in a blur of perfume, wine, and giggles. They smothered me with kisses and hugs.

"Happy New Year!"

"This is gonna be our year. I can feel it."

"Love you, Freya."

Their love and enthusiasm was infectious, and warmth bloomed in my chest at all the emotions coursing through me. I'd always remember this moment. Whatever happened next, I knew I was lucky to have this and to be able to see the new year in with the people I loved.

Talking of which, my eyes automatically lifted, searching for Colt.

Somebody turned the music back up and the heavy bass thumped through the room as I extracted myself from the girls and scanned the room for my man.

I smiled when I saw him just a few feet away at the bar. His eyes locked on mine, and a smile spread across his handsome face. He looked relaxed, leaning one elbow casually on the bar with a beer in hand, but beneath his composure, his eyes burned with so much love as he studied me that it made my chest ache.

Our connection was palpable, even in a crowded room. I could feel the emotion emanating from him as he took a swig of his beer, his ocean-blues never leaving me. So much passed between us in that one look, that any lingering doubts melted away.

My heart was so full of love for him that it felt as if it would burst, because I knew that no matter what happened next, we'd face it together.

The party raged on until well after two A.M.

My very tipsy Dad threw in the towel around one o'clock and turned in. Bowie and Layla only made an appearance to see in the new year with us because Layla was exhausted, the twins took so much out of her.

Just after Dad left, Atlas said his goodnights and made Sophie turn in with him. She was six months pregnant and even though she was enjoying herself, she admitted defeat.

The rest of us sat at the bar and watched the party wind down, chatting and drinking together.

Colt took the stool next to me and threaded his fingers through mine, all sense of pretense gone. He was quiet and I knew his mind was probably going over what was about to happen. I wished I could take it off his shoulders, wished I could make everything better, but I couldn't.

Tomorrow was our D-day. We were finally there.

Cash clapped Colt on the shoulder, pulling him away from his thoughts. "You okay?"

Colt glanced at me and grinned. "Yeah. Just thinkin' about tomorrow."

It went quiet for a while before Kit piped up. "What if Dad's okay with it?"

Cash barked a laugh. "And what if a flying pig decided to glide around the clubhouse?"

Kennedy sent me a sad smile. "I'll miss you."

I rubbed her arm. "I'll miss you too, but we're not emigrating. We'll be able to visit and I'm hoping to God you'll all visit us wherever we end up."

"I think you should look for work in Hawaii," Cara suggested. "I'll visit every weekend."

I laughed. "As much as I like the sun, I also love the seasons."

"You're all actin' like it's gonna be all doom and gloom," Cash remarked. "But you're forgettin' somethin'."

We all looked at my brother expectantly.

"Dad's steppin' down next year. Who's gonna be Prez then?" He waggled his eyebrows. "It'll be my club and my rules. Dad may kick you out, but I won't. When I'm Prez you'll always be welcome. Build on Freya's plot so you've gotta home here. Come for the holidays, hell, come whenever you like. I'll never turn you away."

Colt squeezed my hand. "Thanks, brother," he said before turning to me. "Pick out furnishings for your house. I've got all the measurements. We'll get it sorted."

A weight I never realized had settled on my shoulders suddenly lifted, making me feel twenty pounds lighter. I looked up at Colt. "Can I?"

He slid his arm across my shoulders. "Get whatever you like, baby."

Cara jerked a thumb toward him. "See," she muttered to Cash. "Colt gets it. Happy wife, happy life."

Cash looked up and heaved a breath. "Colt's got more money than he knows what to do with, Wildcat. I haven't."

She stared at me, pursing her lips. "He thinks I don't know about his top-secret savings account."

Cash tensed.

Cara smirked. "If you don't want me knowing about your shit, don't leave your statements lying around for me to come across."

My eldest brother sighed exasperatedly.

I looked around the room to see it was almost empty. It had been a great party. Everyone enjoyed themselves. My heart jolted when I realized it had been a perfect goodbye. I'd always remember this night and all the love and sense of family.

I brought my hand up to cover a yawn. "I think I'm gonna turn in." I glanced at Colt and smiled sadly. "We've got a big day tomorrow."

He nodded. "We'll go to my room for a chat. Sort out what were gonna do."

"What time you goin' to see Dad?" Breaker asked.

Colt shrugged more nonchalantly than he probably felt. "As soon as he's in. I can't see him bein' up and about early though."

"How 'bout we all meet in here at ten?" Cash suggested, turning to Kit. "That way we can go in the office with him. Have his back."

"I'll be here," Kit confirmed.

Cara leaned her head on my brother's shoulder. "I knew there was a reason I loved you."

Cash grinned. "Let's not get it twisted. You love me for my big, fat cock. Doncha, Wildcat?"

Chuckles rose up as Cara slapped Cash hard across his chest. "Asshole."

He grabbed her and planted a long hard kiss on her lips.

Kit stood, gathered Kennedy in his arms, picking her up bridal style. "Come on, Kitten. Let's go fuck the new year in."

She laughed. "Okay, big boy. Take me to bed."

We all said our goodbyes, watching as Kit walked off with his woman in his arms.

Colt stood and held his hand out to me. "Come on, Princess. We got a lotta shit to discuss and we gotta be up early in the morning. We need to get some shut-eye."

Placing my hand in his, he gently pulled me to my feet and locked eyes with me. "You ready to do this?" he asked.

I jerked one nod. "Yeah, Colter. I'm ready."

Turning, I gave Cara a tight hug, pulling back to murmur, "See you in the morning."

Cash smiled down at me and opened his arm for me to walk into. "You'll be okay, pretty girl," he whispered in my ear as I squeezed him. "I'll look after your man."

I looked up into the same golden eyes I saw every day in the mirror. "I love you, Xan."

He dropped a kiss on my head. "Love you too, Sis."

I pulled back and turned for the corridor to Colt's room while he gave Cash a clap on the shoulder and Cara a kiss on the cheek. His fingertips grazed the small of my back, guiding me down the hall in silence.

My nerves jangled with each step, the knowledge of what lay ahead bearing down on my shoulders. I didn't quite know what to expect, which made everything seem more ominous.

Colt's hand pressed more firmly as if sensing my unease.

I glanced up at him, but his stare remained fixed ahead, his stubbled jaw clenched tight. He seemed as on edge as I was.

Colt pulled his keys out of his pocket as we approached his room. After a few seconds, he pushed the door open and gestured for me to go inside.

I stood awkwardly, wrapping my arms around myself as Colt flicked on the lamp sitting on his nightstand. The warm light sent a muted beam through the room, making the shadows dance.

Colt grabbed my hand and led me toward the bed. "Get in," he ordered gently, leaning down, and pulling the comforter back. "You're freezing."

I kicked my shoes off and sank into the bed, breathing in the familiar scent of Creed and watching as Colt took off his cut and laid it carefully over the back of a chair before getting into bed next to me. I shifted until I was laid on my side, so we faced each other.

"I'm scared," I murmured.

"It's gonna be okay," he assured me, pushing my hair back from my face. "Whatever happens we'll be together, Frey."

"Where are we gonna go?" I asked quietly.

"Maybe we could take a vacation?" he suggested. "I've always wanted to go to Bora Bora. Stay in one of those huts on stilts in the sea. We can regroup while we're there and decide where we wanna move to. I'm thinkin' Virginia initially, while I get my assignment sorted and we can take it from there."

I smiled because he'd obviously thought about it. "Sounds amazing."

His hand caught mine. "We're gonna be okay. We just need to get tomorrow outta the way."

"Yeah," I said sleepily, my eyes drooping.

His hand gently swiped a lock of hair out of my eyes. "Go to sleep, baby. I'll wake you up early."

I nodded, so physically and mentally exhausted that I was already falling asleep. The bed moved and I heard Colt's zipper and the rustle of his jeans before he gently undid my skirt and top and slid them off, leaving me in just my panties.

"Goodnight, baby," he whispered, kissing my forehead.

But I didn't reply, I was already dropping off to sleep, my exhausted mind wondering what the hell tomorrow would bring.

A loud banging sound pulled me out of my deep sleep.

Colt let out a groan, his warm body stirring beside me.

"Colt!" a deep voice called out. "You in there?"

I jerked awake, my heart dropping like a deadweight as I lurched to a sitting position and blinked in the bright morning light.

"Jesus!" Colt muttered, leaping out of bed, and reaching for his jeans. "It's your fuckin' dad." He grabbed his phone from the nightstand and cursed under his breath before dropping it with a clatter and pulling his jeans on. "It's nine o'clock. We overslept."

"Colt!" Dad yelled from the hallway. "Open the fuckin' door. Need to talk to ya."

"Fuck! Fuck! Fuck!" Colt spat, zipping his jeans, and going to his dresser and pulling out a tee. "He heard me."

Panic rose in my chest as Dad rapped loudly on the door again. "Who you got in there?" he shouted. "Have you seen Freya? Her bed wasn't slept in last night."

My throat thickened, my stomach twisting painfully. "Shit!"

Colt looked straight at me, his eyes bugging out.

Our shocked stares locked together in silent conversation. I watched the panic in his eyes shift, morphing into resignation. His shoulders slumped and he heaved out a breath that seemed to carry the weight of the world.

"Get dressed, Freya," he said gently despite the circumstances. "I'm gonna open the door."

Tears sprang into my eyes. "Are you sure?" I whispered. "Now? Colt..."

My man heaved out a stoic breath. "It's time, Freya. He's not stupid, and I'm not hiding you anymore."

My heart stuttered in my chest. He couldn't be serious. "But—"

"Get dressed," he ordered again softly.

His words were like a punch to the gut, knocking the wind from my lungs, but deep down, I knew he was right. We couldn't keep lying.

With a jerk of my head, I turned away, grabbed my clothes, and threw them on. My fingers fumbled over the zippers, hands shaking, but I managed to make myself presentable.

Turning back to Colt, I froze when I saw his hand outstretched. I slid my palm against his, lacing our fingers together and squeezing tight.

He went to step toward the door where Dad was still banging but hesitated, glancing at me one last time. "No matter what happens, remember I love you and we've done nothing wrong."

My heart swelled even as it raced. "I love you too," I whispered. "Now. Open the door."

Chapter Thirty-One

Colt

"Now. Open the door," Freya murmured, her golden eyes glistening with tears. She braced her shoulders just as Prez banged on my door again.

Something dark settled in my stomach, twisting in anticipation of the shitstorm I was about to set off. Still, I squared my shoulders and approached the door.

On occasion, my buds in the military told me that just before you died, your life flashed behind your eyes. It was unsettling because with every step I took toward the door, a slew of images sprang to my mind, all of them about my time at the club. Meeting Dagger and fighting by his side. Stepping into the clubhouse for the first time. Feeling like I'd found a home.

But with every picture flicking through my head, a memory of Freya played right along with it. Maybe it gave me the strength I needed, because I reached out, turned the key in the lock, and opened the goddamned door.

My eyes lifted, meeting golden ones.

"What the fuck took you so long to open the door?" Prez demanded, stepping into my room before turning to close the door softly behind him. "I've been knocking for nearly ten minutes. Please don't tell me you needed to put your lipstick on. It's bad enough seeing Atlas in drag..." His stare fell over my shoulder, his voice trailing off as confusion flashed behind his eyes. "What are you doin' in here?" he asked after a beat.

"There's somethin' I need to talk to you about?" I told him, tone laden with meaning.

Dagger's eyebrows pulled together in confusion. "What?"

I stretched my arm out and took Freya's elbow. My eyes never left my prez as I tugged her close to my side and slid an arm around her shoulders. "Me and Freya are together, Prez."

All color drained from Dagger's face, his eyes narrowing as they darted between us. "What the fuck are you talkin' about? You can't be. Freya's off-limits." His hands clenched into fists at his sides as he glared at me. "She's my daughter," he roared. "You had no right to go behind my back."

I met his glower unflinchingly. "I'm tellin' you now, to your face that me and Freya are together. I love her, Prez."

Dagger's nostrils flared like a dragon about to burn me alive.

"Dad," Freya whispered imploringly. "I love Colt. I want to be with him."

Prez's lip curled into a snarl. "The hell you do. You're too young to know what love is." He jabbed an accusing finger at me. "And you! You betrayed my trust. I brought you into my club, gave you a family, a home, and this is how you repay me?"

His words punched me in the gut, but I tamped my unease down, keeping my voice steady. "We didn't plan for it to happen, brother, but we have deep feelings for each other. You've seen us, you must've noticed our connection. You can't deny it, and neither can we anymore."

Dagger let out a snarl. "Brother? You're no brother'a mine."

Freya stepped forward, pleading. "Daddy. Please..."

He held a hand up again to stop her words, his jaw clenching so tight I thought it would crack. For a long, tense moment we just eyeballed each other, cold fury crackling between us, before his eyes shuttered and he turned to Freya. "You've got a choice to make. Him or us."

"Daddy," she breathed. "I—I." She couldn't speak through the catch in her throat.

"Don't you do that to her," I warned. "Don't you fuckin' treat her like she means nothin'. Don't do somethin' you'll regret later."

He gnashed his teeth together. "I'll see ya in the ring. I'll give ya ten minutes to get your ass there or I'll find ya and drag you in by the scruff'a your neck like the traitorous mutt you are." His eyes flicked to his only daughter. "By the time I'm done with him, I want your decision."

Freya's usual warm gaze turned ice cold. "I don't need any time, I already know my decision." She jutted her chin up proudly. "I choose him."

A shocked silence fell over us. Dagger stared at Freya like he didn't know her. "Right," he grated out. "Pack your bags. When I throw lover boy out on his ass, you can go with him."

My beautiful girl let out a snort. "I've already packed. I knew you'd do this; I knew your ridiculous pride would come before me, just like everything else does."

His mouth thinned into a white slash across his face. "How long, Colt? How fuckin' long have you been sneakin' around behind my back, fuckin' my daughter? How long have you looked me in the eyes and lied to me? How long has it been since you began to betray the man who regarded you as a son?"

My stomach churned. "Not long. Couple'a months."

Prez's face darkened, spit flying from his mouth as he roared, "You son of a fuckin' bitch!" My breath seized as he lunged at me, hands curling into claws.

Like a shot, I pushed Freya behind me and braced for impact, but at the last second, Prez jerked to a stop. His chest heaved with harsh breaths as he tried to control his anger.

The sound of Freya sobbing made my heart wrench.

Prez glowered at her. "You've betrayed me as badly as he has. What did ya do to reel him in? Wear one'a your little skirts? Bat your pretty eyelashes?" He let out a humorless laugh. "Ya think I don't know the way you work?"

My gut twisted, my fingers twitching with the need to wrap around his neck and squeeze. "Don't fuckin' speak to her like that. She's a good girl, the fuckin' *best* girl. She doesn't deserve that shit from *you*."

He took a step back and raised a finger, pointing to my chest and spitting, "You're a fuckin' traitor to this club and to this family, and I'm gonna beat the fuck outta ya for it. Where's your cut?"

I nodded toward the chair I'd laid it on the night before.

Dagger stomped over and grabbed it. "You've just forfeited it. You don't gotta cut anymore."

Freya sniffed loudly.

All the tension whooshed from Dagger's body as he turned his head to study me. "Ten minutes. Bring your A game to the ring. You're gonna fuckin' need it." He threw me one more furious look before his stare slashed briefly to Freya, and he walked out of the room, slamming the door closed behind him so hard, the wall rattled.

"Let's just go," Freya whispered. "You don't need to fight him, Colt. He won't let you win; for him it's a matter of honor. If you get the upper hand, he'll do something to turn it in his favor." She stepped toward me and raised her hands to frame my jaw. "Please. Baby," she begged. "Let's just get our stuff and leave."

Still reeling, I lowered my forehead until it touched hers. "I can't, Princess. I've got honor too. Your dad's right. I did fuck up. Don't get me wrong, I wouldn't change a thing, but I gotta take responsibility for what I did, plus I owe him a jab for the way he spoke to you."

"I don't care about that." Her eyes welled up with tears again. "Please don't do this."

My hands slid around Freya's back, gathering her in close. "Sshh, baby. It'll be okay. He can beat the fuck outta me. It won't stop us bein' together. Nothin' will. At least this way I can get the fuck outta here with my head held high. Don't ask me to be a coward, please."

My girl rested her face against my chest and sobbed her heart out.

I pulled back slightly, this time taking her face in my hands, my thumb brushing away the tears trailing down her cheek. "Hey. It'll be cool. I'll still be pretty enough for you after." I shot her a cocky grin, trying to reassure her, even though a sense of foreboding settled in my gut. "Let me do this and we'll go. Just think, tonight we could be on a flight to somewhere warm and exotic, where nothing can touch us. It'll just be me and you, with the rest of our lives stretching ahead of us."

Slowly, Freya closed her eyes and nodded. "At least make sure one of my brothers is there, or Atlas. They can rein him in."

"I will," I told her with a reassuring smile. "I'm gonna be okay. I can fight with the best of 'em. I won't wail on your dad, but I won't hesitate to defend myself."

She bit her lip nervously. "Please be careful. He'll fight dirty rather than lose to you, especially after this. He's got a point to prove, not just to you, but to the club brothers too. In his eyes you've betrayed the Demons, and he needs to punish you, the bigger the audience the better."

My gut stabbed painfully.

Freya was right. I'd seen Prez take on tougher men than me without blinking. He'd do whatever it took to win, and I needed to watch my back, because he'd come at me with everything he had.

The cold, hard truth was that if I wanted to walk away from this relatively unscathed, I'd need to keep my wits about me and hope that Freya's brothers would keep him from going too far.

The murmurs and chatter died down the second I stepped foot into the bar. You could hear a pin drop as Prez, surrounded by about six men stared me down.

It wasn't busy. Most of the brothers were probably still in bed recovering from the party last night. Still, Prez ensured he had his minions by his side for support, which didn't bode well for me in the ring.

I scanned the room, hoping to God Cash was there. My heart sank when I realized he wasn't but luckily, Bowie and Abe sat away from Prez at a table by themselves.

Bowie shook his head at me sadly, while Abe tried shooting me a reassuring smile.

I sent a chin lift their way, a silent signal that I was okay and ready to rumble.

The noise of boots hitting the floor sounded, making me turn back to Prez and his crowd. Bile rose in my throat when the men I'd helped and supported over the years, one by one, turned their backs on me, a message that they didn't regard me as a brother anymore.

I tilted my chin, staring at their backs, feeling like trash. This was the biggest statement they could make. It said I was a traitor, and they wouldn't even deign to look at my face.

A chair scraped loudly across the floor as Abe got up from his seat, pointing a finger at the crowd of men. "Shotgun. Wasn't it a month ago when you got in shit with gambling debts? Who loaned you the green to give to the bookies to stop you getting your face caved in?"

Shot turned to Abe, folding his hands across his chest. "He betrayed Prez."

"That's a matter of opinion," Abe bandied back. "And regardless of who's side you're comin' down on I need to ask somethin'. Did he betray you? Or are you just jumpin' on the bandwagon to suck up to Dagger?"

Shotgun clamped his mouth shut.

"Thought so," Abe huffed out, his eyes sliding to Prez. "What the fuck are you doin', Dag?"

"Dealin' with a traitor," he retorted. "It may not be Shot's, Tex's or even Brew's fight, but when someone betrays the club and breaks the cardinal rules they go against us all. Mess with a Demon, Abe, and we'll raise hell."

Abe's eyes roamed Dagger's face, full of disappointment. "That's just it. Freya's not a Demon."

Prez's lip curled, his face reddening as he shot Abe an incredulous look. "No. She's my fuckin' daughter. He knew not to go there. He knew the consequences of touching her, but he still did it. Am I meant to let it slide, Abe? He broke a club rule. End of fuckin' story."

"You'll regret this," Abe muttered. "One day when you're old and grey, you'll look back on this moment and your conscience will tighten like a noose around your neck. Are you willing to lose Freya over this? Are you willing to lose the grandbabies she'll give ya? The pride in seein' her succeed and know that somethin' in that came from you? Are you willing to push your girl away for lovin' someone you don't approve of, even though as far as I can see, he's a stand-up man?"

Prez's jaw clenched. I could almost see the anger simmering beneath his stony expression. "That's just it," he said flatly, meeting the other man's accusing stare unflinchingly. "He ain't a stand-up man. He betrayed me after I gave him a home and a family."

Abe just stared at him, shaking his head, lip curling with disgust. "Seems to me that you only did it on the condition Colt obey you. That negates all the generosity you extended, because friendship shouldn't come with conditions, John." He pulled his shoulders back, standing to his full height. "As an officer of this club, I vote we do this another way."

Prez's mouth thinned, his eyes immediately going to Bowie. "You're an officer too. What do you think?"

Bowie's eyes rounded so wide that, for a second, he reminded me of a rabbit caught in the headlights. "Don't agree with what you're doin', but you're my prez. I won't go against ya."

Dagger smiled smugly. "Seems you're outvoted, old man. Two officers against one."

Bowie sighed frustratedly. "Fuck!"

"I'll call the other officers in," Abe declared. "We'll put it to a vote."

"Nope," Dagger scraped out. "All officers present got a vote. Colt's goin' in the ring."

My stare went to Abe. His skin had paled, and he looked almost defeated. "It's okay," I assured him. "I'll do it. Just need you to make sure things don't get dirty."

"You don't have to, Son," Abe insisted.

I dipped my chin. "I want to."

His face fell, but he nodded regardless. "I'll be your second. Can't say I can jump in, but I can make sure nobody else does." His stare fell on Prez again. "Don't think for one minute I support what you're doin'. I find it abhorrent."

Dagger's cool façade cracked, just for a second. Hurt flickered across his features before his expression shuttered again. "It's done." He nodded toward the stairs to the basement. "Come on. Time to kick some traitor ass."

Chuckles rose through the air as Prez, and the men with him, made for the stairs.

Abe's hand clasped my shoulder, and he leaned in to whisper, "He'll go for broke. Watch him closely. I've seen you fight, you're good, technically maybe better than him, but remember, he's a street fighter and he'll go sneaky if it means victory. Put him down and keep him down. Show no mercy, 'cause he won't."

I took in everything he told me, nodding along and tucking his advice away to call on in the ring. We followed the crowd of men down the stairs and into the basement where we had a full-sized boxing ring set up, along with top of the range gym equipment.

"We gonna party or what?" Prez called out, his voice booming through the room.

Chest jerking, I stalked toward the ring, adrenaline and nerves battling inside me. I climbed up and opened a gap between the thick, elasticated ropes. As I stepped inside the ring, the men began to call out jeers.

I bounced on the balls of my feet, thankful that I remembered to put a pair of sneakers on. They wouldn't do damage like a biker boot, but at least I'd be lighter on my feet.

"Yo!" Abe called from the corner behind me, passing me a pair of boxing gloves up.

"No gloves," Prez bellowed. "We're doin' this old school. Bare knuckles, anythin' goes."

My gut dragged to the floor. Bare knuckles? No rules? Jesus, he already had the upper hand. This wasn't a boxing match, it was a street brawl.

Dagger's grin was almost feral. "What's wrong, asshole? Not so confident now?"

Taking a deep breath, I tamped down my surging adrenaline, trying to keep my head clear. I shook my arms out, inhaling and exhaling slowly to calm my heart rate as Abe's advice echoed through my mind.

No mercy.

I had to win if I wanted to walk outta this ring in one piece.

Shouts of encouragement for Prez filled the air.

"Clock him, Prez."

"Show him how it's done."

"Kick his traitor ass."

I tuned all the noise out until the only thing in the room was me and Dagger. My heart thumped so hard I could feel it in my ears.

He lunged for me so fast he seemed like a blur, swinging his fists toward my head.

I ducked so his fist caught my ear, then spinning to the side, I slammed a punch into his ribs causing him to grunt and stumble back on his heels.

My heart exploded in my chest with the blood pounding through my veins. I shook my hands out, waiting for him to make the next move, but he just circled me, eyes narrowed angrily.

Before I could react, he charged again, moving to swing left, then at the last-minute dodging to his right. I tried to deflect but I wasn't fast enough to avoid his fist clipping my jaw. Pain ricocheted through my face and my mouth filled with the coppery taste of blood.

Roars went up as the men shouted encouragement to their prez.

I lifted my fists in front of my face, going on the defensive. I just needed him to get cocky and slip up. That was Prez's biggest weakness, sometimes he got too complacent.

The noise from the audience dimmed, and everything narrowed to just me and Dagger. We circled each other, both looking for a chance to strike out. With a grunt he jabbed my kidney making me bend over double with a groan.

I stayed down, waiting for Dagger to come at me. As he neared, I struck upward hard, with the palm of my hand and undercut his chin with a loud crack.

He let out a loud 'oof', reeling backward from the force of my strike.

Standing tall, I heaved in a deep breath trying to fill my lungs with as much air as possible. My breath sawed in and out so forcefully, I almost went light-headed as Prez rushed me again with a feral snarl, shooting straight past me as I sidestepped him again.

He lost his footing and stumbled.

Taking advantage, I pulled his head up by the hair and jabbed his face twice.

With a roar, he jumped up, emitting animalistic grunts as he lowered his head and charged at me, flinging me back against the ropes, and winding me in the process.

Dagger kept up his momentum, lunging with a flurry of punches.

I tried to deflect what I could, but before I could recover from the onslaught, his fist smashed into my temple and I saw stars. Pain exploded as my skin split and blood oozed down the side of my face.

He bounced on his toes, smirking.

My head throbbed. I'd probably gotten a concussion, but I couldn't give in. I shook my head, trying to clear the darkness descending behind my eyes. I couldn't pass out now, Dagger would kill me.

I swung wildly, hoping for the best. It worked, because I connected with his face, causing him to stumble backward against the ropes.

I followed him, pressing my advantage and landing another pummel to his face. He lurched at me until we began to trade blows. Somehow, I got the advantage again and landed a fist to Dagger's nose. Blood flew everywhere and he let out a roar, stumbling to the corner where his minions waited for him.

Staggering to my corner, I looked down at Abe who studied me approvingly.

"You're doin' good," he said jumping up to hang onto the ropes while he spoke to me. "You've got him on the backfoot. You've broken his nose, take advantage of it."

I nodded, turning back to face the ring where Dagger was already coming for me again. With a bellow, he raised his fist, and I caught a flash of metal glinting in the light across his knuckles as he cracked me across the side of my head, once from the right, then again from the left. The pain shooting through my skull took my breath away.

"You fucker," Abe roared. "You've got brass knuckles."

His outraged bellow lanced through the haze of my mind, and I groaned out loud at the pain clenching my brain. I tried to open my eyes, but the world spun, making me feel sick, as the blurred outlines of the baying crowd morphed into a single, menacing entity.

Nausea rose through my gut, and I turned my head just in time to retch. The acidic taste of bile burned the back of my throat, and I did it again.

The sounds of shouts and yells filled the air around me. I was sure I heard Atlas go ballistic about something and Cash curse loudly as boots thudded on the floor, making the canvas shake.

A cool hand pressed against my forehead, and I groaned in pain.

"Colt," Sophie's voice whispered. "You're gonna be okay. We're taking you to the hospital." I felt her fingers check the pulse at the base of my neck. "I'm just gonna check for any breaks before we move you to the truck. Stay still for me."

I tried to nod but the pain lancing through my skull made the world tilt on its axis. A groan escaped my lips, and I tried to concentrate on the softness of Sophie's voice as she checked me over just so I didn't pass out from the pain.

I felt the sensation of being weightless as I was lifted and carried. After what seemed like hours, I was laid on something soft.

"Someone get in the back with him," Cash shouted. "Keep him secure."

My heart fluttered in my chest when Freya's sweet voice called out. "I've got him," followed by a sob.

"Freya," I whispered. "Don't cry, baby. I'll be okay."

"I'm here," she replied softly. "I'm not leaving your side."

Despite the pain, a small smile spread across my mouth. Darkness filtered from the edges of my vision, rising up to envelop me and making me succumb to its comfort.

As long as Freya was with me, everything would be okay.

Chapter Thirty-Two

Freya

Colt had been unconscious all day and night, though the nurses at Baines Memorial kept coming in hourly to check his vitals. He had a fractured jaw and a concussion so severe that there was bruising to his brain. Sophie had done countless CT scans and called in a neurosurgeon to examine him.

She was confident Colt would be okay physically, but I worried how the impact of what Dad had done would affect him emotionally. Colt had always thought the sun shone out of Pop's ass, so I knew his mental state would hurt way more than his physical injuries.

Watching him lying unconscious in a hospital bed made me question everything.

Was it worth him being beaten for? Was it worth all the pain and heartache?

It was easy for me to say yes, we were worth going through all this shit for, but I wasn't the one in hospital with bruising to the brain, a broken jaw, and a mangled face. Colt had lost everything because of me, and I knew nothing would be the same after what had happened.

Watching the steady rise and fall of his chest, I couldn't stop the burn of fury that ignited in my veins.

I'd never forgive my dad for this, or Bowie for not helping Colt in that ring. Abe was incensed that Dad had fought so dirty. It turned out that Pop and Shotgun had planned to take the brass knuckles to the fight in case Colt got the better of him.

My man never stood a chance.

The door opened and Sophie walked in, the squeak of her comfortable sneakers sounding from the tile floor. "How's our patient?" she asked softly, going over to shine her medical torch in Colt's eyes.

"His BP and heart rate have gone back to normal," I informed her.

"Hmm," she drawled. "His pupils are still dilated but not as much as before. Doctor Chen will be back over to check on him after her rounds." Her eyes darted to me. "Have you eaten?"

I shook my head. "I think I'd be sick."

Sophie gave me a pitying smile before coming over to sink down on the seat next to me. "He'll need you fit and strong when he wakes up."

"I know, Soph," I murmured. "I just feel so sick about everything. It's all my fault."

Her hand reached for mine and she squeezed. "No. Colt knew this may happen. He went into it with his eyes open, probably more so than you."

"Maybe you're right," I admitted. "I knew Dad could be stubborn, even violent, but I never expected this." I blinked back tears, glancing at Colt's battered face. "I don't know how he'll get over this."

"He's got you," she smiled. "You'll get him through it." She nudged me gently. "If this breaks you, your relationship was never strong enough to begin with. Maybe it's one of the reasons behind what your dad did, like a test. Perhaps he wanted to put you both under pressure and hope you buckled under the weight of it."

"It wouldn't surprise me," I replied quietly. "I'm starting to see exactly how calculating my dad can be."

"He's an MC President, Freya," she reminded me. "He's got to be calculating to a point. He hasn't made the club as successful as it is by letting what he sees as betrayals pass unchallenged. Your dad's a good man ninety percent of the time, but we shouldn't forget who he is underneath all the joviality."

"I'll never forgive him," I vowed.

Sophie's gaze went back to Colt, taking in the cuts and bruising on his face. "Neither would I if that was Atlas laying there. The problem is, John's family, and although his behavior's been vile, he loves you, and you love him."

"I do," I agreed. "But I'll never forgive him, and I'll never forgive the men who stood by and cheered while he did this. Shotgun's dead to me. So's Tex."

She lifted a delicate shoulder in a shrug. "Again. I can't blame you." She glanced at her watch. "Visiting hours are about to begin. Cash and Breaker are coming in so they'll keep you company. I've told Cash to bring some toiletries and fresh clothes in for you. Use Colt's bathroom. Nobody will know."

I looked up at Soph and smiled genuinely for the first time since everything had happened. "Thank you."

She grinned. "Us doctor chicks have to stick together." She paused briefly, her gaze going to Colt again before she continued. "Love is so fucking confusing, Freya. My ideal man turned out to be abusive and the man who treated me like shit turned out to be perfect for me. You know me and Atlas had a rough time at first but look at us now." She stroked her pregnant belly. "Relationships aren't perfect all the time. You have storms, but as long as you learn to stick together and weather them, you'll make it through."

We both looked up as the door opened and Cash and Breaker came sauntering into the room.

"How's he doin'?" Cash asked, a worried frown creasing his forehead.

"Colt's doing exactly what he should be," Sophie replied. "Sleeping. It's the best healer, but I'm hoping he'll come around soon." She turned for the door. "I've got rounds to make. I'll come back as soon as I can." With a low wave she disappeared.

Breaker handed me an overnight bag. "Here, Sis. Go sort yourself out. The last thing you want is for Colt to wake up to you lookin' like that."

I rolled my eyes good-naturedly. "Asshole."

"You do look rougher than usual," Cash reiterated. "Go wash up, brush your teeth and change. You'll feel better."

My eyes lifted to his. "What's going on at the clubhouse."

He blew a breath so hard, his cheeks puffed out. "It's a shit show. Half the club's on Colt's side, the other half's bayin' for his blood. I've never known the brothers so divided. Pop's holed up in his office with a bottle of Jack, and Abe's stompin' around biting everybody's head off. Nobody quite knows what to say or do. It'll take a while for things to settle down again."

I rubbed at my tired eyes, Cash's words echoing in my mind.

Colt was well liked within the club. He did a lot for people in his role and many of the brothers had a lot to be grateful to him for. Between them, Colt and Cash helped with investments, housing, even college applications for the brothers' kids. I was happy that not all the club was set against him at least.

"Is it okay if I stay at the gallery for a while?" I asked Cash as he stared down at Colt in the hospital bed.

"Why?" His voice was a low rasp. "You've got your room at the club."

"Dad kicked me out." I looked down at my hands, trying to fight back my tears.

My brother's mouth fell open. "What d'ya mean he kicked you out?"

I held my hands up defensively. "It's fine. I wouldn't go back to the clubhouse after what he did anyway."

Breaker's golden eyes never left Colt. "I almost saddle myself with fuckin' April and he doesn't bat an eyelash. Freya falls for a good man, and he kicks her out. Pop's losin' the plot."

"And the respect of half the club," Cash added. "But it's done now. We have to try and deal with the fallout and mitigate the damage."

"We need to call Church," Kit said, "Dad doesn't know the half of it. We gotta tell him about the FBI's involvement and how he's protecting the club from bein' targeted." He nodded down at Colt's bed.

I took a sharp intake of breath as the hospital seemed to shrink in on me a little. "What do you mean Colt's protecting the club? What the hell's going on?"

Kit and Cash exchanged ominous looks before my oldest brother shrugged. "He's joinin' the Feds 'cause they didn't give him a choice," Cash grated out. "They've got evidence of him hacking into their systems and the fuckers are usin' it as leverage against him. You know they've chased him for years, now they've got somethin' up their sleeve to control him with. They've threatened him, the club, even you, Frey. If he doesn't join the FBI, they come for us all."

I wet my lips, which had suddenly gone dry, as my mind went over our past conversations. Colt hadn't said much about it, but still, he seemed okay with everything, excited even. "But he told me he wanted to join, that he could do more good working for them than the club. He seemed excited about it."

"Maybe he is now," Cash grinned. "Especially if it means he finally gets you." His big, calloused hand engulfed mine. "He's not mad about it anymore. Even sees it as a fresh start for you both."

I dug the heel of my palm into my eyes, going over all the revelations from my brothers. "Wait," I said confusedly. "Why was he hacking into the FBI's systems."

My brothers exchanged another ominous look before Cash muttered, "That's club business."

I would've laughed out loud if it wasn't all so fucking ridiculous. "Colt's lying in a hospital bed because of a chain of events that I know nothing about and all you can tell me is that it's club business." I pursed my lips. "Great."

"It won't matter soon," Cash said squeezing my fingers reassuringly. "When your man recovers, you'll leave and start a new life together. Club business won't factor into your life anymore and honestly, Freya, I can't say I'm sorry about it. I'll miss ya both, but you'll be safer away from here."

"You sound like Dad," I teased, my heart warming at the sincerity in his tone.

Cash's lips twitched. "Jesus. Shoot me now."

I chuckled softly along with Breaker but inside I was reeling.

So much had gone on behind the scenes that I didn't know about, and it made my stomach heavy with unease. Colt should've told me all this himself. Instead, I found out secondhand from my brothers of all people. What had happened with Colt affected me too and I was getting sick of him keeping shit from me.

I shook my head, sighing with frustration thinking how it didn't bode well for the future, and how sometimes nothing Colt did made sense, when suddenly, a soft groan sounded from the bed.

Cash's hand squeezed mine. "Freya," he said, his voice a whisper. "Colt's waking up."

Breaker rose to his feet. "I'll go find Soph," he said before disappearing.

I leaned forward just as Colt groaned again. "Freya?"

Touching his fingers, I whispered, "I'm here."

Slowly, Colt's eyes flickered open. "Shit," he rasped so quietly I had to strain to catch the words. "Did I get hit by a Mack truck?"

"Nah, brother." Cash grinned down at him. "You got hit by our dirty fightin' dad. Do you remember?"

Colt's ocean-blues came to meet my soft gaze. "How long have I been out?"

"About twenty-four hours, give or take," I replied gently. "You're gonna be okay. Sophie wants to monitor you for a couple of days, but as soon as she discharges you, we'll leave."

Colt's eyes veered to Cash. "I'm sorry it turned out this way, brother."

My brother dipped his chin. "Wasn't your fault it went south, Colt. If Dad had fought fairly, there would've been a different outcome. I'm just sorry we weren't there to talk him down." He stood from his chair. "Gonna go get some coffees and leave you two to talk for a while." With a loose one finger salute, he turned and stalked from the room.

My eyes roamed over Colt, greedily taking in his face, still beautiful even through the cuts and bruises marring his skin.

"I'm sorry Dad did this," I murmured, brushing a strand of the dark blonde hair I loved so much back from his face. "I tried to help," I whispered, tone tight with guilt. "I went to get Cash and Kit, but by the time they got to the gym it was too late."

Colt's eyelids fluttered. "Not your fault," he barely whispered.

I swallowed hard, clutching his limp hand in mine. I should've gone straight to Cash's room, but I worried if I went through the bar while Dad was still there, he'd have realized what I was doing and done something to stop me. I believed Bowie would protect him, but he didn't do a damned thing. Inside I was seething, but I kept my expression blank, not wanting Colt to see how affected I was.

He blinked drowsily.

"Rest," I said softly. "I'll be here when you wake up. I'll call Cara and ask her to bring some things in for you."

Colt's eyes fluttered closed. "Phone", he muttered, seconds before his breathing evened out and his chest began to rise and fall rhythmically.

I took his hand, lacing our fingers together just as Sophie and Breaker entered the room.

"How you feeling, Colt? The doc asked, but he'd already fallen back to sleep. She took out her little torch again and shone it in his eyes. "Pupils are reducing in size, and it's a good sign he's woken up and spoken. I think we just have to give him some time and let him heal. I'll arrange for another CT scan to make sure the bruising on his brain has reduced, but I think he'll make a full recovery, though he may carry a scar or two."

My shoulders slumped in relief and I silently thanked every God who existed.

"He's too pretty anyway," Kit said under his breath. "A scar will add some character."

"Pot, kettle, and black spring to mind." Soph smirked, heading for the door. "I'll arrange that scan. Hopefully he'll wake up again soon, and for longer."

I bent down and grabbed the bag Kit had brought in for me. "I'll go freshen up," I said quietly, heading into the bathroom and closing the door behind me with a soft click.

Walking to the sink, I gazed at myself in the mirror, noting my dull eyes and sallow skin. I took my toothbrush and toothpaste from my bag and brushed my teeth thoroughly before splashing water on my face to wake up.

I'd been awake for twenty-four hours, but I couldn't have slept, even if I wanted to. How could I when the man I loved was confined to a hospital bed with injuries inflicted on him by my own father? My eyes were sore from lack of sleep and my throat dry through crying, but the pain that took my breath away came from my aching heart.

In the space of twenty-four hours I'd almost lost Colt, but in reality I'd actually lost a father. There was no way back from this, because by hurting Colt the way he did, he'd also hurt me. Tears sprang to my eyes again, but I jutted my chin up, blinking them away. There was no point in crying, I had to pull myself together and be strong for Colt. We had a tough few days ahead of us and I needed to keep my shit together at least for now.

I finished freshening up, washing my body down and spraying deodorant, but the fresh scent couldn't take away the bad taste in my mouth. Something was becoming clearer as the minutes marched on, and as much as it made me sad, it also left me feeling strangely liberated.

There was no way I'd forgive my dad for what he'd done, ever.

John Stone was dead to me.

Chapter Thirty-Three

Colt

The days following mine and Dagger's fight brought clarity along with them.

Freya didn't leave my side unless she went to the gallery to shower and change. Sophie pulled some strings, which allowed my girl to sleep by my side in the hospital bed. She took charge of everything, from bullying the nurses into giving me extra pain relief, to making calls on my behalf.

If I had a kernel of doubt that she was too young or too immature to settle down, it quickly disappeared in a puff of smoke. I'd never seen a woman who just got on with shit like she did, and without complaint. I'd always known she was a little ballbuster, but I'd never seen her in mama bear mode before, and I didn't mind admitting that it made my cock twitch, even though I was the one who usually liked to control my environment.

On my second night, when Freya had left to change, Cash, Breaker, and Atlas visited for an impromptu meet to fill me in on everythin' that had been goin' down at the club.

Cash sat forward, elbows to knees. "You could cut the atmosphere in the clubhouse with a fuckin' blade," he growled, the lines around his mouth tightening. "Nobody's talkin' to each other, and we've got the likes of fuckin' Shotgun crowin' about how he helped Prez put the traitor down."

I pictured the clubhouse in my mind's eye. It was usually filled with music and laughter, but now I imagined the air would be filled with tension, with brothers watching each other suspiciously. Heat filled my chest when I imagined fuckin' Shotgun lording it up about how he helped put me down, even though his actions were dirty and cowardly.

My jaw clenched and suddenly I couldn't wait to get better, grab my girl, and get the fuck outta Hambleton. There was nothing left for us here now.

"What's the mood like among the other officers?" I asked Cash curiously.

He scraped a hand through his hair, his long-sleeved tee ridin' up to show the myriad of tattoos covering his arms. "It's a fuckin' mess. Abe won't even look at Pop, but Bowie won't go against him. The rest of us..." his voice trailed off.

"We can't openly question Prez's decisions," Atlas interjected. "But it doesn't mean we can't let him know in other ways how we're feelin' about what he did. I'm not sayin' you were right with what you did, Colt, but I don't agree with the way he dealt with it. Fact is, brother, I've always thought that off-limits rule was bullshit." His stare slid to Breaker. "What if he tried to tell Kady who to fall for?"

Breaker visibly bristled. "I wouldn't stand for it. I'd leave the club before he treated Kady the way he's treated Freya. My kids won't be controlled by anyone. They can be with whoever makes 'em happy."

"Mom's coming back down in a few days," Cash added. "She went fuckin crazy at Dad."

I let out a humorless snort. "I know. Adele called Freya earlier while she was here. I could hear her shouting down the phone, even though Freya was standing over by the window."

"She's good to have onside," Breaker assured me. "If anyone can make Pop see the error of his ways, it's Mom. She won't take his shit and she'll whip the brothers into shape too. God help Shotgun if he mouths off in earshot of her. She'll punch his lights out."

Chuckles rose through the room.

"So," Atlas muttered. "What happens next?"

My stare swept from one man to the next. "As soon as I'm discharged, we're leaving. No point stickin' around for more shit to happen. I don't wanna put Freya through any more heartache, and I don't think Prez will be over it for a while yet. I don't start my new job until April, and she's only gotta be around for interviews for the internships she's applied for. I was thinkin' of takin' her on vacation until we have to settle in for work."

"Kennedy's place is free if you like the idea of spendin' some downtime in Vegas," Breaker suggested. "We could all go there when the kids are on spring break. She's got plenty of room and a huge fuckin' swimmin' pool."

"I'm up for it," I agreed. "And I'm pretty sure Freya will love the idea of spendin' some time with the kids. She's gonna miss 'em like crazy."

"Wherever you end up, we'll visit," Cash assured me. "And when Dad steps back from the club you'll be welcome back in town. Told ya New Years Eve that things will change when I'm holdin' the gavel, and I meant it. You and Freya will always have a home here as far as I'm concerned."

"Thanks, brother." I smiled gratefully. "Your support means everythin' to me and Freya. Want ya to know that I wouldn't put her or any of you through this unless I was a hundred percent sure that what we had was worth it."

"Saw it years ago, Colt," Breaker admitted.

Cash barked a laugh. "Same."

Atlas rolled his eyes. "Fuckin' pussies."

"We all did," Cash added "If Dad was honest with himself, he'd probably tell ya he did too. It was easy to work out. Even when she was a kid, you protected her. He's buried his head in the sand for years and now it's come back and bitten him in the ass."

"And me," I said ruefully.

"Yeah," he agreed. "But you knew it wouldn't be an easy ride. Okay, so we didn't think you'd end up in the fuckin' hospital but at least you're alive to tell the tale."

He was right. It could've been a lot worse than a concussion and a few cuts and bruises, but there wasn't a part of me that felt lucky. I was gutted everything had gone so far south.

A creak sounded from the door. It cracked open and Freya popped her head around it. "Hey," she greeted everyone softly. "Am I interrupting? I can grab a coffee and come back later."

My heart leaped at the mere sight of her. I struggled to sit up straighter, ignoring the stab of pain shooting through my back.

"Nah." Cash gestured for her to come inside the room. "We're done. Just talkin' about your next steps with Colt."

The door opened wider, and she walked inside the room, making a beeline straight for Cash who tugged her by the hand until she fell in his lap. "How you holdin' up, Sis?" he asked gently.

She burrowed into him. "I'm okay. Just glad it's over and we can leave as soon as Colt can drive without being in pain."

"It'll blow over," Breaker assured her with more confidence in his voice than I felt.

"I'm past caring" she declared. "I don't want anything to do with Dad anymore. He went too far this time. I'm sick of his weird, controlling behavior. I've put up with it for years, but no more. Even if he turned up here now full of apologies, I'd tell him to go to hell."

Atlas's lips twitched. "You're Adele's daughter alright. Scary as fuck when you get a bee in your bonnet."

Freya shot him a knowing smile. "Yeah. I am. She'll be here in the next couple of days and Dad won't know what's hit him."

"I think he's already got an idea," Breaker rumbled. "I was there when she called him this mornin' after speaking to you. Let's just say she screamed at him so loudly I'm surprised she didn't burst his eardrum."

I couldn't help chuckling quietly at the glee in Freya's voice. When Adele got involved, she was like a force of nature—totally unpredictable and completely unstoppable.

Freya rose from her brother's lap and sunk down on my bed next to me. "How you feeling, honey?"

I took her hand, entwining our fingers together. "Let's just say the drugs are workin' great. Shame they're gonna start weaning me off 'em tomorrow."

"It means you're healing," she murmured reassuringly, sweeping my hair back from my face. "You'll be out of here in a day or two. We'll stay at the gallery for a couple of days while you build your strength up, then we'll jet."

I nodded, almost mesmerized by her beauty. Her long, dark hair was loose with its natural curl at the ends. I lifted my hand, catching a lock between my fingers. "Okay, baby."

The door creaked open again and Sophie strolled in. "How's my patient feeling this evening?" she asked cheerfully, picking up my chart and reading the notes.

"Okay," I replied. "Doctor Chen told me you'll probably start reducing the pain meds tomorrow."

Sophie nodded, eyes still on my chart. "Yeah. Your pain level should decrease drastically. The stuff you're on is highly addictive so we try to reduce it as quickly as possible. We'll take you off all meds in the morning and assess your pain levels so we can decide the best course of treatment." She put my chart back. "But I'm very pleased with your progress."

"You can't keep a Demon down for long," Atlas muttered, eyeing his wife up carefully. "You ready to leave work now?"

She sent him a nod and a smile. "Yeah. I just wanted to check on Colt before I left. I'm ready when you are."

Atlas stood from his chair giving us all chin lifts before holding his arm out for Sophie and heading for the door. "Night, boys. Don't do anythin' I wouldn't." He ushered his wife through to the hallway and disappeared, clicking the door shut softly behind him.

"I think that's our cue to leave too," Cash muttered, getting to his feet, followed by Breaker. He clasped a hand to my shoulder before disappearing with a wave, his brother hot on his heels.

"Was it something I said?" Freya murmured as the door closed behind them, leaving just us in the room.

I grinned, pulling her to lay down on the bed next to me, my arm sliding across her shoulders. "They've got women and kids to get home to."

Freya sighed contentedly, snuggling her face into my chest. "Yeah. I know."

My fingers trailed up and down her back. "Can't believe we're leaving in a few days."

She lifted her face to gaze at me. "It's the end of an era but the start of the rest of our lives."

The corner of my mouth tipped up. "That's a nice way to put it."

"I can't wait for us to start living together properly," she whispered. "No more hiding. We can be a real couple at last."

Drawing her hand up to my mouth, I kissed her knuckles. "I don't deserve you, baby."

Our eyes locked and she leaned down to peck my lips. "You do. We deserve each other and all the goodness between us."

My throat tightened with emotion.

Nobody had ever fought for me the way Freya had. Not only had she stood up to John, but staying by my side while I got better also spoke volumes. I swore then and there that I'd fight for her too. No more screwing around. I was in this forever. She was the most incredible woman I'd ever known, and I'd never give her up now.

"Kiss me again," I rasped, voice thick with the love bursting from my chest.

She leaned forward, brushing her lips gently against mine. I savored her warmth, then the feel of her skin and the sweet scent of Coco Chanel that drove me wild with need for her.

I'd never felt closer or more connected to anyone.

When she finally pulled back, her cheeks were flushed.

I grinned like a lovesick schoolboy, my heart swelling with all the emotion I could muster. As long as we had each other we could weather anything her dad or the club threw at us.

In our case, love would conquer all.

The ringing of my cell phone startled me awake.

I sat bolt upright and stared ahead, dazedly wondering who the hell was calling me in the dead of night. I rubbed at my burning eyes, glancing at the time on my cell, which was lit up next to me on my nightstand.

It was just after one thirty A.M.

My first thought was that something must be wrong. No call at this time of night ever meant anything good.

Freya stirred by my side in a deep sleep. My girl was exhausted from keeping a bedside vigil for me over the last few nights. I didn't want to wake her. She needed to rest.

The number displayed wasn't one I recognized, but still, to be ringing this late indicated it was someone of importance. Before the caller rang off, I pressed the green icon and muttered, "Hold on." Throwing my legs over the side of the bed, I padded to the bathroom, so's not to wake my girl. As soon as the door clicked softly closed behind me, I held the phone up to my ear asking, "Who is it?"

"Colter?" a familiar voice murmured. "Is that you?"

My breath seized in my lungs. "Cordy?"

"Oh my God," my sister whispered with a relieved breath. "I was hoping this was still your number. I found it in Mom's phone. Something's happened, you need to come home. I can't believe it Colt. We need you. Mom needs you."

I raised a hand to rub my aching temple. "Slow down, Cordy. Tell me what's goin' on? Are you alright?"

I'm fine," she cried. "But Mom took an overdose tonight. Dad's had her committed to a psychiatric hospital, but they won't let me in to see her." Cordelia's voice cracked. "I don't know what to do. I need your help."

I gripped the edge of the wash basin, knuckles turning white.

My bastard of a father had finally done it. Pushed Mom to attempt goddamned suicide. I knew it would only be a matter of time until his thirst for power pushed Mom over the edge.

"I'm gonna fuckin' kill him," I growled. "Which hospital?" I put my phone on speaker while Cordelia rattled off the name of the hospital and the doctor treating Mom. My fingers flew over the touch screen as I brought up all the details and bookmarked them, before pulling up flights.

"Would Jasper mind if you picked me up from JFK just after lunchtime tomorrow?" I asked. "I can get on the first flight out."

"I left Jasper a month ago," Cordy choked out. "I went to his office to surprise him with lunch and caught him fucking his PA over his desk. I haven't seen him since."

"Fuck!" I ground out. "What did Dad say?"

"He threatened to cut me off if I didn't go back," she whispered. "But I don't care, Colter. I'd rather live on the streets than end up like Mom."

"You've got your trust fund," I reminded her. "You'll be fine. I've got money too, Cordy. I'll give you whatever you need."

"We'll talk about it tomorrow," she assured me. "Tonight I need to concentrate on Mom. It's such a mess, Colter. Dad moved his mistress into the house a week ago. It sent Mom over the edge."

A blaze of heat flared in my chest and my teeth gnashed together. "What the fuck?"

"It's Victoria, Colter," she whispered. "I'm so sorry."

I scraped a hand down my face, not quite believing what I was hearing. "Have they been seeing each other all this time?"

"I don't know," Cordy murmured. "But it's probable. He's no doubt been seeing dozens of women. He's disgusting."

"I'll see where the land lies when I get there tomorrow, Cordy. There's nothin' we can do for her tonight. We'll get Mom outta there, I promise. We just gotta hang tight tonight."

"Okay," she said, renewed steel in her tone. "Send me the details of your flight and I'll wait for you at arrivals."

"Is this your new number?" I asked.

"Yes," she replied. "Jas and Dad were harassing me so I had to change it."

"Okay, baby sister," I said softly. "You did good tonight. Now get some rest. I'll handle Dad." The hardness of my voice brooked no argument. Cordelia had always been the emotional sister, quick to react and even quicker to cry. Dad had wrapped her in cotton wool all her life. Probably to keep her compliant. She needed somebody to take charge in a crisis.

"You're right. I'm exhausted. I'll rest for a few hours." She paused. "I don't know if you're planning on seeing Dad but be careful. You know what his temper's like."

My mouth twisted. I knew exactly what his temper was like. I still bore the scars from the leather belt he'd whip me with when I'd tried to protect Mom from his rage. The memories would always be seared in my mind.

But things had changed now. The little boy starved of affection from his father was all grown up. I was taller, stronger, and smarter than Conrad Van Der Cleeve would ever be. He'd always seen Mom as a cash cow albeit an inconvenient one. Now he was trying to stash her away, out of sight, out of mind, while he played house with his new mistress.

The same girl who just happened to be my ex-fiancée.

Grabbing my cellphone, I quietly opened the bathroom door and crept back to bed. My head pounded from all the bullshit surrounding my father. My blood boiled when I thought of how scared my mom would be stuck in a fuckin' asylum.

Sinking down on the bed, I pulled the comforter over me and reached for Freya, settling her on my chest. That was when it hit me, I couldn't take her to New York, not when my dad would be looking for any weakness he could exploit.

My heart hurt at the thought of leaving her here, but she'd be safer in Hambleton than having to deal with my family drama. I wanted Freya to meet my mom and sisters so much, but with Mom overdosing and my dad acting like Hugh fuckin' Heffner, the timing wasn't right.

I'd come back for her once I got my family away from Dad and set them up somewhere safe. I hated the idea of being away from my woman indefinitely, but she needed to stay behind for her own good.

I swallowed hard at the thought of leaving Freya here after everything we'd done to be together. When morning came, I'd have to explain why I had to leave her.

I only hoped she'd understand.

Chapter Thirty-Four

Freya

Quiet footsteps roused me from my sleep. As I snuggled deeper into the comforter, I heard a throat clear softly, before Colt's voice whispered, "Wake up, baby. We need to talk."

My eyes blinked open and rested on my man, who sat on the bed next to me fully dressed. He wore his usual black jeans, button-down and leather jacket, though the one he'd slipped on didn't have the usual Speed Demons patch sewn onto it.

My forehead furrowed. "Hey. What's going on? Why are you dressed?" I scrambled to sit up, reaching for my sweater which was crumpled on the floor next to the bed.

Colt watched me with an unreadable expression and his jaw clenched tight. He pulled his shoulders back like he was bracing for something.

A tight knot formed in the pit of my stomach as I studied his face. What the hell was happening? Why had he gotten dressed while I slept? "Colt? Has something happened?"

His ocean-blues met mine, a storm brewing behind them.

My breathing sped up. Something was very wrong.

"Baby." Colt dipped his chin, his piercing gaze locking onto mine. "I have to catch a flight."

My heart sank into my stomach. "What?" I breathed incredulously, my mind racing. "What do you mean you have to catch a flight? Where are you going?" My mind reeled with questions as I searched his face for a clue. His jaw clenched tighter and his expression shuttered.

He looked almost guilty.

"Talk to me," I pleaded. "Please explain."

Colt pushed out a heavy breath, his shoulders rising and falling with the effort. He reached for my hand, his calloused fingers threading through mine. I clutched his hand as if it was the only thing tethering me to the earth and braced myself.

"My sister called me late last night," he finally admitted. "I've got no choice. I have to go to New York and deal with it. I'm sorry, I know the timing sucks but I have to go."

My reply came out strangled. "What?"

His fingers squeezed mine. "My mom took an overdose last night. My father's had her committed to a psychiatric hospital. She needs me, baby. I'm sorry."

His words hit me like a sledgehammer.

I blinked in shock, my mind trying to process his words. Biting my lip nervously, I looked around the room, still dazed and half asleep, trying to get my head together. "Okay. Give me thirty minutes to shower and change. It won't take me long to get ready." Scrambling to my knees, I went to get out of bed when Colt took my hand and pulled me back.

He tugged me back down to my ass and framed my face with his hands. "Freya. I can't take you with me."

Tears filled the backs of my eyes and my heart clenched painfully. "What do you mean?"

Colt sighed, running a hand through his hair. His eyes were bloodshot, face etched with exhaustion.

"Please try to understand how bad a state my mom's in. I know her and she hates people seeing her vulnerable. On top of that, I have to confront my dad. You'd be a distraction, and I need to have my head in the game if I'm gonna get my dad to back off Mom. He makes your dad look like a Boy Scout, Freya. I don't want you breathing his air."

Each word was like a shot to the heart.

My eyes welled up. "But you can't leave me here after what's just happened."

His hands angled my face upward. "I'm sorry, Freya. I have to."

"No!" I insisted, my hands raising to grip his shoulders tightly. "We've just come out as a couple, Colt. If you leave me here my dad will think he's won. Everything we've gone through in the last few days will have been for nothing." My voice held a thread of panic, the thought of him leaving me after everything filling me with dread.

"My mom needs me, baby," he rasped. "Please try to understand—"

"I do," I said, cutting him off. "Just please don't leave me here on my own. I won't be any trouble, I promise. I need you too, Colt. You promised we wouldn't get separated again, but you're leaving me."

His forehead rested on mine. "It's just for a few days. I'll sort everythin' out in record time then come back for you. We'll go on that vacation we talked about. Remember the houses on stilts in Bora Bora? We'll go there, I promise."

I squeezed my eyes shut tight to hide the pain shooting through my heart.

My senses were pinging on overload. I didn't know why, but I knew deep down he wouldn't be back anytime soon. I knew if he didn't take me with him, it would be a while before I saw him again. I couldn't explain without looking like a stage one clinger.

Tears filled my eyes at the wrenching pain in my chest.

My palms grew clammy, my knees weak. I wanted to beg and plead for him not to leave me, but I could see by the set of his jaw that he'd made his mind up. Covering my face with my hands, I sobbed.

"Hey. Come on." His hand slid around my nape. "It's just gonna be for a couple of days. I'll go sort Mom, get her some help, then I'll have a little chat with my dad. I fuckin' love you so much, how could I not come back for you, Freya. It'd feel like my heart had been ripped from my chest."

I looked up at him teary-eyed. Studying the flecks in his ocean-blues and committing them to memory. My hand gently ran over his face, feeling every curve and dip.

Colt leaned forward and pressed a searing kiss to my lips before pulling back and getting to his feet. I watched heart-in-mouth as he pocketed his keys, phone, and wallet.

Everything had been perfect when I'd gone to sleep. How could I wake up to him intent on leaving? Everything had happened so fast it felt like a bad dream.

He walked to the door, pausing at the threshold and craning his neck. "I love you." He shot his sexy smirk, but instead of it lighting me up like it usually did, something withered away and died inside me, because I realized something. Colt did love me, but not enough to take me with him. He'd done the one thing he'd promised he wouldn't do, abandon me.

I'd never ask him not to go. If it was my mom in trouble you wouldn't have seen me for dust, but Colt would've been by my side, always, especially in the dire circumstances we found ourselves in. An icy fist wrapped around my heart, squeezing painfully, and a shiver ran down my spine, the premonition hitting me again that if he left me now, nothing would be the same.

"I'll call you when I land," he said huskily, eyes searing into my face as he studied me briefly before turning away and walking down the hospital corridor, each step of his biker boots echoing eerily like a hammer to my bruised and battered heart.

I remained frozen in place, my stare fixed on the door Colt had just disappeared through, my mind willing him to come back to me.

My composure finally broke and tears spilled down my cheeks. I tried to hold back the sobs ripping at my throat, but it was no use. Covering my face with shaky hands, I let the wave of unhappiness drown me, my shoulders wracking with the force of my sorrow.

I wept for him, for me, and for everything that had gone down between us and the club. On the surface, I knew Colt had left to help his family, he believed it down to his soul, but I knew him better.

Loving Colt for so long meant I knew him completely. He thought he'd left for the right reasons, and he had, but he also hadn't. He'd been thrown a lifeline, an opportunity to have a break from everything, including me, and he'd grabbed it with both hands.

My beautiful man clearly needed time to compartmentalize. What Dad had done to him had screwed with his head. Colt needed time to come to terms with losing the only man he'd ever considered a father, and to embrace the changes that had been forced upon him.

After a few minutes, I wiped my eyes, got up to grab my overnight bag and began to shove my stuff inside it. Sophie had pulled some strings and arranged for me to stay with Colt, but he was gone now.

I had to have faith in him, think of this goodbye as temporary, and believe in the connection we'd forged over the months.

Maybe this would be good for us in the long run.

But even as I tried to convince myself, I knew this was a major setback, even though I knew it was something he had to do, or else we could never move on.

I just had to keep the faith.

The only good thing about hitting rock bottom was that over the next few days, I learned exactly who my friends were.

Iris, Cara, Kennedy, and Sophie wrapped me in a cocoon of love and took over my life because, to my shame, Colt leaving me didn't make me stronger.

If anything, I fell apart.

When I left the hospital, I went back to the gallery so dazed, I couldn't function properly. My heart felt like it had been ripped out of my chest, and I couldn't stop crying. Every plan Colt and I made flew outta the window, and for the first time in my life, I didn't know what came next.

I found out the hard way that Dad had cancelled my bank and credit cards.

On the way back to the gallery I tried to buy gas but the card got declined. Humiliated, I had to call Cara to come pay before the manager of the gas station called the cops.

I'd half expected it, and although I had my inheritance money from Bandit to fall back on, I'd planned on keeping it for the year I interned. Even if I got lucky and secured a paid position, it wouldn't be enough to live on. Plus, the money was in a type of high interest account where I needed to give the bank notice if I wanted to access it.

Money magically began to appear in my checking account. Cash, Breaker, Kennedy, even Atlas and Sophie ensured I was okay, but notably, Bowie and Layla didn't, and it broke my heart a little bit more than it already was.

Colt called me that night but couldn't talk for long. He was dealing with a suicidal mother and two sisters who'd never had to deal with real life problems before. I didn't tell him about the money, he had enough on his plate to worry about, and thanks to my brothers and sisters, I was okay for the time being.

Then, two days after Colt left for New York, a tornado rolled into town. Well, not an actual tornado, though the damage she could cause put an F5 to shame, as evidenced by Dad ordering her to stay away. Not that she took a blind lick of notice.

You see there was one person in the world my dad was afraid of.

His ex-wife, Adele Stone.

My mom.

A shiver skated down my spine as an icy cold winter wind blew down Monument Street.

I tugged my coat tighter, trying to get warm, my eyes never wavering from the car that had just pulled up by the metal steps leading up to the tiny apartment I'd been living in above the gallery.

Mom switched off the engine of her rental and slowly emerged from the vehicle, her hands flying to her mouth. "Oh, Freya," she breathed, holding her arms out for me to walk into. "Baby, come here."

It was exactly what I needed. My mom had always been such a source of strength and comfort that I was suddenly overwhelmed. I burst into tears, again, walking into her arms.

After my two-day crying jag, I knew I looked a mess. My face was blotchy, eyes red, and puffy, and so swollen that it looked like someone had punched me, but Mom never said a word, she just stood by the steps and silently hugged me, stroking my hair while I sobbed on her shoulder.

After a while she pulled back slightly, her hands framing my face while she wiped my tears away with her thumbs. "Is this where you've been living?" she asked, her eyes flicking up toward the apartment.

I nodded through my tears.

The hard set of her jaw conveyed how furious that made her. "Come on, tell me what's been going on. Iris told me the important stuff but there's a lot of blanks you need to fill in." She clasped my hand and led me up the steps and into the warmth of the apartment, looking around. "Well, it's nicer than I thought" she said approvingly. "At least he hasn't left you in a fucking hovel."

Immediately, I jumped to Colt's defense. "He had to go. His mom's in a bad way."

"I agree," she muttered. "But he could've made sure you were okay before he went."

My mouth clamped shut because what could I say? Mom was right and I wouldn't insult her intelligence by challenging her on Colt's behalf when I agreed with everything she'd said.

Mom took off her coat and laid in on the foot of the bed. "I'll make coffee, then we'll talk." She looked around, eyebrows knitting together. "Where's all your stuff?"

I nodded to the two overnight bags stacked in the corner. "There. Dad let Cara pack those for me, but he won't let me in the clubhouse to get the rest of my stuff. He's saying he paid for it all and it doesn't belong to me."

Mom's body locked. "What?"

I shrugged. "You know what he's like. He'll calm down soon enough." My forehead furrowed as I watched Mom reach down toward the bed, grab her coat, and slide her arms into it again. "Wait. What are you doing?"

"Come on," she said brightly. "We're going out." Her eyes flashed as she checked her pocket for her keys and ushered me toward the door. "It's about time we paid your dad a visit."

"Mom," I protested. "He'll go crazy if we show up there."

She barked out a laugh. "Do I look like I give a fuck? My only daughter's been cast out by her own fucking father. Do you think I'm bothered about how John Stone's gonna react when I rip him a new one?" Her mouth twisted angrily. "Send Xander a message. Tell him we're on our way."

During the ten-minute drive to the clubhouse, I told Mom everything. She already knew about my lifelong crush on Colt, so I only had to tell her about Denver and the months since. The only parts I left out were the sexy bits, though I'm sure Mom put two and two together on her own.

"How long's Colt in New York for?" she asked.

I shrugged. "He called me last night and said he's gotten his mom out of the hospital, but she's had a breakdown. He has to stay for the time being."

"I'll be honest with you, Freya," she muttered. "I don't like the fact he's left you here all by yourself to face the music. I'd hunt him down for that alone, but I think there's more to it than just his mom's mental health. He told me once about his dad, he sounded like a piece of shit."

"Yeah," I agreed.

"Maybe in his own fucked-up way, Colt's trying to keep you away from him for a reason," she said thoughtfully, turning onto the long road leading to the clubhouse. "He's always been protective over you."

Something twisted inside my chest. "Would his father try to hurt me?"

"Not physically," she argued. "But Colt told me all about him a few weeks after he joined the club. He beat Colt when he was young for trying to defend his mom; that shit stays with a man. As he grew older he subjected Colt to a lot of mind games." She glanced at me curiously. "Did he tell you why he enlisted?"

"Yeah," I breathed, mind reeling at what Mom had just told me. "He walked in on his dad with his fiancée."

Mom nodded slowly. "Perhaps he's keeping you away from his father in case he tries to get to Colt through you somehow."

I slumped down in my seat as Mom's words weaved through my brain.

It made sense. Colt sometimes told me funny stories about his mom and sisters, but never his dad. It was like he tried to cut him out of his memories, and after what I'd just heard, I couldn't blame him. Back when Colt had enlisted, he'd left the upper echelons of New York society and never looked back. Now I knew he had a damn good reason to leave such a charmed life behind.

"I don't think your dad gets his background," Mom added. "He doesn't concern himself with society gossip, it's not in his purview. As far as John's concerned Colt's a man he doesn't want for you because he's in the MC, but maybe if somebody had sat down and explained Colt's background, he would've been more receptive. I don't think you and Colt did anything wrong by falling in love, Freya, but you lied. You should've called me the minute you decided to be together. I know your dad better than anyone. I could've advised you."

I closed my eyes. "I'm sorry, Mom. You're right. I didn't want to put you in an awkward position with Dad, but I've made matters worse."

Mom eyed the clubhouse looming ahead of us. "Freya. Let's get things into perspective here. You didn't murder someone; you fell in love. Am I hurt you didn't tell me? Yeah, maybe a little, but let's face it, Cash, Bowie, and Kit had lied to me about worse things by the age of fucking ten. I'm a mom of three boys, all of them little shits. You're a saint compared to them."

"I wish Dad would see it that way," I whispered.

"He's a product of his environment." She shrugged. "Bandit was the biggest misogynist I've ever met. I tried my best with your dad, but I couldn't knock it all out of him."

For the first time in days, a bubble of laughter rose through my chest, and I giggled.

Her eyes slid to mine, and she grinned. "There she is."

My heart warmed at the look on her face. "Thanks, Mom."

Mom slowed the car as she signaled, before turning into the gates. "You ready for a showdown, daughter of mine?"

I held my breath, watching the gates open wide before Cash appeared, waving us through.

Mom drove straight into a parking space, switched the engine off and turned to me. "Come on. Let's get this over with."

We both took off our seat belts and exited the car just as Cash approached and enveloped Mom in a big bear hug. "Thanks for this, Son," she murmured. "I'm sorry I've pitted you against him."

My brother looked down at our mother with soft eyes. "It's not a thing, Mom. He's in the wrong this time, and I'm not gonna stand by and watch him fuck everythin' up." His eyes came to me. "You okay?"

I nodded, my throat constricting with emotion.

"You been cryin'?" he demanded.

I nodded again, that time smiling wryly.

"Well quit it," Cash ordered. "You're a Stone. You fight back and you definitely don't take anyone's bullshit." He pointed toward the clubhouse. "You stand up to him. Hear me?"

My mouth quirked and I nodded at my incredible brother, marveling at how much he'd changed since he'd gotten Cara back and become a dad. The Cash I knew from five years ago was a selfish, entitled man who always believed he was right.

Somehow, in the last year, he'd learned to listen, and lost the chip on his shoulder that made him a bit of an asshole. I mean, he still had his asshole moments, but they were few and far between. His support had opened my eyes to how much he'd evolved, with the help of Cara and some counselling.

My big brother slung his arm around Mom's shoulders. "Come here, Freya," he ordered, waiting for me to scurry over before he took my hand and guided us both to the doors of the clubhouse.

"Cara, Sophie and Kennedy are in there," he advised us. "They've been givin' Pop a hard time, but he's holdin' up to the pressure. Kit won't speak to him, and Atlas will only reply to a direct question. Iris and Abe haven't been here since the day of the fight. They won't entertain him. Half the club—most of 'em old timers—are on his side, along with the suck-ups like Shotgun. The rest of us are on yours and Colt's side. Bowie says he won't get involved, but he's bein' fine with Dad." Cash glanced at me. "Have you heard from him?"

My heart sunk. "No. I haven't heard from him or Layla."

"Says it all," he muttered as we approached the door. "You ready?"

"Oh, yeah," Mum replied, eyes flashing.

"Should'a known you'd be up for a fuckin' fight, Mother," he said dryly before pushing the doors open and ushering us both through the door.

The sound of chatter and laughter cut the air as we stepped inside. My eyes went around the room taking in the men who'd been like family to me for so long.

I'd always loved the clubhouse. It was my home, a place I'd always felt safe and cherished. I had a hundred uncles, and I loved every one of them, along with their wives and kids. I'd experienced a life so different from other people, and I counted myself as the luckiest girl in the world to never have had to face hardship or abuse in any form.

A cry went up from a table close to the bar. "Adele! Freya!" The sound of a chair scraping against the floor filled the air and Cara appeared like a whirlwind, hurrying toward us.

Silence fell over the room, every eye turning in our direction.

Cara approached, flinging herself at Mom. "It's so good to see you," she cried just as Sophie and Kennedy walked toward us from the direction of the bar where Dad sat, glaring at us.

A shiver ran down my spine at the sneer on his face, his eyes flicking coldly between me and Mom before resting on Cash. He cocked one eyebrow questioningly.

Cash stood to his full height, folding his arms across his chest.

"I told you they weren't to be let in here," Pop snarled across the room. "This is my club, my house, my rules. You just disrespected all three." Slowly, he drained his beer bottle and clambered off the stool. "It's like you're beggin' me to take your patch."

Cash cocked his head, not looking affected by Dad's threat, whatsoever. "That's the thing about takin' a brother's patch away. Club bylaws say you can only do it by unanimous vote. I'm thinkin' there's plenty of brothers who wouldn't take kindly to you involving the club in your personal vendettas."

Dad's nostrils flared. "It's not a personal vendetta when it involves a club member."

"Freya and my mom aren't in the club," Cash retorted. "You never wanted my sister as part of it, hence your weird rule. And I distinctly remember you divorcin' my mom years ago. They're here at my invitation, so unless there's a man in this room brave enough to throw 'em outta that door, I suggest you have yourself another beer and chill the fuck out."

My dad's brow scrunched up, his eyes narrowing on Mom. "You happy now you've turned the kids against me and the club, Adele?"

"I didn't need to, John," she snapped. "You've done a stand-up job of that all by yourself." She moved toward him, her face twisting with disgust. "How dare you treat my kids this way. How dare you throw my daughter out of her home."

Dad's face turned red with fury. "She betrayed me!" he bellowed.

"No!" Mom slashed a hand through the air. "You betrayed her! I told you when we divorced how it would go if you carried on trying to control the women in your life, John. You've got nobody but yourself to blame." She craned her neck to address me. "Go and get your stuff. You're coming back home with me."

Pop snorted humorlessly. "She can get her stuff when she apologizes and agrees to end it with the traitor. I may even call the bank and order new cards for her, if she swears she'll never go behind my back again."

"You're a bastard," Mom spat.

Dad cocked an eyebrow, smirking. "You should know."

"Come on Freya," Mom said quietly. "Let's get your clothes." She turned, grabbed my wrist, and pulled me toward the corridor to my room.

Shotgun stood from his chair so forcefully, it fell back with a clatter. "Prez said no."

Mom threw her head back and laughed. "And who's gonna stop me? You?"

"Touch my mom or my sister, Shot and I'll slit ya throat," Kit rasped.

"You're already on my shit list, asshole," Cash snarled, head swiveling to stare Shotgun down. "Just give me a fuckin' excuse."

The brother lowered his stare and slunk back to his seat.

"She's not goin' in that room," Dad insisted, stomping toward Cash. "Anyone who goes against my orders'll be dealt with accordin' to the bylaws."

"No fuckin' problem," Cash muttered as he walked toward the corridor before turning around to address the room. "Need some brothers to pack up Freya's room. Box everythin' up then load it into my truck."

"I'll help," Arrow offered.

Reno pulled away from the wall he'd been leaning on. "Me too."

Fender stood from his chair, his lips thinning at Pop. "I'm in."

Sophie walked toward the group of men who were about to head to Freya's room. "I'll come too. I don't think Freya wants you guys looking at her underwear."

Dad let out a snort, watching Sophie and the three brothers disappear down the corridor.

"Oh, grow the fuck up," Mom snapped, glowering. "Stop being so pigheaded. What do you want with Freya's clothes and belongings, you stubborn old fool?"

"Should'a known you'd take her side," Dad muttered, catching my eye, and glaring at me like he hated me. "Ain't ya a little old to go running to Mommy, Freya."

"Like you've got a right to judge me," I muttered, my tone cold with fury. "All my life I've done everything you asked of me. School, college, med school. I never wanted to be a doctor, but I did it to make you proud, searching for validation from a man who'll never think I'm good enough. As for running to Mom, why wouldn't I? Unlike you, she loves me unconditionally."

Silence fell over the bar again.

"I love you," Dad bit out. "I only ever wanted the best for you, but you went behind my back for months with my so-called brother. You lied to my face."

"Because I knew you'd do this," I exclaimed.

"So it's my fault?" he demanded incredulously. "You and Colt betray me, and you blame my reaction for the fact you've lied?"

"Yes," I admitted softly. "Because look at your reaction."

His face hardened to steel. "You knew the rules."

"I did, Dad," I confirmed. "So did Colt, but I don't want to live my life according to your rules. I want to live it according to mine. Colt's been nothing but loyal for twelve years. He's everything you ever wanted for me except he wears a Demons' cut."

"Not anymore," he muttered.

"No." I agreed. "He'll be wearing an FBI badge soon enough. He gave up everything for you and your club, but you don't give a fuck about that, do you?"

Dad's head reared back, his stare slashing to Atlas. "What's she on about?"

"Dunno the full story," the SAA conveyed. "But the Feds wanted techno boy to join 'em, so they got down and dirty and threatened the club."

Dad's face turned ashen. "What have they got on us?"

"That's better discussed in Church," Kit interrupted, looking around the room at the men who were watching our exchange with undisguised interest. "Let's just say that Colt joined the feds under duress. He's made a deal so they won't come after us."

Dad's hand scrubbed down his face. "Why am I always the last to know this shit?"

"You're the one who put him in the fuckin' hospital," Cash reminded him. "What did you expect him to do? Pick up the goddamned blower to fill you in on all the latest gossip?"

Dad rubbed his forehead, deep in thought. "Call Church. Five o'clock." He turned on his heel and stomped toward his office.

Cash gave Mom a confused look. "Well, that went weird quickly."

Mom walked over to Cash and stroked his hair back. "Your dad sees the world in black and white, Cash. When you show him grey areas, it unnerves him." She gave him a beautiful smile. "I've never been prouder of you."

"Stop it, Ma," he muttered, ducking his head bashfully. "The boys are watching."

I giggled softly.

Kit barked a laugh.

"Well, that was an eye-opener," Kennedy said, turning to Kit. "Sorry, babe. I know he's your dad and all, but John can be a bit of an asshole."

Chuckles rose through the room.

"We're bikers. That's our job," someone called out.

More laughter filled the air, and the men went back to their conversations, bored now the show was over.

Arrow appeared at the mouth of the corridor, juggling three stacked boxes. "Where we puttin' this shit?"

I sighed, already needing to escape this place and my dad.

"Follow me," Mom told him, heading toward the main doors.

Within twenty minutes Cash's truck was packed full of my belongings.

I stood there with Kit, looking at it ruefully. "Can you believe my entire life fits on the back of a truck," I murmured thoughtfully. "Twenty-four years and everything I own is there."

Kit clasped my shoulder and squeezed. "I've got less than you and I'm in my thirties. When you settle at your hospital, you can start building, Sis."

I glanced up at my brother's handsome face. "I'm scared. All my life I've known my next step. Now, everything's up in the air, Kit, and I don't know what's gonna happen."

"Maybe that's exactly how it should be, Frey," Kit grinned. "You're twenty-four. You've smashed life so far. Maybe you need to just do you for a while. Don't hang around waitin' for Colt. Go and live. He'll come for you when he's ready."

"I don't think he'll be back for a while. If ever," I admitted. "Maybe all this has been for nothing."

Kit's eyes slid to mine and locked. "He'll come for ya, Frey. In the meantime, do what makes you happy. You're out from under Dad's thumb, so go and be free. God knows, when Colt's ready, he'll lock you down in a hot fuckin' minute."

"I wish," I whispered.

He side-eyed me and let out a deep laugh. "Be careful what you wish for, Freya. I've learned somethin' over the past year that I wish I'd known back in the day, when I was imploding."

My brow furrowed. "What's that?"

Kit's eyes went to Kennedy, and a peaceful expression fell over his face. "If it's meant to be, the universe will find a way to throw you together, Freya. You can't fight fate."

Chapter Thirty-Five

Dagger

Later that day, I made my way through the bar toward my office. It was pretty much deserted. Maybe the family drama left a bad taste in the men's mouths, though I doubted it, seein' as they loved to gossip more than the ol' ladies.

Most of the brothers had gone back to work in the auto shop, our bar, or were out on a job as part of the club's construction crew. I'd seen Atlas milling around, but as soon as he saw me, he walked the other way.

As I reached the hallway leading to the offices—and Church—my gaze fell onto the wall covered in old photos and rows of cuts.

One, in particular, caught my eye.

My gaze lifted to the soft, black leather, my chest swelling proudly as I took in the patch. A motorcycle with a single wing on each side. Our name, *Speed Demons MC*, curved over the top, and our state, Wyoming, across the bottom. Nineteen-sixty-eight was stamped inside the design.

It was in September of that year when my pa founded the club and never looked back.

Don 'Bandit' Stone, my dad, was a crazy son of a bitch. He decided there was more scratch to be made on the wrong side'a the law, which caused the downfall of his friendship with his buddy, Bob Henderson, the man earmarked as the future mayor of Hambleton.

Years later, the title of mayor passed to Rob's son, the current mayor of Hambleton, Robert Henderson the Third. The man who stole the love of my life out from under my nose.

I had my own legacy, President of the Demons, which I took over when my pop passed away. The club was a mess back then, so I decided to turn us onto the straight 'n' narrow. We gave up our one-percenter diamond patch and opened successful businesses, which to this day gave us good lives.

My steps echoed down the corridor as I walked toward the room where we held Church. I pressed my thumb to a keypad on the wall to the right, it gave a high-pitched beep while the locks disengaged. I pushed the door open and made my way inside the room I'd always classed as sacred.

It was Colt who'd installed the top-of-the-range thumbprint sensor a few years ago. He'd wanted to bring the club into the twenty-first century.

I didn't understand any of that technological mumbo jumbo; it flew way over my head. I was a mechanic by trade, but I'd admired his abilities and trusted him to do his best for us, which admittedly he did, at least until recently.

I loved him like a son, which is why his betrayal hit me so hard. The more I hurt, the harder I lashed out, as proven by my actions in the last week. A part of me knew I'd gone too far, recognized that the punishment was far worse than the crime, but what they'd done had hit me like a ton of bricks, weighing down on me so heavy that I struggled to see the light.

The last time the light died for me was when I came home after bein' tortured and held prisoner by Adid's forces in Mogadishu, to find the girl I loved more than life had married somebody else and birthed his baby.

My world had been dark ever since.

I pulled the gavel off the shelf, taking it to the Prez's seat and placing it carefully on the table, which had been battered by the same gavel over the years. Every dent in the wood told a story, from back in the day when Bandit was president, and would continue to do so when Cash took over the top spot.

I took my seat, my pinkie touching the block of wood, as if I needed to know it was there, along with the years of tradition and family it represented. The block was smooth against my skin. Comforting almost.

My eyes lifted as the door opened and my oldest friend entered the room in silence, taking his seat. Mere seconds passed before Atlas and Cash came in, followed a minute later by Breaker and Bowie. They all sat down without a word, regarding me with expressions ranging from disappointed to downright fuckin' furious.

I picked up the gavel, whacked it against the sound block, and rumbled, "Let Church commence," before my stare met every man in turn. "I know the last few days have been... difficult," I began. "But it's over now. Colt's gone, Freya's goin', and we need to get back to normal."

"Is that it?" Abe asked, the corners of his mouth turning downward as he addressed me. "You turn this MC on its head and tell us to carry on regardless?" He shook his head disbelievingly. "Fuckin' typical."

"They knew the consequences," I pointed out. "It's been drummed into them both for years."

He stared at me blankly. "Stupid fuckin' rule if you ask me. Tellin' people they can't fall in love." He let out a snort. "What gives you the right?"

My chest panged because Abe being irked made me feel like I was a naughty schoolboy getting berated by his dad. He was a man I looked up to, so losing his respect had an impact.

I looked around the room. "Anyone else got somethin' to say? Why don't we get it all outta the way so we can fuckin' move on?" My stare rested on Atlas. "You're the SAA. Your job's to ensure club members don't break the rules. What's your take on it?"

His eyes met mine and I knew I wouldn't like his reply.

I was right.

"Ya know, Prez. Every time you said you didn't want Freya with a club member, I wondered why we weren't good enough. Don't get me wrong, I never looked at her as anythin' but a little sister, but whenever you gave us the spiel, I wondered what we lacked. Over the years the club got straight. We make bank, and now live according to the law, mostly. We put our women on pedestals and love 'em to distraction. What's so bad about us?"

My throat caught because when Atlas put it like that, no answer would suffice. I had to make him see though. Had to make him understand. "It's the life, Atlas. All our women are in constant danger. Look at what's happened in the last eighteen months. Layla, Cara, Sophie, even little Kady girl got caught up in shit that shouldn't have touched 'em."

"Layla's bullshit happened before the club," he pointed out. "She got kidnapped because Henderson didn't wanna get linked to Sunny. My Sophie got more abuse from her pig ex-husband than the Sinners. Little Kady was marked 'cause she's a little fuckin' beauty and those sick fucks wanted to sell her, not 'cause of the club." His mouth thinned into a line. "We've worked for years to make the Demons successful. Seems to me we're good enough to make you scratch to pay for Freya's education, but that's where it stops, so I'll ask ya again, Prez. What's wrong with us?"

My eyes hit the table, suitably chastised. "Nothin'. I just wanted my girl to have an easy life. It wasn't personal, I promise."

Atlas jerked a nod, but I knew he didn't get it, and after hearing the hurt behind his words, I couldn't blame him.

"Kennedy told me somethin' last night," Kit chimed. "I mentioned Colt's family name and she nearly fell off her chair. Turns out Colt's family isn't just rich, they're the top tier of New York society and part of the top one percent of the world."

"One percenters?" I asked, tone confused.

Break laughed. "No, Pop. They belong in the top one percent of the richest families on Earth. They're up there with Arab princes, kings and queens, oligarchs, and sultans."

Unease stirred in my stomach.

"Fuck me," Atlas muttered.

"Colt is exactly the type'a man you've wanted for her all along." Kit shook his head disbelievingly. "How fuckin' crazy is that?"

Abe busted out laughing.

My throat went dry, my eyes rounding when the connotation of Kit's words hit me. "How did we not know any of this?"

"Vetting hang-arounds came in with Colt," Cash reminded me. "It was his suggestion. He's hardly gonna vet himself and come runnin' to you with info he clearly didn't want known. Nobody asked questions at the time 'cause you're the one who vouched for him."

"He never hid who he was though," Breaker muttered. "Never lied about his name. Just didn't boast about it either."

"Maybe he didn't wanna be treated differently," Abe suggested. "He's probably had people suckin' up to him his whole life. I reckon he just wanted to be part of somethin' real for a while."

My hand came up to rub my beard as I mulled over Abe's words.

Colt had told me about his dad on occasion. He enlisted to get away from him and soon after he left the military, he found us. He always told me we were his chosen family because we lived a life we could be proud of. I'd never really understood the meaning behind it until now.

"Does anyone know about the feds recruitin' him?" I asked the men.

Cash's stare hit the wall behind me.

Kit's hit the floor.

I sighed. "Out with it."

Cash leaned forward, elbows to table. "All I know is that they've been after him for years. Over that time, they've built cases against us, so when they finally moved to reel him in, they could use their evidence as leverage. The last straw was when Colt hacked into their database lookin' for the vehicle involved in the chase the night we followed Stafford. He left a footprint and they jumped on him and threatened to make him disappear. That was when he decided to start things up with Freya, when he knew he was leavin' the club."

I scrubbed a hand down my face, wincing internally.

"There's more," Kit added. "They knew there was more to Henderson Junior's death than we let on. They told him they'd come up with evidence one way or another to take us down."

I glanced at Bowie who'd paled.

"Colt knew you'd take the rap," Breaker continued. "He wouldn't allow you to spend the rest of your life in jail."

Leaning on the table, I buried my head in my hands.

So much had been goin' on behind the scenes, I was shocked Colt hadn't had a nervous fuckin' breakdown. He'd had the Feds on his case and still managed to protect the club, the brothers, and me.

Nausea swirled in my gut because I realized I hadn't afforded him the same protection. If anythin' I'd been the cause of his downfall.

"You didn't know, Pop," Bowie murmured.

"Nah, Son, you're right, I didn't," I rasped through my tightened throat. "But I didn't stop to find out either."

Cash grinned. "Well, I get my hotheadedness from somewhere, right. Just be grateful that your filthy temper didn't land you in jail."

Cash's words sent a cold shiver down my spine, 'cause over the years, it could've done. It was more luck than judgment that kept me a free man. My throat ached from the guilt wrapping around my neck, much like the noose Abe spoke of the day I got in the ring with Colt.

As president of the club, I had a duty to act fairly.

On this occasion I'd failed.

"Where's Colt now?" I asked the boys. "Is he okay?"

"He's fine," Cash assured me. "His mom's in a bad way, mainly 'cause his asshole of a dad's up to his mind game tricks again. He's held up in New York indefinitely 'cause his mom's had a mental break. He'll be back for Freya; he just doesn't know when."

My gut clenched at the mention of my girl.

I'd been a cunt to her and her mother, a woman I liked and respected above most other people I knew.

When I threw Freya out, I'd been so fuckin' blind with fury. By the time I began to waver over my decision it was too late, the damage had been done and changing my mind would've looked weak to the men.

Cancelling her line of credit had been a petty, drunken decision I'd regretted as soon as I'd sobered up. If Freya used her cards now, she'd find they worked again. I'd unblocked them later the same day.

"Where is she?" I asked, my skin itching about what the answer may be.

"Her and mom have gone to Denver," Kit told me. "Freya's friend doesn't go back to school until next week, so they're stayin' with her for a few days."

My gut ached. It seemed that driving my girl away hurt me a lot more than it hurt her. But then again, I had a plethora of sins to feel bad about and make up for. I couldn't blame her for fleeing. I'd let my humiliation get the better of me, and not for the first time. Luckily, my daughter was the forgiving type. I'd give her time to calm down and catch up with her when she returned.

If I'd realized what the future held that day, I'd have got off my ass and driven to Denver to make things right. It would turn out that the repercussions of my actions would stretch far and wide, and last for many years.

Colt wouldn't return to Hambleton until months later and under circumstances that were less than ideal. As for my daughter, she'd come back for a short time but soon move away too. She'd never call Wyoming her home again.

And I only had myself to blame, which I did, for many years, because Abe turned out to be right about something.

That noose pulled tight, every day, for the rest of my life.

Chapter Thirty-Six

Freya

I loved being back in Denver. It was a special place for me; the place where I'd matured, started thinking for myself and began to grow up emotionally. Being with Abi again made everything just seem better. Maybe it was because she took my mind off Colt, whose calls were short and sporadic at best.

Mom came too. She called Tim and told him we needed some mother-daughter bonding time. So, I had my best friends at my side to help me unbreak my heart and get some perspective.

I knew I was falling apart, but I also knew I'd be okay eventually. The rational side of me recognized how I had to face what had happened and start making decisions for my future. It was a shame I couldn't factor Colt into them, but he had no idea what his future held.

I just had to cry him out of my system. It wasn't so different from what I'd already been doing for the last ten years. Colter Van Der Cleeve had brought me to my knees for as long as I could remember.

"What about Sex in the City?" Mom mused from my right, flicking through the TV planner.

"Yes!" Abi agreed from my left. "We could definitely benefit from Samantha Jones's big clit energy. Whenever we get steamrollered by a man, we should ask ourselves, *what would Samantha do*?"

The corner of my mouth hitched for the first time in days. I mean, who wouldn't smile at the phrase 'big clit energy'?

Leaning forward, I pushed aside the blanket covering my knees and grabbed my hot chocolate from the coffee table. "I love Samantha. She wouldn't let a man affect her. She wouldn't live on a couch with her mom, Carrie, Charlotte, and Miranda."

"Carrie would," Mom interjected. "When Mr. Big dumped her and married Natasha, she was a mess."

"I want to be Samantha when I grow up," Abi muttered. "Who wants to sit on the couch and cry over a man like Big. I wanna go out, get drunk on Cosmopolitans, and fuck hot men."

Mom aimed the remote control toward the TV and clicked a button. "Fucking hot men is what got us on this goddamned couch in the first place."

"Hey!" I cried out.

Mom bumped my shoulder with hers playfully. "It's okay, Freya. If I had a dollar for every time your dad made me cry on a couch, I could tell him to stick his spousal support where the sun doesn't shine."

My eyes slashed right. "Dad gives you spousal support?"

Mom's voice turned steely. "It's the least he can do. I pushed four kids out for him, and three of them were huge-headed little bastards. I put up with his club and all their bullshit for years, and he still fucked me over. The rich shit owes me."

Abi burst out laughing. "Take him to the cleaners, girlfriend."

"Even though he's been an asshole recently, John's usually okay. He wouldn't see me go without." Mom smirked. "Plus, he knows I've got too much on him. If he starts his shit with me, I'll humiliate his ass so badly he wouldn't be able to show his face in Church for months."

Abi busted a gut so hard she nearly fell off the couch. Even I had to laugh. My mom was the shit. I bet she could even teach Samantha Jones a lesson or two.

The opening credits to Sex in the City flickered on the TV screen, and an arm slid around my back. I glanced left to meet Abigail's bright blue eyes. "Thank you, babe," I whispered.

Her expression morphed into a grin, which was weird because I was sure her eyes glistened. "Anytime, Princess," she murmured, resting her head on my shoulder.

Tears welled in my eyes, and Mom's hand grabbed mine, squeezing gently.

Glancing right, I took in her warm expression as she watched Abi support me in the way only a best friend could. As much as my heart ached for everything I'd lost, I also appreciated the things I did have. I may have lost Colt for now, but I'd gained a new understanding of friendship.

Time passed, and eventually, I carried on. Colt may have left me bruised and broken, but I had so much love around me it helped patch over the hole he left inside. It wasn't filled, not wholly. Now and again, the aching of my soul seeped through so forcefully it took my breath away, but over the days, I began to come to terms with him being gone. Everything hurt inside though because I could feel his disinterest whenever we spoke on the phone, as evidenced by a call I made to him two weeks later.

The hospitals where I'd applied for internships started getting in touch and arranging interviews. Colt had told me to call him as soon as I heard anything, so, two weeks after I'd arrived in Denver, I picked up my cell phone and pressed on his name, clicking the phone onto speaker.

It rang for ages before the call clicked in. "Hey," Colt breathed.

My heart squeezed when I heard his voice. Missing him so much affected me in ways I couldn't have imagined. I'd see him everywhere, in restaurants, bars. I'd dream of him, and it would feel so real that I'd wake up and expect him to be beside me, only to burst into tears when I realized it was all in my head.

"Hey," I greeted him. "How's things there?"

He paused briefly before sighing. "Fucked-up. My father's fighting me at every turn. We got Mom outta the clinic yesterday, but she needs help. I'm lookin' into places she can go and convalesce, but it's a minefield."

"Have you spoken to Sophie?" I asked. "She may know of somewhere. Or maybe call Mitch's office and ask his advice."

He went quiet for a minute. "Never thought of that."

"Do you want me to call?" I asked him. "I can send any details to your phone."

"Nah, it's fine, Frey. I can do it. I need shit to take my mind off my father and his bullshit antics."

"Let me help," I pleaded gently. "You don't have to do this by yourself. I can fly up there today if you let me."

He groaned. "No, baby! My dad's playin' a game of cat and mouse. The last thing I need is you involved in his bullshit. I'm already livin' on my nerves, worryin' about what he's got up his sleeve. I need you away from here and safe. It's the only thing keepin' me sane."

My heart twisted painfully.

I got it, I really did, but I also wanted to support him so badly. Being separated was killing me, but I didn't want to pile any more pressure on his shoulders. He was already bogged down with so much.

"I heard from Palomar Bay Hospital today," I told him. "I fly up to Maine on Thursday."

"Is that the one in the little fishing town?" he inquired.

"Yeah," I confirmed. "I'm meeting with Doctor Manning. He's head of trauma surgery there. There's one position and they're interviewing ten candidates."

"See," he murmured. "Bet they had hundreds of applicants. You did well to even get an interview and I know you'll impress 'em. You're so fuckin' amazin'."

My throat burned with emotion "Do you think you can work in Maine?"

"There're positions all over the country. I don't think Maine has a big FBI presence though. Regardless of that, I don't want ya takin' a job for me, baby. You've gotta go where you'll be happy and fulfilled. We'll make it work wherever we end up."

Bowing my head, I fought back my tears. We'd taken a step backward again. I hated him saying that shit. Why couldn't he beg me to take a position close to him? It was what a partnership was supposed to be, surely? I didn't mind compromising, it's what you did in relationships, but he had to give me something to work with. Confirming a state would be a start.

"When are you going to speak to your new boss about where you'll be based?" I asked tightly. All I'd done was walk on eggshells since he'd left. I was so scared of putting more pressure on him that I'd ignored him skating over the important stuff, but time was running out. I needed something.

"No," he replied. "I dunno when I will, either. I'm meant to start in April, but with what's goin' on here, I can't commit to much else."

My heart sunk. "Please, Colt. I need an idea. I'm trying to keep us together but I can't do it by myself. I feel like you're slipping away from me."

"No, baby. I'm not," he assured me. "It's just that I can't spread myself any thinner than I have already. If I take anything else on, I'll fail everyone, and there's too much at stake for me to let my dad win. I love you and wherever you end up I'll find you. I'll visit. I'll do everything in my power to make it work."

"Okay," I whispered, my eyes brimming with unshed tears. "I'll let you go."

"Thanks," he muttered blankly, his mind probably somewhere else already "Call you soon."

"Bye," I breathed before clicking the end call button and sinking down into the nearest chair.

Elbows to knees, I held my head in my hands, trying to keep it together.

I was so sick of feeling like an imposition. So tired of the loneliness gripping my heart. It was funny how Colt said he was scared of failing everybody when he'd already failed me. I hadn't seen him for weeks and he wouldn't commit to a future with me, even after everything we'd sacrificed to be together.

Everything was falling apart, but I knew I couldn't. I had to live my life, and hope that one day Colt would find his way back to me. Maybe after everything he still wasn't ready, and I just needed to stop moping and start concentrating on the areas of my life I could control, like work.

If Colt wouldn't give me what I needed, I'd have to make my own happiness. It wasn't what I wanted, but I couldn't carry on the way I was.

I picked my cell up again and began to look for flights.

Maybe a few days in a little fishing town in Maine would be just what the doctor ordered.

Palomar Bay was a beautiful place. I could already tell the rolling seas would be stunning in the summer. The town had a community feel, much like Hambleton. It felt safe and homely, and the feelings of comfort it gave me were wonderful.

The hospital was small, but efficient. My meeting with Doctor Manning went well and he seemed eager to get me on board. A nurse called Vivi showed me around. She was a widow and a single mom and reminded me a lot of Sophie in her personality.

Vivi and her friend Lulu's shift finished at the same time as my interview. She talked me into going for coffee with them and seeing a little more of the town while I was there. The hospital was in walking distance, so we headed to Main Street together, enjoying a stroll in the crisp winter afternoon.

"This is Beanie Love," Lulu told me as we approached a small café with a blue and white striped awning over the door. "It's the hub of the community."

"Don't listen to her," Vivi told me, eyeing Lulu frustratedly. "Palomar Bay is much more than just a coffee shop. We're a coastal town, so summers are busy. We've got some great bars and restaurants, and I can tell you from experience that the schools are second to none."

The warmth of the coffee shop hit me as we walked inside. I looked around, taking in the old-fashioned but clean décor, and smiled. We placed our order and found a seat near the back of the room close to a group of elderly ladies who sat together at a big table.

"Well," one of them cackled. "Who's this young thing?"

"Hi, Pearl," Vivi greeted her. "This is Freya. She's just interviewed at the hospital for the Internship starting next summer."

Her mouth downturned. "She won't do at all. We need a strapping young man to take the job."

Lulu rolled her eyes. "Excuse her. She means well. One thing you'll learn about Palomar Bay is that there's way more women than men. A lot of the guys don't return after college unless they want to be a fisherman or a run a store. We have a firehouse, and of course the hospital, but not much else."

One of the other old ladies looked me over. "You'll do well," she murmured, looking me up and down like a piece of meat. You're pretty, so I'm sure you'll ensnare one of the single men sooner rather than later."

I smiled. "It's okay," I assure her. "I have a boyfriend."

Her eyes lit up. "Where is he?"

"New York," I explained. "He's got family issues at the moment, but if I did move here, he'd visit. My family too. My dad runs a motorcycle club, and my three brothers are officers. I'm sure they'd visit with their wives and kids."

Pearl sat up a little straighter and waggled her eyebrows at me. "Are they anything like that Sons of Anarchy hunk with the blond hair?" She turned to her friend. "Believe me, Doris, I'd clean his exhaust pipe out any time."

"No, they're better." I pulled my phone from my purse and clicked on my camera roll, moving to sit at the old lady table. "That's my oldest brother, Cash," I said, pointing to his picture." There's Bowie and Breaker. He's the youngest brother, but I'm the youngest out of all of them, and the only girl."

"And who's that fine slab of man-meat?" Doris asked.

"My dad," I murmured. "The president of the club."

"Oh my," she muttered. "Look at his guns."

I winced.

Pearl looked directly at Doris. "I think we need to open a motorcycle club in Palomar Bay. I'll let the local newspaper know. You activate the gossip tree. Leave no stone unturned."

I bit back my laugh.

These women could've been Emmy Dixon and Mrs. Fenton. In fact, the entire town reminded me so much of Hambleton, it was uncanny. I looked around, trying to picture myself here, working at the local hospital, and living my life in a small community where everybody knew each other.

It hit me that if I lived here, I may as well just take a job at Baines Memorial, because my life would be pretty much the same. I didn't want that. I wanted something different, something exciting that I'd never experienced before.

There and then, I struck Maine off the list, and hoped to God that the next place would offer me what I wanted, because my list of hospitals were getting smaller, and time was running out.

Chapter Thirty-Seven

Colt ~ February

On February tenth, my mom came home from the clinic Mitch had recommended six weeks before. After thirty plus years, she was finally sober and feeling positive about her future.

I picked her up and took her back to the house I'd rented at Peach Lake, in Putnam County, Upstate New York. My sisters both lived there with us, disgusted at my dad's behavior toward Mom.

I'd been busy since I'd been in New York, gathering evidence against Dad, so when Mom served him with divorce papers, I'd have sufficient leverage.

So far, I had pictures of him in bed with three different women—one of them a well-known escort, the other, a second mistress he had on the side, and of course, the third woman was my ex-fiancée, Victoria.

Vicki had aged well, if Botox, fillers and extensive breast and ass augmentation was your bag. It wasn't mine, but I still couldn't help feeling sorry for her. She'd chosen her path when we were young, and now, in her thirties, she was tied to a man who would never be faithful, good, or decent toward her.

I had no doubt that eventually he'd marry her. She was from a good family who invested in the same stocks and shares he did. Dad always had an agenda, so it felt good to finally have the upper hand. He had no idea I was onto him, and I wouldn't rest until he let Mom and my sisters out from under his influence.

Mom reckoned Valentine's Day seemed like the perfect date to end her marriage. It had been loveless from day one. Mom had loved a boy who her parents disapproved of. They'd made him disappear and she'd married my dad under duress.

The grandparents I knew were kind, so what they'd done to Mom was maddening. When they died all their money got split between us, while my dad inherited their business and merged it with his own. We were all wealthy in our own right, also owning shares in dad's firm. After making enquiries I discovered Dad owned forty percent. Mom was also a major shareholder, owning thirty-five percent of the business. Me and my sisters owned five percent each, the rest split between investors.

I looked across at Mom, who sat next to me in the back of the limo as we headed to Dad's office. Reaching over, I squeezed her hand. Her face whipped around to look at me and I took in her bright eyes and serene smile. "You look wonderful," I told her. "Your new hairstyle takes years off you."

Her hand raised to her blonde locks, patting the stylish shoulder-length bob. "Thank you," she responded. "I wanted a change for so long but he wouldn't allow it."

"You can do whatever the fuck you want from now on," I reminded her.

Mom's blue eyes, exactly like mine, sparkled even though she sighed frustratedly. "Language, Colter."

I smirked. "Sorry, Ma."

Her lips twitched.

Between us, we could take Dad down and end his reign, but after discussing it, we decided to use what we had as leverage instead. We didn't want any part of the business, and Dad, for all his faults as a husband and father, was a good CEO, who'd taken the firm to new heights. It wouldn't hurt if he made us more money.

"I don't mind admitting I'm terrified," Mom whispered.

My heart squeezed. Dealing with Dad wouldn't be easy. We'd probably have to put the squeeze on him in order to get what we wanted, but I'd gladly call his bluff.

"No need to be," I assured her. "I'm here now."

Her eyes flicked over my Tom Ford suit. "You look like everything he ever wanted in a son. A man molded in his image, ruthless and smart enough to carry on the Van Der Cleeve legacy."

"I look like you, thank God," I muttered, eyeing the skyscraper the driver had pulled up at. "And I've got your heart too, Mom. He'll see it soon enough."

She leaned over and cupped my jaw. "Whatever happens today, Colter. Know I'm proud of you and I'll never go back to him."

"I know." I grinned. "We'll move away, after today you can start afresh."

Mom nodded. "Are you ready?"

Before I could answer, the driver opened my door for me. "Looks like I'll have to be," I murmured, grabbing my briefcase, and exiting the car.

I walked around the limo to help Mom out, before leading her into the building. After announcing our arrival, we were sent up in the elevator to the top floor where Dad's office was.

The penthouse floor was exactly as you'd imagine. Its marble, concrete, and glass construction made it cold and clinical. The only soft furnishings were the low-slung leather couches and chairs in the waiting area, but they didn't add any warmth. The floor-to-ceiling windows looked out onto a typical New York winter's day, with grey skies and rain smattering against the glass.

My father's assistant came around her desk to shake my hand and greet my mother. "I've told him you're here," she murmured. "Follow me please."

She made her way toward the door to Dad's private office, which took up half the back wall of the building, the other half belonging to his CFO.

I held my arm out for Mom, who slipped her hand through before we followed the PA.

My heart thudded with anticipation.

This meet wouldn't be easy. My dad wasn't known for capitulation, which made me slightly nervous. However, he also hadn't got to where he was by cutting off his nose to spite his face, which was the one thing giving confidence to what I was about to do.

The assistant knocked on Dad's door, opening it, and giving me my first glimpse of my father in over fifteen years. "Your eleven o'clock is here," she announced.

"Show them in," Dad ordered, voice low and filled with a confidence that could only ever come from old money, and the knowledge that he was a key player in the top tier of society.

I tilted my chin and strolled through the door with Mom on my arm, before showing her to the one chair that faced Dad across his desk.

It was a power play, only having one chair ready. There were more in the room, but instead of dragging one over, I ensured Mom was comfortable before approaching Dad's desk and parking my ass on the edge, looking him dead in the eye. "Good morning, Father," I greeted, setting my briefcase on his desk with a thud. "Still up to your old games I see, how predictable."

Dad tilted his head to one side, leaning back in his chair without a care in the world. "How good to see you, Colter. It's been a long time. How's that biker gang you've been working for? I must say, I thought you could do better than resorting to criminality." A bored look settled over his face "Maybe my expectations of you were too high."

My eyes flicked over his face, still handsome, albeit showing signs of age. "I must say, Father. Mine certainly were. Now, let's get down to business." I opened my briefcase, pulling out a binder full of paperwork and handing it to him.

With a wearied sigh, he took the papers and began to flick through them sheet by sheet. After a few minutes, he slapped them onto his desk, looking straight at Mom. "No, Caroline. There will be no divorce. It's unacceptable for people in our position. I'm afraid you're stuck with me." His eyes lifted to mine. "Next question."

"Conrad," Mom murmured. "I will get my divorce. Yesterday, Colter arranged a board meeting for nine o'clock Monday morning, with all your colleagues, business associates, and investors. Let us show you item one on the agenda." She nodded at me.

For the second time, I went into my briefcase and pulled out another folder, handing it to Dad. "I think you'll find that although we live in a modern world, this kind of scandal's looked down on by people in our circle." I watched, smirking as he flicked through pictures of himself fucking the escort in our family home, along with others of him, Victoria, and his other fuck buddy involved in a threesome.

He threw the sheaf of papers onto his desk. "Nobody cares about this anymore."

"Your major shareholders do," I retorted. "We're moving to have you removed from your position as CEO. The Van Der Cleeves are embarrassed by your behavior, and if we must be associated with you, it will be under duress."

Dad smirked. "I'm the majority shareholder."

"Yes. But when you add your wife's shares to your children's', we own more."

Dad paled. "The girls wouldn't do that to me."

"You're right," I admitted, "They wouldn't have six months ago. Unfortunately, since then, you've shown them the kind of sick fuck you really are, by moving your whore into their family home where their mother sleeps." I nodded to the pictures. "And rest assured, their respect for you is non-existent after seeing those."

I stood from the desk, motioning for Mom to stand. "I'll leave the divorce papers with you. If you sign them before Monday we'll cancel the meeting. If you don't." I smirked. "We'll see you in the boardroom." I motioned to the images scattered across Dad's desk. "You can keep those. We've got copies." I offered Mom my arm again, waiting for her to slip her tremoring fingers through it, before sweeping out of his office and toward the elevator, which was still there from when we came up, seeing as it was for the use of the penthouse offices only.

As we stepped in and turned around to face Dad's office, I caught sight of him at his door, staring at us with a snarl on his face. "You'll regret this, Caroline," he called out.

"No, Conrad. This time, I think you'll be the one with regrets," she replied in a clear, confident voice as the doors closed, cutting him off from sight.

She slumped against me.

I held her firm, until her knees stopped trembling and she was able to stand straight again. "You were perfect," I told her quietly. "I know you hate confrontation, but you had to be there. You had to look him in the eyes and make your demands, or he wouldn't have taken us seriously."

"I know," Mom admitted before angling her face up to study mine. "What happens next? What if he calls our bluff?"

My eyes met hers, I couldn't help marveling at how clear and coherent they were, despite the years of drinking. "Then we go to the meeting Monday morning and oust the motherfucker. I'll find somebody to take over as CEO, but he or she will be on our payroll."

"You're as savage as him, Colter," Mom murmured as the elevator doors slid open and we swept through the ground floor reception area. "Though I must say, I'm grateful for that savagery today."

I caught Mom's gaze and gave her a knowing look. "I may not be my father's son emotionally, Mom, but I still watched and learned from him. I knew one day I'd have to play him at his own game. It's been a long time coming, and when it comes to getting what I want, I learned from the best."

The rest of the week passed by quicker than expected.

We got to know each other as a family again. Mom slowly gained more confidence, and my sisters smiled bigger and more often. We stayed on the lake, which even in the winter months was a beautiful place. We walked around there every day just catching up.

On Sunday morning, we sat in a little café which overlooked the lake, talking.

It was there I told them about Freya and how much I loved and missed her. I'd left Wyoming thinking it was wholly for them, but really, I'd also needed time to heal from losing the only family I'd known for the last twelve years, because honestly, it had gutted me.

"You were so beat-up when you arrived," Cordelia murmured, placing a hand on my arm. "You looked like you had the weight of the world on your shoulders."

"I guess I did," I admitted, my stare taking in the still waters of the vast lake, blue from the reflection of the clear winter sky. "The reaction shocked me. John had been a father figure for a long time. Showed me nothin' but love and appreciation." I grinned. "I met him in a bar fight when I first left the military. He was the underdog, three against one, so I jumped in, and we fought side by side."

"Colter," Mom chided. "You weren't raised to participate in bar fights."

Gracie giggled.

Cordy's lips twitched.

"Sorry, Mom," I said thickly. "It was weird, that night when we spoke, I felt I'd met him before. Then he took me back to his club's compound and I was accepted, just like that." I clicked my fingers. "Over the years I thought of 'em as my family, and then Freya grew up and I buried my feelin's for her, because I didn't wanna disappoint John."

"What made you change your mind?" Cordelia asked, rubbing my arm.

"I guess my feelings for her became stronger than my loyalty to him." My eyes slid to Mom. "Maybe I'm more like my father than I always thought."

Mom tipped her chin, looking up into my eyes and murmured one word. "No." Her hand reached for mine across the table and she squeezed my fingers gently. "You're nothing like him. You did it for love, Colt, something your dad wouldn't be able comprehend, because he's never loved anyone except himself." Her head cocked sideways, blue eyes never leaving mine.

"You didn't betray John, Colt. You didn't go out and collude with the enemy. You didn't go to the police and tell them his secrets. You worked hard for that club, you kept them safe and secure."

The knot that had been strangling my chest since the morning of the fight suddenly loosened.

Mom had a valid point. I'd always done my utmost for the club, sometimes to the detriment of myself. For years, I'd ached for a woman who I pushed away for them, only giving in when I knew I'd have to leave.

Maybe if the FBI hadn't pulled their puppet strings, me and Freya would never have happened, I'd been so intent on doing the right thing.

The thought made my blood run cold. Suddenly the FBI recruiting me seemed like the best thing in the world, because it brought me her.

And then I'd pushed her away.

I brought up a hand to rub my throbbing temple. "I've been a dick to her."

Cordelia and Gracie exchanged a knowing look.

"Son," Mom said gently. "Your only experience with love was with a woman who cheated on you with your father. Is it any wonder you self-sabotage?"

I sat straighter. "I don't self-sabotage," I denied, looking affronted.

"You get to a certain point in a relationship and back away," Cordy agreed.

"But I never have girlfriends," I argued.

Gracie leaned closer to me. "Because you're scared to commit."

"I committed to Freya," I muttered.

"And you've got to a certain point in your relationship and backed away," Mom repeated.

Her words weaved through my head, and I winced.

There'd been a lot of push and pull between me and my girl since we got together. I thought back to all the instances where I'd put up walls, and I realized something that made my throat go dry.

My own father and fiancée had made me so untrusting that Freya had seemed almost too good to be true. All the times I'd pushed her away and been a dick had been my way of testing whether she'd stick by me through thick and thin. Mom was right, I'd been self-sabotaging since the night we got together and I gave her hell because a waiter back in Denver gave her his number.

I buried my head in my hand. "Fuck!"

"Colter, language," Mom snapped.

"Mom," Cordy began. "I think we can ignore it given the circumstances—" she was cut off by mom's ringtone blasting from her purse.

She fished it from her bag, checked the caller display, and froze, all color draining from her face. "It's your dad," she whispered.

"Want me to take it?" I offered gently.

She shook her head, pulling her back straight. "No. I can do it." She looked at us in turn before pursing her lips and clicking the icon to answer the call. "Conrad," she murmured. "What can I do for you?"

I held my breath, studying Mom's expression, trying to work out the tone of the call by her face.

My dad should've called me, not Mom. The fact he'd gone over my head made him a fucking coward. He knew Mom wouldn't stand up to him the same way I would. She was still getting over the years of trauma he'd caused her.

"Okay, Conrad," she murmured. "If that's how you feel, we'll see you at the meeting. Good day." She disconnected the call and put the phone back in her purse. "Your father won't agree to the divorce. He said if I go back to him today, he'll ditch the mistresses and give our marriage a chance. As you just heard, that's unacceptable to me. So, it looks like we have to be up bright and early for a meeting."

"God," Gracie snapped. "He's such an asshole."

"Preach," Cordy muttered.

My heart went out to Mom. "You did good there," I said softly. "I know that was hard for you."

She shrugged. "I didn't expect him to give in at the first hurdle. It's not his style. If there's one thing I know about your father, it's that he's a tenacious son of a bitch. He'll wait it out until the last minute."

"Language, Mom," Gracie said with a giggle.

She waved her hand nonchalantly. "Well. His mother was a bitch, God rest her soul. She spoiled him. I blame her that he can't keep his teeny tiny little penis in his pants. He's so needy."

I sat back grinning. "At last!"

Mom turned to me. "At last what?"

"At last there's somethin' about him that I can honestly say, he didn't hand down to me." I nodded toward my crotch. "Nothin' teeny tiny about me."

"Oh my God," Gracie muttered. "You're such a child."

I grinned huge, my thoughts going back to the time when I'd just thrown Christian the auto mechanic outta Freya's apartment. She'd called me exactly the same thing.

"You'll get on well with my girl," I said huskily. "She gives me so much shit in one breath, then so much love in the next, she makes my head spin." I rubbed at the ache in my heart. I missed her so much, but I didn't know how to make it right from so far away.

"Go to her," Mom breathed. "Explain everything. Be honest."

I jerked a nod. "I will. Just need to see this shit through with Dad first. When I go to her it's gonna be forever. I want this part of my life over, Dad's gotta be gone. I don't want him around my woman or my kids. Not ever."

Every one of my girls comforted me in some way.

Mom hugged me.

Cordy stroked my arm.

Gracie squeezed my hand.

"Let's make a pact now," Cordelia suggested, studying each one of us in turn. "When Dad's gone he doesn't get back in. We all move away and we start fresh. I've already instructed my divorce lawyer. I don't want a cent from Jasper, I just want my freedom."

We all nodded our agreement, grinning.

It was like music to my ears. I'd been trying to get them away from him for years. I realized now that Mom wasn't in the right headspace to leave, and my sisters hadn't seen the dark side of Dad.

Now he'd proven who he was, they wanted out, and I couldn't have been happier.

Two things happened that night.

First, my dad's lawyer called me to say that if we called the board meeting off, my dad would sign the divorce papers. They would both walk out of the marriage with what they took into it. Dad would keep the house and stay on as CEO. We'd retain our shares, plus, Mom would get a lump sum of billions, along with their homes in Aspen and the Hamptons.

Mom cried with relief, but I also think the victory was bittersweet for her. She went into her marriage with the best of intentions and wished she could've made it work.

It wasn't bittersweet for me or my sisters though. We cracked open a bottle of good wine and drank to the misery of Dad and the good health of Mom.

Conrad didn't call to speak to any of us.

The second thing that happened came out of left field.

My phone rang with a number from out of state, and not Wyoming. I recognized it as a Virginia number, because Shepherd sometimes called me from the same area code. In fact, that was who I thought it was when I clicked on the green icon.

When a deep voice said, "Yo. Colt. How ya doin', bud?" my jaw dropped open in surprise.

"Hendrix?" I asked. "What the fuck are you doin' callin' me?"

He barked out a deep, throaty laugh. "Little birdy's been tellin' me you got caught fuckin' your boss's daughter?"

My jaw clenched. "You were told wrong, Drix. Fact is Freya's mine. It ain't a joke or club gossip if it's about the girl you're gonna marry one day."

He paused briefly before muttering, "Saw it, Colt. I think the first time was on her twenty-first birthday when she danced with some random in The Lucky Shamrock. Knew it then as plain as the nose on my face that she belonged to you. Hell, brother, the only fucker who never saw it was your stupid ass."

"You're not the first person to tell me that," I responded. "Is that what you called about? To get the gossip on me and Freya?"

"Nah," he replied jokingly. "Prez told me to call ya."

My body locked. "Prez?"

"Yup," Drix drawled. "He tells me you've been recruited by the FBI."

Understanding began to gnaw at me. "So he knows?"

"Everythin'," Hendrix confirmed. "Cash and Break told him what you did for the Demons, and he relayed it to me. Wondered if you wanted to come down to see my club. Catch up."

"What for?" I asked.

He barked a laugh before saying something that made my OCD rear its ugly head.

"You're supposed to be the smart one, Colt. Work it out."

Two Weeks Later

Hendrix's hotel was gorgeous. It was situated on the Potomac River, just North of Quantico in Prince William County.

The place must have been built in the 1920's because it's art deco interior was breathtaking. It sat on five acres of land, and had a huge ballroom, which was now used as a bar and social room. The kitchens needed upgrading and the rooms were somewhat tired and faded, but I found it made everything feel more authentic.

Hendrix led me through the reception area, unlocked a door, and threw it open. "This is Church." He grinned. "Used to be a room where the guests gambled and played some poker."

"It's fuckin' amazing," I breathed. "You could do with some security upgrades though."

"Yeah," he agreed. "Wonder who I could get to do that?"

"It won't be cheap," I advised him, walking around the room, and touching the shiny new gavel and sound block, which had been placed on the table. "I'll do the work for ya, but you're lookin' at about fifty grands worth of equipment to kit this place out. It's so fuckin' big you'll be payin' through the nose to get cameras everywhere."

"I can do that," he muttered. "All the scratch we earn goes back into the club for now. The men I've got are either workin' a nine-to-five or livin' off their military pensions. I feed and house 'em for nothing until January. That's when we start payin' 'em."

My head reared back. "They're workin' for nothin'?"

"Right now, they get paid per job and I cover their room and board," he advised me. "They're good with it." He motioned toward the table for me to sit.

"How's business?" I asked, sliding into the chair next to his.

"Gettin' there," he said thoughtfully. "We're gettin' known in security circles. I gotta few buds who worked as bodyguards, so we've been lucky there. We're openin' a bar and a tattoo shop in the summer. My only issue is our government contract."

My brow furrowed. "Tell me."

"My contact at the FBI went cold. We were promised jobs that never materialized. Most of the men here were specialists in their field at whatever military branch they were in. We've got pilots, Marines, Rangers, Scouts. We've got weapons specialists and bomb disposal. They're itchin' to get out into the field, but we're bein' blocked somewhere along the way."

I sat back in my chair, awareness dawning on me. "You want me to call my contact? Pull some strings?"

"No, Colt," he muttered. "What I want is for you to be our handler at the FBI."

I froze, lost for words as Hendrix continued. "When Dagger told me about your new job I got to thinkin'. Why don't you patch into my chapter? Your computer skills are second to none. You've got contacts at the FBI. You know how things work, and more importantly, I trust you."

I held up a hand to stop him. "Whoa, Drix. Back up a bit. We both know cops and MCs don't mix. I had to leave Wyoming to become a Fed. Are you sayin' you and your boys are good with it?"

Drix sat back in his chair, arm leisurely flung across the back. "One'a my boys is a cop, his dad was too, and his grandpa was CIA. I've got a guy whose dad was Secret Service, and I gotta retired detective. We're all ex-military, Colt. We're built differently from Wyoming. My club's different. Jesus, we've even got an ex-vet trauma surgeon." His expression softened. "I don't care about you and Freya. In fact, I'd love her to come here with her skills. We're growin', Colt. All my officers are in place, except for one." He grinned. "I need a tech man and there's nobody better than you."

"But I'll be workin'," I argued. "I'll be a fuckin' Fed. Don't you get it?"

"It's you who's not getting' it, brother," Drix pointed out. "Go to your boss. You tell him you wanna be our handler. You'll be our liaison to the powers that be in D.C. I want you to be the man who organizes us and helps us plan and strategize. In your downtime you'll be here as my officer and my brother."

I stared at him open-mouthed, not quite believing what I was hearing.

If I did this, I'd be a Demon again, but the difference was, I wouldn't have to hide Freya.

Drix was giving me an opportunity to have everything I wanted. Interesting work, challenges, but also a link to the MC that I'd missed ever since I left Wyoming. I'd be based here, with the club, and still have access to all the information I'd need through my FBI work.

It was a dream come true.

But could I swing it?

"What do ya say, Colt," Hendrix asked. "Are you in?"

I pulled my cell phone from my pocket and clicked on Shepherd's number, before putting it onto speaker and shooting Hendrix a knowing smile. "Let's find out, shall we?"

Chapter Thirty-Eight

Freya ~ March 31st

A tear ran down my face as my finger trailed over the baby's button nose and rosebud-pink lips. "She's beautiful," I whispered, heart squeezing with love for the new addition to the Speed Demons' family. I tucked a finger under her tiny white hat. "And all that beautiful dark hair."

Atlas let out a curse, pulling the baby away from me. "Did ya wash ya fuckin' hands? Don't want her gettin' your germs."

"Oh my God, Danny," Sophie snapped. "Will you please let somebody else hold her?"

"No!" He huffed, looking at his wife like she was crazy. "She's mine. I'm puttin' her in one'a them baby carrier chest contraptions and she's comin' everywhere with me. I'll feed her, change her ass, and put her in a popper outfit. All you need to do is squirt her milk into a bottle for me and rest up."

I covered my smile with my hand.

Atlas had been an overprotective husband in the last few weeks of Sophie's pregnancy, to the extent that he'd even carried her up and down the stairs in case she tripped, that was when he let her go up and down stairs.

All that protectiveness had transferred to his daughter because he wouldn't give her up.

The door creaked open slightly and my stomach dropped as Dad popped his head around it. "Okay to come in?"

Atlas jerked a nod. "You can't touch her unless you've washed your hands."

Dad sauntered into the room, rubbing his hands together gleefully. "Course I've washed 'em, and I put some'a that gel shit on 'em too." He did a grabby hands gesture. "Give her to Grandpop John."

Atlas turned his back on him. "No. She's mine."

Sophie sighed. "I'm sorry, John. Sooner or later he'll need to pee. We'll get her back then."

The SAA's jaw clenched tight.

Atlas turned back around. "You can come meet her but watch yourself. She's a little lady and very sensitive to dirt."

Dad rolled his eyes but still leaned down to take a closer look. "She's pretty as a fuckin' picture, At. You did a good job there."

Atlas puffed out his chest. "I know."

"What's her name?" Dad asked.

"Belle," Sophie murmured. "Belle Iris Woods."

"Ris'll be over the moon," Dad whispered. "You'll make her year."

"We thought we'd ask her to be godmother." Her gaze came to me. "You too, Freya. Will you?"

My hand flew to my chest. "Really?"

Sophie smiled. "We'd love you to. I like the idea of a doctor looking out for Belle if anything happened to us."

I swiped the happy tears from my face. "I'd be honored."

The door opened again and Cash walked in with his arm slung across Cara's shoulder. He wore a baby carrier on his chest with Wilder inside.

"Where d'ya get those things from?" Atlas demanded. "Want one for my Belle."

"Oh!" Cara exclaimed, extracting herself from Cash and moving toward Atlas and the baby. "I love that name!" Her eyes widened as they fell on Belle. "How did you make her? She's tiny."

"Seven pounds on the dot," Sophie relayed.

Cara glanced at Wilder. "He was eight, six, and had a big head, like his dad."

"Well my Belle's perfect," Atlas muttered. "She's in proportion and I won't have anyone sayin' different."

"Wouldn't fuckin' dare," Cash muttered.

"Yo," Bowie called from the door before it opened wide to allow him, Layla, and Sunny to walk inside. Sunshine skipped toward the SAA. "Assless, please can I holds the baby? I promise I'll be gentle, and I'll love her, and tell her stories, and later Willows will too."

Atlas looked up to the heavens and sighed. He couldn't deny Sunny anything, especially when she was so excited. "Get up on the bed with Sophie," he ordered softly. "Do you remember how to hold a baby?"

Sunny glared up at him. "I'm not stupids, Atlas. I've gots a baby sister, and soon I'll have two baby brothers."

Silence fell over the room.

"Brothers?" Dad questioned.

Bowie nodded. "We've just come from Doe's sonogram. We're havin' two boys."

Calls of congratulations filled the room, waking Wilder up with a start. He opened his mouth so wide we could see his little tonsils, then proceeded to let out an eardrum-shattering scream.

Cash rolled his eyes. "Thanks, assholes."

"But it's two boys," Dad said excitedly. "The next generation's coming along nicely."

Leaning against the wall, I studied Dad while everybody started chatting animatedly.

He'd apologized to me the day after I came back from Maine. I accepted it to keep the peace. I loved my dad, but when he beat Colt, I lost a lot of respect for him, and it would take a while to rebuild.

My eye caught Layla's and she smiled at me.

I returned it, but again, things between us were icy. Layla and Bowie hadn't supported me when I needed them most, and I was finding it hard to forgive and forget. When Bowie treated her badly, I was there for her, even though I didn't really know her at the time. She was a single mom and lived a difficult life, so I'd welcomed her and Sunny into the fold, no questions asked.

Hambleton had been ruined for me in a way.

I didn't see the town as home anymore. All it held were the memories of loving and losing Colt, and I couldn't wait to get away from the crippling feelings they evoked.

Colt's calls were few and far between. He hadn't bothered at all in the last week.

It hurt me a lot. I understood his Mom and sisters needed him, probably more than I did, but his silence spoke volumes. He wasn't ready for me; I could see that now. I had to make my own way in life and stop believing that love could conquer all.

Colt had been breaking my heart since I was sixteen, and I didn't want the pain anymore. I wanted to be a doctor and help people. I wanted to move away and make a life.

I wanted to find myself again, because along the way I'd lost the girl I was.

Everything ached. I'd lost weight when I didn't really have weight to lose. I knew my friends and family worried about me, but I was okay. Heartbreak took its toll for sure, but I'd accepted I was Colt's—I always would be—but Colt wasn't ready to be mine, at least not yet.

He loved me, I knew it. He wouldn't have lied about that, but Colt's love came with too much upheaval and way too many sacrifices. I couldn't even tie him down to a town, so how was I supposed to plan a life with him?

"Freya. When do you set off for your next interview?" Sophie asked from her bed.

The room went silent. All eyes turning to me.

"Tomorrow," I said quietly. "This is my last one. I've ruled out Oregon and California. They don't specialize in the surgeries I want to do. Maine was a quiet town, but on reflection, I liked the place and the work will be interesting. I'll make my decision after my final interview." I shrugged. "That's if they even offer me the internship."

"They will," Sophie said with more confidence than I felt. "Just show them what you already know. Your practical experience is on a level with a resident, not an intern."

"Easier said than done," I replied. "It's not like I can walk into a hospital for an interview and perform CPR is it?"

She laughed. "You never know."

Two Days Later

"What's the holdup," I asked the cab driver, peering out of the windshield from the back seat. The traffic had come to a standstill. My heart skipped a beat at the sight of the accident up ahead.

The driver nodded toward it. "Don't think we're getting through anytime soon."

My stomach twisted with anxiety, and I glanced at my watch.

If I went to assist, there was no doubt I'd be late for my interview, and that probably meant losing the position I really wanted before I even got it.

Closing my eyes, I looked to the heavens, seeking divine intervention, but I already knew what my decision would be. I couldn't in good conscience let anyone suffer when I may have been able to help.

"I'll get out here," I told the driver, voice thick with emotion at what I was about to give up. This job was the one that excited me the most. The hospital was small, but the head of the trauma department was a vet, well-known for his innovative work with veterans and hard-ass surgeries, a lot of which he did pro bono to help his brethren.

"Are you sure?" he asked, his eyes darting between me and the chaotic scene farther up the street.

I nodded, swallowing hard. "Yeah. I'm sure." Sighing again, I dug into my purse and pulled out a fifty, handing it to the driver. "I'm going up there to see if I can assist."

"You a doctor?" he asked, a thread of shock weaving through his voice as he took in my long, thick hair and expertly made-up face.

I shrugged. "Not yet, but I'm working on it." I grabbed my bag and threw open my door, muttering how crazy I must be to give up this opportunity.

As I walked up the sidewalk, past the waiting cars, I went into my bag and grabbed an elastic hair tie, pulling my dark brown hair up into a messy bun. My boots were low-heeled and comfortable, allowing me to walk quickly toward the scene of the accident, which was looking more gnarly the closer I got.

There were two vehicles involved. One was a truck with the entire hood stoved in. The engine was hissing and steaming through the hood, the metal crushed like paper. The other car was a smaller red Ford, overturned from the impact of the crash. A child's cry filled the air and my heart plummeted.

I went to the truck first, purely because it would be easier and quicker to assess the damage, and I could then get on with trying to help the occupants of the car. My heart stabbed in my chest at the sound of a siren, which I estimated was still a good couple of minutes away.

"Looks like it's down to you, Freya," I mumbled to myself as I approached the big, black truck, reaching up to open the door before hauling myself up to the driver's seat and looking inside.

I estimated the driver to be in his fifties. He was starting to come around from being knocked out. The airbag had been deployed and had kept him upright in his seat with his head lolling back.

"Hey," I murmured. "I'm Freya. I'm just gonna check your vitals. Is that okay?" My fingers pressed against the pulse on his neck, which luckily beat strong and steady, though it was slightly fast, much to be expected after a car accident.

After ascertaining the man wasn't in immediate danger, I jumped back down to the ground and headed for the overturned car. I fell to my knees on the approach, assessing the situation.

A woman was trapped among the wreckage, unconscious. My stare swept through the car and was met with big brown eyes, as a young girl, around six or seven-years-old peered at me, shocked, from her car seat in the back.

"Hey! I'm Freya," I called to her as I checked the woman's pulse. "Does it hurt anywhere, sweetheart?"

She shook her head, tears rolling down her face. "Can you help my mommy?" she cried.

"I can't move her yet," I explained, injecting my voice with confidence I didn't necessarily feel. "There's an ambulance on its way though, and the nice doctor will help her."

"But she won't wake up," the girl whispered.

"Her pulse is strong, honey," I assured her as the siren sounded again, louder this time. "Your Mom's alive, and as long as she's got a heartbeat, we've got something to work with. Can you keep talking to her while I speak to the man in the ambulance?"

She nodded her head furiously.

"Are you sure it doesn't hurt anywhere?" I checked again, trying to work out how I could get into the back to check her vitals.

"My hand hurts a little, but I'm okay," she told me as the siren sounded again and I caught blue lights flashing from the corner of my eye.

"The ambulance is here." I gave her a reassuring smile. "I'll go talk to them and come straight back, okay?" I got to my feet and hurried over to the paramedics who were exiting the LSV and taking stock of the situation.

"Who are you?" one of them asked me.

"I'm Freya Stone," I relayed hurriedly. "I'm a med school graduate, headed into my first year as an intern. I've had some field experience. We've got three RTA victims. One male in his fifties in the truck. Two females, one adult, one child in the overturned vehicle over there. Child's coherent, says her hand hurts. She's trapped in the back in a child seat. Adult woman, the child's mother, is unconscious, but her vitals are steady. I haven't moved anyone."

One of the medics got on his radio, requesting a fire crew with cutting equipment and another ambulance. "You wanna hang around?" the other EMT asked. "We may need an assist until another rig gets here."

Checking my watch, my heart sunk when I saw my interview was meant to start in five minutes. I'd miss it even if I didn't assist here and I didn't want to leave the victims, at least until I knew they'd be okay.

Crushing disappointment clogged inside my throat, but I cleared it, and nodded to the EMT. "Of course."

"What's your name?" he asked, looking me up and down. "You look a little young to have graduated med school."

"Freya," I murmured, looking around the scene and smiling wryly.

I'd just willingly thrown away my dream job. There was no way Doctor Locke would see me now. He probably had a day full of interviewing candidates. Why the hell would he hire a girl who couldn't even make it to her appointment on time?

And as I hurried to the truck to check on the driver, I resigned myself to the fact that I'd screwed it up, but I also knew I couldn't have walked by and not helped. I had dreams, sure, but I also had a calling, and to leave someone suffering would have screwed with my head.

My conscience wouldn't allow it.

"His BP's dropping again," Harry the EMT yelled as we rushed the stretcher toward the ER.

The cacophony of blaring sirens and shouts filled the air around us, drowning out any sense of calm I may have had.

I'd never seen such chaos. There'd been another road traffic collision on the other side of town, and the local hospital—ironically, the same one I was meant to interview at—was getting slammed.

"Freya, stay focused!" Harry ordered, snapping me back to reality as we guided the stretcher through some double doors. "We're losing him. Start CPR." He slowed the stretcher down. "Get on and start work."

"Oh my God," I cried. "You want me to start CPR now?"

"You want him to die?" he retorted. "Get moving."

My palms began to sweat as I clambered onto the stretcher, straddling the guy who had been driving the truck, and checking his airways. Tilting his chin up, I breathed down his throat, then, when his lungs were full, I pulled back and began chest compressions.

"Again!" Harry ordered.

I repeated the process, holding my breath as Harry pushed us through another set of double doors into a large, busy ER. Cubicles were lined around the outside of the vast space, leaving the middle free for equipment. The chaos faded into the background as I worked on my patient. The sharp tang of disinfectant filled my nostrils, grounding me as I continued CPR.

"Got a pulse," Harry confirmed, pressing his fingers against the patient's neck.

My shoulders slumped in relief. "Thank God," I said, as if to myself. I hadn't lost a patient yet. This day had already gone down as one of the worst. The last thing I needed was a death. Hadn't life already screwed with me enough today?

Looking around the ER, I caught the eye of a tall, good-looking doctor. His hair was cropped close to his head, his muscles straining against the material of his blue scrubs. His blue eyes flicked over me, straddling the patient and his brows shot up to his hairline as he moved toward us.

"Status report," he demanded.

I started chest compressions again. "Male in his fifties, involved in a vehicle collision, had a heart attack at the scene." I pressed down hard on the patient's chest. "We lost him in the rig and got him back, but he started to crash again outside."

The doctor's lips twitched, amusement dancing in his eyes, despite the gravity of the situation. "And is there a particular reason you're riding the lucky fucker?" he asked. "'Cause if he wakes up and sees you sitting on him, it'll kill him off for sure."

Heat rushed to my cheeks, embarrassment making me internally wince. It wasn't exactly the time for humor, but even I could recognize how absurd I must've looked.

I got up on my knees and threw a leg back, scrambling down off the stretcher. "I guess it does look bizarre," I muttered.

The doctor barked a laugh. "You can't call yourself a doctor until you've done chest compressions while riding a gurney." His stare flicked down me then up again, resting on my face. "Who the fuck are you anyway?" He slid his stethoscope from around his neck and began pressing it to the patient's chest, checking his heartbeat.

"Freya Stone," I replied. "I was supposed to interview here today for the internship with Doctor Locke," I nodded to the patient, "but as you can see, I got caught up and missed it."

A slow grin stole across the man's face. He stepped forward and stretched his hand out toward me. "Grayson Locke," he announced. "But everyone around here calls me Bones."

"Oh my God," I breathed, rubbing my forehead, humiliation making my cheeks scarlet. "Can this day get any worse?"

Bones studied me for a moment, his blue eyes taking in the sweat that clung to my brow, and no doubt the desperation coming off me in waves. I braced for him to tell me I may as well turn around and fuck off back from where I came. I wouldn't have blamed him; I must've looked ridiculous.

But instead, a slow grin crept across his face. "You're hired."

I blinked again, the words weaving around my confused brain. "I'm hired?"

"Wait!" He held his hand up. "First tell me, are you one of those really smart young students who can recite a medical journal but can't take a piss without someone holding your hand?"

I studied him, wondering what planet he'd landed from. "I can take a piss just fine."

He laughed. "Right. See you Monday at oh seven hundred. Get Mommy to pack you a lunch because you'll be eating on the go. I've got five surgeries back-to-back, and you're gonna be in charge of the scalpel. Don't be late."

Bones turned his back to me, barking at a nurse to page a cardiothoracic surgeon and get the patient ready for surgery. His steps faltered and he turned to address me again.

"Get your ass up to HR. They're expecting you." He waggled his eyebrows at me before saying the words that made my stomach flip excitedly for the first time in weeks. "Welcome to Virginia. You better hold on tight, baby Doc. We're gonna have a blast."

Forty-five minutes later—still dazed and confused from my bizarre exchange with Bones—I walked out of my new place of work and was immediately hit by the afternoon sun.

The heat enveloped me like a lover's embrace, soothing away the tension that had built up in my body after my crazy morning. I tilted my chin up, wallowing in the warmth of the orange glow, and smiled.

In my heart, I knew this was my place and that Bones would be an important person in my life. Not romantically—no, I belonged to Colt, there was no question of that—but Bones would be the one to make me a doctor, someone I'd look up to.

Even after everything, the only person I wanted to call was Colt. I'd just gotten the job of my dreams. He'd be so excited, so proud. My chest tightened with anticipation as I pulled out my phone and clicked on his number.

It rang three times before the call clicked in and Colt's rich, deep voice murmured, "Hey, Princess. I fuckin' miss you."

Tears welled in my eyes at the mere sound of his voice.

Being away from him made my soul ache. He was my man, my best friend, the other half of me. He was also a bit of an asshole, but one day, I'd cure him of it. That was if I ever saw him again. At the rate we were going I'd be in my residency by the time he rocked up.

"I've got a job, and it's perfect." My excitement took over and I began to babble. "I'm based in Virginia in Prince William County. On the way to the interview, I saw an accident. I took a patient in with the EMT and had to do CPR. Bones... the doctor who I was meant to interview with, saw me and hired me on the spot. Can you believe it? I can't believe it, Colt. Can you believe it?"

He let out a sexy, throaty laugh and my heart clenched. "I knew you could do it."

All my anger drained away. I didn't want to argue. I didn't want to pretend to hate the only man I'd ever loved. He couldn't help his circumstances. His family needed him and if he was the type of man to not help them, I wouldn't have adored him the way I did.

"I miss you so much," I said, voice husky with emotion. "How's New York? Is your mom okay? Your sisters? Did you deal with your dad?"

"I'm not in New York," he rasped. "Mom needed a fresh start so we all moved to a new state."

My heart did a backflip. "Where?"

He paused briefly before murmuring. "Look to your right, Freya."

My knees began to shake.

Slowly, I turned right and inhaled sharply at the sight before me.

Colt stood, leaning against a black GMC SUV with his muscular arms folded across his chest.

The sun made his dark blond hair gleam like molten gold. He wore black pants and a tee, under an FBI-issue black bulletproof vest. I couldn't see his ocean-blues through the dark lenses of the Ray-Bans covering his eyes, but I could tell by his wide grin they'd be sparkling.

"What are you doing here?" I called over.

He shot me the sexy, crooked smirk that made my skin tingle, "I've been neglectin' my girl lately. Thought I'd stop by her place of work and see if she wanted to go for lunch with me?"

I threw my head back and laughed before my eyes locked with his again. "I have it on good authority she's starving. Your girl's had a busy morning."

His arms dropped to his side and he reached out, beckoning me to him with his index finger.

His presence warmed my skin and my stomach turned to mush as I took in the handsomeness that was all Colt. My feet began to carry me toward him, my body drawn by the force of the man who owned me body and soul, and always would.

He held his arms out for me and I walked straight into them, burrowing my face into the little nook just underneath his throat that was solely meant for me.

Colt's face hit my cheek and he inhaled deeply as if he'd been starved of me. The breeze played with my hair, and I shivered slightly, despite the warmth of the day.

My hands slid around his shoulders and I sighed contentedly because I was finally where I was meant to be. People always told me home was where the heart was. Well, my heart was always his. Colt was my home and I never wanted to leave.

"When people talk about falling in love they never mention right person wrong time," he whispered, his breath warm against my cheek. He pulled back slightly, removed his shades and the depth of emotion in his ocean-blues sent a shiver down my spine. "You meet the girl your soul knows is yours, but she's too young. You watch her grow and the chemistry grows with her, but it's impossible to be together."

He was so close that I could smell the Creed on his skin. The heat of his body radiated into mine and my heart thundered in my chest. He was so beautiful, so compelling, I couldn't look away.

"You lay in bed, lookin' at the ceiling, knowin' you have to trust that the universe has a plan, and one day she'll be yours." He pulled back, his hands framing my face and angled it up until our eyes locked. And he smiled. "The wait has paid off."

My heart skipped a beat.

This was it, after all the years of waiting, we were finally doing this.

Colt reached into his pocket and pulled something out. "You're mine and I'm yours. Ain't gonna ask 'cause it'd be like askin' God to give me air to breathe. I can't live without you, don't wanna try."

Something cold slid onto my ring finger, and my world tilted. "Oh my God," I murmured, eyes widening as I took in the single, solitaire diamond on my finger.

My mind raced, a torrent of thoughts and emotions consuming me. I was so elated that I threw my arms around my man's neck and let out a loud whoop.

"Wanna meet my Mom?" he asked. "She's drivin' me up the fuckin' wall, Frey. Can't take a shit without her asking when I'm bringin' ya around."

I winced slightly. "What if she hates me?"

"She won't." He shrugged one shoulder. "Ma's already got the weddin' magazines out. She reckons our day'll make Harry and Meghan's look bougie."

I giggled. "My mom will love her."

He waggled his eyebrows. "We'll find out at the weekend. Couldn't exactly ask your dad for your hand in marriage, so I called Adele. She's comin' down to check out our house and talk weddings with ya."

"Our house?" I repeated, a thread of shock in my tone.

Colt's fingers trailed up and down my back. "I bought us a place. Got so much to tell ya. I'm gonna be based in D.C. I'll be workin' with Hendrix's chapter too." He nodded toward the hospital. "You'll love the brothers. Bones is one of us. Can you imagine my shock when I told him all about my girl and it came out he was interviewing you for an internship?"

A sharp pain ripped through my chest. "Oh my God! Was it a setup? Please tell me I didn't get the job through nepotism."

Colt let out a snort. "Have you met Bones? D'ya think he'd let anyone in his ER if he didn't think they were the best?" He rubbed my shoulders. "Baby, you didn't get the job because you're connected. He called me after he sent you to HR to tell me he hired you on the spot because you've got gumption, and balls of steel."

A wide smile spread across my face. "Really?"

Colt's blue eyes twinkled, and he leaned in, pressing his lips against mine in a tender, earth-shattering kiss that left me breathless, before pulling away and leaving a lingering warmth on my skin.

"Yeah. Really," he said with a laugh. "Now we need to go. Mom's expecting us, and then I wanna show you the clubhouse. Hendrix can't wait to see ya."

I went to turn toward the SUV but paused, clutching Colt's hand. "Is this a dream? Am I gonna wake up and find none of it's real?"

Colt traced a finger down my cheek. "It's real, baby. This is it. This is everything we've been working toward." He opened the passenger door of his SUV, taking my hand and helping me inside. "Hold on, baby," he reiterated, pulling my seat belt across my lap, and fastening it securely. "And enjoy the first day of the rest of our lives."

That Night

The evening sun cast a warm glow through the room, bathing the worn wooden floorboards in golden light. Low music thumped through the speakers, filling the vast bar with a deep, resonating thud.

I sat with Colt's arm around me, feeling his warmth as we chatted with the brothers. The dim lights cast shadows across their faces, each one a unique tale of secrets and stories that I couldn't wait to discover.

We'd been at Colt's mom's house all afternoon with his sisters, and we'd hit it off straight away. Gracie had teased him about our age difference—her and I were the same age—but his mom just rolled her eyes and asked if we wanted more food.

After living a life of being pampered, Caroline had discovered a love for cooking and baking, not everything she served was a resounding success, but I loved the fact she was trying to live a normal life after being waited on for so long.

Picasso, the brother who would become a tattooist in the new shop Hendrix was opening, took a long pull of beer. His eyes were dark and heavy with thought, but a playful smirk tugged at the corner of his mouth. "You seem to be settling in okay," he said, nodding to Colt. His gaze flicked toward me and the smirk turned knowing. "And I can see why."

I felt my cheeks flush, but I forced my gaze to remain steady.

"Am now," Colt responded, glancing at me. The corners of his eyes crinkled slightly, and a smile played around his lips. In that moment, his whole demeanor softened, filling me with a kind of calmness that warmed me from the inside out. "In fact," he added. "My life's pretty much fuckin' perfect." He lifted my hand, entwined with his, and kissed my palm.

Picasso raised his beer bottle in a mock salute before taking another swig. His gaze never wavered from me although his eyes were glazed over in thought—or was it a memory? Who knew?

The Virginia chapter was shiny and new, like a fresh, crisp newspaper hot off the press. Hendrix and Blade were building the club in a way where I knew they'd do good, decent things and secure their place within the growing Speed Demons organization.

"What about you?" a southern-accented voice asked from beside me. "You think you're gonna like Virginia?"

My smile was wide as I studied Hendrix's dad, noting how much he and his son were alike, even though the man sitting opposite me had more lines around his eyes and greying hair.

Will was a character. At first I would've compared him to Abe, but after getting to know him, I could see their differences. Will had a hardness about him that you only found within military men. His shoulders were always straight, and his walk carried more intent, like he had a mission to complete, and nobody would stop him achieving his objective.

"I love it," I replied gently. "My new job is exciting, and I get to be with Colt. What more do I need?"

Will beamed a genuine smile. "Nothing, girlie. Seems to me like you've got the world at your feet. Taking pride in what you do, and having the love of a decent man should keep your heart beating steady." He patted his chest. "Not like my old ticker."

"Dad," Hendrix said, elbows to table. "Don't try and garner sympathy. Your heart's had so much work done on it you're almost a new man. You've been fine since you had the stents done and your pacemaker fitted." He turned to me, cocking his eyebrow. "Don't let him—"

A piercing scream echoed from the stairs outside the ballroom, followed by a woman's voice yelling, "You asshole!"

We jumped up from our chairs so fast, they clattered back onto the floorboards. My heart pounded as we ran to the door leading to reception and the sweeping staircase leading to the rooms. The dimly lit hallway stretched out before us, and on the stairs, a tall, good-looking guy ducked out of the way of objects being thrown at him by some woman whose fury rolled off her in waves.

The guy was dressed only in low slung jeans, his bare chest wide and muscular as he held his arms out defensively. "Baby—"

"You told me you loved me!" the woman screamed; her voice tinged with anguish. "Then I come to visit and you've got some whore in your room!"

"Told ya, you could'a joined in," he reasoned, ducking just in time to avoid the pot of cream that flew past him, shattering against the wall, its contents spilling on the floor.

"You're cleanin' that up, Rockabye," Will snapped, approaching to comfort the woman who by then was in floods of tears.

"Who's that?" I asked Colt, his hand warm on my shoulder.

"Rockabye," he replied dryly. "The resident manwhore."

"Rockabye?" I asked curiously.

"He *rocks* their world then says *bye*." He shook his head frustratedly. "That's the fourth one since I've been here. He's averaging two a week."

"Oh my God," I breathed. "That could've been Bowie a few years ago."

"This place is even more fucked-up than Wyoming," Colt muttered, leading me back into the ballroom. "The guys here have all got a crazy streak a mile wide. Iceman's one'a the fuckin' sensible ones, can you believe it?" He shook his head. "I'm gonna have a job keepin' these assholes in line."

I slid my hands up his hard chest and clasped my fingers around his neck. "Are you sure this is what you want?"

He looked down at me, eyes clear and free of the demons that had ravaged him for as long as I'd known him. "I've got everythin' I ever wanted in my arms, Freya. The job and the club's a bonus I never expected." The corners of his mouth tipped up. "Your dad called me while you were talkin' to Mom in the kitchen earlier."

My jaw dropped. "What did he say?"

"Asked me if I could keep an eye on the cameras remotely," he told me. "Said things are getting weird in Hambleton and they need all hands on deck."

I beamed a smile. "Did he act like nothing had happened and he didn't give you a concussion at all?"

Colt dipped his chin in a nod.

"That's Dad." My lips twisted with humor. "Means he's over it. He won't apologize but he wants to move on." I leaned closer. "Guess what?"

Colt's eyes sparkled with humor. "Tell me."

"I used one of his credit cards for gas by mistake, and it worked." I grinned. "So I've maxed it out to furnish the bedroom in our new house. Every time we fuck on the new sheets I bought for the bed it'll be courtesy of Dad."

"I dunno if that makes my cock hard or soft," he said thoughtfully.

I giggled. "We'll find out in a few days. We can always give them to one of the brothers if you can't take it."

"I'll give it a good go," he vowed.

My eyes locked with Colt's ocean-blues and my heart skipped a beat.

We'd done it, against all the odds we were together, a couple, engaged, with a new house, new careers, but still lucky enough to have the support of a good club and good men behind us.

"This place will challenge us you know," I murmured. "It's crazy and beautiful but I have a feeling it'll drive us bonkers too."

"Whatever happens," Colt murmured, his words a sacred vow that weaved around my soul. "We'll face it together. You and me, Freya. Always."

Epilogue

Colt ~ Two Months Later

The blinding Wyoming sunshine blasted me with its heat as I ran down the steps of the FBI's private jet which had just landed in a small airfield on the outskirts of Hambleton. Sweat trickled down my back in anticipation of being back here after months, and also because of the shit show I'd just walked into.

"Progress report?" I barked down the phone, tone raw with impatience.

"Slow down, hotshot," Shep replied, his voice calm and reassuring. "He's filling me in now, but her cover's definitely blown. Henderson told our agent to take Duchess to the container with the other women. He was gonna traffic her, though God only knows where she'd have ended up. She's beautiful, but older than the average victim. After everything she's done, I can't let him go through with it—not that he would anyway—so we're risking his cover getting blown too."

I clenched my jaw, trying to suppress the anger threatening to bubble over.

This case had consumed me since I joined the Feds. I'd been helping the Wyoming chapter behind the scenes with their trafficking problem, as well as being the go-between for the agency and my boys. This morning I'd logged on remotely to the cameras I'd planted months ago in the mayor's mansion and saw enough bullshit to make me hop straight onto an agency's private jet.

"I've got everythin' on camera," I relayed, walking hurriedly toward the SUV parked on the tarmac. "He caught her in his safe and beat the snot out of her. She's in a bad way, Shep." Red hot fury rose through my chest, and I whacked my hand hard against the hot metal of the car. "Surely that's enough to bring him in along with all the other evidence we've gathered."

"We need the shipping manifest," Shep confirmed. "If we had that document, we could lock him up forever. Henderson wouldn't last three months in high security."

I rolled my eyes. "I dunno why we can't just shoot him and Bear Rawlins in the head?"

"'Cause we're the FBI," Shep reminded me. "We're the good guys who do things by the book, remember?" he sighed.

"Of course we do," I said sarcastically. "We never color outside the lines."

"I'm not saying that," Shep replied. "But we don't assassinate people. We're not the CIA." He paused briefly. "We've got eyes on Henderson. He's not goin' anywhere." Another pause. "Got an update. Our guy just got her outta there. We need to think up a plan. How can we get Duchess somewhere safe without blowing our guy's cover? If he doesn't take her to the container, Henderson will know something's not right. We need to intercept them without raising suspicion."

A slow smile spread across my face. "Got an idea, but it means getting the Speed Demons involved. I may have to tell 'em what we've been doing and bring 'em in on it."

Shep heaved out a frustrated breath. "We're out of options. We've got to get Duchess safe. She's our key witness. Without her, we've got nothing." He paused briefly before ordering, "We don't have a choice. Do it."

"Call you back," I said thickly, ending the call before clicking on a different name. The phone rang twice before it clicked in and a voice barked, "Yo! Please fuckin' tell me why a dirty-assed Fed's callin' my cell phone?"

I almost grinned at the memories of the brother I'd strangely missed the most, flicking through my mind. "Need your help. There's a transfer bein' carried out as we speak. Can you intercept a black SUV that's heading out of town on the road toward Mapletree in about five minutes? There's cargo I need taken back to the compound and kept safe until I get there. I'm about thirty minutes out. Don't do anythin' stupid until I get there."

"Prez know your ass is payin' us a visit?" he demanded, his voice deep and rasping.

I started the engine, turning the SUV toward the exit gate. "Nope."

The distinctive pop, pop, popping sound only a Harley could produce filled the line before Atlas yelled, "Breaker! Cash! Arrow! We gotta ride out. Now!" Another loud click sounded through the line as Atlas turned his helmet's Bluetooth on. "We're on our way."

"See ya in thirty, Atlas," I murmured, voice thick with emotion at being back at the place where everything started for me. "Ride steady, brother."

Sunlight glinted off the corrugated iron roof of the clubhouse as I looked at the massive old warehouse that used to be my home. The sun's gleam reflected off the whitewashed brick walls so brightly that I was thankful I had my Ray-Bans to protect my eyes. Although I'd only been gone six months, it felt like a lifetime ago that this place was my sanctuary.

Memories of the motorcycle-filled parking lot filled my head, along with the deep rumble of engines and the sound of laughter. My heart ached for those simpler times when brotherhood was all that mattered, before I took the girl who belonged to me, no fucks given.

As much as I missed my time in Wyoming, I wouldn't change my life now for the world. I was happier than I'd ever been, more content and challenged in ways I'd never dreamed of—not only by my work, but also my woman.

As I drove through the gates, a sense of foreboding washed over me. This place held a lot of ghosts and memories of the way everything went down.

I still wasn't completely over it. I'd always feel a thread of resentment toward the man who gave me so much with one hand and took it all away with the other. And after the way he fought me on my last day here, it would probably never go away.

Winding my window down, I shook off the heaviness of the past weighing down my shoulders and sent Billy a chin lift. "Any trouble?"

"None so far," the prospect replied, his eyes turning to scan the perimeter of the gates with natural vigilance. "But we're ready if anything happens." He nodded toward the clubhouse. "Sophie's seein' to the woman, and the boys are down the Cell with the prisoner."

My chest constricted, like an unseen fist had slammed into my sternum. "They've taken him down already? I told Atlas to wait for me."

"We don't take orders from you," Billy retorted with a smirk. "Last time I looked we weren't on Virginia turf."

Cursing under my breath, I drove into a parking space and jumped out of the SUV.

I knew the Speed Demons enough to understand exactly what they'd be up to. Taking a man down to the Cell meant trouble, especially when they had an undercover FBI agent down there.

Pushing the doors open, I walked into the bar where the ol' ladies sat, talking.

"Fuck! Colt!" Cara exclaimed. "Did you bring Freya?"

"Good to see you, honey," Layla called out.

"Well, aren't you a sight for sore eyes," Kennedy drawled.

"How's the woman they brought in?" I demanded. "Is she okay?"

Cara's face fell. "Sophie's seeing to her in one of the medical rooms. John went fucking crazy when he saw the state of her and started smashing up the bar."

"He took the guy they brought in straight down to the Cell," Kennedy added. "I'd hate to see the state of him when Prez has finished."

The gut punch slammed into me again.

I knew exactly what these men were capable of. Hell, a year ago I'd have been down there with them. A heavy weight of guilt settled on my shoulders. I should've given Atlas the backstory. I knew the SAA well enough to understand what his reaction would be and the pleasure he'd take in beating information out of the FBI agent they had no idea was working undercover.

I stalked to the familiar corridor that used to house my office, before turning and hurrying down the stairs. Holding my breath, I held my finger up to the sensor on the wall, breathing a sigh of relief when the locks disengaged and opened. I prowled to the next set of doors, praying that they hadn't removed my prints from the database as I held my thumb up to another sensor. I sent up a prayer of thanks as the locks clicked open, allowing me entrance.

The door creaked as I pushed on it and slipped inside the Cell. As I did, the scent of stale sweat, and the iron tang of blood assaulted my nostrils and memories flooded into my brain.

The dim light barely lit the room, but it was enough for me to make out the sight before me.

Prez, Bowie, Cash, Breaker, and Atlas all stood in line glowering at a man who'd been stripped and hung bare-ass naked from a meat hook attached to the ceiling.

"Who fuckin' beat her?" Prez roared.

"I don't know!" the prisoner retorted; his voice pitchy with fear. His lips pressed together in a tight line, defiance shining from his eyes. "Fuck you!"

Prez snarled, pulling his fist back and launching it forward with every ounce of strength he possessed. The sickening thud of flesh meeting flesh echoed through the room as the prisoner's kidneys bore the brunt of Prez's powerful punch.

I winced, recalling exactly how hard that fucker could hit. His fists were like damned sledgehammers.

"Stop!" I roared.

Prez ignored me, his fist landing on the prisoner's torso again with a crunch.

"You've just cracked a fuckin' rib!" I bellowed, prowling toward the group of men I knew as well as I knew myself. "What part of fuckin' stop don't you get?"

Prez pointed to the prisoner with a finger shaking with anger. "Did you see what he did to her?" he bellowed. "Sophie's scared she might not even pull through." His face was purple with rage, his entire body vibrating with such powerful emotion I worried he'd have a heart attack.

"He didn't do it," I grated out.

"Course he fuckin' did it," Prez snarled. "She was in the back of his car. He was tryin' to get her outta town, to avoid gettin' caught."

All tension left my body. "John," my hand went to Prez's shoulder, "he was getting' her away from her abuser. The mayor, Robert Henderson."

Prez's jaw dropped, his eyes crinkling with disbelief. "What?"

"Elise has been working for the FBI for years trying to help us gather evidence about the trafficking ring run by Henderson and Bear Rawlins. We were wrong, Thrash was involved too. It started years ago when Bandit was in charge. We've never been able to get enough on them to put them away until now. We're so fuckin' close, John. You can't fuck it up."

My stare slid from one shocked face to the next.

Bowie's hand went to the back of his neck, his eyes clouding over as his brain worked overtime.

Cash scraped a hand down his face, looking helplessly between the prisoner and his dad.

Breaker's lip curled and he rolled his eyes, rasping his breath, "What a goddamned fuck-up."

Atlas looked between the men, a huge smile covering his face as he held up a huge, meaty hand. "Wait!" he demanded, brow furrowing questioningly. "If you're FBI, and Elise Henderson's workin' for you pigs, what the fuck has shit-for-brains here gotta do with anythin'?" He jerked his thumb toward the prisoner.

I rubbed at the tension headache forming in my temple, my eyes lifting to the poor fucker hanging like a piece of meat, his cock waving in the breeze. "Brothers," I muttered. "This is my colleague. He's been working undercover for the FBI on this job for seven years. "This is Special Agent Brett Stafford. The poor bastard you've just beat bloody."

Prez's hands went to his waist, and he looked to the heavens, cursing out loud.

"Jesus," Cash breathed.

"I don't fuckin' believe this," Bowie said under his breath.

Kit's mouth pressed into a thin line before he spat, "Fuck!"

And good old Atlas... well that asshole barked a laugh so loud it almost burst my goddamned eardrums.

Fuck my life.

Sophie ~ Two Days Later

I sat, my fingers touching the plain white of the envelope, mind whirring with so many questions it made me dizzy.

When Elise Henderson was brought in three days before, almost beaten to death, of course I stepped up. I loved being a doctor, loved skewing the odds and saving a life, even when I could feel the Reaper circling.

On her death bed, my mom begged me to go to Hambleton. She told me it was my place of birth and maybe the place where I could get my questions answered.

Seemed she wasn't wrong.

The first rule of treating a patient was to take their vitals, check their airways, and if there was any chance of a head injury, get a CT scan. The second rule was to find out if they had allergies to any medication and check their blood type.

After checking her vitals, airways, and carrying out a CT scan, Colt hacked into Elise's medical records to check for allergies and her blood group. When the information came back, I did a double take.

Elise and I shared a B negative blood type.

That in itself wasn't an issue, millions of people had the same blood types. What made it unusual was that mine and Elise Henderson's blood type was one of the rarest in existence. Only one and a half percent of the population were B negative.

At first, I didn't think much of it. Hambleton was a small town, but it wasn't impossible for a couple of different families to share rare blood types, though it was uncommon. I pushed it to the back of my mind and continued treating her as I would anyone, but then I began to notice little things.

When I adjusted her IV drip, I caught sight of something that made my heart skip a beat—a small mole on Elise's top lip, identical to mine, and now Belle's. My fingers trembled slightly, and I brushed it off as coincidence.

Later, when Atlas helped me turn Elise onto her side to check her injuries, I noticed something that stopped me in my tracks. There, on the small of her back was a birthmark in the shape of a strawberry—a perfect match to mine. What freaked me out was that Belle also shared the same marks, the mole, and the strawberry, all in identical places, as if it had been passed down from mother to daughter....

An unsettled feeling hit my stomach and refused to leave. It lingered inside me like a ghost haunting me with questions I couldn't answer, and evidence that I tried to explain away in my mind.

When I got home that night, I sat down with Danny and told him everything. My man was practical. If he thought my suspicions were just wishful thinking, he'd tell me I was being an idiot and to stop reading into coincidences.

He didn't.

What he did instead was call John and relay everything to him.

Prez was dumbfounded, he told me the first time he saw me, he noticed the mole and it threw up memories of Elise from when they were younger. John asked me to return to the club and take a blood test to determine if there was a maternal link between me and Elise.

After we took Elise's blood, I took a vial of mine and sent them both off to a guy I knew in a lab. While we spoke to John, I noticed Danny looking between us both, his brow creased like he was trying to work something out.

The problem was, we couldn't conclude how it could be true,

Mine and Robbie Henderson's birthdays were two weeks apart, him being the slightly older one.

If our birthdays were the same day, we could've been twins, but it was an impossibility for a woman to give birth to two babies, two weeks apart. I wracked my brains, and even checked out medical journals to see if a woman was ever pregnant with twins, and somehow, one was born later, but it didn't make sense to me. Superfetation was a term I'd heard of though I wasn't familiar with it, but deep down it didn't add up.

How could I have a twin who looked totally opposite to me? Elise had green eyes and was blonde. Robert Senior and Junior were blue-eyed and also light-haired.

My features were dark. Eyes, hair, and my skin had an olive tone.

It didn't make sense, and the only person who could shine a light on it was currently unconscious. So, I was left for days, fretting, and making up all kind of crazy scenarios in my head while I looked down at Elise's lifeless body trying to work out if there was a soul deep connection between us.

"It ain't gonna open itself, Stitch baby," Atlas rasped softly, pulling my mind back into the present. "If she's your mom you need to know. If she's not, you need to know, too."

I nodded, throat so tight, I could hardly get my words out. He was right, the sooner I knew, the sooner I could deal with it. Heart racing, I handed my man the envelope. "You do it, Danny." I said huskily. "I can't."

He took the paper from me, glancing at the name and address before lifting his dark eyes to lock with mine. "No matter what this says, I know exactly who you are. You're Sophie Woods. My wife, and mother to the most amazin' baby girl in the world. You're smart, strong, and the most givin' woman I've ever known. In a word, you're spectacular. But best of all, you're mine and will be until the day I meet my maker."

A tear tracked down my cheek and I nodded. "I love you."

He jerked a nod before looking at the envelope and tearing into it.

His eyes moved left to right as he read the words on the piece of paper. "Fuck me sideways," he muttered.

My heart clenched so hard, I found it difficult to draw breath. "What does it say?"

Atlas's eyes raised and met mine and softened before he said the words that changed my life forever.

"It's a match, baby. You're Elise's daughter."

THE END

Thank you for reading.

Colt's playlist can be found here ~

https://open.spotify.com/playlist/58Go17XFK49gH
ifT71cFu3

Authors Note

Awwww the revelations....

All will be revealed in the next book where we go back in time to the eighties and nineties to look at what happened between John and Elise—and of course, Sophie—and get the answers to all your questions.

We'll get to meet a young Abe and Iris, and also, Bandit, who's a lunatic. LOL.

Thank you to Nicola, my right hand woman who keeps me sane. You're a Godsend and I couldn't do any of this without your support. You alpha, you edit and proofred, and you keep me going when I want to curl up and cry. Bless you. X

Jayne, thank you for taking care of my ARC team. You do a fab job.

Talking of the ARC team, thank you to my lovely ladies who read and review for me. You're a lovely bunch and our chat group is hilarious. Thanks for the laughs.

Mylene, Jayne, Nicola, and Nads, alpha readers supreme... kept you busy with this one, right?

My fabulous Tribe, thank you for your love for the Demons, and your enthusiasm for every book that's released. This one was a wait, and I thank you for your patience.

And last but least, you, the reader. Thank you for reading my boys... I appreciate you all.

Love and light
Jules
xoxo

Stalk Jules

Jules loves chatting to readers

Email her

julesfordauthor@gmail.com

Join her Facebook Group

Jules Ford's Tribe | Facebook

Instagram

Jules Ford (@julesfordauthor) • Instagram photos and videos

Printed by Amazon Italia Logistica S.r.l.
Torrazza Piemonte (TO), Italy

55385959R00317